JAY TINSIANO

Frank Bowen Conspiracy Series: Books 1-3

I

False Flag

False flag (or black flag) describes covert military or paramilitary operations designed to deceive in such a way that the operations appear as though they are being carried out by other entities, groups or nations than those who actually planned and executed them.
Wikipedia

Prologue

1991

Chiu Wah On smiled at his old friend; metallic black, compact and powerful. He felt the weight of the SIG Sauer P225 Pistol in his coarse hands and checked the recoil actions to ensure everything would work perfectly.

Lighting a cigarette, Chiu inhaled and blew out grey smoke that wafted upwards, dispersing against the whirring ceiling fan. His fingers ran over the long scar that went from his forehead and around his left cheekbone; a constant reminder of that bloody night, before settling on the solid form of the weapon again.

Chiu knew the weapon inside out, as if it were an extension of his body, and had handled it many times in training. It was a widely used handgun and not easy to trace or be attributed to any particular source.

The first time he had fired the pistol felt like it was only yesterday. The execution yard in Nanjing, capital of Jiangsu province, under a stark, grey sky. Two People's Liberation Army guards escorted a shackled prisoner into the empty concrete yard, pulling off his cloth hood to reveal the broken face of a man aged around twenty, eyes wet with tears as they settled on Chiu in anguish.

His superior handed Chiu the loaded P225 and gave him a level stare. He took it and looked into the eyes of the prisoner for a moment, before swiftly raising his arm and firing point blank into the forehead. Every detail, every sound, was crisp in his mind. The shot, followed by the slump of the body on the hard concrete ground, and finally the words of praise from his superior. His first live kill gave Chiu a grim satisfaction, enabling him to move on from years of raw frustration.

The cheap Bangkok hotel room was low lit. Net curtains across the open window wafted in the breeze and the walls faded into a sickly brown from years of stale cigarette smoke. A television flickered silently in the corner and the occasional roar of a moped or tuk-tuk filled the room. He had not left the hotel for three days now and it felt like the walls were closing in on him. Thankfully, the killing would soon begin.

Chiu wrapped the pistol and cache of bullets in a cloth, tucked them into a red canvas bag and then placed it back into the bottom of the wardrobe. Patience, he kept telling himself, over and over. Patience.

Chapter 1

Two months earlier

A strong wind swept the rain across the dual carriageway and through the valley where Frank Bowen had killed time in his teens. There would soon be dozens of red brick houses built and he wanted to hold and embed that place in his memory before it changed forever. There was something comforting to him about the trash and old car tyres lying abandoned on the unused road.

"Here, boy!" Frank whistled to Scotty, who was sniffing around the ground and ignoring him, as he followed a scent trail. He was Jodie's pet, but walking him made for a great excuse to get away from the flat.

Thick droplets of rain began to build and then within seconds, it came down as a torrent. A nearby derelict car garage offered shelter and Frank ran inside. The windows were now broken black holes that had not seen occupants for over a decade.

Further up the hill, the last solitary houses stood on the rain-washed road set against the grey shapes of two North London tower blocks. He had heard the developers were waiting for the owners to either move or die, so they could get on with their big project.

He considered going to look at the old house where he'd grown up with his parents before the accident, but the rain was coming down harder and it was getting late.

Scotty, bored with being soaked, finally scurried over to join Frank in the dry and shook himself off, spraying his trousers.

"Thanks for that," Frank sighed. As the terrier investigated the inner corners of the garage, Frank stared out at the relentless downpour. The rain always had a therapeutic effect on him, almost like a comfort blanket for the soul.

Scotty came trotting back and looked up at Frank in anticipation. "Want to go home now?" The dog merely looked up at Frank, his tail wagging excitedly.

"Great. Let's get out of here."

***

The following morning the skies remained threatening as Frank jogged along the docks past the endless offices and suits making their way to work. His dark hair and heavy set appearance made him look older than his twenty-six years. A fact not lost on him when he was younger and looking to get served in the pubs. An old man in combats and a tweed jacket tossed pieces of bread to a group of swans in the water. They rushed at the surprise snacks, beaks pecking gratefully.

A sudden screeching noise pierced the peaceful calm. A sickening crash followed by painful screaming came from the main road that ran parallel to the docks. Frank slowed his jog down to a walk and moved towards the commotion. A man in his mid-twenties was lying on the cobbled street, his body contorted– along with his mountain bike – under a car. Several pedestrians stopped and gawped; some continued to walk by.

"Quick! Somebody! Get an ambulance!"

A woman had already jumped out of the driver's seat, her hands on her head as she took in the scene in front of her.

"Oh Jesus, I didn't see..."

A burly man in a grey suit stood transfixed as dark blood soaked the dusty, cobbled road. Frank knelt over the man, trying to comfort him, impossible though it was—his face white and contorted, shrill screams and moans, short quick gasps for breath, eyes wide with fear. Eyes that were transfixed onto Frank's.

"It's ok, mate ... what's your name? It's ok. An ambulance will be here soon." Frank turned to the crowd: "Has someone called a bloody ambulance?" He looked back at the man on the ground, eyes frozen, staring skywards.

"On its way!" shouted a voice. The driver of the car was weeping and being comforted by another cyclist. After an agonising wait, the ambulance eventually pulled up, quickly followed by other emergency services. A paramedic rushed over and immediately felt his pulse and for any sign of a heartbeat, but the young man's life was already over.

***

Frank put down the keys on the kitchen bar and glanced at a pile of letters on the sideboard.

Jodie came in with a quizzical look from the living room where a home decoration programme blared out, exclaiming the delights of living room renovation.

"Hi, Frank. There's some post for you."

"Yeah I saw, thanks," he said, ignoring the letters. "How was your day?"

"Oh you know, the usual. The excitement never starts," she smiled at him thinly. "So, you're home early?"

"Yeah. I skipped work after what I saw going in. Some poor guy got killed. A cyclist was hit by a car."

Jodie's face turned to shock.

"Oh God!"

"It was nasty, horrible. He really suffered. I don't think he was much older than me."

Jodie rubbed Frank's arm in a rare show of affection. They embraced, her hands moving around him tentatively, as she patted his back. Frank bristled. She had been doing that a lot lately. He recently read in a body language book that it was a subconscious sign the person was not entirely comfortable with what they were doing.

"Makes you think doesn't it?" he whispered.

She pulled away from him and tilted her head. "About what?"

Frank moved to the kitchen bar and grabbed an apple from the fruit bowl.

"Life ... and its rich tapestry. It's so bloody short."

Jodie rolled her eyes.

"How many times have we had this conversation? I know you lost your parents, Frank, and then your grandad. I know how hard it's been for you. I just don't know what to say anymore."

"What? I didn't say anything about my parents or grandad."

"But that's what you meant! And what about me? What about us and a family?"

"What about..? Jodie, I've just seen a guy, lying in his own blood, die in front of me!"

The dog barked and disappeared into the living room.

"Don't shout in front of Scotty."

Frank shook his head while Jodie glared at him and snatched her keys off the kitchen bar.

"I'm taking him for a walk. Away from you." The door slammed.

The death of Frank's grandfather, Larry Bowen, a few months earlier had put a hold on the bickering, but now a return to past form seemed to be back on the agenda.

Frank took a bite from the apple and flicked through the letters. He didn't recognise one as a bill and opened it. It was from his grandfather's solicitor, entitled 'Inheritance'.

He read the words slowly. It told him how he had inherited five thousand pounds from his grandfather's estate. There was just the matter of signing a few forms at his convenience.

Five grand. It was a nice rounded amount, not life-changing, but handy nevertheless. He had expected to receive something but had no idea how much it was going to be. Larry Bowen had always scrimped and saved, despite not earning a great deal.

Frank did a quick calculation. He had around three or four thousand pounds of debt to pay off from the inheritance, which, on any other day would have irritated him. Today, however, he had seen a young man die and that experience had put all into perspective.

He carefully folded up the letter, went to the bedroom and placed it inside a book that lay on his bedside cabinet and then sat on the bed, staring at the wall.

The eyes of the young cyclist stared back at him as his life ebbed away. Frank supposed that at least someone had been there to comfort him at the end. Snuffed out, just like that. Going to work one minute and then...bang! Game over. It was life, but it was no easier to comprehend.

Then a thought came to him and he went to the wardrobe and took out a cardboard box. Inside was an assortment of his grandad's possessions, including letters, photographs, a watch and a leather-bound book. Frank hadn't really looked through all this stuff before and browsed through the items.

The images offered a very brief snapshot of his grandfather's life. Larry as a young man in the boxing gym where he had been a keen fighter for a few years; Larry and his late wife, taken in the 1970s; Larry standing tall, with a group of other men, all proudly posing in their British army uniforms, smiling broadly at the camera—handwritten on the back in faded blue ink, read: 2nd Infantry Division June 1945.

Then Frank noticed one of his parents that he hadn't seen before: young, happy, together. Frank found himself wondering what it would have been like if they had still been alive. Would he have taken them on a trip somewhere as they had aged? Visits on Sundays for a slap up roast, maybe? Helping his mum with the parsnips that she always forgot to do, even though they were his favourite ... listening to Dad moan about his beloved West Ham United. Yes, he would have done all that. No doubt about it, he would have been there for them.

Frank realised he was tightly gripping the photograph, tears escaping his eyes. He was recycling memories again, memories that didn't even exist. "What an idiot you are, Frank," he whispered out loud. He could not remember feeling more alone.

Chapter 2

The Waterfront bar, nestled on the Thames, bustled with the after work milieu of white-collar workers spilling their work gossip of bad bosses and good bosses. Frank spotted his friend, Carl at the quieter end, gazing over at the boats that lined the dockside. He caught his eye and gestured with his hand as to whether he wanted another drink. Carl gave the thumbs up.

"Alright, Carl?" Frank planted down the drinks and slipped into a chair.

"Great, thanks. So, Mr Bond, how's tricks?"

Both men clinked glasses. "I'm thinking of leaving Jodie, Carl."

Carl's face switched from a smile to shock in an instant. He stared at Frank, waiting for the punch line. None came. "Oh Shit."

Frank nodded grimly. "I know she doesn't love me anymore, Carl. And I'm seriously confused about how I feel, but one thing I do know; I'm not feeling good right now."

Carl exhaled slowly and stared at nothing in particular on the plastic tabletop.

"Sorry to hear that mate. That is a shocker," he said quietly.

He looked directly at Frank and added, "Most people who are unhappy can't bring themselves to make that decision. They hide from it. But we're only here once right? Anna and I are tight, but I'd be lying if I said we didn't have our ups and downs."

Frank sipped his pint and then looked out of the window at a couple strolling along the waterside. "I hear you. Part of me still wants it to work out, but I can't see how it will."

"How long have you been together?"

Frank sighed. "Four years, give or take."

Carl nodded silently and took a sip of his ale.

"Listen, Carl, I know you have a lock up garage. I wanted to stash some of my things for a while."

"Oh? Well, of course, you can. Going somewhere?"

"Yeah, to travel for a bit. I want to see some of this beautiful world before I pop my clogs. Also, I really should be getting some sun. This non-stop crap weather is getting me down."

Carl smiled. "I'll second that. Good for you. Whereabouts?"

"I'll start with Goa in India. Then go to Thailand and then see what comes up."

Carl gave a whistle, "Nice! I'm jealous. Just avoid the Middle East right now. There's definitely going to be a war kicking off over there."

"Oh right? Yes, I'd heard something about that. No chance of avoiding it then?" Frank hadn't bothered too much with the news recently. He had other things on his mind and, although he worked at a newspaper, his department dealt with advertising rather than the stories of the day.

Carl leaned forward and lowered his voice. "Not likely. Saddam could basically dance a jig and sing the Star-Spangled Banner; it wouldn't make a blind bit of difference. The Iraqi government somehow got the impression they had the green flag to invade Kuwait, but things have changed."

"Well you can't go around invading countries, no matter what," replied Frank.

"No, you certainly can't."

Frank manoeuvred the ashtray and sparked a cigarette. "So, how is life in MI6?"

"Busy. Between you and me, you ain't seen me, right?" Carl tapped his nose, winked and they both laughed. Carl had been an intelligence officer for six years and wasn't able to speak about any aspect of his job to anyone. It had never bothered Frank. In fact, he didn't want to know.

Frank took a large gulp of his Guinness and Carl looked serious again.

"I'm really sorry about Jodie. I'll help out any way I can. Just think of it as a new beginning, mate," assured Carl.

They clinked glasses. "A new beginning."

Chapter 3

The sleek black W126 S-Class Mercedes travelled north alongside the Temple of Earth Gardens in Beijing. Years before, Zhang had regularly visited with his parents, running along the tree-lined paths that cut through gardens. The walkways converged on the central altar, Fang Ze Tan, where Emperors of the Ming – and later Qing dynasties – had made sacrifices to appease the gods and help the nation.

It had been so long since he had visited any of the Temples, the others being the Temple of the Sun and the Temple of the Moon, which had all played an important part in the city's history. Zhang considered taking a walk there later that afternoon if only to offer credence to the sacrifices he himself was about to offer to the nation.

The Mercedes turned east onto Hepingli North Street, along the north border of the Gardens and into a quiet residential road, coming to a stop outside a restaurant. Zhang ordered his driver to stay put and climbed out of the car, walking up the steps to the glass doors, above which red lanterns hung, glowing in the dim light. He caught a reflection of himself in the glass – dark, swept back hair with his goatee beard, brown suit – and wondered if he would still be enjoying these privileges after the coming operation had played out.

The head waiter greeted Zhang as he came through the door and showed him into the empty restaurant, escorting him to his favourite table. He preferred it because it was near the window and more importantly, away from the ears of the kitchen. Three waitresses lined up to receive him, menus in hand; their uniforms immaculate, ironed and crisp. Zhang had earlier ordered the restaurant to be closed to the public.

The first waitress asked him what he would like.

"Green tea. With two cups. My associate will be here shortly. Also, please bring my Xiangqi board."

The waitress nodded and the three of them scuttled off as Zhang removed his jacket and placed it on the back of his chair.

A tall, gangly, middle-aged man in a dark suit entered and shooed away the head waiter as he walked across the carpeted floor, weaving between the empty tables. Zhang looked up and nodded as Peng Quan, his strategic advisor, hung his jacket over the spare chair and sat down, his sharp breaths suggesting he had been running.

"Peng, have you been working out?"

Peng raised his sharp eyebrows in confusion as he looked at his superior for illumination.

Zhang sighed as he bounced one end of his unlit cigarette on the table top. "Maybe you need some exercise. You're out of breath from walking from the car?"

Peng grinned sheepishly as he understood, "My driver parked down the road, I just jogged a bit. Sorry, I'm late."

The waitress returned with a tray holding a pot of green tea and two small china cups, decorated with gold patterns, and placed it on the table. She arranged the cups in front of the men and poured tea into each one. Zhang nodded his thanks and a second waitress appeared, holding a wooden box.

Zhang took it and placed it to his side, opening the lid to reveal the board and game pieces within.

"Thank you. That is all. Please do not disturb us."

The girl nodded and immediately disappeared.

Zhang opened the box and took out the lined game board and placed it in the middle of the table. He then carefully counted out the disked pieces that were engraved with a combination of red or black Chinese characters. The game, also known as Chinese Chess, was a popular strategy board game representing a battle between two armies and the object was to capture the General. In the middle of the board, a gap represented a river between the two opposing sides.

"I hope I can beat you this time, Peng," Zhang smiled broadly. "But then, on the other hand, beating my best strategic advisor might not be a good omen."

Peng laughed, taking his first sip of green tea. "We shall see, Ho Zhang."

Zhang had worked with Peng Quan for over twelve years in the intelligence community and he was the first person he requested for his small team when setting up the fifth department—a department that did not exist in any official documents or paperwork.

The Chinese apparatus consisted of four main bureaus: the General Staff Department that included organised sub-departments for artillery, engineering, armoured units, operations, training and a host of others, through to the Second Department for military intelligence. The Third was for monitoring of foreign armies and, finally, the Fourth that held the electronic intelligence portfolio, responsible for electronic countermeasures.

It had been Zhang's idea to form an elite unit specifically for 'off the record' black operations. The Fifth's agenda was to enhance and forward China's overseas influence without leaving footprints and, wherever possible, leave false trails to foreign agencies.

Zhang believed this was perfectly in keeping with the ministries' charge by the General-Secretary. That was to ensure "the security of the state through effective measures against enemy agents, spies, and counter-revolutionary activities designed to sabotage or overthrow China's socialist system."

The risk, however, was significant and the buck was always going to stop at Zhang. Such were the sensitive circumstances of the bureau's role, that there had even been a serious discussion about making it financially self-sufficient, even if that meant illegal activities like drug trafficking. Zhang was relieved when this idea was thrown out as it would have, no doubt, given him a myriad of headaches. He would rather leave that type of business to their Triad friends.

Peng Quan moved one of his soldier pieces forward one square, to start the game.

"We need to make a decision on our other game plan," said Zhang as he studied the board and moved one of his own soldiers.

"Yes, yes, I know," Quan replied.

"There are still two pieces missing," Zhang continued.

"Everything else has been set up and is ready to go," said Quan, his voice flat as if Zhang was chastising him. He moved another soldier forward on the board.

Zhang already knew this, having spent over two years involved in the planning. Every detail of the operation had been scrutinised and approved by him and yet there were still vital cogs that needed to be put in place. He scanned the board of play; wondering how he could get his cannon to control the middle of the board as soon as possible. He moved his piece, took a sip of tea and rested his eyes on the man opposite him.

"Without those two players, the game cannot commence and now is the time, Peng. All eyes are on the Gulf."

Quan advanced his horse on the same flank to counter Zhang's cannon.

"Has agent Bashe come up with anyone?"

"Not yet, but I'm hoping he will." As he spoke, Zhang's eyes moved over his opponent's pieces on the far side of the river, which was represented by the middle of the board, trying to second guess him. He moved a soldier piece forward onto Quan's side of the river.

"What about Orchid? Anything new come through?" Quan asked, casually, as he deployed one of his chariots one square forward. Zhang's eyes narrowed. He figured Quan must be looking to get it into his left corner, ready to threaten his general—a possible déjà vu of a previous game, where a 'Jiang si le,' checkmate had occurred almost before the game had begun. He contemplated moving his right advisor diagonally for a moment as he lit another cigarette, inhaling and slowly blowing out a plume of grey smoke that snaked up to the high, dark red ceiling.

"No, Orchid is standing by and will be called upon. You did a good job recruiting our flower over there, by the way. They have been a great help working to an arrangement with our Triad friends for the handover." Zhang moved his right advisor disk.

"Thanks," Quan replied, but he was frowning at the board. He moved a long arm across the game of play and captured one of Zhang's soldier pieces.

Zhang smiled and considered a move that would surely involve the sacrifice of his castle but could enable him to push his Cannon up his opponent's right flank.

Sacrifices were always needed in war, he mused.

Chapter 4

Flight BA377 touched down at Goa airport at 4.20pm local time. Frank strained to see what he could out of the small window but gave up. The man next to him was just too large and had obscured his view for the whole journey. Reflecting on the difficult and emotional past few weeks Frank still wasn't sure if he was doing the right thing.

Moving all his remaining possessions into storage and saying goodbye to Jodie after four years together was a sad time and their parting had been far from amicable.

Maybe he deserved every scream and shout that had been directed at him, followed by the tears. She had looked forward to some kind of future between them and being five years older had anticipated having a family with him. At twenty-six Frank just felt he was too young. There were things he wanted to do with his life. Experiences to be had. Maybe someday he'd be ready for kids but not yet. Jodie had screamed that he was refusing to grow up. Maybe he wasn't ready to grow up. Had she considered that?

Frank felt drained and tired, mixed with a rising sense of excitement as he stared out at the deep blue sky through the windows opposite. He had been yearning to do this for so long. Every time he had walked past a travel agent, with their posters of beaches in paradise, he had stopped in his tracks and stared longingly at the flight prices.

The heat hit Frank like a wall as he stepped off the Boeing 757 and he immediately broke into a sweat. The air-conditioned arrivals hall provided some relief as well as a scene of chaos, as hordes of passengers stumbled around looking for their salvation. An Indian soldier chatted to customs officers, his weapon slung over his shoulder, plastic and shiny. The uniform he wore had a newly pressed and ironed look, reminding Frank of a life-sized action man.

His first destination was Anjuna beach. According to his hastily purchased travel book, it was a vibrant place to start. The plan was to find a beach and settle in for a month or so of relaxation and fun. Frank felt he deserved it. After all, he had been working non-stop for the last few years and it had felt like a hard slog. Pleasant in parts, but ultimately a humdrum period of his life.

As he stepped out of the airport doors, a posse of Indians, holding up pictures of their rental houses, swamped him and the other travellers. He felt like a monkey in the zoo and waved them away.

"No huts, thanks. I want a taxi."

A small, skinny Indian man grinned at Frank with yellow teeth, "I have great bungalow, cheap prices."

"No bungalows, thank you." The man nodded his head from side to side. "OK, mister. Taxi is no problem; I have one just up there."

Frank followed him across the dusty road to an old yellow Bristol car from the bygone British Empire. People were bustled into other vehicles, which kicked up clouds of dust as they drove off. Frank bundled into the back of the vehicle with three other travellers whom the driver had rounded up. He nodded a greeting to them.

"Where you from, mate?" asked a shabby haired, blond Australian man in the middle of the back seat. On the other side of the Aussie was a smart looking woman with a pierced nose. Her long, blonde, curly hair was pulled back into a ponytail; her face was soft and understated, yet classically beautiful. She turned and smiled at Frank.

"Just in from England; same as him," Frank gestured to the large man who'd been next to him on the flight, now welded into the front seat. He tried to turn around to acknowledge Frank for the first time, but couldn't quite manage it and gave up. The car occupants made small talk as the driver drove like a man possessed, swerving around potholes in the road, sometimes failing to avoid them at all. An occasional bump and shudder caused the passengers to grab onto anything remotely stable as they sped past Portuguese-style villas lining the roads.

Everyone in the car smiled despite the concern in their eyes and tried to talk over the noise. At last, the journey ended and Frank left the others to find a quiet spot, eventually finding what he wanted. It was a small beach house, set away from the crowded drop off point, yet close enough to the bars that adorned the beachfront.

He dumped his gear and immediately ventured out to his new surroundings. The air was sweet with the scent of jasmine and the deep blue sky opened up endlessly overhead. Closer to the beach, sun-kissed travellers milled around the bars, taking in the late afternoon sun and generally hanging out. There were characters that looked like they had been here for years, encrusted with the elements and destined never to leave. Everyone seemed to have beads hanging around their necks, sporting heavy tans, their movements slow in the heat.

An old Indian man in bright red football shorts played some kind of instrument that sounded like bagpipes and was paid to move on by a couple of sunbathing women. Dogs ran around wild, scavenging for food, and were consistently waved away.

Frank clocked a lively bamboo hub of activity called 'The Brazil Bar' and mooched up the wooden steps. Dub beats boomed from the stereo, spilling onto the beach. He ordered food and beer before sitting down to take in the scene.

"Hey, how's it going?" an American voice interrupted his thoughts. A young guy with shoulder-length blond hair sat down, uninvited, and slurped his Kingfisher beer.

"I'm good, just came in today," Frank said.

"Yeah, I thought so. You look a bit pasty if you don't mind me saying. You'll love it here though, this place really rocks. I've been here for two months. I was supposed to be headed to Thailand but haven't managed to leave here just yet," he gave Frank a broad smile.

"I could think of worse places to get stuck."

The American saw someone he knew and called over: "Theo, hey! Over here!"

A tall, middle-aged, Indo-Chinese figure moved over towards them, dressed in a white, short sleeve shirt, slacks and leather sandals, his jet-black hair tied back into a ponytail, eyes razor sharp, blue and piercing. He made for an impressive figure. Frank shook hands with him.

"Hi, I'm Frank."

"Theo." The man fixed Frank with a direct look and smiled warmly.

The American grinned. "Yeah, I'm Claude by the way." He shook hands with Frank as well, almost as an afterthought.

Theo talked slowly and deliberately, in direct contrast to Claude who seemed to race through his lines, as if speaking through a panicky oral exam.

"Here in Goa, life is about enjoying yourself and nothing else. You leave your worries at home and that's it."

Theo rolled up a joint as he spoke; piecing the papers together like it was the most natural thing in the world. Frank thought his accent was a strange mix of mid-Atlantic, but more British than American, and he reminded him of a Colombian villain from a T.V. series.

"If there is anything you want, I can get it for you. But be careful of the Takkas; the cops. They usually dress in plain clothes, but you will see them a mile off. You will learn this. I know some of them, so if you get into trouble, let me know."

"Good guy to know, huh?" Claude thumbed towards Theo.

Frank nodded, "Great. I'm not planning to get into any trouble though."

After a few minutes, Claude left to chat to a couple of women on another table and Frank talked with Theo for an hour or so. Theo told him he had been the only son of a Vietnamese mother and an Indian father. He hadn't settled and took off at every opportunity, travelling widely in Asia, but he had not yet visited any Western countries.

They touched on their lives and aspirations and Frank decided he liked Theo. He had a calm demeanour about him as if he regretted nothing and rolled with life like a leaf on a wave.

Frank decided not to go wild that night and hit the sack about ten.

Early the next morning, he awoke to the sun beaming in through the window blinds. It felt fantastic to smell the first morning abroad. Frank found a place to get breakfast and then walked along the beach towards a quieter part and sat watching the waves crashing onto the golden shore for a while. He wondered why he had never appreciated it like this before on all those trips to the seaside in England.

England. It seemed a million miles away now and a new life beckoned.

A figure approached from the market end of the beach, stopping occasionally to gaze out to the blue horizon. Frank watched the figure move closer and realised it was a woman dressed in an Indian style one piece dress. She stared toward Frank and he saw it was the curly haired blonde woman from the taxi. They hadn't really communicated in the cab, due to the Australian dude stuck between them.

She waved and walked over to Frank.

"Hello there. How are you finding it so far?' she smiled, her hand playing with a seashell. Frank noticed she had a necklace around her neck made from small coloured stones and sported a native look of a red dot on her forehead, just above the middle of her eyebrows. The third eye.

"So far, so good!" Frank gestured to her to sit down. "I'm just enjoying the sea," he said.

"It's beautiful, I love watching it," she agreed, parking in the sand next to him and brushing back her hair. Frank immediately noticed a delicate grace about her, as he had the day before.

"It's very therapeutic. It concentrates the mind," Frank said.

"A lot of the beauty is spoilt throughout India though. There's crap dumped everywhere. People have no idea what they're doing to the environment."

She gestured towards a mound of plastic bottles that had congregated nearby. "This is exactly what I'm talking about," she said, with contempt.

"Yeah, that is pretty bad. People are just here to party I guess. I'm Frank by the way," he held out his hand.

"Nice to meet you, Frank. I'm Maria."

They gazed out to sea and he noticed her painted toenails and jewellery. It suited her well, Frank thought.

"You've travelled around India quite a bit then?" he asked.

"Yes, I love it. I flew to Mumbai and went to Matheran and the Sahyadri hills. It's much cooler there and a really great place to relax. Then I came down to Goa on the train."

"That sounds great. I'm going to stay here for a while, and then I plan to move onto Thailand."

"Yes, I have to go there at some point, I won't stay long. I'd like to go to Indonesia then back to Hong Kong," Maria said.

"You live in Hong Kong?"

"My Father is based there. He's English and works for the Legislative Council of Hong Kong. They're all very busy preparing for the 1997 handover to China at the moment. Although it's still six years away you wouldn't believe the panic behind the scenes."

"Oh? What's going on?" Frank was intrigued.

Maria momentarily held her hands above her eyes to shield them from a glare of sunlight as she looked at him.

"Well, you remember the killings on Tiananmen Square a few years ago?" He nodded. The footage of the student standing in front of a line of tanks had become a powerful iconic image the world over. "It certainly hasn't helped put minds at rest," she said. "Then there's the power struggles as groups jostle for position. I also heard the triad gangs have done a deal with Beijing not to interfere."

"Hmm, really? Yes, there's probably a lot at stake," he said.

She gave him a broad smile. "I hear all about it from my Dad. All the, what's the English word? Gossip? I hear it all."

She looked serious again. "But there are a lot of worried people in Hong Kong right now."

"Do you think there'll be trouble?" he asked.

She leaned back; her elbows wedged into the sand and narrowed her eyes at a distant ship on the horizon. Frank couldn't help but cast his eyes over the contours of her body. She was beautiful and clearly relaxing into a favourite topic of hers.

"When there are governments fighting over land, with their agencies of limitless power, there's bound to be trouble."

Chapter 5

Pulsating beats drifted across the beach and a cyclone of colourful rays belted out over the top of the dancing masses as the moon winked over the calm night waters behind them. Frank spotted Theo through the crowd and moved towards him.

Theo turned and grinned. "Hey Franky; you enjoy?"

"Fantastic! Happy as Larry."

"Larry?"

"Oh! It's just an English saying," explained Frank.

Theo laughed and scanned his eyes through the dancing party-goers. "Hey, check out the beautiful girls over there!"

"There's way too many for me, mate," Frank said, smiling at Theo in the dim light.

Frank looked around for Maria but she had disappeared. After meeting on the beach they had walked to the flea market; a busy scene with snake charmers and old travellers flogging their junk. Then they had enjoyed some dinner together, some of the best fish Frank had ever tasted, before joining the beach party.

Theo motioned for him to move towards the edge of the crowd. Frank felt a cold sweat, his shirt sticking to his back. Theo began building a joint, but Frank suddenly craved water as he slowly became aware of his heart pumping hard.

"I'm going to find a toilet, Theo. I'll catch you later."

"Sure, Frank. See you later."

After pushing through the heaving mass, Frank eventually found a vacant toilet at the back of a bar and, on returning, pondered whether to stick around or call it a night.

"Hey!"

He turned to see a scowling, stooped, man leaning heavily on the bar. His white hair straggled around his bony brown neck and shoulders which held a bunch of necklaces, adorned with shells and what looked like bone fragments.

"They call me the dawg!" he growled at no one in particular. It sounded to Frank like his voice was scarred by a forty a day habit and penchant for whiskey chasers. The man then peered at Frank from under bushy, untamed eyebrows.

"How's it going, Dog?" Frank extended his hand for the Dog to shake, but he just stood staring over his shoulder at something behind him before walking off without another word. Frank shook his head in disbelief and turned around to be faced with a tall, blond, German man.

"Zat dog," he stated," is a legend around here!"

"I can tell he is," Frank said, sarcastically, wearily moving away to the exit, suddenly deciding he would call it a night after all. He strolled along the path amongst the palm trees and huts and as he glanced toward the trees near the parallel road, noticed Maria walking along a path that converged with his.

"Hey, Maria."

She turned her head at the sound of his voice. "Hey, Frank." Even in the limited light, he could make out her full beautiful smile.

"Did you have a good time? I lost you."

"Yes, it was busy. I went for a wander along the beach, and then went back, but I couldn't see you," she said.

They strolled through the moonlit palms. The beams from the

beach party behind them continued to streak across their path like a myriad of beacons.

"Were you looking for answers in that view of the sea again?" he quipped.

Maria laughed, her hands still toying with a seashell, perhaps the same one she had earlier. "Yes, I didn't find many there though. It was much too dark to see anything."

They arrived at Frank's hut. "This is my grand abode," he said, catching her eye in the faint light before moving closer. He reached a hand to caress her cheek and their lips met hastily. Maria opened up to him, while Frank's hand moved around her waist, pulling her into him until her breasts pressed against him.

They moved inside the small hut and into the bedroom. Frank scrambled around for his lighter and lit his oil lamp, regretting his decision to go for a cheap hut without electricity. Maria took off her long, Indian style gown and unclipped her bra as Frank opened the mosquito net.

"Quick! Hop in!" he urged, smiling at her as he removed his shirt and shorts before diving in behind the safety of the net.

"I wouldn't want to share you with any mosquitoes," he whispered.

Frank felt her heart beat against his chest. Her skin felt smooth and warm against his and he welcomed it. She smelled sweet and it reminded him of something; a smell from the distant past.

***

An hour later, Frank ran his hand over Maria's slender curves as she lay on her stomach with her face turned towards him. He moved his hand up the small of her back to where the end of her curly hair lay easily on her skin. She looked at him with half-closed eyes;

her face and mouth obscured by her arm, and let out a satisfied sigh. The flickering oil lamp danced animated shadows across their bodies and seemed comforting to Frank somehow, like the rain that transfixed him back home.

"What are you looking for out here?" she asked softly.

"Sun, sea and Dutch women," he said, with a cheeky grin.

Maria laughed. "I see."

Frank returned his gaze to her soft skin, listening to the sound of the lapping tide just outside the hut that seemed to draw closer as if closing in around their feet.

"I had a major urge to take off and leave. I broke up with someone. We didn't want the same things," said Frank.

"People drift apart every day, in the same way, they're pulled together," she said and slowly moved her hand over his chest. "Was it a long relationship?"

"A few years. We were supposed to get married. Kids; the works," Frank said.

"A pretty serious relationship then?"

"Oh yes. It was serious," he whispered, almost mockingly.

Frank turned his body towards her. "What about you? Any Dutch hunks waiting for you at home?"

Maria expelled a loud laugh.

"No, no. Not in Holland. I had a boyfriend in Hong Kong for a while. Nothing came of it."

"Chinese?"

"No. A Frenchman."

"A Frenchman in Hong Kong. Sounds like a novel."

"My life has been a bit of a novel, you could say," she said with a wry smile.

"I look forward to hearing all about it," said Frank, reaching for a cigarette.

"Any other family?"

Frank quietly sighed, wondering whether he wanted to continue this conversation. Usually, he didn't, when asked. He'd just lie or make something up, anything to avoid going down that road.

"No, unfortunately, they've all gone. My parents were killed in a car crash when I was seven. My only surviving relatives were my grandfather and Uncle. Grandad passed away a few months ago."

Maria turned onto her side, looking at him with genuine sadness, "I'm sorry Frank. That's awful. It must have been extremely hard for you."

Frank watched the spiral curl of bluish smoke waft up through the mosquito net.

"The pain recedes over time, but it never goes away. I do miss them, I really do. But I was so young. The memories of them are," he paused. "Kind of faded, you know?"

Frank stubbed out his cigarette and placed the ashtray outside the net.

They lay in silence for a while. The light gush of the tide seemed to slow down and sleep took them quickly.

***

Lightning forked across the black sky overhead, a power of nature that Frank had never seen before. It lit up the endless flat fields that surrounded their cottage for miles. He could even see the trees by the farm where he played army with his friends. There was a tree house there, where they kept their plastic toy guns. The endless dykes acted like trenches and in a field next to the farm stood unused tractors that had been left to rust for years.

She held his hand tight.

"It's OK sweetheart. It's just a storm."

They waited for Dad on the cottage doorstep, clutching their coats as protection against the downpour.

"Come on, Patrick, we're late," his mother shouted.

Frank's father appeared behind them, his anorak rustling as he sorted through his keys. "Right, get ready and make a run for it," he said.

The three figures sprinted down the pathway to the Ford Escort parked on the road and they all clambered inside as quickly as they could.

Patrick turned to his son in the back seat. "You all belted up, Frankie boy?"

"Yes, Dad."

"Good lad."

Patrick started the engine and the windscreen wipers kicked into action, barely keeping the torrent of rain at bay.

"God, would you look at that?" His mother stared across at the field opposite the house.

Patrick and Frank followed her stare and saw the cow, lying on its back with one hind leg stuck upwards as straight as a pole. The carcass looked frozen as if it had been struck by a spear from the sky.

"What happened to it, Dad?"

"It must have been hit by lightning. In the wrong place, at the wrong time. Poor cow," he said and laughed.

The car slowly moved off, momentarily getting closer to the strange sight in the field as they drove by. Frank's small face stared out of the window at the dead animal, and then he looked away.

Chapter 6

Frank opened his eyes with a shudder, breathing heavily, his body covered in a sheen of sweat. As the sound of his heartbeat inside his head receded, the familiar cricket noises and distant voices of early morning beach wanderers took over.

He turned to find Maria had gone and felt a pang of disappointment in his stomach. Something he said? Probably gone for a swim or breakfast, he thought, as he watched specs of dust float against slithers of light that beamed through the hut slats.

Eventually, he climbed out of bed, grabbing his wash bag and towel and padded out to the shower area; another perk of cheap boarding. The cool water rushing over his aching head felt like heaven and he let it stream down his body, eyes closed as he relished the feeling. He reached for his wash bag and fumbled around inside for the shower gel. A piece of paper fluttered down onto the concrete slab, narrowly missing the puddle of water that circled around his feet and landed on the hard, sandy ground.

Frank picked it up with one still dry hand and looked at it quizzically. It was written in neat, perfectly formed handwriting.

Thanks for a perfect night. If you're ever in Hong Kong:

(344) 37484 44

Maria x

Frank could only wonder why she had left him the message in

his wash-bag. She had obviously decided to move on to her next destination but it seemed strange that she had left so quickly. Had she felt like their night together had been a mistake? Feeling slightly aggrieved he tucked the note back in the bag. It would have been nice to spend more time with her but he decided to just get on with having a good time.

***

Lazy days drifted into party nights, the alcohol and drugs all part of the routine and, like a kid in a sweet shop, Frank was there: taking it all on.

He'd catch breakfast around four in the afternoon—if he could stomach it—with the regulars at the Brazil bar, then soak up the last of the sun and drift aimlessly in the blue sea. After a brief relaxation, it was time for beers and cocktails. Theo, Claude and a regular motley crew played cards and backgammon, turning the bar into a kind of beach style scene from Casablanca. Party night was every night. There was rarely a night off.

The comedown was hard and swift. One afternoon as he lounged on a hammock the pain hit him in the stomach, tying it up in knots and spitting it out again. He crawled to the safety of his bed as the sickness took hold; tiredness beating him up with sticks, weighing him down, preventing movement.

His appetite completely vanished, mouth dried up like a prune and he spent too much time in the toilet, wishing he had an en-suite bathroom. The terrible nights blanketed him in darkness, shrouding him in their cruel shadow, like a mocking demon. In his fever, he promised to look after himself, quit smoking, bump the drink, and be healthy.

It seemed to Frank that you were at your weakest exactly when you felt invincible.

After a few days, Theo came to see Frank and was visibly shocked at his appearance.

"Bloody hell, Frank, you look terrible!"

"I feel terrible, Theo; I think I'm going to die," Frank groaned.

"I doubt it." Theo looked closely at Frank, narrowing his eyes as if reading his health meter.

"My friend is a doctor; I'll go get him."

"Anything. Can you get me some more bottled water? I'll give you money for the Doc." Frank tried to move across the room to get to his cash.

"Forget it, Frank. You lie down."

When the doctor arrived he had Frank popping the antibiotics in no time. After a long period of praying and puking, Frank began to slowly recover, almost to his former self.

It was time to move on to his next destination. Thailand had always been in his travel plans and he was suddenly keen to get there.

Frank made a vague arrangement to meet Theo in Bangkok. As they drank tea in the Brazil bar, Theo recommended a guesthouse near the Khao San Road and pointed to it on a map.

"It's a great place, good price and very comfortable."

"Great," said Frank. "It's good to know where to go, saves a lot of hassle."

Frank found himself thinking about Maria again and wondered where she had gone. He hoped she was still around Goa and that there would be a small chance they would bump into each other again. He wanted to hear her seductive Dutch accent one more time, but it was not to be.

Chapter 7

Mu Heng banged the top of the small television that sat in the corner of his desk, attempting to get the picture back. It had been steadily getting worse for the past few weeks and had finally died. He eventually gave up and switched it off; slumping back into his chair. Heng checked his watch: 2.37am.

Where the hell was the team?

Patience was not one of his better qualities and the waiting had been going on for months. This had to rank as one of the most boring cover jobs he had ever been assigned, although at least the booth was quiet, he supposed. It was the slow passage of time that got to him. Still, at least now the waiting would soon be over.

Tonight was the night it would finally start to happen.

He flipped through the Hong Kong Times and then lifting his stocky figure up, walked outside the booth and lit another cigarette. Heng then paced up and down on the shiny tiled floor of the Kennedy Town Mass Transit Railway station, brushing imaginary dust off his grey uniform.

The shrill ring of the phone punctured the silence and he quickly picked it up and heard a low, rasping voice.

"Package is here, waiting."

"OK! On my way," said Heng. He slammed down the phone, grabbed a bunch of keys, his walkie-talkie and then made his way out of the booth and along the platform in the stark, artificial light.

Heng slid the metal gate linking the platform to the exit tunnel aside, where three grim looking Chinese men, each carrying heavy duty holdall bags, stood waiting. The man in the middle – with the arched scar – nodded and, without a word, they followed Heng back across the platform towards the booth, their footsteps echoing behind them.

Chapter 8

Bangkok. Khao San Road.

The smell of fried chicken hit Frank's nostrils as he jumped from the taxi. The thick air seemed almost unbreathable. A Westerner grinned at him from a café table as if Frank were a patsy in a creampie joke. He shoved some baht notes at the driver, determined to find this guesthouse as soon as possible.

It took a while for Frank to get to the guesthouse that Theo had recommended. He almost considered going to the first place he saw, but then decided against it and soldiered on. Eventually, another English tourist pointed him in the right direction.

The room in the 'Sunny Beach' was clean; the ceiling fan provided cool comfort for half an hour as Frank smoked cigarettes and watched the propelling blades slice up the grey cloud. A high-pitched whine stung in his brain. Frank decided to lay off the alcohol for a while. Those drinks on the flight from India hadn't done him any favours.

The outside eating area was a small courtyard where he'd come through from the side street earlier and was decorated on all sides with beautiful mosaic tiling, featuring a Buddha dominating a Thai landscape. It was a quiet spot, well away from the frantic Khao San, and Frank felt relieved he'd followed Theo's advice.

He wanted a drink and a bowl of noodles, and then remembered he was off the booze, but when the waitress came over he decided to order a Singha beer anyway. Looking around at the clientele, Frank could see a few Thai office workers and old travellers killing time at the tables. An old, silver-haired, tanned guy in a red shirt read the Bangkok Post and smoked a cigar.

Another man stopped at his table. He had a young Dirk Bogarde look about him, with jet black hair, sideburns and a five o'clock shadow on his chin and wore typical English attire: long sleeved shirt and white slacks.

"Mind if I sit here?" he asked.

"Of course, no problem," said Frank.

"Just arrived?" the man enquired.

"Yeah, I came from Goa. I'm headed south as soon as I can get out of here."

They introduced each other as Frank's beer and Thai noodles arrived.

"I'm Richard."

"Frank."

Richard ordered himself a coffee.

"Bangkok is an extremely interesting city. It can be a tad daunting on first arrival though."

"It's manic. I've only been here a couple of hours but I'm not planning to hang around."

"Well, you can't leave until you've visited the infamous Pat Pong." Richard winked at him.

"Oh, what's that?" Frank asked, sucking in his noodles.

"You don't know about Pat Pong? It's girlie bar central, Frank. It's where the action is," said Richard. He noticed Frank didn't look convinced and added, "Don't worry, we'll just look around and have a laugh."

***

The tuk-tuks swarmed through the early evening traffic, weaving past helmetless bikers and Japanese cars. The pollution rose in the air like a mist, making the city's buildings look like grey husks through the taxi window. Golden roofs of little temples tucked away amongst the shanty huts, jutted into the dimming sky.

The two men paid the fare and joined the crowd that milled around two parallel roads of Pat Pong. It was packed with T-shirt stalls, girly bars and prostitutes of every manner. There was certainly a seedy feel about the place. Richard warned that it was easy to get ripped off, but he knew a good place to go.

They were constantly harassed by gangs of girls or Thai pimps. Frank glanced into a passing bar and caught a glimpse of a beautiful Thai girl, dressed in a bikini, gyrating around a silver pole. She was closely watched by a gaggle of men at the bar.

Richard turned to Frank, smiling, as they fought through the crowd and pointed towards a side street. "I was down here last week," he started saying as they negotiated the crowd. "I saw a group of Rugby lads fight their way out after they were asked for an extortionate amount of money for their beers."

They paused to let a group of singing young German men pass them by.

"Another time there was a chap who had to flee for his life from a strip bar," Richard continued, "he was chased by machete wielding Thais who ran the place."

"What did he do?" asked Frank.

"I heard later that he accidentally insulted one of them. And he groped one of the girls which obviously didn't go down well." They turned left into an alleyway.

Great, thought Frank, sarcastically, as Richard rang a doorbell to a sinister looking metal door. A slot zipped open for a moment before the sound of a bolt unlocking the door revealed an older Thai woman peering out from the darkness. She held a torch to their faces and Richard quickly gave her some money. The two men followed the torchlight along a blackened corridor which led up a series of steps. She knocked on another door and babbled something in Thai before it opened to a buzzing interior, tinged with red light.

A bar ran all the way around a raised stage where people hunched over their drink and watched a group of dancers swing their stuff. To the back of the dimly lit room lay further tables and seats on different levels. The two men took seats at the bar and ordered beers. A group of young Thai girls in bikinis immediately surrounded them.

"Buy a drink for lovely girl?"

"Wanna try nice girls like us?"

Frank smiled at them. "We're just here for the show and a beer."

"Beer shit. Try hot Thai girl," one of them said. Frank laughed, wondering how he had been persuaded to come here.

Richard ordered drinks for the girls, which consisted of an inch high measure of orange juice and cost the same as their beers. He gave them to the girls who made small talk before leaving them to find more willing customers. After a while, a young couple came on stage and started a live sex show for the crowd. Twenty or thirty positions later, they trooped off. Their bored expressions throughout the entire spectacle indicated it was just another day at the office. Frank took in the seedy atmosphere and drank the beer in quick gulps.

"There's a free table at the back, let's grab it," said Richard.

"You're a sad old man, Rich, knowing these type of places," Frank said jokily.

Richard laughed. "Yeah. Just red-blooded. But it's all part of Bangkok's rich tapestry, you know."

Richard gestured for more drinks from the waitress dressed as a Playboy bunny.

"I like to live a certain type of life, Frank." He lit his tenth cigarette of the hour. "I can meet people here. For the kind of business, I do."

Frank sensed a change of tone in the conversation.

"There are ways of staying out here and making money and that's what I do. I'm not a traveller Frank, I live here."

He smiled again, but Frank could tell by his eyes he wanted to get something off his chest.

"I guessed as much," said Frank. "So how does someone from the old country make a living here?"

"Well there are all kinds of business one could get into. Asians love to do business, Frank. It's in their blood. That's what I love about it over here. No bullshit."

"Yeah I can imagine," nodded Frank.

Richard continued to talk about the black market, currencies, precious metals like gold, even selling snakes. It was a crash course in being a hustler in Thailand. After a few more beers, Richard mentioned he had a problem. He needed someone to bring some gems to Bangkok from the south. It was an easy deal, easy money. No borders to cross. He used travellers all the time, apparently.

"Thanks for the offer, Richard, but it's not really my line. Not right now anyway," he said.

"No problem, Frank." He searched his wallet and gave Frank a business card that only had a Bangkok phone number on.

"Just give me a call if you change your mind."

Frank took the card and slipped it into his wallet.

Chapter 9

The night bus left Bangkok in the early evening, heading south. Frank's head felt like it was lagging a few feet behind him, due to the relentless drinking nights that Richard had persuaded him to go on. He exhaled in relief and was glad to be leaving the manic city behind him and fell into a deep sleep.

Around five o'clock the following morning the coach pulled into Surat Thani; the bright sunlight already bathing the streets in a yellow glow despite the early hour. Frank grabbed his bag and headed off to find out the boat times to Koh Samui. Scanning the timetable, Frank could make no sense of it and wandered over to a nearby café to ask the owner. A tall, burly, dark-haired man had the same idea and was turning back from talking to the small, jovial faced proprietor.

"There's a six-hour wait," he said to Frank's unasked question.

"For the boat to Samui?" Frank asked.

"Aye. You'd think they'd put 'em on more regular, like."

The big man slung his huge backpack down next to a table in a way which suggested he was going no further. Frank joined him for breakfast, ordering banana pancakes and coffee whilst the Irishman ordered half the menu. He offered his massive hand to Frank.

"Jimmy," he said, a smile forming across his broad, deep-set features. Jimmy was a bus driver from Lisburn, Northern Ireland.

But driving buses was just one of a long list of occupations. He'd taken off two years previously and had been over the Americas and was now covering Asia. They drank bottles of rice whiskey to pass the time until finally their 'Coconut boat', a two-level transporter that crammed in as many travellers as possible, was available for the crossing.

Once they had both finally arrived on the island, the two men found a tuk-tuk and headed for a stretch of beach called Choeng Mon, which Jimmy had heard about. They found a bungalow each, behind the guesthouse restaurant but only metres from the beach. They did their own thing in the day and met up for meals in the guesthouse restaurant, Frank burning his mouth on Coconut Soup and Thai style curries, which he was developing a taste for, and Jimmy trying everything without hesitation. The menu was geared to tourist 'Farangs' and wasn't very adventurous, but Jimmy managed to persuade the waitress to deliver 'off the menu' real Thai food.

One balmy evening, after dinner, Frank took his leather waist bag with his money and passport to the reception to book a boat trip, while Jimmy decided to stretch his legs and walk up the beach. Then he spotted that the best hammock on the beach was free and decided to grab it.

Swinging lazily, Frank watched the sun disappear below the horizon amid magical colours of the emerald sea. Daydreaming of the next stop on his trip; he weighed up whether to head to Penang in Malaysia or to carry on down the coast of Thailand to Kota Bharu.

The light faded fast and Frank finally went to return his money bag to the guesthouse safe, but no one was around at reception. He walked back to his hut, stashed the bag in the bottom of his rucksack, locked the door and headed for the beach to see if he could catch up with Jimmy. A Thai man in black shirt and long shorts walked past him, avoiding his eye.

The beach became deserted once past the last busy bar that catered to a happy drunk crowd, apart from the sounds of the lapping sea. Pink and neon blue lights winked in the darkness ahead and Frank moved towards them, stumbling in the thick darkness. The lights turned out to be a small lonely bar and Frank made out a Thai woman serving a man. Getting closer, he recognised Jimmy's distinct Northern Irish accent.

"Hey Jimmy, had a good night?" Frank said as he patted him on the back and pulled up a stool.

"Hey, Frankie, how're ya doing there? This is Mimi," he gestured to the middle-aged woman, who gave Frank a broad smile.

Frank eased onto another stool and slapped his Lucky Strikes onto the bar top.

"Very nice to meet you, Mimi. I'll have what he's having."

Mimi grabbed a bottle from the cooler and put it in front of Frank with another beautiful smile before disappearing around the back.

"So, been in touch with anyone back home?" asked Frank, as he started to pull off the bottle label, bit by bit.

"Home? Yeah, haven't been back there for a while. To be honest, there are a lot of bad memories back there," Jimmy's huge forearms dominated the bar and he shrugged.

"Ahh, sorry to hear that, Jimmy. We're all running from something I guess."

"Well, my da' was killed in an I.R.A. bomb when I was fifteen or so. He was a policeman. It was a kick in the teeth for a lad to lose his father like that."

Frank shook his head. "I'm really sorry mate, I didn't realise. I lost my parents when I was young. Car crash."

Jimmy grimaced in sympathy and he held up his beer: "To loved ones." A clink of bottles. "Yes, let's drink to that."

The light began to break as the two men staggered through the sand. The orange glow of a rising sun sparkled on the sea, revealing a fishing boat out on the bay.

"This is the best thing I ever did, so it is," Jim started, admiring the same view Frank was.

"All those shitty days of packing, driving and shovelling crap in people's gardens. It's like, why doesn't everyone just take off, leave it all behind? This is what I'm gonna do from now on, Franky boy, jus' work when I can and travel and enjoy the world's beauty whenever possible."

"Exactly right," Frank agreed.

As they approached their line of huts in the early morning light, Frank noticed something was wrong. The towel he'd left hanging outside was strewn over the steps, his door was slightly ajar and, with a sinking feeling, he suddenly noticed the damage of a forced entry on the frame. Inside, his clothes were strewn over the floor. He dived down into his bag, desperately looking for his money and passport. Both were gone.

"Shit!"

"I'd better check my hut too," said Jimmy and he quickly moved across the yard.

Frank tried to retrace his steps in his alcohol-riddled mind.

Jim returned after a couple of minutes.

"My place too, only I left my valuables with the restaurant owners."

Frank stood up, looking around, flushed with anger. "Shit! I just cashed in a large travellers' check!" he punched the wooden wall suddenly, with the side of his fist, and stepped outside, looking around angrily, as if the culprit might just still be hanging around.

He slumped down on the steps to his bungalow, sobering up quickly as the realisation hit that he was now virtually penniless, apart from the small amount of money he had on him.

***

"Hi ... Richard?" There was a pause on the line.

"This is Richard."

"It's Frank, from Bangkok. We went to Pat Pong. Remember?"

"Oh yes, Frank. How are you? Enjoying the sights?"

"Yes, or I was. I have a little financial problem. I was thinking about your offer."

"I see. Sorry to hear that. Where are you now?"

"Well I'm at Suret Thani, I've just been to Koh Samuri."

"Can you go to Krabi? I have a friend there."

"No problem."

"Great. Find the 'Bird House' in Krabi town. It's very quiet down there. You'll meet a guy called Greg. Be there by the fifteenth; that gives you a week. He'll give you everything you need."

"Thanks. Listen, I've a friend in the same boat, we both got robbed at the same time. He's an Irish fella. Is there anything he could do? He's broke as well."

Richard exhaled slowly over the line.

"I'm not sure. Probably not right now, not this time, but we'll see ... maybe something later. What's his name?"

"It's Jimmy Duffy, but it's no problem, Rich. Thanks, mate."

"Goodbye, Frank." The line went dead.

Chapter 10

Theo left his rented condo overlooking the beach in a short-sleeved white shirt and slacks. A Toyota pick up truck stood outside, its engine purring as Theo climbed in. He nodded at the driver and they pulled away.

The Toyota moved fast down the Mapusa-Anjuna road towards the town of Mapusa inland.

"Take it easy," said Theo, in Chinese Mandarin.

The truck paused at a crossroads while a herd of goats were shepherded across, and Theo leaned and spat from the window. His mirrored sunglasses glinted against the hot sun, turning towards an old man who was sitting outside a makeshift wooden snack stop. His watery eyes glanced up at Theo briefly, considering him for a moment before looking away. He reminded Theo of photographs he had of his late father, Daaruk Kumar.

Daaruk had come from Southern India and had always wanted to help people throughout his life. Born in the Bengaluru region, he had moved to study at Mumbai University and made the decision to join the International Red Cross. The war in Vietnam had begun and Daaruk found himself based in Saigon at the Red Cross Vietnam Southern branch where he met Theo's mother, Pham Thi Qui, a Vietnamese nurse. Eighteen months later, Theo was born – as Amith Kumar – in 1968, just as the combined forces of the North

Vietnamese Army and Viet Cong launched the Tet offensive against U.S. army positions.

Daaruk's work required him to be based up towards the war zone for a while, just as the war intensified. On a particularly humid hot day in May 1969, Daaruk and his small team entered a village to bring medical supplies. A passing U.S SeaCobra attack helicopter sweeping the area mistook them for Viet Cong and attacked them with machine gun fire. There were no survivors.

The young Amith and his mother weathered the storm until 1975 when Saigon fell to the Communists. The bitterness at his father's death stayed with Amith throughout his youth and he was won over by the communist cause, joining the party and becoming an active member.

At the age of twenty, Amith travelled to Hanoi in northern Vietnam and worked for the administration of the party. Being mixed race, Amith had to work extra hard to prove his loyalty, but he didn't care. His aim was to make a difference in the way he saw the world, his motivation was a kind of vengeance.

After a few months, Amith got an opportunity to visit the Hong Kong branch of the Chinese Communist Party with his boss, for a strengthening of ties between the two parties. Amith was amazed at the wealth he saw on display there but equally disturbed by the hidden poverty embedded in the urban concrete jungle that was shown to them by the local party leader, Hu Lam.

"See how Capitalism divides and pushes down the poor here. They never show you this side of Hong Kong, do they?"

Amith had seen his share of poverty but had to agree it didn't make any sense considering Hong Kong's high per capita wealth. He was then introduced to a tall man from Beijing called Peng Quan. Quan told him, due to his cultural background, he would be a useful asset to the mainland's cause. China was soon to take back Hong

Kong from the British and there was a lot of preparation required. And so Amith's involvement with the 5th department of Ministry of State Security had begun.

The truck negotiated the swarms of tuk-tuks, beaten up cars and scooters as they entered the town. It was market day; stalls and traders peddled their wares selling everything from fresh fruits, vegetables and livestock to carved wooden monkeys and fake branded clothing. The main street thronged and heaved with a mass of locals and the odd traveller checking out the offers.

The truck turned off and parked up in a quiet street, scattering a group of street dogs.

"I'll call you in a few hours and you can take me to the airport," Theo said, jumping out of the truck. The driver nodded and drove off. Theo unlocked a door that led through a garment shop, nodding to the owner, who impassively sat staring out toward the front. He then proceeded to climb a creaky stairwell and unlocked another door to a sparsely furnished office. There was a single desk, a filing cabinet with a fan on top and a table with a few papers scattered across it. Theo switched the fan on and removed a painting on the wall which revealed a safe door. He dialled the combination and pulled out an M-125 Fialka electro-mechanical cypher machine, which was the size of a typewriter, and placed it on the desk.

Theo then plugged it into a socket in the wall and connected it to the phone line before typing in the words: *Frank Bowen*.

Chapter 11

Frank shuffled along the shore from the phone booth and headed to the bus station with his heavy bag in tow. He had decided to travel to Krabi early to check everything out.

Krabi was indeed a quiet town. The streets ran in squares across each other and there was a main road along the riverfront, which moored various tourist boats and a seafood restaurant. Small islands jutted out from the emerald water as reaching for the clear sky. Frank had heard 'James Bond Island' was around here where they had filmed 'Man with a Golden Gun', but that little excursion would have to wait.

Frank looked at the notes he had jotted down when speaking to Richard. They included the name of the place with a rough map. The guesthouse café had an array of photos of local beach places to stay. There was no sign or mention of this 'Bird Cage' place though?

"I want to go the Bird Cage, tomorrow?"

"Bird Cage?" said the jovial, moustached, Thai man. 'There is a place called the 'Bird *House*' just outside town."

"Ah right. Yes, that's probably it."

"Run by Mr Ron."

"Uh huh."

"Do you bird watch?" the proprietor asked, looking at Frank intently through his shades.

"Uh? ...oh yes ... sometimes."

The man babbled Thai at a bored looking kid playing the computer game in the corner of the café and then picked up the phone and spoke to Mr Ron. The bored kid strolled past Frank and got onto a scrambler bike, revving the engine impatiently.

"Yes, he take you there now," the café owner gestured for Frank to jump on the back.

They scooted up through the town and up a steep hill where the countryside began. He busted a left through an open cast iron gate hidden from the road and, suddenly, they had arrived. It turned out Frank could have easily walked there in ten minutes, but at least he now knew where it was. He offered the bored boy a ten baht note, but he just smiled and took off without a word, leaving Frank alone in the undergrowth.

Plants grew high in the small, secluded garden and the grass was badly in need of a trim. Small insects buzzed in the evening ambience. There was a scent of sweet flowers lingering in the air and an old rusty bike leant against a white building that ran parallel to the path. Here were the guest rooms, a line of eight doors and a toilet and shower area at the end. Frank walked past the bike and saw the man sitting on the patio through the gloom.

Mr Ron stood up from his chair, sporting a white linen suit, and greeted Frank. He was average height, but more western looking than most Thais. It was the prominent nose and chin that made him look like an Englishman.

"Hello," he said, slightly effeminately, "I am Mr Ron. Can I help you at all?"

He seemed surprised at having a visitor but was warm and friendly and spoke fluent English with barely a trace of an accent. Behind him, there was a wide wooden patio with a railing extended over, what seemed like a marshland. The panoramic view extended across the horizon, revealing long grass, palm trees and little shack huts dotted in the distance. Beyond the jungle overgrowth, mountains rose on the landscape; grey hazed mounds for their distance.

"I know it's out of season and everything, but I wondered if I could hire a room for a week. I prefer a quiet spot like this, to staying in the town," said Frank as he walked slowly over to the railing, gazing out at the view.

"It is indeed a beautiful spot,' the Thai man agreed, moving elegantly to what looked like a disused dusty counter at the side of the bar. He took a key from a hook that belonged to pigeonhole shelves and handed it to Frank.

"Somewhere for the birds to come; that's why we have bird watchers stay here," he said, smiling.

"Yes, I can imagine."

Frank paid for a week and, as Mr Ron began to walk away, the Thai turned back to face Frank. "There's a fridge behind the counter, help yourself. Just write down what you've had."

With that, Mr Ron disappeared on his bicycle down the path, moving awkwardly through the long grass.

Frank had a smoke on the patio and gazed at the view again. Did Mr Ron have a connection with Richard or this Greg character? He was supposed to meet Greg here in five days time, but right now the place was completely dead. There was no one else there at all.

He looked in the fridge and saw a couple of beers and some lemonade Sprites. The bottle tops were slightly rusted and, on closer inspection, all the drinks in the fridge were long out of date. Cardboard boxes filled with old newspapers lay neglected behind the counter. Opposite the bar were more boxes piled up and an old sofa that had definitely seen better days.

He then checked out the room, which seemed clean and in order, then looked in the toilet and showers. Dead leaves fluttered across the pale tiled floor and large cobwebs lurked in the corners. It didn't look like there had been any guests for some time.

Frank lay on his bed, watching the ceiling fan whip through its rotation, and felt his eyelids flicker as they became heavy.

***

As if it were a harbinger of the death to come, a black crow flew across the road ahead and perched on the dark tree that looked evil to Frank's eyes. The bird hopped along towards the end of a branch and then suddenly froze as if to watch them drive by.

"You're driving too fast, Patrick!"

"No, I'm bloody not. It's a dual carriageway, a 70 miles per hour limit..."

Frank pulled his coat tighter around him as if to blanket out the anxiety.

"It's still too fast, I don't like it!" his mother shouted from the passenger seat.

"Stop arguing, I hate it," Frank whined, his little fingers fidgeting uncontrollably. His father turned his head slightly to address Frank. "Sorry, Frankie. Your mother, she's..."

"Watch out for that bloody lorry. It hasn't seen..."

The memory dimmed; time slowed down, taking its toll; spinning and rushing forward into the blackness. And then only a boy's scream remained.

A light faded into the darkness, circling slowly and then the face of a concerned woman filled his vision. "Are you awake?"

A dull pain on the side of the head helped bring the face into sharp focus. A nurse, with brown friendly eyes, clicked the torch off and stared down intently, brown wisps of hair fell around the back of her ears.

"Can you speak?" she asked.

The boy coughed and mumbled something which the nurse could not hear. "Do you want something to drink?" The boy shook his head.

"Where's my mum and dad?" he asked before coughing again.

"Shhh. It's ok. You try and get some more sleep, now."

***

Frank opened his eyes, his mouth felt like sandpaper and there was a distinct buzzing in his head. He sat up slowly and decided to stroll down to Krabi town for a bite to eat as the contact was not due for a good four hours.

Draining his beer bottle in the empty bar, Frank looked at his watch, a fake Omega he had picked up in Bangkok. Finally, it was nearly time to meet his Greg character.

After a walk back up the hill from the town to sit on the veranda at the 'Bird House' and listening to the crickets, Frank watched the odd starling fly across the horizon. He did a batch of press ups to burn off some energy and then paced around the patio.

About an hour later, Greg arrived and shook Frank's hand. He was French, average height, with a dark ponytail and goatee beard. He wouldn't look out of place on the backpack circuit. They went to Frank's room and Greg gave Frank a pack of two hundred cigarettes.

"Thanks. And the gems?"

Greg looked at him quizzically for a moment and then smiled.

"They're in one of the packs."

"Gems, not drugs, right? That's what we agreed."

The man looked offended for a moment.

"You can check. Definitely not drugs."

"OK. So where do you want me to go?" asked Frank.

Greg moved to the bed and took out a map of Bangkok, laying it flat on the yellow sheets, and pointed to a street near the Bangkok railway station with a pen.

"There's a country and western bar called 'Texan Bill's'. Richard will meet you there and pay you. Get there for the eighteenth. Seven o'clock in the evening."

He folded up the map again and put it in his pocket. His eyes flicked around the spartan room as he held out his hand.

"That's all. It's a piece of cake. See you again, perhaps."

Greg left the room and Frank listened to the hum of his car disappear as he stared at the Lucky Strike cigarettes on the bed. He picked them up. They were shrink-wrapped in clear film as if brand new.

The following day, Frank took the overnight tourist coach back to Bangkok. He hardly slept and his mind flipped between Jodie, his new friend Richard and then once again, Maria.

It was a strange way to say goodbye, disappearing like that. Still, she didn't owe him anything. It wasn't like they were an item. Frank couldn't help wondering if he'd see her again. There were so many faces while travelling, he thought, most of the time they turned up again somewhere along the trail.

Frank didn't intend to hang around Bangkok for long. He wanted to sort out a new passport from the Embassy to replace the stolen one and get his money.

Texan Bill's was a themed country and western bar, where the waitresses wore cowboy Stetson hats and a small band played bluegrass to the delight of what Frank assumed was Bangkok's American ex-pat community.

Richard was in a corner booth and waved at Frank.

"Well? Easy peasy, right?' he said, grinning at Frank as he sat down. Frank had the cigarette pack in a plastic carrier bag and held onto it tightly. Richard nodded, immediately understanding Frank's expression that told him he wanted to get straight down to business.

"OK, I need to check the goods...in the back." He jerked a thumb behind him towards the toilets.

Frank hesitated for a moment and then slowly pushed the bag across the table and watched as Richard disappeared with it into the restroom. A waitress took Frank's order for a beer and then he waited, trying to ignore the growing tension in his stomach. He needed that money badly and as he closely watched the toilet door, began to wonder what would happen if the man called Greg and just given him a normal carton of cigarettes, with no gems. Frank hadn't checked them. Deep down, he hadn't wanted to know.

The door opened and Richard made his way back towards him, expressionless. Easing back into the booth, he placed the carrier bag onto the bench next to him. His hand moved under his shirt and he unclipped a shoulder money pouch and handed it over to Frank.

"Sorry about the sweat, mate. But it's all good. Here's what we agreed."

Frank took the pouch and checked the contents under the table. He allowed an internal sigh of relief at the sight of the notes inside.

"Have you ever been to a Thai boxing match, Frank?"

***

The atmosphere was heavy with smoke and the cries of a thousand Thai yelps as the opponents literally kicked the shit out of each other. Their combination of punching and kicking blurred fast and furious in the caged ring, jabbing at each other like furious cockerels.

Richard turned to Frank, sweat glistening on his forehead. "This is what it's all about, eh Frank?"

Frank nodded silently, unsure of a reason to argue.

"So, why could Greg or someone else not have brought them up?"

"Simple logistics, Frank," said Richard. "Yes, any number of people could do it, but people I work with are very busy. Also, I need Greg in the south at all times. Anyway, I trust your face and you're from the old country." He patted Frank on the back in a jovial gesture of friendship.

At that moment a short, stocky Thai man came up and spoke to Richard in Thai. Frank couldn't hear them anyway and continued to watch the match. The man in the blue corner was getting the upper hand and getting kicks and punches through his opponent's defence.

"Frank, this is Police Lieutenant General Chatri Anuwat of the Thai Royal police, for the Bangkok province."

Frank shook hands and felt slightly unnerved that Richard was introducing him to a Thai policeman, a very high level one at that.

As if reading his mind, Richard winked at him. "It's OK."

The police lieutenant smiled at Frank but said nothing. His eyes studied him for a moment before returning to the boxing ring. He drank some kind of liquor from a paper cup and was approached by another Thai man who took a wad of Thai Baht notes from him. Frank guessed that the police lieutenant was having a fairly hefty bet on the outcome.

Chapter 12

Richard walked past the Grand China Hotel on Thanon Yaowarat and then crossed the busy road that bustled with Chinese street traders hawking their exotic Asian dishes. He stepped into a secluded bar and moved slowly to the back, looking around for someone. His eyes took a while adjusting to the low lit interior which was illuminated with dark blue and pink lights fixed inside paper lanterns. Finally, he saw the familiar, smartly dressed figure of a striking mixed race man with shoulder length hair sitting in an alcove near the back.

"Hello, Theo."

"Hello Richard," said Theo, acknowledging him curtly.

Richard sat down on the expansive leather seat and signalled the waitress for a drink.

"So, how is our friend?" asked Theo.

"He's made contact. He's in. I had him do an easy courier job from the South," Richard replied, evidently pleased with himself.

"Good," said Theo in a matter of fact manner.

"He mentioned a friend called Jimmy Duffy, who might be up for something."

Theo didn't mention he already knew who Jimmy was and had arranged the theft of both their possessions and money in Koh Samui. Unfortunately, Jimmy hadn't been so careless to leave his main valuables in his hut. But with Frank almost out of money he was more likely to take up Richard's offer.

"That is good to know. Does Frank trust you?" Theo took a slug of beer, his sharp blue eyes settling on the Englishman.

"Yeah, I think so."

"Well, he had better. We'll probably need his friend too," Theo whispered.

"So what's this all about?" Richard asked, before immediately holding up his hands in a defensive gesture. "Sorry, I know I shouldn't ask."

Theo ignored him and fished a five hundred baht note out of his wallet, tossing it onto the table next to his half-finished beer and stood up.

"I'll be seeing you," he said and walked off. Richard held his beer up, glancing sideways as Theo disappeared past him. "Great to see you too, Theo," he said.

Chapter 13

Frank walked along the Thanon Yaowarat road and glanced up at the address Richard had given him. It was an old, dilapidated, concrete building with a heavy steel door. A metal plaque had the name, 'Stokes Consultancy' etched into it, with an intercom just underneath.

For the past few days, Frank had been weighing up Richard's latest offer. "It's great money," he had said. "Less than a day's work and a trip on an aeroplane," Richard had grinned as if that was the icing on the cake.

"It doesn't involve drug or gem smuggling does it, Rich? Because you can bloody well forget it."

"Absolutely not, Frank! It's completely legal, working with Asian Government agencies. The only reason this has come up at all is because I know people in Government circles."

Frank figured it was worth hearing them out. The alternative, as a sympathetic Swedish traveller listening to Frank's woes had suggested, was selling his passport and reporting it stolen to get a replacement. A Swede called Bernt knew an African gang and he could make the introductions. Frank did not even consider it but he was worried about his finances.

The gem run hadn't paid that much and he knew his cash wouldn't last. There wasn't even enough to get back home. The alternative was to run crying to the British Embassy and he didn't fancy that at all.

Frank pressed the buzzer.

"Good afternoon."

"It's Frank. To see Richard Stokes."

"Hi, Frank."

The door buzzed and Frank let himself in. Richard had explained to him that he used different names. A vital contingency in his line of work, he had explained.

Inside the sparse room, there were two desks and a large table, as well as various computers, phones and a fax machine. Richard greeted Frank with a smile and a handshake and introduced him to the Thai police lieutenant he had met at the boxing match, who once again smiled and said nothing.

"This is Dean Whiteman." Richard gestured to a tall, officious, western man in a grey suit who peered at Frank through his gold-rimmed glasses.

"How do you do, Frank? Thanks for coming," he smiled and gave Frank a firm handshake.

Richard offered everyone drinks, said a few words and then handed over to Whiteman.

"I'm from the Legislative Council of Hong Kong. We are mainly dealing with the transfer of Hong Kong to Chinese rule in 1997. However, we've been asked to help the Hong Kong authorities and the Special Duties Unit test their counter-terrorism responses in a drill."

Whiteman paused and sipped from a glass of water.

"What we're basically looking for are volunteers to help with the exercise. You will be compensated and I'll come onto that in a moment."

Frank glanced around at the group of men. He remembered Carl had once mentioned something about similar drills taking place in England. It made sense.

"The exercise will involve various journeys that must take place at a certain date and time. I can't emphasise the importance of this enough."

Frank nodded in agreement.

"We'll pay you $5000 US and naturally you will receive the travel expenses to Hong Kong. Half in advance. It'll be a same day return flight so no accommodation is needed. Does that sound agreeable so far?" asked Whiteman.

Frank leaned back in his chair. "May I ask why this has all been arranged in Bangkok and what the Thai police connection is?"

"Fair question, Mr Bowen. Exercises such as these are carried out throughout Asia, usually as a planned blueprint. So each nation, and this has included South Korea, Vietnam and Malaysia, have an agreement to share intelligence when it comes to counter-terrorism. The agreement includes exercises of this kind."

He paused again and, when no one spoke, continued: "Your reference to the Royal Thai police and the police Lieutenant General here, simply ties in with that. That's really all I can say without breaching confidential information."

Frank nodded his head, satisfied. "Ok."

"Richard mentioned you may be able to bring in a friend. We need two people for the exercise ideally. It's the same deal for him if he's interested?"

"I should be able to get hold of him, I'll ask," said Frank.

"Good. It has to happen on the 2nd of February, which is one week from today. As I said, dates, times and places are very, very important. There are a lot of resources being devoted to this. Do you understand?"

"Yes loud and clear. Like I said, I'm happy to do it. I need the money to stay out here for a bit longer and then get back home," said Frank.

"Great. Any further questions?"

Frank shook his head.

"Richard will brief you on the details and will give you all the documents you need."

With that, Dean Whiteman shook hands with Frank and left the room.

Richard smiled at Frank, patted him on the shoulder and offered another round of drinks. The remaining men in the room seemed to eye him with a curious regard.

***

The next morning, Frank managed to track down the number of the hostel where Jimmy was staying. He had already moved on but had left a forwarding phone number as promised. Eventually, Frank got through and filled Jimmy in with the details.

"Sounds like it'll be worth looking at. I certainly need the money, Frank. It'd be great to catch up again anyway. I'll get the overnight to Bangkok."

Jimmy Duffy met with Frank a few days later, as arranged at his guesthouse, and they caught up over a few beers.

"So it's all kosher then, you think, Frank? I can't afford to get into any murky waters. I didn't mention my ma. She's sick. Breast cancer. I received a letter last week. So after this, I'm off back home."

Frank looked pained and leaned over to put on a hand on Jimmy's shoulder. "Jimmy, I'm really sorry to hear that mate. You should get back there and be with her."

"It's ok. I need the money. I can use it to help her or take her on holiday. Hey, any excuse to stay in the sun, eh?" he said, winking at his friend.

Looking out onto the street he was facing, Frank watched a group of builders as they scurried along rickety bamboo scaffolding as if they were on a tightrope. He had gone over the details with Richard and it all made sense to him. The money would keep him on the travel trail for a long while yet. He could do the rest of Asia and then the rest of the world beckoned. Australia, New Zealand? The prospect was truly exciting.

"If you're absolutely sure, Jimmy?"

The Irishman nodded.

"OK. It's just an exercise; which is pretty common in most countries. I know my friend who works at MI6 said it was pretty standard practice at home," Frank said.

"Well, if you're happy, I'm happy. Here's to Hong Kong, Frank."

The two men clinked beer bottles to their new found adventure.

Chapter 14

The plane from Bangkok banked a hard left as it came into Hong Kong International Airport at Kai Tak that jutted out into Kowloon Bay over the impressive skyline. It was touted as one of the world's most dramatic air descents and the two men would certainly have agreed with that as they stared at the sky-high buildings flashing past their window.

As instructed, Frank and Jimmy parted company at the airport terminal, shaking hands and confirming their meet rendezvous, before Frank headed out to find a taxi. The flight had been late and neither of them had time to lose. Frank waited in line for about ten minutes and jumped in with his small backpack when one became available.

"Tsim Sha Tsui star ferry please."

Studying his map carefully, Frank plotted out his route once again. He needed to take the short ferry journey across to the island and from there get the 11.30am MTR train to Causeway Bay. He glanced at his watch which read 10:45. He was already sailing close to the wind.

The taxi crawled along the road and Frank looked across at Kowloon, shimmering in the dusty heat. Eventually, they reached the Kai Tuk tunnel where bright sunshine was replaced by the artificial glare of the tunnel lights. They reappeared onto the East

Kowloon corridor and headed towards the west of the city, where ramshackled buildings, covered in Chinese graffiti, towered over them on each side.

After cutting through a number of side streets, they rounded a corner and the majestic scene of Hong Kong Island, with modern, jutting skyscrapers and the mountainous peaks behind them, came into view.

At the ferry terminal, Frank paid the driver and joined the crowds of locals mixed with tourists, moving slowly through the turnstiles into the waiting area.

Climbing up to the upper deck Frank leaned against the rail, gazing across the water as the ferry began its short journey. Another ferry passed them; heading in the opposite direction and a tugboat scooted across their path up ahead.

He glanced at his Omega for the umpteenth time. The layered ferry terminal slated on concrete pillars grew closer and Frank moved towards the exit bay to get off quickly. Once clear of the departing crowd he jogged towards the main Connaught Road, asking general directions on the way, hardly waiting for the details. After getting lost for five precious minutes, Frank spotted the entrance and ran down the steps, joining a small queue at a ticket office. The time was 11.28am; he had two minutes. It was the train he had to get, no earlier, no later. That was the instruction.

He wished he had pushed for an earlier flight as his heart pumped in his chest, waiting behind an old woman, as she spoke to the official behind the glass.

Finally, she had her ticket and Frank stepped up to the booth quickly, ordering his, before bolting through the turnstile. His quickening steps weaved through people on the escalator down to the platform, where he caught a glimpse of the last passengers getting onto his train. The doors clunked shut just as his feet reached the smoothly polished platform.

Frank swore out loud as the train moved steadily away from him. He watched the glint of the end carriage disappear into the darkness, the rumble on the tracks fading until it had disappeared completely, leaving him staring at the dark red tiles of the tunnel wall.

"There goes five grand," he said out loud, dropping his haversack onto the ground in despair. "Shit!"

Frank loitered for a while, pacing the platform and then decided to leave the station. He walked back out onto the road and briefly glanced into a bar with a television that had attracted a small crowd. It was time to think this through and figure out how he was going explain this screw-up and, more importantly, figure how he could get the rest of the money.

The smoke filled bar was darkly lit, despite the hour, and he nodded to the barman who was making himself busy whilst glancing at the nearest television screen.

Frank sipped his beer and tried to think. All he could do was meet Jimmy at the rendezvous hostel and take it from there. His eyes wandered to the screen that a group of Chinese businessmen and locals were watching so avidly.

The anchorman spoke hurriedly in the local dialect against backdrop footage of rising smoke coming from a familiar skyline. Hong Kong's skyline. The shot changed to a reporter on the street talking to the camera. Behind him was a scene of chaos with policemen, ambulance crews and wounded civilians.

What followed next ran an ice cold chill through Frank's entire body—a still photographic mug shot of his friend, Jimmy Duffy, suddenly filled the screen.

Chapter 15

An hour earlier, Jimmy Duffy jumped onto the double-decker, North Point bound tram right on schedule. He looked around the crowded space and grabbed a free hand rest dangling down, before peering out at the busy King's Road. The tram faithfully followed the snake-like rail line into the Chun Yeung Street market.

Jimmy checked the next stop on the map and confirmed that it was his. He jumped off the tram as it slowed down and started to walk back, past the endless food stalls that grabbed the interest of passing tourists and locals alike.

"A quick coffee and I'm done," he thought.

The force of the explosion that ripped through the busy street from behind threw him onto the ground. The dense shockwave seemed to run through his entire body. Jimmy lay still for a few seconds, hearing nothing but a high pitched tone deep inside his ears. He slowly turned onto his side and looked back at the tram he had just stepped from and saw it was opened up like a sardine can. The roof spewed dense smoke, billowing into the sky.

For a moment, he supposed that somehow this was all part of the exercise. His brain trying to make sense of what his eyes were seeing.

That notion didn't last very long as, to his utter horror, he saw moving figures inside the burning carriage, flapping around wildly as they tried to escape.

Jesus Christ.

People lay huddled on the ground and then he saw the body parts, burnt clothes strewn across the road and pavement. A dense, sickening smell invaded Jimmy's throat and he turned and vomited hard and fast.

A woman staggered around screaming, part of her arm was missing and thick blood sprayed uncontrollably from the wound.

The smoke spread across the entire area like an attacking fog, turning the busy street –that had been enjoying a sunny afternoon – into hell on earth.

A bomb? Why a real bomb?

And then Jimmy realised.

He used all his strength to get onto his knees and felt wetness on the back of his trousers. Dark red liquid spread fast. He hacked and coughed as the smoke reached him, rushing past and spreading into nearby buildings and shops.

***

Thirty minutes previously, Lieutenant Chan of the SAS trained Hong Kong Special Duties Unit, or the 'Flying Tigers' as they were nicknamed, had listened closely to his earpiece. His four-man team had been on standby for several hours. Fully briefed, each man was in position one level up in the small hotel overlooking the Chun Yeung Street market.

All Chan knew from his superiors was that they had to focus on one man, whatever happened. The tip-off was that a dangerous Caucasian man was likely to be in the area at the time of the explosion and most likely to be on the tram. In the unlikely event of him surviving, they were to take him out.

When the explosion ripped through the street, Chan and his men were initially surprised, despite having forewarning but their professionalism rapidly kicked in and the job in hand became paramount.

"Ok let's go!"

Agent Xeng scanned the square through his field glasses. His colleague, watching through the sighting of his Lee-Enfield L42A1 sniper rifle, also scanned the street around the scene of the explosion. The two agents were positioned in a building that looked down the market street at the rear of the burning tram. The billowing smoke had started to obscure Xeng's vision and he caught glimpses of burning bodies and bloodied limbs, strewn on the concrete road. Several screams filtered back down the street. He breathed deeply and swallowed hard, trying to concentrate and stay focused. In his entire fifteen-year career, he had never seen anything like the scene that lay before him now.

He watched his fellow colleagues, dressed in black combat gear with helmets and night vision visors, holding their Colt Automatic Rifles in attack mode as they moved, one at a time, towards the scene of the explosion. Occasionally pausing behind street stalls, they checked ahead before moving forward again. Frightened civilians who were crouching or had been thrown onto the ground looked at them in astonishment.

"Any sighting, Bravo 9?"

"No, nothing yet. I ...wait!" As he was speaking, Xeng caught sight of what looked to be their target. He was a large man in a white shirt and on the ground on the far side of the tram. Then, drifting smoke obscured his vision.

"Ten metres ... keep going to the corner, he's right there."

Chan moved to the edge of the building and glanced behind him. Sun was right with him and the other two agents were on the opposite side, covering them both. He caught his breath and quickly looked around the corner, seeing the target at once and just as fast, moved his head back again.

Chan gestured silently with his hand, pointing it towards the tram and Sun moved quickly across behind the burning carcass of the carriage to the other side. A young teenage girl on the ground held out an arm towards the running figure, but he ignored her.

"Agent Sun, can you get a shot on the target?" Chan spoke firmly into his radio.

"Too much smoke, Lieutenant"

"Xeng. Can you see the target?"

"Yes, target has not moved; looks like he is wounded."

"Can you see a weapon?"

"Negative. But the smoke is getting worse."

"Ok Agent Sun, let's do it."

Chan moved around the corner, moving slowly toward the man as Sun simultaneously moved in the same direction from the other side of the burning tram.

***

Out of the mist, Jimmy saw a tall, padded, dark figure, closely followed by another figure a few metres apart. They wore some kind of gas masks, or visors, and were pointing their weapons directly towards him.

The fatigued clad figure closest to him seemed to adjust his weapon. Jimmy held his hands up and opened his mouth to speak; to tell them he'd been duped and this wasn't part of the plan. No words left his mouth.

Jimmy Duffy's last vision was a flickering flash from the muzzle of the assault rifle aimed at his head.

Chapter 16

Frank moved into an alcove at the back of the bar where another television was streaming an English version of the news. He strained to listen to the low volume.

"...Tram explosion on Chun Yeung Street market. No reports yet of the number of casualties."

The live footage showed a bird's eye view of the square with smoke billowing up alongside the city's skyscrapers. The tiny red and blue flashing lights of dozens of ambulance and security vehicles peppered the screen.

Frank's shaking hand could barely hold the beer bottle and he placed it on a table. His mind raced. The same mug shot of Jimmy filled the screen once again.

"Reports are coming in from eyewitnesses that police engaged and shot a western Caucasian man at the scene. We are still waiting for a statement from the Special Duties Unit."

Frank's head fell into his hands and he felt utterly crushed. Total confusion, fear and panic all seemed to combine into a potent cocktail of emotion, rushing through him like an injection of some powerful vaccination. He gripped the edge of the table hard and tried to clear his head, fighting the welling tears.

Think Frank, Think!

He and Jimmy had been set-up big-time. How the bomb had been planted on the tram he had no idea, but he was certain Jimmy wasn't carrying any device. It must have been there already, or put into his bag?

An intense fear run through him and his heart started pumping hard. His eyes moved down to his haversack. There couldn't be anything in there; he had rummaged through it at the airport. He tried to remember if he had left it unattended at any point and concluded he had not.

Nevertheless, Frank slowly and carefully opened the zip and removed the small number of items, one by one—his wash bag, spare clothing, moneybag and passport. He very carefully searched each of the side pockets. There was nothing out of the ordinary. Frank exhaled slowly.

"...a secondary explosion has been reported at the Causeway Bay MTR station. The East Concourse has been badly damaged."

Frank looked up at the screen.

Causeway Bay! The station he hadn't been able to get to for the arranged time.

I can't believe this!

Frank was fixated on the screen and thought about Jimmy getting shot. That meant he must have been specifically targeted and that also meant Frank was probably in danger too. It was time to disappear fast and get out of sight.

Seeing the gentlemen's toilets, he went inside. He had to change his appearance in any way. With soap lather, he greased back his thick black hair in a way he would never usually have it. He already had a pair of shades and would need to get some kind of hat. Unsure of whether it would make any difference he quickly changed his shirt, just in case it might help make him less recognisable.

Had he already been flagged up as some kind of bomber? Frank didn't particularly want to hang around to find out. He pulled out his wash bag to get freshened up, almost as a way of procrastinating before having to face the streets.

The small piece of card with its scribbled phone number fell out into the sink as he rooted around for his face wash. He stared at it blankly for a second, remembering how, in Goa, he had found it and then stuffed it back inside. It had stayed in there ever since.

Maria.

He remembered her saying she had family or some connection in Hong Kong. He took the piece of ripped card and put it safely in his wallet. That could well be the only option he had.

Chapter 17

A second Special Unit team had been dispatched to Causeway Bay and had split into four groups. The teams were not in full combat gear like their colleagues at the market but wore heavy navy vest jackets hanging over their T-shirts. They also had air-filtered masks hanging from their utility belts.

There were five exits for the station and they were all covered by agents. They mingled with the crowds heading in and out of the station and awaited their orders.

Causeway Bay was one of the most crowded areas in Hong Kong, with a shopping centre above the station that proudly hosted all the big brand shops carrying products from Japan, Europe and the United States.

Team Alpha waited around by the East entrance on Great George Street while Team Beta waited at the West entrance, with other teams covering other exits.

Each two-man team had only just got into position. Team Alpha, which consisted of Charlie Wo and Joe Yi, felt a distant roar and vibration underneath their feet. Both men instantly knew it was no train. Charlie Wo looked at the tall frame of his colleague, "That could be it. Did you feel that?"

"Radio it in," Agent Yi replied gruffly. Charlie nodded and pressed the disponder on the radio strapped to his right shoulder.

"Agent Wo here. We are just in position at the East Concourse and felt a tremor."

There was a slight pause before he received a response. "Move down to the station and look for the target and keep low. Emergency services are on their way," the radio hissed back at him.

Charlie nodded to his colleague and they quickly moved down the steps towards the underground station. A few metres down the subway, they heard distant screams and a wall of dust came rushing up the corridor, choking the two men and the handful of other people in the area.

Charlie and Joe quickly put on their masks before continuing down to the platform.

A stream of terrified civilians came running from the opposite direction, attempting to escape the scene. The two agents scanned their faces looking for the male Caucasian before gesturing to them to make their way to the exit. The chaos seemed to increase rapidly the nearer they got to the platform and the smoke thickened making it impossible to see anything. Everyone was choking and coughing and Joe spotted the first casualty, a middle-aged woman covered in blood, staggering around in a daze.

"Are you OK, Madame? Emergency services will be here any minute. Please make your way out now," he held her arm and manoeuvred her in the right direction.

"This is crazy!" shouted Joe.

"I know, I know. Keep focused. Remember, this man is supposed to be very dangerous." The target in the photograph they both had was Frank Bowen.

The two agents moved slowly towards the platform, occasionally helping a distressed passenger who had been lucky enough to escape with minor injuries. A chorus of wails and the sound of misery greeted them as they stepped down to the platform that was drenched in blood. They were soon stepping over limbs and bodies. A red heat blew from the carcass of the train that had exploded in the station. The carriages still contained passengers who desperately fought to escape the furnace.

Joe Yi caught his breath in his chest as he looked around at the pandemonium unleashed before him. He immediately depressed his radio disponder.

"Team Alpha at location. No sign of suspect. Multiple casualties. Where are the emergency services?"

"Right behind you. They'll be at the scene any moment. Just keep looking."

An hour later, all the teams reported that there was no sign of their suspect. Dead or alive.

Chapter 18

Theo Kampala sat at his desk in the Bangkok Hilton hotel room and prepared to make contact with his superior, agent name Oracle, within the MSS – Chinese intelligence – for just the second time in the year. He scribbled down the coded message, encrypted it and then input the letters into the modified Soviet M-125 Fialka cypher machine. His message: Operation Dizang successful but the Redshank bird has flown.

After sending the message, Theo waited as the crackling radio fizzed against the background hum of the air con.

In Beijing, a radio operator waited patiently, standing to attention in front of the large desk that Ho Zhang sat behind in his officious leather chair. He read the message sent by agent Bashe and was not happy at all. If one of the terrorists had escaped, then how was the operation a success? This had to be dealt with as soon as possible.

Zhang dismissed the operator and then walked to the window and looked across the river towards the hazy cityscape of south Beijing, his mind drifting. His office was in the Hang corporate building and looked exactly as if it was another department in the corporate infrastructure, but of course, it wasn't. No other employees of the Hang Company knew what the department on the 34th floor did.

He paced up and down, weighing his options and then returned to his oak desk to write another message on his notepad. Picking up his phone, he called through the internal line to the radio operator and asked him to return to his office.

"Send this to Agent Bashe," he said, handing the operator the slip of paper.

In Bangkok, Theo watched the Fialka cypher machine spit out the encrypted message onto a sheet of paper; his response from the Beijing station. He ripped off the sheet and translated the encryption.

It was an order to find the escaped bird and clean up. Theo stared at the message. Cleaning up meant tracking down Frank Bowen to kill him.

The television screen showed the latest images from the war in Kuwait. The eyes of the entire world were focused there. The operation seemed to be perfect timing. No doubt they planned that way.

Chapter 19

Frank dialled the number from a phone booth that was hidden down a side street. A female voice answered.

"Is that Maria?"

"Yes?"

"Hey, Maria. It's Frank. We never quite got to say goodbye in Goa."

There was a pause.

"Frank? How are you?"

"I'm fine, kind of. Listen, I'm in Hong Kong and wondered if I could see you?"

"Sure, come and visit anytime."

"Erm. Sorry for the short notice, but can I come over now?"

Maria laughed, "Ok, no problem. I'll give you the address."

Frank studied his battered map and thought about the best way to get there. He wasn't sure whether his photo was now plastered all over the media and needed to get to Maria's place undetected. Hopefully, his slightly changed appearance would help. He noticed – with worry – that Happy Valley was fairly close to the Causeway Bay, an area he obviously wanted to avoid.

Frank hailed a taxi and asked for Deep Water Bay on the far side of Hong Kong Island.

Thankfully, after some initial small talk, the driver didn't pay close attention to his passenger, enabling him to lie low in the back seat. The journey seemed to take an age and Frank relaxed once they had reached the island.

At Deep Water Bay, Frank hailed a different cab to the Hong Kong Cricket Club. He asked the driver to stop nearby and waited until it had disappeared before crossing the main road and climbing secluded steps that weaved up the hill through a wood. The roads were set on hills that offered occasional fantastic panoramic views of the sea and other small islands that appeared merely as grey shapes in the haze. All the low-set houses were protected by walls and gates.

The bell rang, a distant low chiming that seemed to fit perfectly with the calmness and tranquillity of the neighbourhood. It seemed a long way from the hustle and bustle of central Hong Kong. A familiar face answered the door.

"Maria?"

She beamed a welcoming smile that brought back why he had been so attracted to her.

"Hey, Frank. Wow, really nice to see you again."

They hugged and Maria gestured for him to follow her. "Come in."

The house had the typical décor of an expat residence. The wall of the hallway was covered with paintings and photographs of landscape scenes from Amsterdam and London.

Frank heard the distant faint background sound of Budgerigars punctuating through the house. The slow fans whirred overhead as they entered a large living room area with tall windows that overlooked Kowloon. Chinese art, depicting ancient warriors and dragons, hung on the wall and a large, beautifully decorated vase sat on a low table near the door.

"Are you ok?" She looked at him, frowning, sensing the tension in him.

"It's been an insane day, Maria. I'm still taking it all in, to be honest. I need to clear my head and figure out what the hell is going on."

Frank accepted tea and explained the day's events. It sounded unbelievable, even as he uttered the words, but he continued. Maria stared at him in disbelief, her mind obviously whirring like a motor. After he had finished his story her head was in her hands.

Frank looked at her with a hint of harshness. "You *do* believe me, right?"

"Yes Frank, yes, of course." She went over and put her arms around him. She whispered, "What are you going to do?"

"I've got to go through the whole thing. It seems I've been set up as some kind of dupe for this bloody mess and I was obviously supposed to die in that tube explosion. I can't believe I was so stupid. Now I'm some kind of target. Yes, I could give myself up, but everything points to me ... and Jimmy. I can't stop thinking about him. I pulled him into this and now he's dead."

Frank felt the anger rising inside him; anger mixed with desperation and confusion.

"I'm caught bang in the middle of some bullshit. If I give up I'll be framed, I know I will. That bastard Richard set me up. I need to get to Bangkok and find him as soon as possible."

Frank was letting his anger run forth and Maria seemed to know better than to start to argue.

"Who else was in Bangkok?" she asked.

"This Dean Whiteman guy. Very officious. He said he was part of the Legislative Council of Hong Kong."

"Wait a minute, yes. My father works for them. Remember me telling you? Maybe he can help."

"I doubt very much that this Mr Whiteman was part of that

department; he was just a very slick conman but it might be worth checking out. There was also a Thai police lieutenant. I can't remember his bloody name."

Maria frowned. "That's pretty high up in the police rank. Was he in on it, do you think?"

Frank shook his head.

"No idea." He looked up at Maria. "Listen, do you think your father could get me a passport? A fake one, I mean?"

Maria paused, "Hmm, I'm not sure. I'll try, Frank. He's actually coming by soon, so you can meet him."

"Great. I stashed most of the money they paid me in Bangkok, thinking I'd go back there. Maybe I should get it back. I think I'm gonna need it."

Maria stroked his arm. "Hmm, that all sounds a bit dangerous at the moment. Please don't worry about money, I can lend you some."

"Thanks, Maria, that's appreciated. But I also need to track down this Richard guy."

"I don't think that's a great idea either."

Frank stood up and walked to the window, staring across the city skyline.

"I know it's not a great idea but ... shit, I don't know what to do," he said.

"The British Embassy?"

"No. It's too risky. I don't know who's involved." He turned to Maria. "You know what's so funny about this mess? I was running for that train like my life depended on it and if I had caught it I'd most likely be dead now. That's pretty ironic, huh?"

Chapter 20

Christopher Johnson, Chief Inspector of the Royal Hong Kong police force, shifted through the report shared with his department by the Counter Terrorism Response Unit telling him there was a second Caucasian terrorist at large in his city.

He stared at a photograph of Frank Bowen. According to the report, his suspected connections included MI6, the Ulster Defence Association in Northern Ireland and various drug cartels, although no direct evidence was offered for this. He was also deemed very dangerous. It claimed that he had been involved in various criminal activities from an early age and in 1988 – facing drug trafficking charges – had co-operated with the authorities to help bring a larger network of criminals to justice.

However, Johnson could see no reference to actual criminal records or the specific trial mentioned. He frowned and quickly clicked and rotated a pen in his hand over and over.

His team was scanning C.C.T.V. footage at that very moment but nothing had come up so far. The Police were also watching all main transport hubs and he had ordered extra men to patrol the city.

Johnson picked up the phone and asked for Lim Su Sung, his senior inspector of police, to come into his office. After five minutes, Lim knocked on the open door and entered. He was a tall, prominent figure, wearing round glasses, and a workaholic who had served well for the force. The two men had worked together for over five years.

"Hi Lim, have you looked through this?" said the chief inspector, gesturing to the report in front of him.

"Yes, I read through it."

"It came through from the local MI6 station," the chief said, almost as a question.

"Apparently so, Sir."

"Take a seat." He gestured to the chair opposite him and the senior inspector dutifully sat down and looked at the chief expectantly.

"It's interesting that MI6 passed on this information so readily. It's not their usual style."

"Yes and very quickly too," agreed Lim.

"I know it's not usual practice, Lim, but can you get in touch with your point of contact in London and get confirmation of this report for me? Also, request any further information they have on this Frank Bowen."

"Right away, Sir."

***

Detective Inspector Douglas Brown walked down the East Concourse at Causeway Bay station, surveying the echoes of destruction which became starker as he neared the platform. Broken glass, plastic and metal had spread across the polished tiles on the ground, spreading a sea of blackened dust and debris, only punctured by dozens of cut-out shapes where bodies had fallen since removed from the scene. Dried blood had stained wide areas of the platform and the thick atmosphere made Brown feel a wave of claustrophobia for a moment.

He laid his eyes on the charred husk of the train that had every single window blasted out, giving it a ghost-like aura. Where the windows had been; only inky black gaps remained. Yellow ticker tape sealed off entire areas and a white-suited forensic team, with masks and gloves, painstakingly picked through the debris and bagged anything of interest.

Brown carefully stepped over to the train and spoke to the officer in charge who walked him along to the carriage where the explosion had detonated. This carriage, almost in the middle, was blacker than the rest.

"This is where the explosion and the resulting fire were at their most intense," said the Officer, dryly. "A large fireball ripped through the remaining carriages, both ways."

Brown peered inside, through the blackened gaps of the windows. The plastic passenger seats had melted into unrecognisable shapes and the whole floor seemed to have been ripped upwards as if some incredible force had punched its way through. Shards of metal from the train floor streaked in all directions. Brown couldn't begin to imagine what it had been like to be caught up in this horror.

The detective inspector took an hour looking around the scene, taking notes and mopping his brow with a handkerchief to wipe away the floating dust that clung to his skin, before walking back up the concourse. He found his car and sat in it for a moment, breathing heavily, trying desperately to dispel the nausea.

He glanced at himself in the car mirror; his swept back, grey hair seemed to him to be verging on white and he adjusted his thick-rimmed, black spectacles. He had definitely aged rapidly since moving to Hong Kong, he noticed solemnly.

Swapping from the London Met to the Royal Hong Kong force was not something he had expected five years before, but meeting his Chinese wife on a holiday break in Hong Kong had set him on an entirely different path in life. She worked in a department store, a fashionista. Yet her feet were firmly on the ground and he loved her for it. Funny how life turned out if you were open to change, he'd thought, and the moment that he decided 'to hell with it' would always stick in his mind. He married the girl and put in for a transfer.

Hong Kong was not without its problems. Triad activity seemed to be on the increase and a new kind of anxiety had gripped the city, especially with the Chinese handover six years away. And now it looked like a new fear was going to close in; the fear of terrorism.

The detective inspector started the engine and headed west, skirting around Victoria Park, then along King's Road towards Chun Yeung Street market and another scene of carnage.

Chapter 21

Maria's father walked into her living room. He was tall and cut an imposing, confident figure. His cropped silver hair was a stark contrast to his tanned skin and he wore a dark suit with a white shirt, no tie. The man stared at Frank for a moment with a hint of surprise which quickly turned to a broad smile.

"This is my friend, Frank," said Maria, before turning to Frank. "And this is my dad, Peter."

"Pleased to meet you, Frank." Both men shook hands. Peter Chapman spoke with the confidence of a man who knew what he wanted and how to get it.

Frank felt an uneasy tension for a moment as if Peter was aware of what he was about to ask. Perhaps Maria had mentioned something to him on the phone?

Maria made some green tea and they sat around the coffee table in the breakfast room that held a spectacular view across Tai Tam Country Park. The clock chime signalled the passing of another hour from the hallway.

"First time in Hong Kong?" asked Peter, carefully pouring tea into each cup as if it were a practiced art.

"It is." Frank felt unable to elaborate further and instead asked permission to smoke. Peter waved him on, his face impassive and unreadable. He finished the tea and his blue eyes moved onto the stranger in his daughter's house.

"So, I'm in a situation," Frank began. "Some kind of messed up intelligence exercise I got involved in. I take it you've seen the news?"

Peter nodded, "I have." He clasped his hands together in front of himself, elaborating no further and instead crooked his head slightly, signalling Frank to continue.

After going through the story once again, Frank drained his tea and fixed Peter with a level stare. "I have been completely stitched up and now I'm in serious trouble but I was definitely nothing to do with what happened. You do understand, Mr Chapman?"

Peter simply nodded in acknowledgement and then turned his teacup on the saucer and took a sip. Placing it back on the glass table top, he leaned back in his chair.

"Well. It certainly sounds serious. I'm tempted to say you need to get to the British Embassy, but I'm sure you've already thought of that."

"Yes," Frank replied, "But right now I don't know what I'm dealing with or who's involved. I just want to get a passport in another name so I can get out of here. I need to figure things out."

"To be perfectly honest it sounds like you could have been a bit more wary before making the decision to do this...exercise."

"It all looked legitimate. They had the credentials, the paperwork. There was no reason to think I would be set up and put on some death list," said Frank, raising his voice slightly. He knew he had been foolish and suddenly felt the need to justify his decision.

Maria's father leaned forward and stared at Frank sternly.

"I don't want my daughter mixed up in this, you hear me?"

Frank held up his hands. "Believe me; I didn't know what else to do. I don't want that either. I just want to figure this out."

"Dad! He needs help. He's not just some guy I met whilst..." Maria seemed to catch herself and quickly looked away.

Her father gave her a sideways glance, leaned back in his chair again and settled his eyes back onto Frank. He exhaled slowly as if making a considered decision.

"I cannot afford to get directly involved in this either, as I'm sure you'll understand. But, as you are a friend of my daughter, I want to help, of course. I can give you a name of someone who can help you. But that's all."

"I understand and am really grateful for your help Peter," said Frank. He glanced at Maria who smiled at him reassuringly.

"Also, I know this is a long shot," Frank continued, "as he probably used a fake name, but there was a man calling himself Dean Whiteman in Bangkok. He appeared to be in charge of the exercise and said he worked for the same Council as you." Frank described the man he had met as Peter and Maria listened.

"Hmm, can't say I know anyone with that name or description, but I'll ask around for you if you like."

Frank nodded, relieved at the feeling that he had some support, no matter how small.

***

The following afternoon, Frank walked through hanging beads into the cramped store that seemed to be stacked high with everything from toasters to Chinese lanterns. It was empty of people and Frank moved to the counter glancing around at the ceiling high stacked consumer goods. Jasmine incense lingered in the air.

A distant sound of a babbling television drifted through a door behind the counter and then, unexpectedly, a face of an older woman appeared, eyeing Frank suspiciously.

Frank put down a black card onto the counter and she glanced at it without picking it up. She turned and shouted in Chinese into the back room. A young man appeared with a cigarette hanging from his mouth, dressed in a vest that had seen cleaner days and yellow knee length shorts. The older woman disappeared behind the back again.

"Hi there. I'm Frank." He gestured to the card on the counter. The young Chinese picked up the card and peered at it for a second.

"Friend of Peter?" he asked, narrowing his eyes at Frank, yet clearly unhappy that this foreigner was standing in his store.

"That's right. He's helping me and I wondered if you could too?" asked Frank, hoping that the visit wasn't going to turn into a waste of time. He had to get this passport.

The young man certainly knew Peter Chapman. His father, a successful Hong Kong businessman, held him in high esteem. The English expat had helped him secure a contract with a British company and, in the spirit of the Chinese term "guanxi" – a favour for a favour – this was obviously repayment time.

Eventually, the young man nodded and lifted up the counter hatch to let Frank through. They walked through more cluttered rooms and Frank saw the old woman sitting on a sofa watching the television. She glared at Frank and said something in Chinese. The young man shouted back and soon they were walking down some steps into a basement which housed, even more, boxes of televisions and other white goods.

At the back of the windowless basement room, was a clear space with a desk, a filing cabinet and piles of papers. The young man gestured for Frank to sit in an old armchair while he slumped down behind the desk.

"I'm Li," he said, briskly.

"I'm Frank," Frank said for the second time. "I need a passport."

Li nodded. "It will cost five thousand US dollars and I need you to supply a photograph."

Frank shifted uncomfortably in his chair.

"Five thousand? Your friend ... our friend, Peter, said you would help me out. I wasn't expecting it to cost that much," Frank stared at Li apprehensively.

"It's a risky business. Cannot be done cheaply. But you friend of Peter, so let's say two thousand."

That's quite a drop from five thousand, thought Frank. He decided not to look a gift horse in the mouth and pulled out a wad of notes that was rolled into tubes. Maria had kindly lent him the money.

"Ok, I'll give you a grand now and the rest on delivery," said Frank, handing over a roll.

Li considered the money and then grabbed it. "Sure, no problem with that. You have photograph?"

Frank handed over a passport photo he had taken earlier that day in his new look of combed-back hair with the beginnings of a beard he was growing.

"And the name?" asked Li.

Frank thought for a moment. "Make it Joseph Burns, that's all I can think of."

Li nodded and wrote down the name. "No problem. A few days, OK?"

"Thanks for helping me out, Li."

Chapter 22

"Hello Carl," said the voice at the other end of the line. Carl recognised Frank's tone immediately and sensed a hint of tension.

"Frank? How are you? Back already?"

"Not quite. I need your help with something."

"Sure, no problem."

"I need you to find out some information for me, on some names. I can't explain everything right now, but I'm in a spot of bother. Life or death situation, mate."

"Oh right? I'm sorry to hear that. I'll try to help you as much as I can, Frank. Is there anything you can tell me?"

Frank paused on the line, the cogs in his brain turning.

"The fact is, I'm finding it hard to trust anyone, possibly even you, so I can't really say too much. It's connected to that Hong Kong thing. I was set up."

"Frank, what the hell's going on? Did you say Hong Kong? I read something about a couple of bombs but it wasn't widely reported here. There's a war in the Gulf that has everyone's attention."

"Yeah. Look, can you help me or not? If I give you some names, can you look into them?"

Carl paused and flicked his pen around in his fingers.

"Of course I'll do what I can, Frank. I don't want to get into trouble though."

"No, it's just getting background information on some names. They set me up, said it was a drill. Richard Desmond – also called himself Richard Stokes – based in Bangkok. There was another man, Dean Whiteman who said he worked for the Legislative Council of Hong Kong. If there's anything you can find out about them, that would be appreciated, Carl. I don't know if these are real names though. I'll ring back sometime tomorrow if I can."

"Sure, but Frank, that's not a lot to go on..."

The line went dead.

Carl replaced the handset and thought for a moment, frowning heavily.

Chapter 23

Chiu Wah On – or agent Tian, as was his codename – stamped on the cigarette butt and ground it into the concrete with his heel. The message had come through at his safe house to go deliver on his orders—the moment he had been patiently waiting for. He strolled briskly across the road and pushed back the beads that hung in the doorway.

The young Li looked up from his newspaper at the smart gentleman entering the store. He presumed he was a white-collar worker. His second thought was this man was no ordinary office worker, judging by the long scar that arced prominently on his face.

Chiu smiled warmly at the young man as he cast his eyes around at the stacked wares for sale. A sudden movement caught Li unaware and the man grabbed the back of his head and smacked it down onto the counter in one swift action. He felt the cool butt of a gun pressed against his temple. Chiu pressed hard against the back of his head, keeping Li in place.

"Listen very carefully. You raise any alarm, shout or struggle, you are a dead man. You do exactly as I tell you and you will live … understand?" Chiu whispered menacingly into his ear.

"Yes understood," Li mumbled. His face was pushed so hard against the wood he could hardly speak. Chiu pulled his head back up.

"Now shut the shop."

Li did as he was ordered and flipped the sign over to display 'closed.' His mind raced; so many questions. But for now, he decided just to co-operate.

They moved behind the counter, out of sight from the street and into the back room, the man signalling for Li to sit at the table.

"Your Western friend, where is he?"

Li hesitated, scared, but he knew straight away who this man was referring to—his recent visitor from Peter Chapman, his father's friend.

"Western friend? I know quite a few expats."

Chiu took out a photograph from his inside jacket pocket and held it up in front of Li's face.

"No, I don't recognise him."

"Do not lie to me, my friend, otherwise I promise you will not see out the next minute." The scar-faced man levelled his gun towards Li's face. His eyes seemed to darken, like dead coals.

Li glanced at the gun; his heartbeat seemed to speed up in his chest. He believed what this man was saying, yet his instinct was telling him to keep as much information from him as possible, especially the connection with Peter Chapman. On the other hand, he didn't want to die.

Li closed his eyes. "He came here, into the shop. That is correct."

He felt the gun barrel slowly press against his forehead. Li dared not open his eyes, as though looking at death would somehow encourage it.

"He came in for a fake passport," Li spoke slowly, wishing he wasn't speaking the words that came from his mouth. "He picked it up this morning."

"Show me," the calm voice replied.

***

Theo Kampala picked up his latest message, translated the encryption and then burned the piece of paper. He quickly packed a small bag, placed the encryption machine in a case and left his small room, glad to be on the move, and stepped onto the busy Bangkok street. He hailed a taxi and headed to the train station, watching the blur of traffic swirl around him.

The train station was the usual scene of chaos and he shuffled his way up the line to buy his ticket south. Theo figured Frank Bowen, hunted like a dog, might end up at a familiar hideaway. The same place Richard Desmond had sent him on his gem run.

Chapter 24

Detective Inspector Douglas Brown flashed his badge at the policeman who stood guard outside the front of the shop and made his way through to the counter and then down the steps to the basement. A forensic team of two, dressed in white overalls and masks, were just finishing up their procedure of sweeping for prints and blood samples. Li's body was at the centre of the room, sat upright and slumped against a pile of boxes, his head hanging forward. He had been shot in the head from the front. A claret red splash cast a stark pattern against the cardboard box behind him. His hands were bound behind his back with cord and his feet were also tied.

Brown nodded grimly at the police sergeant at the scene and cast his eyes over the body. 'What have we got?'

"Victim is named Li Wu. Multiple cigarette burns, especially around his face. Fingernails extracted. Looks like he's been tortured for information. Cause of death is most likely the bullet to the head."

"You don't say?"

The sergeant ignored his quip and stood staring straight ahead.

"Not a robbery then?"

"It doesn't look like it at this stage, Sir. Nothing was taken as far as we can see. An eyewitness says he saw a Chinese businessman enter the shop sometime around noon. Another local woman said she came around 12.30 and the closed sign was up."

Brown thought for a moment. "Take down their statements and then send them to me together with the forensic report when it's ready. What about the victim's family?"

"His mother's in the kitchen with an officer. She was out at the time and came back to find him like this. We are in the process of locating the rest of the family."

"I'll talk to her before I leave. Anything else?"

"Yes, crucially there's evidence the victim was involved in passport forgery. A few stamp blocks, lactate film, a variety of blank passports and all the tools. I've gathered them up for evidence."

Brown scanned the gloomy basement one more time. "Thanks, Sergeant." He climbed the steps to the rooms above and spoke briefly with the sobbing mother who had found her son's body, trying to give her some comfort. As he left, Brown asked the officer with her to ensure a statement was sent to him as soon as possible and then returned to his car.

Chapter 25

Distant lights flickered from across the water in Kowloon and, apart from the familiar chorus of crickets and occasional noises escaping from the harbour miles away, the neighbourhood stood in near silence. Chiu crouched low and still, his eyes and ears straining with alertness from behind the large palm leaves, where he waited at the bottom of the garden. His main focus was on the tall windows of the living room. He caught a brief glimpse of a shadow move momentarily across the ceiling before disappearing again.

Maria set down a glass of red wine in front of Frank and slumped down next to him on the living room sofa.

"Thanks," said Frank, sipping the wine slowly. "So do you own this place?"

"My Dad does. I just live here and keep it warm." She patted the sofa arm.

"That's great," Frank almost whispered as he lost himself in the distant city lights.

"I know, I know. I'm such a lucky girl."

"There's nothing wrong with luck," he said. He could sure do with some himself, he thought.

"What's with the horse?" Frank gestured towards a finely sculptured piece, expertly crafted from dark wood that stood defiantly as if standing its ground.

"In Chinese culture, horses symbolise success, courage and loyalty among other things. That particular horse is older than Christ."

"Wow. It must be valuable."

"It is," she smiled, knowingly.

"My kingdom for a horse," he said, drily. Maria wrinkled her nose and laughed. Frank smiled at her and studied her face. The perfect lines of her eyebrows shaped to perfection, and the delicate tilt of her lips seemed to comfort him, as if everything was normal and fine, just for that moment. Her green eyes seemed to shine and intensify at his gaze, before glancing away, self-consciously.

"I'm sorry about all this, Maria. Barging in on you and everything. I really wished – hoped – the circumstances would be so different."

She took his hand in hers. "Hey, don't worry. It's lovely to see you, Frank. Despite the ... crazy circumstances."

Frank pulled her towards him, kissing her gently on the lips. They became lost in each other and for a second Frank had forgotten all his troubles.

He leaned back and gave a satisfied sigh.

"How about some snacks before bed, hmm?" she asked.

"That sounds good."

Maria walked across the room towards the kitchen and then stopped and froze as she glanced towards the hallway door.

Frank looked up at her, "What is it?" He turned towards the direction of her surprised stare to see a Chinese man in a navy boiler suit, half obscured by darkness, pointing a pistol at her. Frank made to get up and the intruder swung round, aiming the weapon at him, which made him stop dead. The man smiled benignly.

"Frank Bowen?" he asked.

"Who the hell are you?" Maria asked. Carefully, the man moved further into the room revealing a cold, hard face; his smooth skin severed by a moon-shaped scar. Maria held her hands up, her face fixed in an expression of fear as she ever so slowly inched forward toward him. "Please don't hurt us, please..." she continued.

The intruder levelled his gun at her, "Stay still."

"What do you want?" Frank asked. He was slowly standing up from the sofa. The Chinese man turned the gun on him, taking his attention away from Maria. "Stay where you are," he rasped.

Whatever he had come for, he seemed to be hesitating.

Maria acted instinctively, without thought of consequence, grabbing the vase resting on the table that she had slowly edged towards. In one swift action, scooping up the ceramic piece, she threw it at the man's head with all her strength. His left shoulder jerked upwards but he failed to protect himself as its full force smashed into the side of his skull. The intruder slumped back towards the wall, off balance, and Frank, seeing he was raising his gun, leapt at him to grab his arm before jerking it upwards, smashing his hand against the wall.

The gun fell onto the sofa and Frank followed up with a quick punch to the intruder's stomach as hard as he could, bringing his full body weight in behind the blow. The man's stomach was hard, well protected by muscle, but the force of Frank's punch still made him keel over and groan out loud.

Despite his obvious nausea and disorientation, the Chinese hurled himself at Frank, keeping his head low as he butted his chest. The momentum threw Frank backwards onto the coffee table, crashing the wine bottle and glasses onto the floor. Suddenly there was a hand on Frank's throat, gripping tighter around his larynx so he could not breathe properly. Before he lost control of the situation, Frank fiercely jerked his knee into the intruder's groin. The grip loosened and now it was his turn to gasp for air.

Maria quickly moved over to the sofa and grabbed the weapon.

She went around behind the Chinese, whacking him hard across the back of the skull with the pistol butt, grunting with the effort. His head slumped onto Frank's chest like a rag doll as the fight in him suddenly receded and then she quickly changed the gun around in her hands and pointed it straight at the back of the intruder's head. Frank slowly hauled the body off the top of him and climbed to his feet. Maria's whole arms were shaking.

"Great work, Maria. It's ok, it's ok," he said, almost whispering.

Maria nodded and handed Frank the pistol.

"Keep an eye on him; we'd better tie him up. I'll go get some rope," she said, finding her composure again.

As Maria left the room, Frank held the weapon in his hand, staring at it. He looked at the Chinese man slumped on the floor and wondered at Maria's calm, but powerful, response to the situation, glad of it, nevertheless.

"Don't you think we should question him?" asked Frank when she returned.

"No. I think we should get out of here," she said.

"Yes, you go to your father. Just..."

"No Frank. I'm coming with you."

Frank shook his head as he wrapped rope around the unconscious intruder. They needed to get out of the house first and then he would argue with her.

Chapter 26

Frank and Maria slowly shuffled forward in separate queues towards the customs checkpoint at Kuala Lumpur airport. Frank had his hair greased back and with his maturing dark stubble, his appearance had changed. He clutched the passport he had managed to get from the young man, Li Wu, in Hong Kong. A smart young Malay customs officer, sitting in a box, gestured him forward and checked his passport. He glanced at Frank and back again at the photograph, then swiftly stamped the page and handed it back, nodding without a word.

Frank waited briefly for Maria to come through and they headed to the luggage collection point together, giving each other a reassuring look. Maria had packed hastily after they had tied up the intruder, cleaned the gun of fingerprints and dumped it in the trash in downtown Hong Kong. At the airport, Maria anonymously phoned the police about the Chinese man tied up in her house.

It's not that they were running away, just buying time, as Frank had put it. He had questions he wanted answering, first in Krabi to see if Mr Ron or that Greg character were around and then to Bangkok to see if he could get the money he had stashed. It was a pretty loose, spontaneous and probably insane plan, but neither of them could think of a better option.

Maria insisted on tagging along and had vehemently dismissed going to her father for help, out of hand. Frank hadn't lied to her father when he said he didn't want her involved but Maria wouldn't say goodbye.

They made their way to the exit area of the impressively modern airport and caught a connecting bus to the railway station, a colonial-era landmark in the heart of Kuala Lumpur. The ticket office under the high canopy roofs sold them their tickets for the overnight sleeper to Hat Yai in Thailand, then they grabbed some refreshments and sat in an air-conditioned waiting hall, sipping their ice teas.

"I just have to go to the bathroom," said Maria, picking up her cotton shoulder bag.

"Sure," Frank nodded.

Frank returned to the thoughts that had been churning around in his mind on the flight from Hong Kong as he watched Maria walk away. He had been wondering about her lightning-fast reaction to the intruder and the ease with which they had overcome this, apparently, well-trained assassin. Maybe she had surreptitiously left him her Hong Kong number as if it were a backup plan to reel him in, if something went wrong, as it had.

Frank glanced around the waiting hall and then strained to see Maria disappearing through the crowd. At the same time, he couldn't really believe that she was involved. She had been nothing but a saviour and had, after all, attacked the intruder. But how had he found them? He knew the location of Maria's house. It didn't make sense.

Frank leaned towards a businessman reading a paper nearby.

"Excuse me, could you just keep an eye on this for one minute?" Frank asked, pointing to Maria's suitcase. The man nodded. Frank took his money bag and left the waiting hall, looking around for Maria.

A train had just come in and streams of people hustled their way towards the exits. Frank moved forward through the crowd and glanced around the platform area. Across towards the exit, he spotted a reflection of Maria in the glass of a café, making a call from one of the phone booths.

Chapter 27

Chiu Wah On felt an intense throbbing pain in his head, his whole body felt constrained as if wrapped in a coil and, before even opening his eyes, he knew he was tied up, wrapped in rope. The room was dark, except for the distant lights of the city that cast long shadows across the floor. Chiu tried to move his hands and loosen the rope slightly but it was tightly done. Fragments of broken glass lay scattered around him and he manoeuvred his body so he was sitting upright against the wall.

He breathed in and out, allowing his chest to expand and shrink and then shuffled and shook, slowly loosening the grip of the coiled rope around his torso. With a sliver of more flexibility, he was able to move his body around and get a broken fragment of glass into his hand. Slowly and deliberately, Chiu worked his fingers, sawing at the rope that bound him.

An hour later, the intruder was flexing his arm, repetitively opening and closing his fingers to get rid of the numbness. He looked at his watch; two hours had passed. He searched the room for his gun and, on not finding it, proceeded to search the house for anything else that might give a clue as to where they were headed. Finding nothing, he left the way he had come in and retrieved a small backpack that he'd previously hidden at the bottom of the garden. It was several hundred metres to his car where he retrieved the keys from his pack before driving to the nearest public phone booth.

Chiu spoke in rapid Mandarin to the voice at the other end and recited the passport details that he had forced out of the young Chinese at the shop. Then he hung up and headed to the airport. There was other work to do.

Six hours later, Chiu had checked into a hotel under an assumed identity in Bangkok.

***

After three days of hiding himself in the hotel, Chiu switched off the television and wiped down all the surfaces that he may have touched during his stay there. It was highly unlikely it would be a problem, but he liked to take precautions. He attached a residential services badge to his white shirt and picked up his red canvas bag that had been in the bottom of the wardrobe.

Checking out of the gated hotel under his false identity, Chiu walked up the relatively quiet Sol Prida promenade towards the main Thanon Sukhumvit road. The street gradually became busier as he walked in the fading sun. Street food carts sold their spicy dishes; restaurants and bars competed for business. A couple of office girls glanced at him as they passed. The air hung thick and humid, as it always did.

There was a bar, sheltered by umbrellas that seemed to sink into the sidewalk, with a sign offering happy hour drinks. Chiu slipped onto a table hidden from the road, ordered an espresso in fluent Thai and fixed his eyes on the apartment block opposite.

An hour later, Richard Desmond wiped his brow with a handkerchief as he descended the stairs to his apartment. He was looking forward to getting the payoff for delivering Frank Bowen to Theo's little operation. It would give him some much-needed breathing space as a few debts were starting to get out of hand.

What would happen to Frank? Desmond didn't much care. He was just another sucker tourist who had arrived in the land of Siam looking for adventure, although he was sure his fellow Englishman had a hidden intelligence behind that mask of nonchalance.

Richard's train of thought was interrupted by a knock at the door, which in itself was strange, as no one could get into the building without buzzing first. *Must be that fat prick from next door wanting to borrow something again,* he thought. Desmond peeped through his spy hole and saw the side of a Chinese man, glancing down the corridor.

"Who are you?" he said through the door.

The face – that bubbled into an oval through the fish-eye lens – turned towards the door and smiled.

"Mr Thang ... building maintenance services. I need to look at your air conditioning unit, Sir." He held his identity card to the spy hole.

"Really? You need to look right now?"

"If that is possible, Sir? There is a problem in other apartments and we want to make sure there isn't a possibility of failure during the night."

That would be a nightmare, thought Richard. Air con was the only way to sleep in Bangkok. He unchained the door and opened it. The man smiled at him and picked up a red canvas bag that he had placed on the floor. Richard stood aside and waved him in. He wondered, for a moment, how a service engineer came to get such an ugly scar but thought it might be rude to mention it.

Richard pointed towards the kitchen, "It's in there, pal."

The engineer moved towards the kitchen and glanced around the apartment.

"I hope it won't take long. I just need to check something," he said.

"No problem," Richard said as he turned to walk back into the living room, looking around for his T.V. remote. He found it under a newspaper on the sofa and pointed it at the screen, frowning in surprise as he caught the reflection of the engineer moving silently up behind him.

Chapter 28

Detective Inspector Brown shuffled into his desk chair and was glad to see the forensic report from the shop murder waiting on his desk. It told him what had been obvious; that the gunshot had killed the man and he had been dead for three hours by the time the body had been discovered. Various fingerprints had been found – most of which were Li's – but there was another set which had, so far, turned up no matches.

The Detective's phone rang and he picked it up immediately. "Douglas, it's Chris… Can we talk in my office?"

"Sure, Chief Inspector. I'll be right there."

Inspector Brown entered the chief inspector's office and closed the door behind him. The glassed box offered little privacy from the rest of the department, which Chris Johnson hated. He did have blinds, though, and pulled the cord to close them as was his routine.

He smiled at the inspector and gestured for him to sit down.

"Did much come up on that murder in Mercury Street?"

Detective Brown still had the forensic report in his hand and placed it on Johnson's desk. "Light torture followed by a single headshot that killed him. Still running fingerprint searches but nothing has materialised as yet."

The chief nodded and seemed to pause for thought. "I've asked for a meeting with the Special Unit chief in regards to the recent terrorist attacks," he said. Just then, there was a knock at the door; the figure of the staff sergeant was visible through the frosted glass, waiting outside.

"Yes, come," said the chief.

The staff sergeant held a report in his hand, eyes darting between the chief and the inspector. "I thought I'd better get this to Detective Brown as soon as possible."

Johnson gestured to the Detective, "Be my guest."

Brown took the report, dismissed the sergeant and read for a moment. He handed it to the chief who scanned his eyes over it and raised his eyebrows. "As I thought, there is a connection to the attack." The report in his hands featured a grainy photograph of Chiu Won On.

The chief stood up and started pacing the room. "So this Chinese intelligence agent has been placed at the murder of Li Wu, with fingerprints. He was obviously not very careful unless he wanted us to know. This is a very difficult situation, politically."

"Sure, but if he's murdering people in our city he needs to be found. What's your theory?"

"The Intel on those two British men paints them as double agents with criminal elements, but there are no records of any trials or convictions in the UK relating to the charges mentioned. We checked with London on Bowen and Duffy; according to them, they are not on any watch list nor have any records. They're clean." The chief fished around for the MI6 report in his filing cabinet and handed it to Brown.

"Can you look into it, Detective? I'd be interested in your angle."

Brown took the report and started flipping through it before looking up at the chief.

"You think this is fake?"

"It certainly seems that way. If it is, I need to know, especially if

Chinese intelligence is involved. Officially, this is counter intelligence territory, but I'm also meeting Teng from the Special Unit to try to get some co-operation. They were at the scene of the attacks soon after and seemed to be privy to this Intel. I want to know what the hell is going on. Can you tag along to this meeting, Douglas?"

Detective Brown looked up from the papers in his hand, "Yes, of course, Sir."

Chapter 29

Raksami – or 'Mr Ron', as he was better known – stepped into his small house just outside of Krabi town, having finished another day of teaching English at the local school. The familiar sound of chirping birds greeted him as he put down his briefcase and hung up his linen jacket in the hallway. He and his partner, Deng, had lived there for five years. They had made short work of the garden that his partner nicknamed the 'little paradise'. It was a favourite place for the butterflies and wildlife and the two men would often sit in the shade, talking and admiring the delicate bloom of white, lilac and purple parrot flowers, so called because of their resemblance to a parrot in flight.

He called to Deng, who answered from the back in the kitchen, asking him if he'd like tea. The phone rang and Raksami picked it up, thinking it was probably the school.

"Hello. Is that Mr Ron?" The voice was flat and spoke to him in English.

"Yes, this is him," he replied with his usual courtesy.

"Ah, excellent," the voice became more friendly. "My name is Mr Lee; I am visiting Krabi and would like to look at a room at the Bird House. I believe it is out of season but I am keen to have a few days' bird watching. Are you available today?"

Mr Ron had started opening his briefcase to search for his diary.

"Oh, today? Yes, of course. Are you nearby? I can meet you there in about an hour?"

"Excellent. I shall see you then." The man hung up.

Chapter 30

The overnight train journey was quiet and uneventful. There seemed to be very few people travelling. Maria suggested they take advantage of the opportunity to sleep and they both slumped, exhausted, into their bunks. Frank stared at the lights flicking past the window and listened to the rhythmic chug of the tracks.

Jodie's face came into his mind and he wondered what she might be doing at that moment. He remembered a snapshot, one of many, when she would stare at him with her mock pleading, brown eyes; the rest of her face covered by the duvet. It was always a signal to him to get her something, like a cup of tea or toast. Frank would always relent, playfully hitting her with the pillow as he climbed out of the comfortable sanctuary of their bed.

It had been over three months since he'd seen her and he realised that he might not ever see her again. He should have sent a postcard to at least let her know he was alright. They had been together for over four years, after all, and their split had been on good terms. He felt a wave of guilt for not doing so, followed by a moment of sadness. At least he could trust her. Then the terrifying thought came to him of her reading the papers or seeing the news and gasping in shock as he was named as the main suspect for that horrible attack in Asia.

Had the British press picked up the story? Did all his friends currently think he was some kind of secret operative blowing up innocent people for some political agenda?

He made a mental note to ask Carl about the press coverage and drifted into a troubled sleep.

In the morning, the train pulled into Butterworth; across the water lay the island of Penang. They hung around for an hour and then boarded a one carriage train to Hat Yai. Pulling out from the station, Frank saw the wreck of a train on unused tracks that stood like a ghost, a shell of its former self, left to rot and rust. The front engine carriage looked like it had been in some kind of collision. As the train picked up speed, the rooftops of Butterworth changed to fields and dozens of palm trees scattered across the landscape, with the waterway and the island of Penang shimmering in the distance. A wisp of cloud was the only contrast against the wide, deep blue sky.

Ironic. Penang had been somewhere he had planned to visit when he was travelling as a tourist. Now it was passing him by as he fled as a fugitive.

A jovial faced man, sitting opposite, tried to engage Frank and Maria in conversation, but they were both reluctant to talk or give anything away about themselves. Frank closed his eyes and tried to fend off the craving for a cigarette.

In Hat Yai, Frank and Maria hired a Toyota Corolla and they headed north towards Phattalung and then cut across country, west towards Krabi, along the quieter roads of the rural south. On either side, there was an endless sea of palms and fields, interspersed with the occasional dwelling.

Maria glanced at Frank, "Your beard suits you."

Frank scratched at it, "Believe me, it's not out of choice. I can't wait to get rid of it." He paused and let a silence pass before speaking again.

"You never did tell me why you ran off in Goa," he said, eyes fixed on the road.

She looked at him quizzically for a moment and then laughed. "Oh that. I so hate long goodbyes. Why? You think I should have made you breakfast?"

He smiled and stroked her thigh, playfully. "Breakfast would have been icing on the cake."

"I thought it was a one-off thing, at the time," she studied her fingernails. "Besides, you weren't long out of your relationship. I didn't want to be your rebound."

"And then I knocked on your door, a hunted man ... begging for help."

She wrinkled up her nose and laughed. "We'll laugh about it one day."

"We're laughing now, aren't we?" he grinned at her and they both giggled.

After a few miles, Frank glugged at a bottle of water and passed it to Maria. "You handled that chap pretty well, back at your house."

"Yes, I've done a few martial arts classes in my time. It's a handy skill to have."

"Are you a black belt or something?"

"No, nothing that advanced. Just a few classes."

That kind of makes sense, thought Frank as he pressed his foot down on the accelerator and overtook a lorry that had slowed him down.

"It's funny how we managed to overcome him, don't you think? I mean, for an assassin, he seemed pretty unprepared," he said.

Maria gave him a look and frowned. "Yeah, I guess so."

"I mean, if he wanted to kill us he could have easily."

Maria fixed her pale eyes on Frank once again, as if trying to read him and then shrugged. "I've no idea. I'm very glad he didn't though."

He caught sight of Maria's bare leg as she shuffled position in her seat, covered in those light freckles that also adorned her face, and couldn't imagine that she was anyone other than who she claimed to be. Frank let it drop and decided his mind was playing tricks on him.

Chapter 31

Frank parked the car a few yards from the entrance to the Bird House and stopped the engine. He turned to Maria.

"Stay here and I'll have a look."

"Let me come with you," she said. He took her hand in his and smiled at her persistence.

"I'd rather you stay here. Please. I won't be long."

Frank walked up the path that had overgrown even more since his first visit that seemed like an age ago. The chirping of the hidden crickets seemed to intensify in the midday heat.

As Frank followed the curve of the pathway he caught a glimpse of Mr Ron's bicycle, propped up against the outside shower room wall. *Good.* That meant he was here and Frank felt a rising optimism. Perhaps he would get some information and answers after all.

Flies spun around chaotically in the air as Frank approached the dilapidated guesthouse. It seemed they were coming from inside the communal area. He peered into the open space to see the familiar sea of palms and overgrowth on the other side, past the veranda set, like a framed painting in the gloom. An old armchair was planted in the middle with its back to him facing the marshland. As Frank's eyes adjusted to the low light, he saw an elbow leaning on the armrest. Mr Ron seemed to be enjoying the view.

"Mr Ron?"

No answer. The buzzing of flies seemed to intensify. Frank suddenly felt something was wrong and he felt his skin go ice cold.

"Mr Ron?" he repeated, more cautiously.

Frank slowly stepped towards the chair. A sickening smell hit the back of his throat, almost making him gag. He clasped his mouth and nose with his hand and inched closer. Now he saw the side of the head and a curious wire that seemed to spring out from his neck. The waxy skinned corpse of Mr Ron sat upright in the chair, buttery fingers grasping the armrest like an alert spider. A thin wire was tightly wrapped around his neck, cutting deep into the throat, and had opened a flow of dark red blood, soaking his chest and stomach through his tropical shirt.

Frank stood transfixed, unable to fully comprehend the sight or move away from the corpse. Mr Ron's eyes stared out across the veranda in frozen terror. Flies crawled over his face, dancing like demons.

"Hello Frank," rasped a low, quiet voice from behind him. Frank spun around, his entire body tense and electrified, heart beating almost out of control.

Half hidden by junk, the figure of Theo slumped on an old sofa, almost in a leisurely pose—had it not been for the dark red spread across his stomach, a violent contrast to his white cotton suit. He clenched the wound, his skin like a pale moon in the shadow, whites of eyes pointed toward Frank, pleadingly.

"Theo? What the hell are you doing here? What happened?"

Frank's eyes stared, disbelievingly, at the familiar face and edged away from the stench of Mr Ron.

"What the hell is going on here?"

Theo somehow managed to grin, despite the intense pain, his handsome face distorting something close to caricature.

"Big gangfuck, Frank. Wouldn't you say?" He coughed and

gasped, bile oozing from his mouth; his face sheened with sweat.

Frank swatted a hand at the flies. The air was thick like syrup and he badly wanted to leave, but instead, he stepped towards Theo.

"I'm sorry about Hong Kong, Frank. But you did well … you're smart." Theo struggled with each word. Frank stopped walking and stared at Theo in disbelief.

"Hong Kong? You were involved in that?"

Theo's eyes rolled and he was near passing out. Frank moved towards him and shook him back to consciousness. "Theo! Who did this?"

"Be careful Frank … he's … psychopathic."

Theo's glazed eyes focused on Frank for the last time, before the life ebbed away from him. Frank shook him again but knew he was dead. He glanced around once more at Mr Ron and slowly moved away from the sofa before turning to run down the pathway as fast as he could.

"Everything OK?" asked Maria, glancing at him with concern.

"Not really," Frank said drily and started the car. "Mr Ron and Theo were in there—both dead. Well, Theo died in front of me. I don't know what the hell is going on. Let's get out of here."

Maria held her hand over her mouth in shock. "Oh God!"

As they drove down towards the town to get onto the main highway, a blue Nissan weaved past them in the opposite direction.

Chapter 32

Chiu caught a flash of Frank – at the wheel of the car driving past him – looking like he'd seen a ghost. Chiu didn't think the Englishman had seen him. They must have been at the Bird House and seen his handy work. He had gone down to the town to get supplies, intending to clean up the scene and hide the bodies, but had been delayed for days as he waited for a local contact to get him new equipment. Now, an opportunity had arisen to finish off Frank and the woman. He stopped the car and backed into a driveway to turn around and sped down the hill until he saw the back of their hired white Toyota.

Chiu bitterly regretted not taking them both out back in Hong Kong when he had a chance. Why had he hesitated? He had never flinched when it came to his work before. Stepping into the room, the sight of the woman had thrown him. A thought had come to his mind. He had heard there was a double agent based in Hong Kong but was never privy to the identity of that agent for security reasons. No one was, apart from Oracle. He wondered if his hesitation was because for a split second he had thought it was her?

Or was it because he blanched from killing female targets? He found it hard to do, even if they were the enemy.

Chiu had been brought up by women. His mother and aunt were all he could remember and, as there had been no men around, he became the man of the house. It had helped his self-confidence no end. He fought his peers like a mad dog, never afraid of anyone and he felt aggrieved, angry that his father, who constantly worked away, in a different province to the north, never came back. There were rumours of course. That he had met another woman or had been kidnapped by bandits and his family could not afford to pay. Chiu bore the brunt of constant teasing about it from his school peers which only fuelled his frustration.

Then, he seemed to find solace in one thing—killing. First, it was animals; he would capture a dog or a cat and torture it to death, enjoying that moment as the last flicker of life passed through the animal's eyes. This seemed to calm his inner rage for a short time.

Chiu could not wait to get his P.L.A. army papers, but no opportunities that involved actual kills to satisfy his dark lust seemed to come his way. It was all training, crawling through mud, grappling over walls and roll calls. Only a move to Special Operations Forces would give him what he wanted, what he craved. Or so he thought. In his whole time with the unit, he had only racked up one kill and that was at long range.

Then he was visited by the military intelligence head, Oracle, and his life became dramatically more exciting. His first test: the prisoner in the yard at Nanjing.

And now the Hong Kong clean-up operation was becoming the perfect catalyst for his murderous side. It was what he had been waiting his whole life for.

Chiu lit a cigarette and flicked the ash out of the window, keeping just out of sight from the white Toyota ahead. His thoughts drifted back to Bangkok and the last few weeks. He regretted having to kill Richard the way he did. It was over way too quickly for Chiu's liking. He would have much preferred to have taken him out more slowly but unfortunately, his orders were to make it look like a gangland hit.

A shot in the back of the head took less than a second and it seemed like a big anti-climax; there had been a distinct lack of satisfaction.

Then he had the chance to give the Thai police chief the heart attack sermon. Now that had been fun. The wide-eyed fear as he struggled to stop Chiu stabbing the verminous liquid into the police chief's bloodstream and then watching the violent spasms of a full-blown heart attack.

The young man in the shop. A need to try and get information on Bowen's whereabouts had given him the perfect excuse to torture and inflict pain.

And then there was the guesthouse man, Mr Ron, who he had garrotted with piano wire. He claimed to know nothing as he begged for his life but he did say he had put up Frank Bowen. Chiu guessed he probably also had a connection with the criminal, Richard Desmond. Not that it mattered.

It was also unfortunate Theo Kampala had turned up at that moment. He had eventually believed Chiu when he said the victim was an enemy agent. Of course, Theo was his main concern, he needed to be hit, too many loose ends. Despite turning up at the birdhouse, with the same mission to kill Bowen, Kampala had served his purpose.

Yes, despite his doubts about the blonde woman's true identity, he would not hesitate to kill her or the main target now. This had to be wrapped up and quickly.

It had been a roller coaster ride and was just beginning as far as Chiu was concerned. He wouldn't stop now. Once he had disposed of Frank and his girlfriend, he would continue his killing spree. There was no going back.

Chapter 33

Lieutenant General Teng of the Special Unit leaned back in his chair, forehead creased with lines and a greying mop of hair hung loosely around his ears. He glanced at the gold watch that his wife had given him and wondered if she'd be offended if he bought himself a new one.

Opposite him sat Chief Inspector Christopher Johnson and Lim Su Sung, his senior inspector of police. There were jugs of water on the table as well as numerous files and papers spread over the surface but there already seemed to be a tension between the two groups.

The inspector read a paper in front of him before meeting Teng with a level stare.

"What we need to know is why Chinese intelligence is trying to kill Frank Bowen."

Teng raised his eyebrows, "Chinese intelligence?"

Inspector Johnson pushed a report across the desk. It was a file on Chiu Won On, his known history, military record and recent C.C.T.V. photographs of the same man in Hong Kong. Teng took it and frowned as he read. "You should have shared this," he said.

"I'm sharing it now. Anyway, this known assassin recently killed a shopkeeper who had helped Frank Bowen get a false passport. He then tracked them to the house of a Maria Amerman Chapman, where they reportedly overpowered him. It's worth pointing out that she is the daughter of Peter Chapman who works for the Legislative Council of Hong Kong. We received an anonymous call, but he had already escaped. We found fingerprints, so we know he was there."

Teng shrugged, "Yes, we stormed the house before your men got there."

"I know you did, contaminating a crime scene. That, we could have done without," remarked Johnson quietly. Teng frowned, "We were tracking a suspected terrorist for God's sake."

"Reports sent through from MI6 put Frank Bowen and Jimmy Duffy as main suspects for the attack, but they were certainly not working alone. We also had problems confirming these intelligence reports," said Johnson.

Teng said nothing, his face a mask of mild annoyance.

"You had a team at the market very soon after the explosion. You had a tip-off; can you tell us anything about that?" Johnson asked, his eyebrows arched in anticipation.

"I can't reveal anything about our sources, I'm afraid, except that we had reliable information about this operation," Teng snapped.

"And why weren't we told?" interjected Johnson.

Teng slammed his hand down onto the oak table, "We had no time! We had to move a team in fast and even then we were too late to stop the attack," the lieutenant stared hard at the chief inspector, clearly irritated.

Lim Su Sung leaned across and whispered into Johnston's ear. He nodded and turned once again towards Teng. "We'd also like to know the exact source of the reports about the suspects and this tip-off, Lieutenant General."

Teng waved a dismissive hand, his voice raised. "I cannot tell you that right now, maybe in time. But we have a job to do and that is tracking these terrorists and protecting Hong Kong."

"Yes and we have to do our job," retorted Johnson, "We need to find out what the hell is going on. There could be more attacks if Chinese intelligence is behind this and it looks like they are trying to frame MI6 for carrying out a false flag operation. We need your co-operation, Lieutenant."

Teng breathed heavily as if trying to hold in his temper.

"Of course we will co-operate, Chief Inspector."

"Then tell me the source!"

Teng paused and stared down at the table, "MI6," he said.

Johnson frowned, "So they knew about the attack beforehand? They told you and you went to the locations? Why weren't—" He stopped himself, frustrated.

Teng shuffled in his seat. "I'll level with you. The message was to keep your boys out of it, initially anyway. As I said, we were given very little time."

Johnson felt even more confused and he had several questions in his head. But he only asked one more, "Can you give the exact MI6 codename of the source?"

"There was no information on where it came from exactly. It was anonymously delivered."

Johnson and Su Sung glanced at each other. "Alright. Thanks for your help, Mr Teng." Chairs scraped as the meeting ended.

Chapter 34

"Yes, Governor Wilson, I'll keep you informed. Goodbye." The chief inspector put the phone down and glanced up at Lim Su Song, senior inspector of police.

"The Governor's anxious about the investigation. Is the detective inspector ready?" asked Johnson.

"Yes, he's already in the situation room," answered the senior inspector.

Johnson and Lim Su Sung walked into the long, bright room where Detective Inspector Brown was tinkering around with the window blinds to block out the fierce sunlight. A board on the wall had photographs, maps and notes pinned all over it, resembling a puzzle. Johnson and Lim Su Song sat down at the large table that dominated the room and slapped down their files.

The detective inspector cleared his throat, "I'll start with what we know so far."

"One bomb detonated on the number 61 tram at Chun Yeung Street market at 10.45am on the 2nd February. Then the 11.30am MTR train to Causeway Bay blew up as it entered the station at 11.37am, causing seventeen deaths and multiple injuries." Inspector Brown gestured to photographs of the immediate aftermath on the wall. He then produced the same passport photograph of Jimmy Duffy that had appeared on the news from a briefcase on the table in front of him.

"This man, who we had identified as Jimmy Duffy from Northern Ireland, was shot dead by the Special Unit at the street market immediately after the explosion. They had apparently been tipped off about the attack and were at the scene minutes after the explosion. We're still trying to find out where this tip-off came from. According to his file, he has Ulster Defence Association connections, but we're treating that with a big pinch of salt."

Brown moved to the other side of the board and pointed out Frank Bowen's passport photograph.

"Frank Bowen ... who is still at large and could be linked to the Causeway Bay attack. He arrived in Hong Kong on the same flight as Jimmy Duffy and they split up at the airport."

"This is where it gets interesting. Frank Bowen's fingerprints have been placed at the scene of the murder of Li Wu, who was a passport forger. There were also fingerprints of Chiu Wah On, an operative of MSS and former People's Army. We believe him to be operating for a division within Chinese intelligence. Witnesses also have placed a man of his description entering Li's shop before the time of death."

Brown paused and sipped his water before continuing. "An anonymous call, which was traced to Malaysia, tipped us off about an intruder in the home of this woman, Maria Amerman Chapman. Apparently, the intruder had been tied up, but we only found cut rope and signs of a struggle. No sign of Maria Chapman. We did, however, find fingerprints, from both Frank Bowen and our friend, Chiu Wah On.

Right now I'm coordinating a concerted effort to track down Frank Bowen and Maria Chapman. Frank Bowen is most certainly travelling on a false passport. We already had the airport security unit and all exit control points notified, but we can't rule out that he's already left Hong Kong."

Detective Brown paused and looked up at the two men sat in front of him. "Any questions so far?"

Johnson gestured for him to continue.

"So, we need to find these two suspects as soon as possible. Also, I've asked the sergeant to question her father; see if that brings anything up."

Lim Su Song shifted his weight in his chair, "It might be an idea to go through all their background files again to see if we may have missed something—an alternative to our current source if possible. It would be good to have a second opinion."

Johnson chimed in, "The two men, Bowen and Duffy. They came in from Bangkok, what's the track on their movements?"

"Our line of enquiry with the Bangkok police has revealed they stayed in a guesthouse on Khao San Road. I'll put a full list in the report."

Johnson clicked his pen, flipping it round and round in his hand. "Do we have any idea where the explosives came from?"

Brown sighed, "Not at the moment. It's much too early to tell. Forensics is still going through the crime scenes."

Johnson thought for a moment and then opened his file for the first time, almost hesitating. "Well, the location of the MI6 station that supplied the false Intel to the Special Unit came through and it's pretty worrying, to say the least."

He handed the sheet to Detective Brown, whose eyes quickly fell on the paper and widened as he saw that it was the station right there in their own city; the Hong Kong station.

Chapter 35

Frank found a phone and dialled the same number he had before, pouring Baht coins into the slot. It took a while; several redials later, Frank heard Carl's voice.

"Frank, good to hear you. There's nothing on a Dean Whiteman, no one with a record anyway. I have some other news though. Your friend Richard Desmond is dead. He was found in his apartment, classic execution style. He was just a lowlife villain, but a connected one, doing anything for the highest bidder. He also had a record in the UK, petty stuff, drug trafficking."

Frank took in the words as he watched a dog lying flat on its side, sleeping on the shaded platform as though it were dead. "He was assassinated?"

"Yep. Right or wrong, he's out of the picture."

"Jesus!" Frank paused before continuing: "Listen, I've got another name for you. Theo Kampala. I met him in Goa but I found him in Krabi with a dead guesthouse owner. He admitted involvement and then died before I could get anything more out of him. He'd been shot and the other guy had been throttled with piano wire."

"That doesn't sound good."

"What the hell is going on? Why are they doing this, Carl?"

"Frank, it's pretty complicated from what I can see. We've got the Hong Kong authorities screaming the same questions. It looks like a False Flag op. Basically the Chinese have set this up and tried to make it look like a MI6 gig. There are stories in the Chinese press that it's a Brit operation and the authorities are sticking to that story and accusing us of murdering Hong Kong citizens. To what end I do not know. You should get the hell out of there and come home."

"And get locked up for God knows how long? You know as well as I do that I'm still blamed by the Hong Kong authorities and probably by your lot, officially anyway. Maybe not by you personally, Carl, but I don't trust anyone at the moment."

"Look, I'm trying to find out all I can. Hong Kong Police did contact us trying to verify a report we allegedly sent them. It claimed you were connected to us as well as a few terrorist organisations."

"What?"

"It came from Hong Kong, not here. But Frank, listen, we'll sort this out, don't worry."

Frank fell silent as the line crackled badly for a few seconds before returning to normal. He was about to say something and then thought better of it as a thought crossed his mind.

"You OK, Frank? Hello?"

"Yes, Carl, I'm still here. Listen, what is the British press saying? Please tell me my photo isn't plastered all over the bloody Sun newspaper?"

"No, we buried it. There was a small piece in the Times but it's hardly made the news. Everyone's attention is on the Gulf war."

Frank sighed in relief. "OK, I'll call you later, Carl. Thanks for your help mate." He put down the phone and walked back to where Maria was waiting outside Surat Thani train station.

"Is everything OK?" she asked.

Frank forced a smile but his mind was still taking in what Carl had said. "My friend gave me some background but the Bangkok situation has changed slightly. Want to get a drink?"

Frank wondered for a moment if the report Carl had mentioned had been doctored by someone in London, not Hong Kong. Had he been involved somehow and was now attempting to cover his tracks by telling him?

Now that Richard was dead and God knows who else, there was no reason to go to Bangkok, except, of course, to get the money he'd stashed there. But going to the Thai capital now seemed too dangerous.

"Frank?" Maria studied him, her hand touching his as they sat in a café near the train station. He shook his head and smiled. "Sorry, I'm miles away."

His face went serious. "Maria. The guy I wanted to get some answers from in Bangkok is dead. I think you're right. Going there was never a good idea."

She looked at him, shocked, and then asked how. Frank told her and she looked relieved that he had scrapped that plan.

"I think I need to lie low for a while. I read about a great place. It means a train back South again, I'm afraid, and possibly a boat. If you're game, that is?"

"Well, well. You are the dark horse, Mr Bowen." She gave him a full smile, the one he could never resist.

Neither of them noticed the blue Nissan parked opposite.

Chapter 36

Ho Zhang looked out across the Beijing skyline; the grey smog settled leaving only vague shapes of buildings visible as if it were a painting. He suspected that he might be seeing the view for the last time and put on his jacket before checking himself in the mirror. He then made his way down in the lift, stepping out into the humidity, and told his driver to take him to the headquarters of the Ministry of State Security.

Zhang stepped warily up the polished steps to the building and entered the vast lobby area that echoed his footsteps up to the ceiling. He reported his appointment and verified his identification before sitting down on a long bench. After half an hour of waiting, a guard walked over, dressed in immaculate uniform, and asked him to accompany him to the lift.

On the top floor, Zhang waited another fifteen minutes before being called into the office. He bowed and sat down nervously in front of Xu Yun, the agency head, who nodded as he finished off writing on a notepad in front of him. Yun had a bullish red face and large bags under his eyes. A reflection of nearly fifty years in the intelligence service, thought Zhang as he glanced over the framed certificates on the wall behind him. There was a photograph of a much younger Yun shaking the hands of a man that he did not recognise.

Yun stood up and Zhang quickly followed his lead and they shook hands.

"Thanks for coming, Ho Zhang," he said gruffly and pulled a folder out that was set aside, opening it to reveal Zhang's file.

"So," he began, "Mr Zhang. A graduate of The University of International Affairs?" Zhang nodded in agreement. He had enrolled at the University in 1979 which had re-opened a year earlier, following a hiatus due to the Cultural Revolution. The University had been brought under the control of the Ministry of Public Security in 1965 and was charged with training intelligence agents for the Investigation Department, which later became the Ministry of State Security.

"And you seemed to be in the right place at the right time when the National People's Congress established the Ministry of State Security under the State Council?" Yun looked up and peered at him from under a pair of thick eyebrows.

"Yes, you could put it like that, yes." The MSS had indeed been established out of the old intelligence service, the Central Investigation Department of the Ministry of Public Security under Deng Xiaoping, perceiving a growing threat of subversion and sabotage.

Yun flipped the pages and came to one that he stared at momentarily before shutting the folder entirely and leaning back in his chair.

"The operations your department have been carrying out are, I'm sure, all in the interest of our great country. I've been receiving your reports. The Hong Kong situation..." The old man paused as if reluctant to mention details, "Is it under control?"

Zhang cleared his throat. He had prepared for this.

"Everything went according to our wishes, it was very smooth, Sir. The operation took two years to plan and we anticipated most things. We did have a slight problem in that one of the terrorists escaped the theatre of operation. I, therefore, sent our agent Tian to take care of it. This is still in progress and I have no doubt this will be concluded very soon," Zhang paused, unsure whether to carry on. The shadows under Yun's eyes seemed to darken and he leaned forward.

"We have had to respond to the changes in this operation. Denying it all, of course, and our press agencies have pointed fingers at the British, but if any of this gets out it will be severely damaging, you understand? Your plan to use Orchid to lay the trail to MI6 was a good one. But it seems to be unravelling, is it not?"

"Sir. The only problem is the terrorist, which we're on top of, I assure you."

Yun suddenly grabbed a Bangkok Post newspaper and threw it onto the desk in front of Zhang, jabbing his finger at a prominent story on two bodies found in Krabi.

"There are bodies piling up all over Asia. Your agent is cleaning up a little too publicly!"

Zhang bowed his head. "It won't happen again. I will send orders..."

"No, it will not happen again because you're going to shut down all operations as of now. The department is closed until further notice." Yun's face seemed to become almost as red as the Chinese flag on the wall.

Then, as quickly as he had exploded in anger, the old man seemed to calm again, "The State Council is concerned and asking questions. It's put me in a very tricky situation. I have no choice. Don't worry, you will not be arrested. You will be reassigned."

Zhang held his eyes shut for a moment and nodded. He began talking slowly and quietly: "Most of the agents I can recall. As I'm sure you're aware, agent Orchid is a quality product who delivers us very useful information from within MI6. How do you suggest I handle it?"

"I know losing such a valuable asset is not easy to take, Zhang, but they are going to be compromised sooner or later. Cut the agent loose."

Chapter 37

The curtains opened and Frank could make out the outline of Maria's hair in the gloom.

She climbed into the cramped space, astride Frank, finding a comfortable spot that suited them both. Their lips met and soon their bodies were intertwined in a quiet urgency. No words. Just a need to be close.

Yet the uncertainty of who she really was floated at the back of Frank's mind as they made love, both fighting to keep their gasps quiet.

Could she really be some kind of honey trap? Right then he almost didn't care.

As they lay together, letting the rhythm of the train envelop them, Maria gently stroked a loose wisp of Frank's hair back into place.

"Do you think if we get out of this there'll be something for us on the other side?" she whispered.

Frank smiled, moving his hand up and down her bare back.

"I'm sure there'll be a lot for us if we want there to be." He realised for the first time the risk she was taking by coming with him. She could just have easily stayed well out of it and pointed him on his way.

"Thanks for being with me," he said.

Frank's body absorbed the gentle rumble of the train carriages that vibrated the bunk bed. He wanted to drift off to sleep but he realised, with irritation, that nature called.

Untangling himself from Maria, he pulled on his shorts, slipped into flip-flops and made his way down the quiet, dimly lit train.

He had to pass through an empty catering carriage and then another sleeping car before finding a toilet. He closed and locked the door to the cramped cubicle, splashing cold water over his face from the running tap. Staring at himself in the mirror, he wondered when he was going to be able to shave off the bloody beard. Frank hated it. He then proceeded to take a leak.

A moment later, he opened the door to come back out and caught sight of a Chinese man passing by. He seemed familiar, even from behind, and Frank could see the edge of his scar. The intruder in Hong Kong! Amazingly, he hadn't noticed Frank, but it was definitely the same man. He knew it. Frank thought fast, realising that this guy was probably looking to quietly kill them in their sleep.

How the hell did he find them? Was it coincidence? No, it couldn't possibly be.

Frank stepped out of his flip flops and crouched low, waiting for his moment, whilst frantically looking around for some kind of weapon. The Chinese wasn't looking in the sleeping berths, instead walking purposefully along the narrow corridor, reading the berth numbers, obviously knowing where they were sleeping. The assassin approached the catering carriage, sliding the door to go through. Frank had to act soon. If the intruder had looked around behind him at that moment, he would have seen Frank stalking after him in nothing but his shorts but the Chinese continued through the sliding doors. Frank just managed to catch the door with his hand before it slammed shut and slipped through, immediately spotting a fire extinguisher placed just inside the carriage.

Struggling to release it from its grip Frank glanced up and saw that the killer was halfway through the catering carriage and would soon reach his and Maria's beds. He wobbled the whole of the canister to free it from its bearings but age seemed to have welded it in place as it stubbornly refused to budge.

Finally, with one final effort using all his body weight, it came free in his hands, almost throwing him off balance. He moved fast, running down towards the end of the carriage to build the momentum of speed, as the killer approached the doorway. The noise of the train hid the sound of his footfall. As Frank got to within three metres of him, Chiu started to turn around as if he sensed the movement approaching.

Frank threw the fire extinguisher at him with all his force. The Chinese instinctively dodged the canister but it still bounced off the side of his head, ricocheting off the plastic carriage door back onto his neck, throwing him forward onto his knees. Frank used the momentum of his speed to shove him over again with his foot, stubbing his toes on the man's shoulder.

Ignoring the shot of pain, Frank went to grab the fire extinguisher again but the killer adopted a defensive stance, kicking the inside of his knee. Frank fell back onto the ground, yelling in agony. Jabbing violently at Chiu with his feet; he tried to crawl backwards, the adrenaline pumping hard in his veins. The assassin attempted to pull himself to his feet by using the side of a table to lever himself while rolling back the canister out of Frank's reach with his foot.

Then Frank saw a chilli pot on the table and grabbed it, immediately throwing the powder at Chiu's eyes with a swoop of his arm. The man cursed in Mandarin, holding up his hands to his face as Frank followed up with a full kick onto his chest to force him back down against the carriage door.

Frank had to prevent the assassin from getting near him as he had seen first-hand, at Krabi, what he was capable of. He went to kick again and this time the killer grabbed his leg, twisting it at the same time, making Frank yell out in agony as he was pulled down to the floor. Chiu managed to lunge forward, throwing himself onto Frank, one hand grabbing his neck while the right hand came around, holding a syringe, pointing it directly at Frank's chest. Frank grabbed the arm holding the syringe, to prevent getting jabbed. The two men's faces were inches apart, Chiu's bloodshot eyes glaring at Frank with pure hatred; teeth bared as saliva dripped onto Frank's neck. Frank used all his strength to prevent the needle going into him—if that happened he knew he was dead.

Frank shouted for help. No one could hear above the chugging tracks and, besides, the doors both ends were shut. He was strong, but the Chinese seemed stronger and the needle inched closer. He felt his strength ebb as the hand gripping his throat seemed to close up his windpipe, draining him of air.

At that moment, a pair of hands appeared low down through the sliding door to grab the canister from the ground. Frank saw it was Maria and jerked his head; butting the killer's face with his forehead to distract him.

Maria held the fire extinguisher above her and brought it down at the back of the assassin's skull with all the force she could conjure. There was a sickening crack and Chiu's head slumped against Frank's shoulder, blood streaming from his wound.

Frank pushed the limp hand away from his throat, coughing and wheezing, spitting drool out of his mouth. Maria helped pull the lifeless body slumped on top of Frank aside. Frank managed to get free and crawled onto his hands and knees, coughing thick bile onto the ground. It was several minutes before he could speak.

"Thanks, Maria. This is becoming a habit," he rasped, voice almost gone as he somehow managed to flash her a grin.

"Can we get out of here?" she asked urgently.

"What about him? You think … he's still alive?" asked Frank. They both looked at the still unconscious body.

"Not sure." Maria leaned down and held his pulse for a moment. "Yes, just."

"Let's get rid of him, out the door," said Frank, slowly pulling himself to his feet.

"Throw him out of the door? That would definitely kill him, Frank."

"He was trying to kill me. This is the second time he's caught up with us. No more chances," Frank said, a look of grim determination on his face. Then he looked at the syringe gripped in Chiu's hand and eased it free, holding it up to the flicking carriage light to study the liquid content.

"God knows what this is. Maybe I could give him a dose of his own medicine?"

"We haven't got time for this!" Maria was looking back through the inner door window into their carriage, clearly worried.

"OK, let's do it. All clear?" asked Frank as he began to drag Chiu towards the door. Maria went through into the carriage and used all her strength to push open the main door which buttressed against the force of outside air that rushed by. The door swept back, banging against the carriage metal, and she quickly stepped back to allow Frank to drag Chiu to the doorframe.

A moment later, the body had disappeared into the inky night, along with the syringe and Frank pulled the door closed. He rested against it for a moment before gesturing to Maria. "We'd better clean up and get off this train."

Chapter 38

Douglas Brown pressed the buttons on the vending machine and watched his coffee cup drop down onto the tray and fill with black liquid, quickly followed by white, frothy milk. He grabbed it, winced as he burned his fingers and walked back to his desk where another pile of paperwork had magically appeared. The detective inspector cleaned his glasses on his shirt and blew the top of the coffee in an attempt to cool it down. The first report was from the forensics at the scene of the explosion in Causeway Bay.

He read for two minutes then jumped out of his seat, walking briskly to the chief inspector's office and knocked rapidly before poking his head around the door.

"Chief?"

Johnson nodded, gesturing for him to come in.

"Report from forensics. The explosion at Causeway Bay was caused by a device underneath the train, not inside the carriage. The force of it ripped up through the floor." He paused and handed over the report. "I actually saw that myself, but it didn't register at the time."

"Anything from the tram attack?"

"There's nothing in yet," Brown replied. "I have a feeling it will be the same."

Johnson leaned forward. "Douglas. Find Frank Bowen. We need

to talk to him. Tell him he's in the clear, but on the condition, he comes back to Hong Kong from wherever he's hiding. I'll make a call to MI6. It's time we compared notes."

Chapter 39

A row of clocks in various time zones on the pale, flaking wall had faithfully displayed the time for over twenty years. Mary Lo didn't hold much love for the windowless room that sat in the centre of the MI6 Hong Kong station but was thankful she was able to lose herself in her work to block it out at least.

She ran her eyes down the Personals advert column of the Hong Kong Times once again. It was a painstaking task to which she had devoted a few hours a day, unless she saw a lead and then she'd be off like a dog with a bone, working through the entire evening. The word 'orchid' written into one of the ads seemed to stand out, turning tiny cogs in her brain. It was one of the keywords on her list; words that cropped up that may have significant meaning and even be part of a message.

Having the job of checking the Personals column had, of course, drawn plenty of comments from her male colleagues. "You're secretly looking for Mr Right, eh Mary?"

"Yeah, no real men around here," she'd usually fire back.

Mary walked over to a filing cabinet and flipped through previous issues that she had marked and catalogued. She found the page that she was looking for and looked over one of the ads again, spreading it open over a nearby table.

"To my loving K. My flame is growing every day. Miss You -

Orchid."

Another said:

"My darling K, I could not share you with another. If our love is to grow I must have a reply. Orchid."

She started to follow the trail and look for possible responses to the message in editions a day or so afterwards, messages that would consistently fit and look as if they were connected. She couldn't initially see any obvious culprits, but then that was the idea with hidden messages.

Mary went through the ads one by one and wrote down each letter, matching them to common code encryptions until she had a group of numbers in rows. She ran through the numbers in Chinese dialects – Mandarin, locally known as Guoyu, Cantonese, Hakka, Yin – as well as English. It was a thinking process more than anything. One which took time. Plenty of time.

Messages could be transmitted in a variety of ways, depending on the circumstances. They could be via the World Wide Web, a technology that was increasingly being used by universities, groups and enthusiasts. Then there were various levels of Cryptography. The Data Encryption Standard (DES) and the Advanced Encryption Standard (AES) were block cypher designs which had been set as cryptography standards by the US government but were unlikely to be used by Chinese intelligence.

Mary mainly focused on 'In Plain Sight' messages where the mailbox was public, such as newspapers and magazines, even radio messages. Benjamin Fowler, an intelligence officer based at the Hong Kong station for over twelve years, entered the room and nodded at Mary.

"How's the world of Miss Lo? Breaking those codes?" he smiled. His short, cropped, blond hair seemed to get lighter by the year, Mary thought.

"Oh yes. Firing through it, almost done," she joked, sarcastically. She glanced down at her notes as if pondering something. "There is something."

She explained her hunch about the personals as she flipped through the papers pointing out the marked suspect adverts.

"Orchid huh? I'll throw it at matey boy downstairs and see if it shakes any leaves," Fowler said, his eyes scanning over the newsprint. "You never know."

Fowler left Mary to her notes to fetch his colleague and question their suspect. The pressure had been building on him and he was acutely aware he needed answers, especially one that dug deep into his psyche and had kept him awake in recent weeks.

He remembered getting wind of the fake report naming Frank Bowen and Jimmy Duffy as terrorists that had been supplied to the Special Unit purporting to come from MI6. Worse, it had since come to light that it had come from his station. Finding the agent responsible, from the twenty or so operating in the area, was proving to be more difficult than he had anticipated, especially with the evasive experience they all had.

Fowler opened the door to the room and nodded at the large, burly man studying a wall map inside.

"Ready, Grant?"

The man grunted and followed Fowler back out into the corridor. They descended metal steps down several floors, lit only by faded bulbs set into the hard walls.

***

Underground, in the anonymous concrete building, a Chinese man paced around a clammy, windowless room, relief brought only when the ceiling fan kicked in for around five minutes every half hour.

Aside from a simple fold-out bed and a solitary table, there was nothing in the claustrophobic space. He unconsciously ran a hand across the bruising on his cheek and then massaged the back of his neck, trying to guess the time. He thought it might be the afternoon, but was unsure. He reckoned this was his third day or so of captivity with very little sleep. The fluorescent tube of light that stretched across the ceiling stayed on permanently. It was a shame the fan didn't stay on, he thought. Both these technical hitches were obviously deliberate.

He thought back to the night his captors wanted to know more about. Three months as a security guard – sitting in that booth every night and watching hours of crap on T.V. – and then the night his comrades came and the three figures had walked down the platform.

Where it came to an end at the tunnel, the three men took out torches from their bags and jumped down onto the rail track and Heng handed them down the heavy bags, one by one, grunting at the weight of them.

The scar-faced one had looked up at him as the other two slowly moved off into the darkness of the tunnel, their torch lights dancing around the tracks.

"The model number?"

Heng had nodded and taken a piece of paper out of his inside jacket pocket, quickly checking it again before handing it over. Scarface looked at it: "This is definitely the right one?"

Heng met the dark eyes and jerked his head confidently. "Definitely."

"Ok, good work. Stay here and guard." And then he had disappeared into the blackness.

The thick iron door to the room rattled with the sounds of keys struggling with the lock before the imposing figure of Grant appeared, filling the door frame.

"Time for a tea break, mate," he said and the Chinese man voluntarily held out his wrists which Grant quickly clasped in handcuffs. They walked a short distance along a dank corridor that had never seen a shred of daylight and entered another windowless room where Benjamin Fowler was opening a metallic briefcase. He hooked leads from the Ambassador Polygraph machine that was housed in the case to an external monitor sitting on a table next to him. The Chinese man held out his hands again, letting Fowler release his cuffs, before sitting down in the same chair he had sat in four times previously. Before that, he had been kidnapped by masked figures, blindfolded and brought to this shithole.

The big man wrapped a black blood pressure armband around his left bicep and attached two monitor devices to his chest.

Fowler glanced at Grant, "Ready to rock and roll?"

Grant gave the devices attached to the Chinese man one more glance, "Yes, go ahead."

"I want to see my lawyer," said the suspect, giving the two intelligence officers a steady glare.

"Fuck your lawyer," smiled Grant. "With respect," he added. The Chinese exhaled slowly, it was the same answer he'd received in the previous four times of asking.

The questions began with the regular familiarity. What is your name? Where do you live? Did you place the bombs at Causeway Bay or Chun Yeung Street market?

The Chinese had not answered anything and had refused to speak, however, he was beginning to deny some of the questions, which the polygraph machine seemed okay with. Grant chain-smoked as he ran through the routine questions and felt a rising sense of frustration, even though he knew that this was a long ball game. There had been many deaths on their turf and there was still a distinct lack of progress as far as the public was concerned, although the finger had very much swung in the direction of Beijing.

"Who planted the bombs?"

"I don't know anything about the bombs," he said quietly. Fowler glanced at the monitor line, which remained steady.

"Did you plant the bombs?"

The Chinese man, Mu Heng, who had not revealed his name, kept his eyes on the wall behind his interrogator and his breathing and heart beat had remained steady. Beating a polygraph machine wasn't easy, there was a distinct method. Polygraph examinations looked for significant involuntary responses in a person's body when they were subjected to stress. Stress associated with deception.

"Who is Orchid?"

Mu Heng blinked quickly. He knew of Orchid. He shouldn't have been aware of that codename, but he had heard stories from fellow operatives. Something about that question had surprised him and Fowler noted – with satisfaction – that the monitor line darted erratically up and down.

Both men made their way back upstairs to the main operations room and studied the monitor print-out.

"He's definitely lying or hiding something," Fowler said.

"Yes, I know he's involved in the bombing, you know he's involved. But why does nothing show up in the graphs for that line of questioning?" asked Grant, clearly not satisfied.

"He wasn't expecting us to ask about Orchid though. He was expecting the bomb questions and has been ready for them from the beginning, but this clearly threw him. Maybe he's not specifically trained for long-term interrogation. We've had him for four days. Maybe the lack of sleep is kicking in?"

Fowler saw that Grant looked unconvinced. "Don't worry about it. This is good. Orchid could be the link."

From briefings with the Hong Kong police and the Special Unit, Fowler had begun to string together what they were dealing with. The prisoner had worked as a watchman at the train terminal for just over a year, where all the trains on the island were serviced, refuelled and checked. After a tip-off, he had been taken by officers of the MI6 Hong Kong station before the police could get him. He had traces of explosives on his hands. At his address, they found bomb-making equipment as well as a whole pile of other evidence. In Fowler's mind, he was guilty as surely as the sun rose in the morning. It was the network behind the watchman Fowler needed to break. As soon as possible.

The phone rang and Grant took it before handing it over to Fowler. He listened to the voice for several moments and uttered a thank you before putting down the phone.

"Cody hasn't turned up to his job again."

Cody was a codename for one of their agents who had been missing and uncontactable for several days, and it was beginning to seriously concern Fowler.

Chapter 40

Frank and Maria sat on the top deck of the aqua green painted ferry that transported locals and the odd traveller from Parapat across to Samosir Island, a volcanic landmass that sat in the middle of Lake Toba in Sumatra. The air was fresh at this higher level and clouds hung low, obscuring parts of the mountains in the distance. They disembarked at a small drop off point that consisted of a wooden platform and walked to the reception and restaurant area that rented out traditional Batak houses that sat alongside the lakes.

The proprietor was a short, stocky Indonesian with a jovial face that reminded Frank of the British comedian Benny Hill. "For you, I have lovely Batak house just available," he had said with unbridled enthusiasm and charm. He had led them back down to the lake, ushering them into one of the beautifully painted Batak houses at the end of a row. It stood so close to the lake that it was possible to dive in right from the door. Frank and Maria decided to take it straight away and settled in, unpacking their bags before sitting outside on two fold up wooden chairs to take in the scenery.

Sunlight skimmed across the surface of the water, the only sound seemed to be the squeak of a water pump some distance behind them.

"I spoke to my father, rang him from the station in K.L.," Maria said suddenly, staring out at the lake, "I just wanted to check he was alright with everything that was going on. I'm sorry, I should have told you. He said he loved me very much," she looked at Frank, her eyes wide and glistening.

Frank nodded, remembering his suspicions. "I'm glad he does love you Maria, wouldn't be much of a father if he didn't."

"I know, but you don't understand. He has never told me that in my entire life," she said. Her face seemed etched with questions.

"Oh? Well, maybe he thought it was overdue? He was worried about you," Frank offered.

Maria shook her head in disagreement. It had played on her mind directly after the phone call, but she had pushed it to the back of her consciousness. She felt now, more than ever, something was wrong.

After a few days, they took the highly recommended walk to a village a few miles up the road. As the road climbed higher into the hills, they admired the breathtaking view of the rice fields stretching into the distance that resembled a patchwork quilt.

When they returned to the restaurant, the owner beckoned Frank over and Maria went ahead to the house. Frank had asked that he let him know if anyone came snooping around.

"Man with grey hair, English man. He ask for you. He not stay here, came after you left," he said, excitedly.

"Did he say who he was?" He had not.

Several hours later, Frank sat outside the Batak house and watched a figure walk towards him. He wore a black shirt – that was in a military style, with shoulder lapels and two pockets across the front – and white slacks. His hair was grey, swept back, and he wore black-rimmed glasses. Frank guessed he was in his mid-forties. The man nodded at Frank as he approached and then stopped in front of him.

"Frank Bowen?" Frank froze and narrowed his eyes. "I'm Douglas

Brown, detective inspector at the Royal Hong Kong police force. Don't worry, I'm here unofficially. I just want to talk."

"I don't suppose you have I.D. to prove that, do you?"

"Yes, of course." He fished out his wallet and flipped it open, revealing the badge. He held it towards Frank to give him a clear view.

"Something you bought in Bangkok?" Frank asked, eyebrows arched. The inspector laughed out loud. "Well I know you can pretty much buy anything there nowadays but, no, it is genuine, trust me." Frank decided to do just that. Trust him. He wasn't in a position to do anything else and, besides, he hoped this inspector had some answers.

"How did you find me?" asked Frank.

"Indonesian customs reported it. There were no arrest warrants in place but we wanted notification. I've spent quite a while tracking you down. Have to admit it's been an interesting experience, running around Sumatra after your tail. It wasn't that difficult though," he smiled, a look of satisfaction on his face.

They sat at the water's edge, on a makeshift wooden platform that acted as a diving point to the Lake. The inspector dangled his feet over the edge, hovering just above the water.

"It's a beautiful spot," he said, gazing over towards the far mountains. A cloud of mist hung, obscuring the far side.

"It certainly is. Quiet and peaceful, something I've been badly in need of recently," said Frank, a hint of regret in his voice as if he'd been sloppy in covering his tracks.

Brown looked at him and smiled. "Yes, I can sympathise with you there," he said.

Frank leaned forward, turning to face the man from Hong Kong, "What happened to me exactly, inspector? I've got my theories, but I'm dying to hear yours," he said.

"Off the record," he paused to take a gulp of beer that Frank had brought from the house, "You were set up, we know that now."

Frank laughed, "Yeah, that's one thing I do know."

"Some element in MSS decided to carry out a false flag operation. By launching attacks, they made Hong Kong look weak and incapable when it came to their own security. Among other reasons it was to give the Chinese an upper hand in the takeover negotiations."

"Jesus, that's crazy," Frank almost spat in the water.

"Maybe, but hardly surprising," said Brown. "Emperors, governments and intelligence agencies all have a long history in false flag operations, including our own. In fact, we pretty much pioneered it. A British Army Officer, Frank Kitson, wrote a book on it: 'Low-Intensity Operations - Subversion Insurgency & Peacekeeping.' He wrote that if there's an organisation or group and you want to discredit them, you create your own parallel organisation. You send them out to commit atrocities which will be blamed on the original relatively benign group, and they'll be discredited, demonised, and you gain political advantage. It's on my bookshelf at home."

"Intelligence agencies, Governments and their power plays," said Frank quietly.

"What I don't understand is Richard Desmond's involvement. He's just a criminal, no intelligence links that we know of," Brown said.

"I think I can help you there," said Frank, peeling off the beer bottle label. "I met someone calling himself Theo Kampala in Goa. He suggested I go to this guesthouse in Bangkok, which I did, and that's where I met Richard Desmond. Theo turned up in Krabi and admitted his involvement before he died. That's all I know."

Brown nodded slowly. "Yes, I saw a report on that. Theo's real name is, or was, Amith Kumar and he worked for Chinese intelligence as a scout based in India. From what we know, it seems his job was to pick suitable patsies—Western travellers with few, or no, family connections. He put you in touch with Desmond and fed your information, as well as Jimmy's, back to the Beijing station."

Frank shook his head.

"I'm sorry, Frank, you were pretty unlucky."

Frank managed a laugh and took a swig of beer.

"So, by putting out false information on you and your friend, making out you were connected to MI6 and so forth, they created a story, an illusion," Brown continued. "Rogue operatives, backed by British intelligence or a terrorist group, whose plan was to plant the timed explosives on public transport—except, in your case, you were to go up with it. The story would be it was an accident and that you hadn't timed it right."

"So they weren't going to paint us as some kind of kamikaze suicide bombers?"

Brown sighed, adjusting his spectacles. "I don't think so, but I could be wrong. We'll never know, probably. The big picture is that it was all to deflect attention away from the Chinese. But you survived. You should have been blown to pieces on that train, but by missing it they had to find you. It seems to me, once they tried to clean up the loose ends, things went from bad to worse for them. The main culprit was their agent: Tian. The one hunting you."

"Yeah, what a bloody psycho he was!"

The inspector glanced at Frank. "His body was found beside a train track near Alor Satar. So he's out of the picture, you'll be pleased to know."

Frank smiled thinly, his heart racing as he forced himself to keep a calm exterior.

"That's great news to me, Douglas," he said, a little too loudly. Brown looked at him quizzically for a moment, before looking back across the lake at another brightly painted ferry coming in from the mainland.

"Someone at MI6 was responsible for setting you up, you realise that, Frank?" Brown's tone was deadly serious again. Frank frowned at the inspector.

"The reports we received about you and Jimmy, as well as the tip-offs about the exact location and time of the attacks, all came from within MI6."

"Shit!" Frank's head slumped downwards, his eyes staring at his own reflection in the dark water.

"The exact agent source was unidentifiable. We double checked officially and an intelligence officer confirmed that the information sent was not bona fide. Essentially, it was false information."

Frank jerked his head to face the inspector, "Who?"

"We don't know. But it's got to be a mole. There has to be a Chinese agent deep within their organisation."

Chapter 41

Orchid picked up the phone and thought he heard a click but wasn't sure. Replacing it back in the cradle, he moved to the window, which was covered by a closed blind, and peeked through it, out of habit more than anything. He paced around the back room, churning the situation over in his mind. It wasn't good.

There had been no response from Oracle to his last three messages. Even if he had to bail out, he wanted assurances that he could defect back to the nest, but none was forthcoming.

Keep calm, he told himself, but deep down he knew it was only a matter of time before he was uncovered.

He had done everything they had required and more and this is how they repaid years of service? He had filed constant reports right up to informing them where to find Frank Bowen's passport contact.

The obvious way was to disappear and yet there was a loose end that he could not ignore, one that pulled at his stomach, tying it into knots, making him feel sick.

The tall man slumped down in an armchair, mulling through his decreasing options, and poured the Jim Beam bourbon into the thick crystal glass before taking a lug, gratefully swallowing the burning liquid that eased down his throat. It gave him solace and, at the same time, courage. Courage for the decision he now knew he had to make.

Chapter 42

Frank sat still for a moment, letting it all sink in. He was half thinking of smoking a cigarette but quickly cast it out of his mind. He was proud of his whole month without having one.

"Is there anything you can tell us? It might not have seemed important at the time but could certainly help." Fowler said, studying Frank carefully. They sat in Detective Brown's office at the Royal Hong Kong police headquarters, where Frank had agreed to come back for questioning. He had been offered a deal by Brown which was; help with their investigation for which there would be no charges.

Frank had already covered everything he knew; his movements from Goa to Bangkok to Hong Kong. He told them who he had met from Richard Desmond to Theo Kampala and the Thai police chief—all of whom were now dead, except one, as far as he knew ... the man they called Mr Whiteman, who had seemed to be the brains behind the so-called drill. Whiteman was not one of the faces in the photographs strewn over the desk, most of which Frank had identified one by one. He leaned back slowly, feeling the fan cut through the air, chopping through its methodical rhythm.

Frank described Whiteman again, the silver-white hair, the aura of authority. "He said he worked for the Legislative Council of Hong Kong. The same crew Maria's Dad said he worked for."

Fowler exchanged a glance with Grant.

"You met Maria's father?" asked Fowler, cautiously.

"Yes, briefly. At her house, after the attacks," said Frank.

"You didn't mention that before," Grant frowned at him.

Frank shuffled in his chair with impatience. "I forgot. He gave me the passport contact; Li. Detective Brown, here, said Li was murdered."

"Will you excuse us for a moment?" said Fowler and the two men left the room, shutting the door behind them. Fowler shook his head and looked at the floor as Grant stared at him as though his world had just caved in around him.

"Are you thinking what I'm thinking, Ben?" Grant said quietly.

"What? That Cody is a Chinese plant?" Fowler couldn't bring himself to believe it. Cody had worked as an agent with the Hong Kong station for over ten years, his cover with the Legislative Council had been a perfect front. Now it seemed he had been using that position as a two-way channel with the Chinese.

"Yes, that he's the mole," Grant couldn't take his eyes off Fowler. Neither man wanted to believe it.

Frank sipped his black coffee from a paper cup and grimaced at the taste as he watched the two MI6 men outside behind the frosted glass. The pieces had all taken time to slot into place like a dovetailing line of parallel roads in his mind. There was something there, just out of grasp, its shape unclear as if a fog hung in front of him... Something Maria had said...

Detective Inspector Brown sat in the corner, where he had been observing the interview in a white shirt that stuck to his skin with the sleeves rolled up. He looked up at Frank, curiously, as if trying to read his thoughts.

The two intelligence officers re-entered the room and sat down in their seats, barely hiding their perplexed shock.

"Can I ask you a question?" Frank asked, glancing from Grant to Fowler. Fowler nodded.

"Does Peter Chapman – Maria's father – work for you, by any chance?" Again, the two men glanced at each other furtively.

"We can't answer that, I'm afraid. Confidential," answered Grant abruptly, focusing on a report in front of him.

"Because if he does," Frank leaned forward, "He's probably a good bet for being your mole."

Fowler stood up, banging his fist on the table. "How the hell do you know about a mole?" His voice was loud with barely restrained anger, but he was staring, wide-eyed, at the detective inspector. The Detective Inspector held out his hands in a defensive gesture. "What does it matter now? Are you going to find him or not?" he asked.

"The fact that we have a Chinese double agent in MI6 is a national security issue, Brown. And you tell a civvie?" He gestured towards Frank. "That was confidential information!" Fowler was yelling now, shaking with anger.

"This 'civvie' was framed by the Chinese, probably helped by your man!" Brown shouted, standing up as if to rise to the rage that seemed to be at boiling point in the room.

"That's enough!" barked Grant, who had been drumming his fingers on the desk throughout the confrontation. "We need to get over there."

"I'm coming with you," said Frank.

"No you're bloody not," retorted Fowler, who hadn't quite calmed down.

"He's with me and I'm going," said Brown, in a steady, low voice. Fowler shook his head in disbelief. "You're responsible for him, then. Grant, get some armed backup, in case."

Chapter 43

The blinds blocked out most of the light, shrouding a veil of darkness across the living room in which Peter Chapman sat in his favourite armchair. Hesitation and indecisiveness had clouded his mind in the previous few weeks. A suitcase, packed with his most treasured possessions, stood ready in the hallway, but he was unable to leave and wasn't even sure where he would go.

It had become obvious that his paymasters in Beijing had abandoned him to his fate and might even be considering killing him. That had closed off the option of defecting to the Chinese but, more importantly, there was Maria. The guilt of involving his beautiful daughter kneaded at his stomach like an untreated wound, growing more infected with every day that had passed since the attacks. He gulped another mouthful of Jim Beam and clunked the heavy crystal glass back on the side table.

A creak made him turn and his eyes blinked as if to reconfirm the sight of his daughter standing in the doorway.

"Dad?" her voice was quiet and uneven. He leapt up and went to her, his eyes welling with tears as he wrapped his arms around her. A huge wave of relief swept over him.

"Maria! Thank god you're alright. I thought I'd never see you again." She tried to speak, but a lump caught in her throat making her gulp. She looked up at him, her eyes filling with a wetness that dulled their usual emerald clarity. "Are you OK?"

Peter nodded and they moved into the room. He cleared a space on the sofa that was draped with clothes that he had previously been sifting through.

"I'm so sorry about everything. I need to tell you something," he said quietly. She perched gently on the leather sofa, looking around at the mess. It was a surprise to her as he always kept his house immaculate.

Peter sat next to her and breathed heavily as if preparing himself. "I did a terrible thing that you might not forgive me for. I wouldn't blame you. I'm not supposed to tell anyone, but I have been working for MI6 for over ten years." He paused, allowing Maria, who nodded grimly, to take it in before he hung his head and continued.

"Obviously there are serious consequences to me telling you this. But this is not the half of it. I've also been working for the Chinese MSS." Maria's eyes widened in surprise, her mouth remained closed.

"I was passing information to them regarding the 1997 takeover, as well as intelligence secrets. I had information on the recent attacks before they happened, no details though and I was not involved in the planning or anything like that. You have to believe me, Maria."

Maria squeezed her eyes shut as a tear ran slowly over her left cheek and then she got up suddenly and stood with her back to him.

"I had no way of stopping it or knowing the details of where it would take place. I did, however, pass the false information about the two lads," he paused, "Jimmy and your friend, Frank."

His daughter's face contorted with anguish, lower lip quivering uncontrollably. She gasped, suddenly desperate for air. "All those people...You knew?"

"I gave Beijing the information about Li Wu arranging a passport for Frank," Peter continued grimly as if his window of confession was about to close. "If it makes any difference, I had no idea they would track Frank down to your house. That mess with the killer. I would never have knowingly put you in danger, Maria. You have to believe that." He looked at her, pleadingly.

Maria looked up at the wall, tears streaming down her face, fixing her sight on an old colonial painting of Hong Kong harbour. She remembered it from when she was a little girl, like an old friend that anchored her to a happy childhood. Now it seemed to be cruelly taunting her as everything she thought she knew about her father was evaporating like some kind of mirage.

"So you met Frank at my house, gave him Li's information and then told the Chinese about Li. What did you think would happen then? You must have known they wanted to track Frank down and kill him?"

"I needed to give them something. They already knew that Frank had met you. There are always casualties in war," he said, as firmly as he could. "I didn't know everything that was going on, Maria, and I wanted to keep you out of it, to protect you!"

Maria snorted with derision as she paced up and down the room, shaking her head.

"Look, it's all been a shitty mess. I regret it all. You are the most important thing in my life. All I can do is apologise and ask that you forgive me, somehow," Peter said.

She looked at him through weeping eyes, shaking her head. "I don't know. I really don't know. I need time."

He looked at the floor. "Unfortunately that's something I don't have," he said quietly. A silence hung in the air, only the low background hum of the air conditioning filled the room.

"Do you remember when we were on the beach on a visit to Cornwall in England? You, me and your Mum... You were about five, I think. A boy was wandering around in the sand, crying his eyes out. He had completely lost his family and we looked after him for hours."

Maria stared at the blinds on the window, as if seeing the view of the city that lay behind them. She spoke quietly and smiled at the memory. "Yes, I do. I helped him build a huge sandcastle. You helped him calm down. You told him not to worry and that he'd see his mum again. You were always really caring like that," she said.

Peter breathed out heavily: "I'm still your father, Maria. Still your dad. The same man. Please don't remember me as anything else."

Maria glanced at the bottle of Jim Beam on the side table. "I think I need a drink. I'll get a glass."

"Maria," he looked across at her, the pain still very much apparent on his face. He held his hands out to her and she went to him. Peter Chapman held his daughter tightly for a moment and then looked into her eyes before nodding. "Go," he whispered, smiling faintly.

Maria stepped into the kitchen and opened the glass cabinet before grabbing a crystal whiskey glass. A distant thumping at the front door caused her to inhale quickly.

As Maria had left the room, Peter had walked to a mahogany wooden table in the corner and opened one of the drawers. Inside it was a Glock pistol that he had loaded before Maria had turned up, which he now picked it up in his sweaty hand. He knew that this was the only way. There was a high chance they would target Maria to get to him. If not, he would be hung out to dry in a long drawn out trial for treason, putting his family through hell.

He had shamed himself and nothing was going to change that. The banging at the front door seemed to focus him as if signalling that it was time.

The loud sound of the gunfire reverberated throughout the house, a shockwave that made Maria drop the glass, smashing it into hundreds of shards on the hard, marble tiled floor. A sickening horror careened through her body – as her legs automatically carried her back into the living room, glass cutting into the soles of her feet; pain she didn't feel or acknowledge – fear realised in the worst possible moment of her life as a daughter as she stared wide-eyed at the limp figure of her father, sprawled on the floor. Her mouth opened to scream without a sound as she scrambled onto her knees, pulling at his bloodstained shirt. Then an agonising wail shook at every wall in the house as if willing them to succumb to its force, closely followed by sudden loud crashes from the front door.

Benjamin Fowler inched into the room holding an automatic pistol, looking around as he took in the scene of agony, followed by Brown and Grant. Frank pushed past them and stood over Maria, who was desperately punching her father's chest.

"You don't get out of this that easy, you fucking bastard!"

Her whole body heaved with violent sobs as she shook her father by the shoulders as if willing him to wake up from a dream. His face was frozen by the impact of the bullet that had ripped through the back of his head. A splatter of brains, blood and sinew plastered the wall that had been behind him when he had taken his life a moment earlier.

"Jesus," Frank uttered and he leaned down to touch Maria's shoulder and comfort her. She ignored him and continued to clutch Peter's lifeless body.

Grant and Detective Inspector Brown were now in the room, looking down grimly at the tragedy that had just unfolded.

"Check out the rest of the house could you, Grant?" asked Fowler, quietly. His colleague nodded and disappeared out of the door. "Inspector Brown? Can you get your men to secure the perimeter, just as a precaution?"

Brown nodded and immediately turned to the sergeant who signalled his understanding and disappeared quickly from the room.

Fowler circled round to get a better view of Peter's body and looked at Brown, sadly, as if to confirm that he was definitely dead.

Chapter 44

"Dean Whiteman was probably just an actor or a conman. Without a positive identification, it's hard to know, but we have the photo fit from your description on file, so you never know," Carl said.

Frank and Carl sat in the sunshine on the Victoria Embankment by the Thames, watching a large group of tourists clambering onto a ferry.

"I know you're close to Maria. She knew nothing about her father; the whole Hong Kong situation, and wasn't involved in any way."

Frank nodded. He had long stopped suspecting her of anything and now just felt incredible pain for her. He remembered Maria telling him that her dad had told her how much he loved her on the phone in Malaysia. He was probably saying goodbye, thinking he would never see her again.

"At least she got to see him," Frank said, continuing his own thoughts. "Before he topped himself, I mean." He sighed and shook his head. "What he was thinking, shooting himself like that?"

Carl patted Frank's shoulder sympathetically. "He was looking at a charge of treason. I guess he couldn't handle it. Perhaps, not mentally all there at the end."

Maria had said little since that horrendous incident a month previously. She'd given no hint on what her father had told her and Frank hadn't forced it, just repeating that he was there if she needed him.

"How is she?"

Frank shook his head again. "Not very well, I'm afraid. She needs time. She's with her mother in Amsterdam at the moment. She's mad at me, her Dad, she's...in a dark place. I'll go over there, soon. See if I can help. Got to do something."

Carl nodded and the two men stared out across the water, under a blue sky, as the tourist ferry passed them, slipping through the dark water.

"The part Peter Chapman played in this whole sorry affair will be kept under wraps by the Official Secrets Act, for now," said Carl as he stood up, clapping his gloved hands together.

"Come on, Frank. Let's walk along the river for a while."

II

Pandora Red

"The technotronic era involves the gradual appearance of a more controlled society. Such a society would be dominated by an elite, unrestrained by traditional values. Soon it will be possible to assert almost continuous surveillance over every citizen and maintain up-to-date complete files containing even the most personal information about the citizen. These files will be subject to instantaneous retrieval by the authorities."
Zbigniew Brzezinski.

Chapter 1

March 1999. GCHQ Cheltenham, England.

Sarah Edwards glanced at the wall clock, noting it was 23:17 hours. Nearly time. The plan was to get started as the shifts changed to the night staff. During late shifts, the hexagon shaped green building, flanked by prison-like towers, had the feeling of a ship silently moving through the night. There was a faded sound, like a distant roar from outside the double glazed windows of her office, a downpour of rain Sarah could see coming down in sheets from an external building light.

The main GCHQ building was planted in the sprawl of the Oakley site in Cheltenham, England, where she had been an employee for six years. As Intelligence liaison officer, Sarah had access to top secret information that would never become public, even under the official secrets act. The glass walls of her office reflected artificial light across the floor and she glanced outside into the main section once again. A few people were still milling around, their flickering screens displaying worldwide operation updates, while the central heating hummed in the background. She moved her slight figure back into the large swivel chair and tapped once again on the keyboard, logging herself out of the main network. To access and copy the information meant using another terminal on the floor above.

Sarah cast her eyes around the office for the last time. The feeling weighed heavily that after tonight, she would possibly never see her family, her friends, or anyone she cared about again. She wouldn't be able to say goodbye either, that was the most painful part of it. For the last three months, she had churned the decision over and over in her mind and kept arriving at the same conclusion.

She put on her jacket, grabbed her bag, and slipped out across the thick carpet along the corridor, caged by metal and glass partitions that seemed to go on forever. Her feet quickly ascended the metal steps at the end, the echoes adding to her anxiety as she left G block and an entire lifetime behind her. No more after work drinks with the boys. No chinwags with her friend in the service, Janet Chambers. How surreal it would all soon seem.

She could only imagine the shock of her colleagues when the news spread about what she had done. They would understand, in time. Surely they would?

In a few years, this site would be empty of its machines, the people and the families in the housing complex would all be moved to the new GCHQ location at Benhall. The new 'doughnut' shaped complex would be state of the art at the cost of hundreds of millions and Sarah knew the security would be much tighter there, another reason to act now.

A quick flash of her identity card on the wall scanner and she was allowed through to the floor above. It would only be a matter of time before her access and subsequence actions were traced back to her but by then, all shit would have hit the fan and it wouldn't matter anymore.

Even now, it wasn't too late and she could still turn back. She could leave the building as normal and continue her life, keep her friends, and stay in touch with her family. She shook that idea out of her head quickly. This was no time for second thoughts or doubt.

It seemed like a dream but she steeled herself and pressed on across the carpeted floor that hosted rows of cubicles, a haphazard mix of screens that flickered in the darkness as if watching her progress. The truth must be leaked, no matter what the consequences.

She stopped at a monitor, sat down, and quickly typed in her login and encrypted password to access the main system. There seemed to be a temporary freeze on the screen and Sarah frowned while she waited.

'Access Denied' flashed at her in large letters on the monitor.

She cursed under her breath. There was no logical reason she would be denied access at this level. Sarah retyped, her fingers stumbling across the keyboard, and she hit return to see the same 'Access Denied' once more.

Come on, Sarah, keep it together!

Slowly, she re-typed, voicing the letters and numbers in her head and breathed a sigh of relief as the familiar green coded access came up. She carefully plugged in the thumb drive that had been meticulously moulded to look like a keyless entry remote for a Honda Accord Acura TL, the exact same car she owned. It had been made through a contact that she had outside of the agency. Working with those outside the law had its benefits and discretion was essential.

She immediately hit the shortcut keys to launch the Shell access command line and typed in a sequence to bypass the computer's automatic security scan of her device.

Once again, she needed to fill in her login credentials to the remote server and then the black console screen filled with a fast moving list of file names as they copied from the 'Project Oculus' folder.

These were the very same files that she had found and read with increasing alarm and exasperation over the previous months. She had not liked what she saw one bit.

"Good evening," the voice came from behind her, making her

gasp out loud. Game over, before she had even started. The sounds of the footsteps grew nearer and she spun around, squinting at the night guard. He smiled at her, nodded, and walked on by. Sarah felt her heart pumping so loud, she was sure he could hear it. "Good evening," she replied.

Time slowed down, the file transfer was still reeling through its list and there was nothing Sarah could do to speed things up. There were a lot of files to copy.

She thought about her mother and father, seeing life drift by from their Brighton semi with a fine view of the sea and the pier. Had she really forsaken them? Would she really never see them again? Sarah refused to believe that. She would find a way.

She remembered first seeing the GCHQ advert in the newspaper. It was a test to find an apprentice and Sarah's mother had encouraged her to apply. Sarah had always been top of her classes, wiping the floor with everyone else and her future glittered like gold. But dark shadows loomed in the corners of her memory: the bullying. There were a few in her class who had targeted her. She could only guess it was because of her intelligence or maybe the social inadequacy.

The only thing she lived for was her studying, the knowledge that she so eagerly soaked up like a sponge and the books she buried herself in.

She passed the test, a puzzle to decode a series of seemingly random letters and then after a yearlong selection process, began her intelligence career, working in the foreign sources section and then later transferring to anti-terrorism monitoring.

It was at the 'firm' she met her first real friends. For the most part, anyway. There were a few comments from some of the male colleagues, but all in all, it was like a family. Besides, Sarah had always seen herself as a trailblazer, working hard to fight her way into a male-dominated environment.

A beep sounded and the copy was complete. She took the drive and slipped it inside her bag then typed in: *sfc /purgecache* in the command line to delete the cache and dump any record of her folder access before shutting down the workstation. She didn't want to leave unnecessary breadcrumb trails.

Sarah braced herself for getting out of the building. For obvious security reasons, no files of any kind were allowed to leave the walls of GCHQ. She knew the routine and just hoped she had thought of everything. There was a risk. There always was.

She moved quickly now, passing the endless monitors, workstations, and desks that seemed to blur past her. She rode the lift down to the ground floor, taking even, deep breaths to calm her nerves. The lift opened and she walked up to a set of double doors, passing her entry card over the scanner, which opened them with a gentle hiss.

Without hesitation, she stepped through and placed her leather handbag with the car key lob inside onto the x-ray scanner conveyor that was manned by Gilly, the elderly night security man. He smiled at Sarah and briefly glanced at the monitor that exposed the contents of her bag. It was a well-worn routine.

"It's a bit late for you, innit, love?" he asked in his thick welsh accent.

Sarah smiled weakly at him, the thumping in her chest once again seemingly growing louder with each beat as she brushed a strand of light brown hair behind her ear. "The devil's work is never done," she heard herself say.

She stepped through the frame of a large metal detector, not unlike those in airports and held her breath as she did so. Despite there being nothing incriminating on her person, the prospect of the alarm sounding haunted her. To her relief, no alarms were triggered and she stood at the end of the conveyor, waiting.

Gilly adjusted glasses on his wide face and scrutinised the monitor and shapes of items inside her bag; her purse, cosmetics, notepad, the Honda key–less entry remote...

He glanced at her for a moment, a hint of regret on his wrinkled face and sighed.

"I'm really sorry, luv, but I have to do a random check. You know how it goes."

Sarah stared at him for a second, half thinking he was joking and then realised he wasn't. She had only been subject to a couple of random checks in her whole time there and it had barely registered as a concern in her planning. Did he know something? It wasn't possible.

His face then turned into a grin, trying to make light of it. "It's your lucky night, obviously."

Sarah then managed a smile in return but it was not good news. A random check meant a more thorough search and possibly a body check. The risk factor was rising.

"It's no problem. You've got a job to do," she said evenly.

The handbag came through and the guard began to take out the items one by one, placing them on a long table. Sarah fixed her eyes on the contents of her bag as he checked; looking inside the cosmetics pouch, flipping through the notepad at her meaningless scribbles. Most of the items had been placed in there for show; the plan always being to mix everything up in the bag. There were also random items such as food receipts or a tube of mints thrown in for good measure. She wondered if the cosmetics were overkill, especially as she barely ever wore much makeup.

His hands reached for the key lob and he picked it up, spinning it around in his fingers for a moment.

"Any weekend plans?" she asked, a forced cheery ring to her voice.

The guard turned and grinned again.

"At the allotment if it's not raining but we'll be lucky, won't we? It's bound to rain, innit?"

"Almost definitely," she said, clenching her fists inside her jacket pockets.

He sighed as if regretting something and began placing the items back in the bag and handed it to her.

"Have a lovely evening now," he said. She took the bag and smiled in genuine relief. "You, too. Fingers crossed for the weather."

The rain-washed streets cast reflections from the street lamps, the echo of Sarah's footfall bouncing off the walls of red-brick houses lining the complex where the GCHQ employees had built their lives. No one was out at that hour and a quietness hung in the air like a blanket.

No more friends.

She unlocked the front door to her cosy 2-bedroom semi where she had lived for almost seven years.

No more family.

Grabbing the large holdall bag that waited in the hall, she then walked to her Honda Accord parked in the driveway and slung it into the boot. There was no point in going back to the house. Everything she could think of had been done, cleaned down, or shredded. Anything she had not wanted them to find had been taken to the landfill, five miles away. Her entire life was now in one bag.

The car weaved its way past the red brick houses and grey block buildings, away from the complex and toward Cheltenham train station.

Chapter 2

Frank was running across the underground concourse, weaving over the charred bodies, victims of some kind of fire. Their dark shapes seemed to melt into the polished marble floor and the inky black liquid congealed around his feet, making it more and more difficult to run. His pursuer's heavy breathing was close behind, yet he dared not look.

The lift service hatch was just ahead, yellow and black stripes beckoning - his escape route clearly marked. And now, worse still, the arms of the dead, constrained by the dark liquid, seemed to move and reach for him, their bony blackened hands gripping at his legs and feet. Frank's heart pumped hard in his chest and it was difficult to breathe as if air was been sucked right out of his lungs.

To his horror, the service door began to slowly close with an eerie scraping sound, like the echo of train tracks in a distant tunnel.

Five feet away.

He had to get there. Kicking away the clinging hands, Frank accidently stood on a body, the sickening crunch of brittle bones sounded underfoot but he ignored it, striving on through the sticky residue.

Four feet away.

The doors ground closer together like a slowly snapping jaw. With a leap, Frank threw himself forward with all his energy, hands clambering to hold them open so he could lever his body forward. Somehow, he found strength again and hauled himself forward over the slippery floor and into the lift. As the doors closed behind him, he caught a glimpse of the bodies of the dead crawling after him and that of his pursuer, who had now become one of them. Burnt black and red, the skin falling away from flesh. Staring right at him through sunken sockets was the unmistakeable bloodied face of Chiu Wah On, the assassin he had thrown out of a train eight years earlier.

The sheets, soaked from sweat, were wrapped tightly around him as Frank fought to free himself, breathing hard and disorientated. He knocked the side table, pushing a glass of water to the floor, which cracked and rolled, soaking the carpet and his unread books.

"Jesus," he muttered, untangling himself. The bed looked like he had been wrestling with an army of demons. Pillows were strewn over the floor, the sheet lay twisted across the mattress. He rubbed his eyes and slowed his breathing, relieved that the nightmare was over. Every now and then, it would re-appear and he wondered why. It had been so long since Hong Kong and there had been many other demons to fight afterwards.

Frank switched on the radio and padded his naked frame over to the en-suite bathroom before turning on the shower, hesitating at the door until the water had a chance to heat up.

After a quick blast and scrub, he dried himself, checked his unshaven face and dark hair in the mirror, and threw on a T-shirt and jeans. He headed down the hallway to the kitchen and opened the fridge, glancing into the bare interior. Had Maria asked him to get the shopping in? She had been talking to him when he was half asleep that morning, which was always a bad idea. Where was she anyway? Then he remembered that she had taken the boys to see a friend and then get shopping.

A dull pain throbbed in the back of his skull but he still didn't hesitate to grab the last can of beer.

It had been a difficult reunion after Hong Kong and the horrific suicide of her father. They had been sitting in a café on Amsterdam's Raadhuisstraat two months after her father's funeral, watching the rain hammer the streets and trams trundle by the window. Maria had avoided his eyes as he uttered sympathetic words and he knew they weren't getting through. They had something, hadn't they? They'd been together under the threat of death and helped each other through those terrifying weeks that neither would easily forget.

Then it had happened. The gunshot in the living room. The sight of her dad lying on the Chinese rug, the blood and brain tissue marking it like a chaotic map.

"You blame me, don't you?" he had said. "If I had never come into your life, maybe it wouldn't have turned out like that. Is that what you think?" She shook her head, brushed a hand through her curly blonde hair, but said nothing and continued to stare at the rain, or was it his reflection in the window? He couldn't be sure.

"Of course I don't blame you, Frank. I just don't know where I am right now. I'm all lost," she said without looking at him, her green eyes seemed duller than he remembered. He tried to take her hand but she moved it too soon and they sat in silence for a while as the coffee machine growled out another customer's Americano.

He gave her his new contact card, carefully placing it on the table. When she didn't acknowledge it, he stood up, scraping the chair on the stone floor.

"Just call when you're ready," he said quietly as he followed her gaze out into the rain. "If you need to," he added.

It was too soon for her to pick up any thread they'd had in Asia. That much was obvious. She needed more time but he feared losing her. The chance of never seeing her bright green eyes and freckled face again cast a shadow over his thoughts.

Frank left the café, running for the tram in the hacking downpour, convinced he would never see her again. He certainly didn't envisage that Maria would contact him only a week later with the news that would change his life forever. The news that she was pregnant.

Adventure. Breaking up the boredom. The fact that he was certain the relationship with Maria was over. There were many reasons Frank agreed to join Carl at MI6 after he had returned from Asia.

The dark truth was he had also experienced a real adrenaline buzz throwing the Chinese assassin from that train in Thailand. And with his death, knowing the killer would never try to kill him or Maria again, just put the icing on the cake. He got the job done. Dead was dead. There was no coming back from death. Except in your dreams. Frank smiled at the irony.

Death. Once you let it pervade your life, it took a hold, became 'normal', a way of dealing with things. Something changed in Frank after that killing. He had become a different beast and knew it. A beast capable of darker acts. Kill or be killed.

No more office job BS. No more being the hamster in a wheel, a wage slave just existing to work. No, he was going to grab this chance and run with it. Run bloody fast.

Adventure, excitement, travel. That was what had driven him before. Now? Now, he had responsibilities. He needed to build a safety net. A home.

Frank nursed his beer in the stark living room and flicked to the news where footage of Riot police and demonstrators clashed in Seattle. He watched impassively as police charged the line, petrol bombs stinging the air as batons pounded heads and limbs before the newsreader moved the story quickly on, his mind still wandering.

Maria did love him now, he knew that, more than words could ever describe. When she said she was pregnant, everything had changed. Then Joe had come along, and now they had Zak as well. As the news continued, Frank wondered what kind of world he had brought his children into.

Chapter 3

Maria Chapman walked with the pushchair that her youngest, Zak, was dozing in. Her older son, Joe, shuffled along a few paces behind as they made their way from Barnes Bridge Station and along a passageway that led to the main road. They scurried along to the end and turned, cutting through the streets and pausing occasionally to study a folded up map. Finally, they reached the address they were looking for.

The houses were four stories high, in semi-detached blocks of two. The adjoined house Maria and Joe both stared up at was painted with a graffiti style collage. The centrepiece was a painting of an old wry tree that stretched from the ground all the way to the top, its branches reaching across the width of both houses, spreading like a spider's web on the brickwork. The end of the branches morphed into television screens, periscopes and satellite dishes.

"Why are we here?" Joe asked, still staring up at the artwork.

"Seeing an old friend," Maria replied, pressing the doorbell.

The buzzer crackled into life and a bored-sounding male voice answered.

"Hullo?"

"It's Maria. I'm here to see Rosie Connelly."

"Okay, one minute."

Maria unbuckled the belt around Zak and hauled him out of

the pushchair onto the doorstep as Joe, now fully trained in the procedure, snapped the hood back of the buggy and folded it up.

A tall girl with braided hair and piercings on her nose and ears opened the door and beamed with delight. She threw her arms around Maria. The two had met whilst travelling in India eight years before and swore to keep in touch. They had bumped into each other a week before on a tube train and made the arrangement to meet.

"It's so good to see you again," Rosie beamed. She looked down at Joe and Zak with equal delight. "And who are these lovely boys?"

Joe placed the folded up pushchair on the ground, grinned, and held out his hand. "Joe," he said.

Rosie cooed at the manners and shook his hand. "...and very well brought up, I see."

"Hmm, maybe not so much," said Maria and laughed. She picked up Zak and they all walked into the hallway. The visitors' eyes were drawn to a huge montage of photographs of various people that had been arranged onto a cork board.

"Pictures of all the people who have lived here over the years."

They all began to study the photographs as Rosie gave a running commentary on each one.

"So what is this place?" asked Maria finally.

"A big happy family. A community of like-minded people. We're very particular who lives here. The activist, John Rhodes, owns it. He lets a select few of us run the place. Have you heard of him?"

Maria nodded her head. Rhodes, a man in his early forties, was an outspoken voice against what was being seen as a rising tide of globalisation and corporate greed spanning the world. He was also behind the alternative media group, Liberatus, that produced a weekly newspaper and had recently started publishing their content online. Maria had heard him speak on the local radio and found herself agreeing with pretty much everything that he had said. Rhodes presented his arguments in an intelligent fashion, backed by facts, and had ripped his interviewer apart as they had tried to dismiss and pigeonhole him as a conspiracy nut.

"Well, he's speaking in a few days, I think. I'll give you the details. Anyway, come on in."

Rosie led them into a spacious dining room that was adjacent to the kitchen. There was a large bay window that overlooked the truss arched Barnes Bridge and Maria walked over to peer outside. The Thames, much narrower in this part of London, along with the flat greenery of the sports clubs opposite, reminded Maria of Holland.

A shabby looking young man, with dark wispy hair and a faint outline of growth on his chin, was sitting at a large oak dining table and looked up at them from behind a Toshiba laptop.

"Maria and Joe, this is Matt. He's a kind of journalist for John's newspaper."

Matt leaned back with an impish smile on his face.

"When you say 'kind of journalist', I'll take that as a big compliment then?" Maria noted a light accent but couldn't be sure where.

"You know what I mean. *The Liberatus* isn't exactly *The Guardian*. It's nothing about your journalistic credentials, which are, of course, first class."

Matt shook his head and continuing typing. "Very nicely redeemed, Rosie."

Rosie offered her guests drinks and they sat down around the table.

"So, what are you writing?" asked Maria, bumping Zak up and down on her knee.

"We're finishing off an investigation into a major corruption by our most trusted and elected members of parliament," Matt said and looked at Rosie. "And, as a matter of fact, the mainstream papers are picking up on the story."

Rosie smiled and rested a hand on his shoulder. "So I heard. You're doing a great job, Matthew." She turned to Maria. "Come on. Let's go out into the garden while the sun's out."

Rosie led them down the hallway towards the back of the house and through a utility room at the end, where the light of the garden seemed to be flooding in.

As Maria and Joe followed her outside, they heard a shriek, where they found a boy with blonde hair around the same age as Joe with a scowl of discontent on his face. Another older boy with dark brown, matted hair was crying, holding his cheek and pointing at him.

"Troy, did you hit him? That's very naughty!" She grabbed his arm and made him apologise but it was evident he was used to being told off. Instead, he just stared at Maria and Joe quizzically. Maria bent down to comfort the other boy.

After five minutes, the commotion was forgotten and the three boys continued playing on a large wooden climbing frame.

As the mini-drama receded, the two adults sat around a large wooden table set outside and Rosie disappeared into the kitchen to fetch glasses and a bottle of Rioja.

"Troy is John Rhode's son," she said on her return. "A right handful as you can see."

"Who?"

"The blonde one. He's staying here for a while. The other one is Tom, my first."

Maria smiled and glanced at the children, as they clambered over the frame like monkeys. "So, this John Rhodes. Tell me more about him and this talk you mentioned."

Chapter 4

The sound of the door slamming forced Frank out of his thoughts and a familiar rush of feet thundered up the stairs to the flat.

"Hi, Dad," Joe said before disappearing into his room. Maria shouted from the stairwell. "I need a hand here."

"Joe, help your mother, don't just disappear like that." Frank put his newspaper aside and reluctantly got up from the sofa.

"Why don't you do it? You haven't done much today," shouted Joe from his room.

"Hey, less of that! Come and help your mother now!" Frank's authoritative loud tone boomed through the hallway and soon, a reluctant footfall followed Frank as they went back down the stairs to the front door. Frank gave Maria a peck on the lips, bent down and picked up Zak from next to his mother and a pile of shopping bags.

"Hey, big man. How's the boss of the house doing today?" he cooed in the toddler's ear. Zak chortled and waved his toy fire engine at Frank. "Mr. Fire Bug been on big adventures, has he?

"Big adventure indeed," said Maria as she handed a shopping bag to a sullen looking Joe, who ran quickly back upstairs. "Three hours I spent in that supermarket. It was total chaos."

"Blimey, that doesn't sound good. Did any of that time include lounging in the café by any chance?"

Maria narrowed her eyes at Frank. "And what if it did? Don't I deserve a coffee break?"

Frank started to make his way up the stairs, holding his youngest son.

"Of course you do. But that's why it takes so bloody long."

Frank put Zak down and walked into the kitchen where his eldest son was pouring orange juice into a glass. "Did you go to Cubs today then, Joe?"

His face remained sullen. "Yeah, we did some knot tying."

"Oh, right? What kind?"

Joe glugged down the juice and then put the glass down.

"What do you care?"

Frank tensed.

"Hey, I asked you a question. The least you can do is answer your old man."

Joe's face turned into a scowl.

"I did a bowline, halter hitch, and the carrick bend." He then promptly left the kitchen, belching as Maria came in.

"Joe! Don't do that!" Maria rasped.

"Sorry."

She began stacking tins of food into the cupboard as Frank shook his head.

"What is wrong with that boy?"

"I don't know. You need to spend more time with him. Tonight's a good opportunity as I want to go to a meeting. Can you look after them this evening?"

He sighed as he grabbed a loaf from the bread tin. "This evening? Hmm, I don't know..."

"You have something special lined up?"

Frank shrugged and moved to the fridge for some ham and cheese. He didn't have anything lined up, it was just a habit of never volunteering for anything.

"What's the meeting?"

"Well, it's more of a talk. By a man, I heard on the radio. It's all about Liberty and Social freedom."

Frank rolled his eyes. "Oh, God."

"It's important stuff, Frank!"

"Suit yourself. We'll be fine. We'll watch a stack of films or something."

Maria nodded, feeling annoyed at him but saying nothing. It was about the world that their children were growing up in. What could be more important than that?

Frank rapped on Joe's bedroom door. "Joe?"

"What?"

Frank opened the door and popped his head through to see Joe sitting on his bed with his arms crossed.

"What's wrong?"

"Just bored. You never come with me to Cubs when you're home. All the other dads go. You're away all the time and when you're here, you just drink beer and do nothing."

Frank dropped his head. "I'm sorry, son. I'll try and make the time. I work really hard when I'm away and just need to relax when I'm home."

Joe stared down at the floor and said nothing.

"Hey. Your mum's out tonight. Fancy a late film night?"

Joe's face seemed to light up at this and he nodded his head.

"Great. Just don't choose that one with all the animals that talk again."

The boy smiled. "No, I'm well bored of that one."

Chapter 5

Maria Chapman moved along the aisles of chairs in the busy windowless community hall and took her place alongside the other people who had come to hear John Rhodes speak. At the front, there was a raised platform that acted as a stage with a long table set back near the back wall. The audience included a wide span of ages, races, and gender, a typical selection of a London community.

An Afro-Caribbean man and a woman went and sat down at the table, as a white-headed figure adjusted a microphone.

The murmur of conversation in the hall hushed.

"Good evening, gentlemen and ladies," he said and gave the audience a warm smile and applause rose through the small hall.

He held his hand up. "Thank you for coming, everyone. Today's meeting is a forum, not just for me but everyone here. We are all affected by the marching globalisation and criminality that casts its shadow and we all need to be involved as one voice." Rhodes took a sip of water and cleared his throat in the hushed room.

"It was the science fiction writer, Philip K. Dick, who said, 'There will come a time when it isn't 'They're spying on me through my phone' anymore. Eventually, it will be 'My phone is spying on me'.'"

There were chuckles from the audience.

"Today, we are living in a society that is on a slippery slope to a modern type of totalitarianism, where the governments are using deception and manipulation to create the society they want. One that deals in the trade of perpetual death through the Industrial military complex, a society that creates wars for profit."

Rhodes put on a pair of glasses that hung around his neck on a chain and opened a sheet of paper from his pocket.

"I want to quote a speech by an American president, just several years before his assassination."

Rhodes cleared his throat before continuing.

"'We are opposed around the world by a monolithic and ruthless conspiracy that relies primarily on covert means for expanding its sphere of influence — on infiltration instead of invasion, on subversion instead of elections, on intimidation instead of free choice, on guerrillas by night instead of armies by day.'"

Rhodes took off the glasses and returned his gaze to the crowd.

"Although J.F Kennedy was speaking in 1961, and referring to the system at the time in the US, I believe we are facing the same enemy today. They have *not* gone away. Closer to home, the surveillance culture is increasingly creeping into our lives. Nearly four million CCTV's in the UK shows how far we have gone towards an Orwellian reality. The dark shadows behind government know they can't bring in mass surveillance overnight. No, that would, or at least should, ignite a revolution. Instead, they wait, boiling the frog degree by degree over time whilst slowly dismantling our civil liberties, brick by brick. Soon, they may try to engineer some terrible event; the finger pointing at a convenient foe to advance their agenda. They've done it before, countless times, and will probably do it again."

Rhodes walked up and down the stage, moulding invisible circles with his hands.

"All around the world, there is a sense that something is not right. Growing anger and discord is rife. We live in troubled and changing times where the gap between the populations and the global controllers, whether they are governments, corporate and banking interests, or the military apparatus that serves them, grows ever wider. There is an increasing suspicion, not just here in the UK but across the western world, that democracy is an illusion and a rigged game, designed to keep us in line within a system that benefits only those controllers."

Rhodes had stopped pacing the stage. "Bush talks about the big idea of a New World Order but let us talk about the big idea of resistance against that order. What was it H.G. Wells said? 'Countless people...will hate the new world order....and will die protesting against it.'"

He waved his hand in the air to emphasise his point and then took a sip of water from the table.

"We are pawns, fodder even, in a dangerous game that is not only making us all poorer but more worryingly, controlled and surveilled. Should we lie down and accept this? Will we wake up one day and realise we have allowed something terrible to happen...that we have allowed them to get away with it?"

Rhodes started to pace the stage again, looking around the room, mixing eye contact with gestures and a steady voice, raising and varying his tone like any good orator. He let out a huge sigh.

"So what does this have to do with us? We're busy. Trying to scratch a living, pay the bills. Are we not already walking around free in a democracy? Free to do what we want, within the ever increasing laws, of course." Chuckles.

"And what is Liberatus? What can we, as ordinary people with busy lives struggling to scratch a living, do anyway? So many questions, so little time." A few murmurs of agreement from the audience.

Rhodes leaned forward, his hands clutching the back of a chair.

"My vision for Liberatus is a common cause that rejects capitalism, feudalism, and the interests that promote destructive globalisation. Instead, we look to the construction of local alternatives: an organisational philosophy based on decentralisation and autonomy. A system that is based on sustained communities, linked around the globe. A self-efficient, self-governing entity that is prepared to defend itself.

A community that is based on mutual respect, not a society where war seems to be the ongoing instrument to boost the economy. A system that is self-sustaining rather than sucking the world's resources dry like a swarm of locusts. A future that benefits all of mankind and the planet, not the current Ponzi scheme of the stock market that we've all been suckered into!

And freedom! Freedom from being watched by the Global surveillance powers that do not have our best interests at heart. That is the way we need to move forward. That is the society we must have!"

He stood straight again, holding out his arms as if reaching out to the people in the room. There was a crescendo of rapacious applause from the crowd. Others had filtered in at the back and joined in clapping with the occasional loud whistle and shout.

A beaming Rhodes gave a wave and sat back down. A woman sitting at the organisers table leaned into her microphone, clapping along with the audience.

"Thank you very much and thank you, John Rhodes," she said.

After the clapping died off, she turned to face a smartly dressed middle-aged Afro-Caribbean man on her left.

"Okay. Now I think we're going to have a question and answer session, is that right, Marcus?" The man nodded and leaned into his microphone.

"Yes, if anyone has questions, please hold up your arm and we'll take them one at a time." A sea of hands rose and the session lasted a further thirty minutes.

Following the Q and A and a call for volunteers, a small group of people made their way to talk to Rhodes. Maria felt invigorated and excited. She had not felt this inspired since she had been involved in a human rights protest group in Amsterdam.

Maria squeezed through the bodies to sign up and then she had decided to talk to Rhodes himself. She had been profoundly affected by his speech and wanted to get involved. Everything he said had resonated with her at every level of what she believed in and she wanted to be a part of it.

"Hello there, did you enjoy the meeting?"

Maria turned to the direction of the voice and found herself looking at a short, chubby man with dark brown eyes looking pointedly back at her. His black hair was shiny with grease and mounded into a cow-lick at the front.

"Oh, yes, I certainly did," she said, smiling politely. She made to move ahead through the crowd.

"Forgive me, I didn't introduce myself," came the voice again. "Nigel. Nigel Harrison."

"Oh, yes. I'm sorry. I'm Maria. I was just looking to speak to John." He shook her hand limply. "Please let me introduce you to him myself."

Maria nodded uncertainly. "Right. Thank you."

She followed the figure through the crowd.

Chapter 6

David Devlin walked briskly down the GCHQ corridor at Oakley in the depths of the iconic green building that had been a landmark in Cheltenham for decades. He passed the main offices of M block, where hundreds of employees sat at their cubicles, all focused on their own tasks. His newly shined black shoes clicking on the polished surface, a leather briefcase, containing the report that had turned his day upside down, in hand. This was red alert time of the highest order. Options swirled through his mind but he tried to dismiss them to focus on the simple facts that he was about to spill at the meeting.

He reached the door at the end and swiped a card that activated a green light on the control console, followed by a click on the huge door lock. The door slid open to the operations meeting room, where other suited figures awaited his presence.

Percy Braithwaite, the MI6 director, stood tall, a striking figure who had aged well for his fifty-five years, coffee in hand as he chatted to Fiona Geisheim from the Foreign Secretary's Office. The group finally all sat down at the large boardroom table; papers and reports were placed on the table in front of them.

All eyes fell on Devlin as he sipped a glass of water and opened a report.

"We've had a breach. One of our intelligence analysts, Sarah

Edwards, managed to take a significant amount of data relating to some of our surveillance projects and has since disappeared. She has almost certainly left the country. It's not clear at this stage exactly what information she has and what she intends to do with it but we're working on finding that out. We need to assemble our response as soon as possible, find this ex-employee, and decide on the course of action going forward. Firstly, I'll say that we intend to keep this as quiet as possible."

Devlin looked around the table and caught Fiona Geisheim's eye and raised his eyebrows and nodded, indicating for her to go ahead with the question she evidently wanted to ask. She was an attractive woman, in her late thirties, with blonde hair tied back into a bun. Only crow's feet around her eyes betrayed her age but the steely green pupils sparked intelligence. Devlin noted she was unmarried or didn't sport any kind of ring at least, and momentarily wondered if she was single.

"So are you suggesting we do not seek extradition?"

"It depends on where she turns up but I would suggest we avoid that route, to begin with." He gave the minister his most charming smile.

"Firstly, what kind of data are we talking about and what damage is it likely to cause? Secondly, why isn't this on the agenda for the next Joint Intelligence Committee?" she asked, the charm evidently failing.

Devlin shifted slightly in his seat and leaned back.

"Oh, it will be on the agenda, Minister, rest assured. Regarding the information copied, it's related to a joint project with the NSA, specifically Internet surveillance working in conjunction with several telecoms companies."

"Operation Oculus," injected a voice from the MI6 Director.

Devlin sighed. "Yes, Oculus. The proposed piping of all Internet data. It's a powerful commercial product, one that can intercept and monitor real-time precision targeting of any type of IP traffic including webmail, email IM chat, and VoIP. There's a lot more to it than I can go into at the moment as I'm sure you'll appreciate."

"So once this is in place, sitting in the middle of any network, it potentially has access to all of the data flowing over that network?" Fiona Geisheim asked.

Devlin nodded in agreement.

"And the consequences of this getting out?"

"There will be a shit storm, that's for sure. The liberals will scream from the rooftops and it could severely damage the current government. There's a high risk that it could be sold or fall into the hands of terrorists, or any number of rogue governments. For this reason, I would strongly argue that an extradition leading to some kind of public trial along with all the media attention would also be inappropriate. It also looks very bad for us. This is Top Secret material and we have to aggressively track down this operative," Devlin finished defiantly.

Percy Braithwaite finished his coffee and cleared his throat. "I think we're all in agreement as to what needs doing here."

Geisheim leaned forward. She hadn't finished and stared at Devlin.

"This Oculus project, I take it the Foreign Office was going to be notified at some point?"

"Yes, absolutely, Minister, a full report is being written as we speak. This is very early stages and would probably not be operational until 2004 at the earliest."

This seemed to satisfy the minister and she nodded and returned to her notes.

"This could be extremely damaging if leaked. Everything must be done to track this rogue employee down. Have you made any headway?" asked Braithwaite.

"We have a signit team on it," said Devlin.

"Maybe you need some help from our chaps, considering the seriousness of the matter, don't you think, David?"

"We can handle it," Devlin retorted.

"Really? You might need bodies on the ground and considering it's a security issue where the target is likely to end up abroad, well, that's very much our department."

Devlin bristled inside but kept a stony straight face. He had never really clicked with Percy. The man was very much an old-school Etonian. Cricket and Champers on a Sunday and a very stiff upper lip.

"I want very much want to keep this as an internal GCHQ matter," replied Devlin curtly.

"I think there needs to be a compromise on this. This calls for an emergency meeting of the Joint Intelligence Committee and I am going to recommend that a covert team is set up. A little venture between MI6 and GCHQ," said Geisheim, flashing a grin at Devlin.

Devlin leaned back in his chair, swore silently, and rapidly clicked his pen. "Are there any further questions?" When none came, it was a signal for the meeting to end and folders snapped shut, followed by the scraping of chairs.

The GCHQ Director wasn't particularly worried about the data Edwards thought she had; that was bound to leak out eventually. If it did, it would cause a lot of problems with their associates across the pond and for all the companies involved but he knew it would be a storm in a teacup compared to what else the intelligence communities were up to. No, it was the darker restricted files that she didn't even realise she possessed that had kept him awake for the past two nights.

Devlin had been recruited into GCHQ at Oxford in the days when an approach was made; usually by one of the professors in the mid-eighties. *Those ways were drawing to a close now, of course,* the director reminisced to himself with a wry smile. Recruitment was going to become a lot more open and transparent in the coming years.

He had risen through the ranks, made connections, and played the game until he found himself perched at the top of the tree. That view gave him the realisation that certain things needed to be done at high cost and that even he was a mere cog in a wheel. Devlin had learned that there was a plan, decades in the making. Almost every major world event, be it regime change, a downturn in the economy, or terrorist attack, were all notes in a grand orchestral piece.

This latest development was one note, however, that could prove most jarring.

Chapter 7

Carl Paterson buttoned up his shirt in readiness as he approached the old red-brick grain warehouse that sat astride the Limehouse Cut Canal. Once a hub of activity for bringing trade goods into East London from the Thames in the 1700's, the impressive building was now converted into commercial units for media based companies. Carl had no idea why he had been summoned here but it was a long trek from 'VX', as the MI6 HQ at Vauxhall was known.

Large loading bay doors dominated the building from the street side and Carl scanned the buzzers for 'Studio 31', the anonymous sounding front company for the project he was being pulled into.

Secrecy was a priority regarding this meeting and he had been verbally warned that it was under the radar and outlined in no uncertain terms by a Senior Officer that once he had agreed to the meeting, for which he knew nothing of the agenda, it would be extremely difficult for him to back away. It was an almost impossible position but Carl was never one to shy away from challenges. He was in one hundred percent when it came to the agency. It was his life and there was nothing else. Anna, his partner, had long gone, leaving him to decide what road he wanted to go down and when this 'offer' had emerged, Carl hadn't needed long to make a decision.

Once buzzed in, Carl climbed the metal stairway to the third floor, where he was met by a large man who looked like an ape in a suit, the kind of thug who wouldn't think twice about throwing you down a disused well. He was told to wait in a reception room that was still a work in progress with step ladders and a half painted wall. On the opposite side was a framed image of a logo for Studio 31, bold and iconic.

A meeting with the Director of MI6 meant something big. What was he walking into? Carl felt anticipation, fear even, but an excitement that had driven him in this line of work. It was what fuelled his blood and made him get up in the morning.

Perhaps he was going to be deployed again in another hostile environment? It could be the Balkans theatre. The war over Kosovo had begun and was currently plastered all over the media. Or the Middle East? There had been covert operations to destabilise Saddam Hussein ever since the 1991 Gulf conflict.

"Carl. Thanks for coming, I very much appreciate it," came a voice from nowhere. Carl turned around from the picture to see Braithwaite, his light blue shirt sleeves rolled up to the elbow. Carl shook the director's outstretched hand.

"The pleasure is all mine, Mr. Braithwaite."

"Please. Call me Percy. Do you want any refreshments? Although it's not the most comfortable of surroundings at the moment, we can do coffee."

Carl indicated that he was fine and they began to walk to another room on the Canalside. The vast space was devoid of furniture, except a couple of chairs and a table at the end. The large windows streamed in rays of light that revealed dust floating in the air. Carl sensed activity behind a shut door to his right but he didn't look, instead, focusing his attention on the director.

They sat down, Braithwaite behind the makeshift desk, his grey eyes appraising Carl.

"So you've had a talk with Keller?" he asked. The director was referring to the Scottish Senior Officer who had given Carl the brief, and the warning. Keller was a figure in the agency most were wary of. The short but ferocious Scot seemed to have ears and eyes everywhere and most of Carl's colleagues referred to him as the Rottweiler.

"I did but there were few details," Carl replied.

Braithwaite smiled. "Good, otherwise, I'd have to reprimand the old dog," Carl noted the sly reference to his nickname. He obviously had a sharper ear to the ground than was realised.

Braithwaite changed the tone suddenly. "Okay, let's get down to business. What we have here is a new completely *off the record* project. This isn't mentioned in any paperwork or on any file. You will not find a mention of this anywhere, apart from conspiracy theorists, maybe." They shared a light chuckle.

"The Joint Intelligence Committee wants our two little bands to work closer together and frankly, I agree with them. There have been a few examples recently where closer co-operation would have had much more satisfying results in recent operations."

Braithwaite leaned back, his gaze pointedly fixed on Carl.

"I want you to work with Keller, who will be overseeing several operations. He's a good chap and has put together a tight working team. It's extremely important to know that this is the highest level of secrecy. You're the man to lead this, Carl. The buck stops with you. There'll be no official benefits, no pension scheme, but you will be rewarded in many ways. You want something, a brand new Mercedes? Just let Keller know. A holiday in the best hotel in the Caribbean? No problem. Officially, you'll still receive your compensation from the company, of course."

Carl brushed a hand over his jaw in thought.

"Are you saying the responsibility of this op ends with me?"

"Not just this operation, Carl. Your team, possibly one of many within Ghost 13, the name of our little team, will be under your wing, with guidance from Keller. This is the first op, one of many to come, that needs urgent attention."

"What op?"

Braithwaite chuckled. "I certainly won't be giving you the details. You'll hear soon enough, providing you agree to move forward."

It all still sounded ominous and vague to Carl. Exactly the type of carte blanche that gave Intelligence agencies the self-appointed approval to do what the hell they liked, but he had already decided.

"Is there any kind of indication of what it might involve, sir?"

Braithwaite seemed to grimace momentarily at the formal address and then smiled and nodded.

"You'll be locating a target and then putting that target under surveillance. National security is at stake. Initially, that would be all, but it needs to be a flexible op."

Carl seemed to contemplate this for a second. "Why me?"

"Discretion and a fairly good track record. There are others who would snap this up, Carl. I'll make sure you're handsomely rewarded. There is a fast ladder to higher places in this organisation that you'll be helped up, take my word for it."

Carl nodded. "Count me in."

"Welcome to Ghost 13, Carl."

The director stood up and Carl followed his lead. Both men shook hands. Carl left the building and headed back to central London, wondering what he had got himself into.

Chapter 8

The sleek black S Class Mercedes moved slowly up the ramped car park levels to the top and pulled into a free space. The cityscape view of Hammersmith shimmered under a threatening dark sky and the patter of heavy raindrops began to rap on the windscreen until a downpour opened up and the city lights blurred into abstract shapes through the glass.

A white van pulled up beside the vehicle and the driver of the Mercedes nodded at the face looking back at him. The figure turned off his engine and jumped into the passenger seat of the Mercedes.

"Viktor. How nice to see you again. You're late."

Viktor nodded to the man he knew only as 'The Marquis' and slammed the door shut.

"Traffic is a bitch in this city…so why don't you sue me. Why am I here?"

The Marquis reached to the back seat for a leather pouch. "I have a job for you. Very important. High level. I trust you still have a good team?"

Viktor nodded, pulling out a pack of Russian cigarettes.

"Not in here," the man said, looking at him with mild contempt, his eyes falling on the Russians' neck tattoo of barbed wire, creeping up to his chin. Viktor shrugged and ran his hand over his neatly trimmed goatee beard as if smoothing ruffled feathers.

"So what's this important job that MI6 can't take of itself?" he asked, with a hint of mockery in his tone.

The Marquis pulled out a report from the pouch and turned to face the Russian.

"You know who I work for and you're well aware of their reach, their power, even to your country. I don't need to tell you that trust between our two parties is paramount."

Viktor grabbed the report from the man and stared at the photograph of a young woman with dark tied back hair. "Yes, yes, you don't need to lecture me on these matters," he said, irritated. "How many times I let you down? Zero. So, Operation Whisper Hunt," he said, reading the title of the report. "Who is this?"

"An employee of GCHQ. Sarah Edwards. She has disappeared with a lot of top secret information."

"What kind of information are we talking about?"

"Secret information, that's all you need to know."

Viktor flipped through the pages, scanning over Sarah Edwards' personal details, and history.

"Will there be other interested parties?" he asked.

The Marquis flicked the lever for the windscreen wipers once and for a few seconds, they had a clear view of the city.

"There is going to be a small team on the ground, the official but covert team sanctioned by the agency. I'll do my best to keep them out of your way but the most important thing is the mission. The information and the woman are the two things you need in your sights at all times. She cannot live through this, do you understand me?"

Viktor turned back to the photograph of Sarah Edwards. "Yes. Big shame. She's very attractive."

"I will be in touch when we have more information on where she might be."

"This other team you're sending, how many? What is their capability?" Viktor asked, concerned.

"For now, I can tell you that their squad will be three men and possibly a local contact. Two of them are ex-special forces and a surveillance officer. I'll get you more details."

"Where is the woman?"

"She could be anywhere, we just don't know yet. Now, what is your price?"

"A ballpark? Five hundred thousand dollars per man by transfer before and then the same amount after completion. I need four or five men."

"That seems a bit excessive to track and deal with a woman, Mr. Kozel."

Viktor laughed. "And the covert team that you mentioned. They might get in my way and I'll need weapons, transport, and communications equipment. This is not cheap."

The Marquis sighed and handed him a phone from his inside jacket pocket. "Three hundred thousand. Now, take this and I will be in touch with further details. Assemble your team, Mr. Kozel, and be ready."

Chapter 9

Maria typed in the key code on the door and quickly climbed the steps to the small, cramped office of Liberatus News on Soho Square, where she had been working for just shy of a month. She had talked Rhodes into allowing her to volunteer to help with the research for the stories and features that syndicated out through the paper and website. John had been impressed with Maria's structured approach to projects and he offered her a part-time job to help organise the activist newspaper. For the last few weeks, she had worked tirelessly on re-organising their structure and workflow to help refine the process of news research and gathering.

Their main benefactor was more than generous, yet no one knew who it was, not even Rhodes, or so he said. This had made Maria uneasy and she felt that it may come back to haunt them but without that funding, they would be in deep trouble. So she had set about finding ways to build additional income streams like web advertising and sponsorship, which wasn't easy considering the group's stance towards big business.

Maria had also become privy to John Rhode's other project, an activist pressure group, which he rarely talked about but was increasingly spending more of his time on. He needed help in providing a clear mandate, which Maria had been central to bringing about: to influence the legislative branches of government and expose corruption in governments and corporations. It still needed an incredible amount of work but was a start, a stepping stone to something she hoped would become a worthwhile entity, a cause worth fighting for.

Maria beamed a smile at Jillian, the general secretary, and sat down at her desk, working through her mind what she needed to focus on today after the usual morning chaos of getting Zak to the nursery and dropping off Joe at school. She read through a list that included a myriad of phone calls and finishing the writing of some key policy documents.

"There's still some coffee in the pot but there's no milk. I'll go and get some. You want anything else?" asked Jillian, getting up from her desk.

Maria glanced up and smiled as she fired up her computer. "No, I'm fine, thanks, Jill." Her footsteps faded as Maria focused on her first task of the day.

"Good morning, Maria." She looked up to see Nigel Harrison standing in the doorway, his dark brown eyes shifting to the side before falling on her.

"Oh, morning, Nigel," she replied, glancing up at him before turning back to her screen. He was the IT guy who John had brought in to manage the servers.

"Erm...I read the early drafts of the mandate you've been working on. It's very impressive." He moved closer to her desk and she looked up again, noticing a sheen of sweat above his lip.

Maria smiled politely. "Thanks. That's very kind of you."

"John showed me. I hope you don't mind? It was because he was so pleased with your progress."

Maria smiled at him, in much the same way she did to her oldest boy. "Ah, thanks, Nigel. I really appreciate that. There's a lot more tweaking to do yet I'm pretty sure."

Harrison hovered slightly, as if reluctant to move on.

"Well, good luck with it. Speak again soon." He didn't take his eyes away from her for what seemed like an age to Maria. She smiled again, tightly this time.

"Thanks, Nigel. See you later."

"Yes, see you later." His wide frame finally moved away from her and she noticed a large sweat patch on the back of his white shirt. Maria shook her head to herself. She couldn't figure out that man. It was obvious he had some kind of 'thing' for her, like a schoolboy fancying his teacher. She had no idea how someone so child-like in nature was a technical whiz on computers.

Chapter 10

Five years earlier

Frank ran as fast as he could, skipping over fallen branches as a whistling bullet flew over his head, hitting a tree in front of him and spraying splinters of bark onto the sodden ground. He swore under his breath and kept running, moving in an uneven line so as not to make himself an easy target. Clocking a ditch yards ahead of him, he made it his goal. As soon as he was near enough, he dived, his body curling into a fetal position as he rolled into the shallow, muddy water at the bottom of the trench.

He lay there for a moment, listening hard, but could hear nothing except for his own heavy breathing and the distant bark of the dog. A glimmer of relief that he was hidden from his pursuers, if only for a short time.

Got to keep moving.

He glanced both ways along the ditch, still lying in the sludge, and saw that one end curved away from the direction of his pursuers. He forced himself to manoeuvre onto all fours before crouching his body into a sprinter position and then he bolted along the trench, keeping his head down and out of sight.

A shout echoed through the woods followed by a series of barks that seemed closer all of a sudden. They were gaining on him and that dog worried him. It was only a matter of time before he was caught. All was surely lost now but he refused to give up; he would make the bastards work for it.

They must want him alive or he'd be dead by now...surely? Were they a terrorist cell? Hardened criminals? Enemy intelligence? Carl had told him bugger all and he felt a rising bitterness at this complete cock up. The targets had known he was watching them. How had this been possible?

***

Twelve hours earlier at 1600 hours, Frank sat with Carl Paterson in a near derelict cottage that sat isolated and hidden in the vast broadleaved woodland in New Forest.

Frank had been picked up by Carl in his Land Rover and they had headed onto the M3 from London towards Southampton. On the far side of the River Test lay the beautiful landscape of New Forest with its two hundred square miles of meandering heathland, woodland, forests, rivers, and fields.

Frank wondered if the Marchwood military port in Southampton was of any relevance. Frank had read that the port had been built in 1943 to aid the D-day invasion of Normandy and was later used as support for the British Falklands war. Whatever it was about, he guessed he'd know soon enough.

Carl Paterson and Frank Bowen had known each other since school days, when they both neglected their work, more interested in hiding out in makeshift dens smoking and drinking stolen beer. They would often scheme about how they could make a few extra quid on the streets of London.

One of their crew, Kieran, had been badly beaten into a coma by a group of older lads for no other reason than being Irish. Both boys visited the hospital every day and, as advised by the nurse, spoke into his ear about what they had been up to. It was important to talk to victims in a coma, in case they could hear or at least some of it slipped through to their subconscious.

Six weeks after the incident, Frank and Carl had turned up at the hospital and found Kieran's very upset parents standing in the entrance hall. They informed the boys that their son had lost his fight and passed away. The culprits who murdered him were never caught, leaving a simmering rage in both Frank and Carl, and the bond of friendship between them only strengthened.

At fourteen, Carl was moved to another school, and under pressure from his parents, finally applied himself to his full ability and did well. His educational journey, along with financial help from relatives, eventually landed him at Oxford University and the intelligence connections it would bring for him.

Frank had moved to London when he was five years old to be brought up by his grandfather after his parents were killed in a car crash. The move from the quiet, flat landscape of Lincolnshire to the hectic, tough London streets was a bit of a shock to the young lad but he soon took to it as he grew up, making friends, getting into football, and becoming a part of the streets. From then on, it was a move into petty crime, drinking, and dabbling in drugs, which led to an ultimatum from his grandfather: Clean up or leave.

***

Frank's memory was jerked back into the present as the 4x4 heaved along the forest track until a cottage appeared and both men entered the dark, abandoned shell of a building. Carl threw down a bag onto an old wooden table and pulled out a map, a flask, and two porcelain mugs. He poured tea and handed Frank one before opening out the map on the table top.

"Target is holed up at a house in this location," Carl said, pointing to a series of lines and a dot at the edge of a vast forest.

"All we need you to do is move into position on foot where you can monitor any movements from the safe house. If there are any prisoners, or if any of the targets leave by car, foot, or any other way, it must be photographed, with notes of exact times." Carl pulled out a compact prototype Nikon camera from his bag and placed it on the table top.

He then continued to lay out a various assortment of equipment on top of the map: binoculars, night glasses, a handheld VHF frequency-range tactical communications radio, a Francis Barker M88 Prismatic compass as well as army issue food packages, three Mars bars wrapped in cling film, a large flask of water, water purification tablets, and dried nuts.

Frank packed them into his backpack alongside his own gear, which included a woollen hat, gloves, and a Swiss army knife.

"No weapons?" asked Frank.

"It's a pretty safe op, mate. Just a bit of standard surveillance. We'll need you to watch the targets for forty-eight hours, so you'll be shitting in the woods I'm afraid. Just try not to leave any tracks."

Carl then pulled out a brown folder and handed Frank a report. Photographs of a woman and two men stared back at him. The woman was attractive, with glasses and dark brown hair, while the two males, one dark haired with a beard and the other with short cropped blonde hair, appeared to be in their mid-thirties. They all wore grim, murderous expressions and certainly weren't the types you'd want to get in a ruck with.

"Who are they?" Frank asked, slurping his sweet tea.

"Sorry, can't tell you," beamed Carl, grabbing the report from Frank before tossing it into his bag and zipping it shut. Frank followed Carl outside from the small, sparse cottage they had marked as the rendezvous point: Codename: Alamo.

"What about civvies? This is a National Park, isn't it?"

"Not where we are. It's private land right up to the target area. If you do see anyone walking their dog, which you shouldn't, you're just a rambler." Carl climbed into the Land Rover.

"You have about four hours of daylight left, by the way," said Carl, with what Frank could swear was a smirk but wasn't quite sure. "See you back here in forty-eight hours," he said cheerily as he gunned the engine into life.

After a minute, Frank was suddenly alone, looking down the empty, mud-ridden track.

He had a few other questions, to say the least, but knew better than to bother asking. He returned inside and studied the map, plotting his route in his mind to cut down on stops. He needed to head south-west to a stream that would take him to the far side of the forest edge near a main road where the target house was. It was probably only three miles as the crow flies but he knew it wouldn't be a simple stroll. He grabbed his pack, checked he had everything, and started walking into the dense woodland.

As he made his way through the quiet, sprawling woods, he made a note to himself to bring his young son, Joe, somewhere like this. Get him away from the city and into some fresh air and closer to nature. He wished his grandad, Larry Bowen, had been around to meet Joe. They would have got on like a house on fire. Larry had always been full of stories from the war. Joe loved that stuff.

His mind wandered back to returning from Asia again, and the decision he had made to work with the 'company' as MI6 was called by its own employees.

The first step was to put himself through three months of basic army training, paid for by the company. It was something Frank had insisted on as soon as he had returned from Asia; to get 'match fit' as his trainer, Sam Keane, had said. Sam was a veteran army man, short, stocky, and tough, a through and through army man who had spent his entire adult life in the Royal Marines. His tour list was extensive: the Balkans, Oman, Iraq, and Africa.

They had spent many a weekend running up through the Brecon Beacons with a rucksack filled with bricks. "Sweat it out, lad. Then you can drink all the beer ya like!" Sam had yelled as they stumbled across the rocky terrain, the Welsh hills shimmering in the background.

He had used this fitness regime as a foundation for the other skills he wanted to add to his bow.

Many weekends included a strict series of sessions with a qualified hand to hand combat expert specialising in Combat Ju-Jitsu, old school fighting techniques originally from the Samurai era and taught to Special Forces in the First World War.

Then he had covered night manoeuvres, weapons handling, basic survival, H2H (hand to hand combat), signalling, marksmanship, all under the shadow of a strict schedule.

Frank opened his M88 compass as he lay hidden in the braken that covered the floor of the dense woodland. He checked his bearings to make sure he hadn't accidentally wandered off course and was at least going in the right direction. Looking up, he noted the dark grey clouds that moved quickly overhead and inwardly groaned as he packed away the device.

He checked the map again, which was wrapped in a clear plastic folder and traced a dotted line with his finger. The target's safe house was marked with an 'X' and sat next to a lonely road that snaked through the forest.

Frank estimated his current position on the map and figured it was another eight hundred metres or so away, as the crow flies. He put the compass and map away in his backpack, checked his Nite

MX10, noting it was 18:15, and moved quickly through the trees, stopping every twenty metres to listen out for anything unusual. It was difficult with his beating heart and heavy breathing.

Hearing nothing, he moved again, weaving between the continuous tree trunks, their canopies darkening his path as thick raindrops began to patter into the hard ground ahead. The woodland thinned out quickly, and he was soon back out in the open and moving upwards to a ridge that would hopefully look down onto the target.

Frank crouched down as he came into sight of the ridge top and crawled the last few feet before peering over the edge down onto the rolling valley below. The rain hacked down at an angle onto his face, which made it virtually impossible to see anything clearly. He took out his field glasses and scanned the area and could only see the grey landscape of fields and woodlands. Then as he moved his glasses down to the bottom of the rocky hill in front of him, he caught a glimpse of a rooftop, partly hidden by a cluster of trees. That was it: the target house.

He continued to crawl along the ridge to get a better view as the rain hardened, coming in waves, soaking his canvas fatigues.

"What the hell am I doing here?" he muttered aloud. But he already knew the answer: It was the woman in his life and their son, Joe. He was trying his hardest to shield them from the hardship and poverty that he himself had grown up with. When he was single, it hadn't mattered to him so much, not being a materialistic type, but suddenly having a family to think about had spun an entirely different angle on things. He couldn't afford to be the old, selfish Frank anymore.

After ten minutes of crawling, he had a good view of the house and peered once again through his binoculars. The cottage was old, grey stone that had made it hard to see, with two outhouses facing into a courtyard at the rear that looked across an open field. It didn't look like anyone was home; there were no discernible lights and no vehicles around the property.

Frank fished for his handheld communications radio and held it close to his mouth.

"Charlie-two-zero Alpha...This is Echo Sierra five niner. Radio check, over."

Silence.

"Charlie-two-zero Alpha...This is Echo Sierra five niner. Can you respond, over?"

Still, there was no answer. Frank checked the radio settings once again and went through the same routine. When that failed, he put out a general call:

"Charlie Charlie...anyone there, over?"

Still, silence. It was as if the radio was missing a vital component.

"Useless piece of shit," he muttered and put it back in the backpack.

The light began to fade quickly, sinking the cold landscape into darkness. Frank swapped his binoculars for night vision monoculars and continued to watch the house through a green haze. Five minutes later, a passing bright light caused Frank to put down his field glasses and watch as the car headlights drew closer, dipping out of view occasionally before a dark Ford Transit van turned into the front drive of the house.

The van stood stationary for what seemed like an age before the engine and lights died and the house and surroundings fell back into darkness. Frank returned to his night visions and watched three figures exit the vehicle, all dressed in black fatigues and beanie hats that made any ID impossible, although one of them was definitely a female. They opened the rear doors, temporarily hidden from Frank's sight, and reappeared carrying large metal boxes that they heaved into the house. One of the figures lingered for a moment, walked around the van, glanced up the road and then chirped the locks with their remote keys before following the others. A window lit up with a slither of light on the nearest side of the house, but the curtains were already drawn.

After twenty minutes, nothing else happened and Frank placed the monoculars into his backpack and edged down the ridge a few feet before rummaging around for a chocolate bar that was wrapped in cling film. He ate gratefully and silently cursed the cold wetness of his surroundings. His feet ached from the trekking and he longed for the sweet tea he had had earlier but flasks were strictly forbidden in case the steam gave away his position. Sipping water instead, Frank wrapped a waterproof poncho around his shoulders to fend off the elements, although it seemed futile.

The rain pattered against the material, like distant drumbeats, ebbing and flowing into his consciousness. An hour passed and the noise of the downpour faded into blackness.

A distant bark snapped Frank's eyes open like an alarm. Shit! He had fallen asleep.

The steady light of an approaching dawn spread across the sky. The rain had stopped and it looked clear. Had he heard a bark? Or was he dreaming? He quickly crawled up to the ridge and slowly peeked over the edge. His heart felt like it skipped a beat, followed by a nervous trill in his stomach as he raised the binoculars for a closer look.

***

Two figures, dressed in the same black fatigues they had arrived in, armed with rifles slung over their shoulders, stood in the yard. The taller one held a German shepherd dog on a leash as it paced impatiently in circles. They both seemed to be talking and simultaneously glanced in Frank's direction. Instinctively Frank lowered his head. They couldn't possibly see him, could they? He was well hidden, or so he thought. He took another look and saw the black figures walking quickly out of the yard in Frank's direction, across the small field that ended at the foot of the hill at the top of which Frank was positioned.

There was no time to mull over why or how he had been blown. It was time to move – fast.

Frank grabbed his backpack and poncho, rolling it up as he ran towards the line of trees where he had come eight hours before. As his feet pounded the ground, taking him across the clearing back to the main woodland, Frank turned over his options.

Head back to the Alamo? Or go an entirely different direction and hope he could lie low and wait it out? The dog was a problem. It would track him, yard for yard, and he didn't fancy tackling a huge German shepherd, let alone his masters, who looked armed and dangerous.

He decided to head for Alamo, with a possible detour to confuse his pursuers if he could, but the question was then what? Carl wasn't due to rendezvous with him for another forty hours.

Keep calm, Frank. And keep moving.

Once back in the shielded woodland, he stopped and hurriedly took out his binoculars to scan the area he had just covered. Movement in the far tree line. A bark. They were definitely coming after him.

He continued to run across the sodden ground, his boots grinding wet leaves and bracken into the mud as he headed north. The important thing was not to get lost. He just had to find somewhere to hole up until he could think of something. A cold sweat soaked his shirt to his back and all he could think was what a great scent that would leave for that bloody dog.

Suddenly, a crack whistled over his head and hit the tree in front of him. Five minutes later, Frank was lying in the ditch he had spotted and dived into, thinking in staccato, *Move, run. Get to Alamo. Ambush them? How?*

He ran along the ditch, head down, and then, at last, it turned away from his pursuers, well out of sight. After a few metres, the ditch levelled out back into the wood and Frank heard a running stream ahead, where a fallen tree lay across forming a bridge. He scrambled over, almost losing his footing on the uneven track before jumping onto the other side. Landing awkwardly he felt a twinge in his ankle and cursed his luck.

Frank limped on, looking behind him, and upon seeing no one directly on his tail, threw his bag down and slumped down next to it on the wet ground. He rummaged around in the backpack and gulped down the cool water that felt like ecstasy in his throat and then retrieved the Swiss army knife and put it safely into his side cargo trouser pocket where he could get to it easily. Not that it would be any use against guns.

There was no time to check directions; he would have to wing it. Then, an idea. There was a tree before the stream that he reckoned could easily be climbed. If he tracked back the exact same direction and hid in the tree, maybe it would confuse the dog and they would at least get beyond the stream. Just maybe he had a chance. It was the only idea he could come up with. Limping onward, he would be caught, there was no doubt now. He had to move quickly though, otherwise, he'd run right into them.

Frank manoeuvred back through the water next to the fallen tree this time and climbed the bank back to the path he had come. He moved slowly, pausing every now and then in case they were close. He spotted the tree with low branches and hauled himself up, ignoring the shooting pain in his ankle, levering his body higher and higher upwards toward the sheltered crown. He reached a point where he was sure he couldn't be spotted easily from the ground and stopped. It was still a long shot but the only one he had. A cool breeze swept through the canopies, which felt so good against his face. He took more water and then waited.

After what seemed like an age, but was only ten minutes, Frank heard a sound, followed by another. Footfall in the dead leaves on the ground. He strained to listen. No dog? Just one of them. The sound grew closer below him and then he spotted one of the pursuers moving cautiously through the wood, his weapon slung over his back.

Frank looked behind the figure, trying the spot the dog handler but there was no sign. They must have split up? Why? Maybe the other guy thought they could head him off and encircle him somehow. It was likely they knew the woods better than him and anticipated that Frank was heading to one of the main roads. It made sense.

The figure clad in black fatigues moved slowly under Frank's tree, looking around in every direction. Frank dared not breathe. His heart thumped away in his ear like an African drumbeat. He held the Swiss army knife in his grip, inside his jacket pocket, if only for comfort. The man stopped suddenly and Frank imagined he had seen something on the ground.

Shit.

Had he dropped something from his backpack? It was game over if he had and a vision came to him of the pursuer looking slowly up, setting his stare onto Frank.

But after a quick look around, the man casually walked up to a fallen dead tree trunk and proceeded to take a piss against the dark moss covered bark. Frank scanned around the woodland again, looking for the other guy, but there was still no sign. It would have been a perfect ambush situation if he was nearer the ground, but he was too far up the tree and there was no way he could get down there in time without making a noise. Frank cursed to himself. He guessed his life was on the line, but maybe they just wanted to get information out of him. Whoever the hell they were.

Frank watched as the figure below zipped up and proceeded towards the stream. Once just out of sight, he gingerly eased himself down the tree, branch by branch, checking the coast was clear, winching with pain every time pressure was applied to his right foot.

The sane option was to head in the opposite direction and put as wide a gap between him and the other guy as possible. Find another way back to Alamo. Get the hell out of there.

But the hunters were determined to find him, whatever their reason, which Frank was becoming increasingly convinced was to shoot him dead. They had plenty of places to hide his body in this vast, unpopulated area. The thought of leaving Maria and his boy gnawed at his stomach, making him feel nauseous and cold.

No, he had to go on the offensive. The man was on his own without the dog and therefore easier to take on. Every fibre of his body screamed at him to keep running. Instead, Frank turned and walked towards the stream.

***

Frank stayed well out of sight as he, once again, heard the flowing water just ahead through the dark trees. He just caught sight of the figure reaching the far side, before disappearing into the wood opposite. Dark clouds moved overhead; it would rain again. He followed the same route and waded through the shallow water and then crawled on his stomach up to the grassy bank, slowly peering over the edge.

There was no sign of his adversary. He kept low as he moved

to the tree line, thankful for the noise of the stream that covered his footfall. As he slowly walked into the wood, he froze as a dead piece of branch cracked under his boot, sounding way too loud to his sensitive ears. Frank quickly moved behind a wide girthed pine that hid his entire body and listened hard, his heart pounding in his chest. There was a ditch by the tree and he contemplated moving down into it for a second as his hand rummaged around in his cargo trouser pocket for the Swiss army knife.

Suddenly, there was a movement to his left side and a rush of pain hit his jaw that felt like a freight train. Frank managed to keep on his feet but only because his body hit the tree trunk as a dark figure appeared in front of him.

He must have doubled back!

Frank lunged, attempting a quick jab with his fist but the man swivelled himself out of the way and elbowed Frank's ribs, blowing the wind out of him as he fell, hitting the ground hard. The figure stood over him, blue eyes surveying him closely. A thin smile emerged. But he stood too close. With all his strength, Frank scissor-kicked his legs, forcing his opponent to the ground with a bump.

He didn't stay still, throwing himself onto Frank to take advantage of his weak position. He pulled back his right arm to start striking. A sudden buck of Frank's hips put him off balance and Frank blocked his hit, counter-attacking with a knife hand strike, a blow with the side of his outer hand.

The man's eyes opened wide as he struggled for air, gagging and choking. He tried to grab Frank's throat, attempting to close off his windpipe with his free hand. Frank shoved him off and rolled away down the slope that morphed into a ditch below them. He quickly got to his feet as the blonde thug pulled himself up, and for a moment, the only sound was of both men breathing heavily into the crisp air.

A roaring laugh followed by a series of barks caused them both to turn around.

"Enough rolling around in the mud, boys," came the mocking tone from the second bearded man who stood with one hand holding up his weapon and the other holding back the growling German shepherd as it strained at the leash.

Frank dropped his head in defeat. It was definitely over now.

He was blindfolded by one of the men and could almost feel their triumph and then they led him back towards the stream.

Chapter 11

The blindfold came off and Frank found himself staring into the eyes of his friend and operations leader, Carl Paterson. It didn't make any sense. He then realised he was inside the same cottage where he had started from. The shaven blonde thug leaned against the wooden table where Carl and Frank had talked earlier and returned Frank's stare with a smug grin.

"Hello, Frank," Carl smiled uneasily. Frank looked at him and then at the two men in half surprise, half contempt. Carl slapped his hands down on his knees and stood up.

"You did well. Not great, but well. I'm sorry for the unorthodox methods but we needed to see how you performed under, well, difficult circumstances, shall we say," he paused but the only response was a deafening silence and the surprise in Frank's eyes that was quickly turning to anger.

"You left some tracks. Where were they, Steve?"

The blonde man nodded. "Up by the hill. It made a good starting point for the mutt." He winked at Frank.

"But nothing serious, right?" said Carl, more of a statement than a question. He turned back to Frank, smiling weakly. "You avoided capture longer than some, that's for sure."

Frank's eyes seemed to darken as he spoke. "You bastard, Carl." The man winced.

"I thought I'd never see my kid again!" He pulled momentarily at the rope binding him to the chair and then lunged his body forward, head down, with all the force he could muster towards Carl, who, already sensing the attack, side-lined his body out of harm's way. The side of the chair clipped Carl's shin, making him shout out in pain. Frank, with the chair bound to his back, lunged halfway across the room before hitting the floorboards hard with a sickening crack.

"For God's sake, Frank, I'm not the bloody enemy here!" Carl rubbed his shin and then shrugged off the dark-haired man who had jumped up at the commotion, holding onto him protectively.

"Get him up," he ordered the two men. Frank spat blood from his mouth onto the floor as he was hauled back upright. A nasty yellow bruise slowly darkened his cheekbone, as if in slow motion.

"Let's stop this silliness, huh, Frank?" Carl said, short of breath. "It was an exercise. One that might bloody well save your life one day." A silence followed, punctuated only by a heavy breathing from both Frank and Carl.

"Can you untie me now?" Frank asked quietly. Carl hesitated and then nodded. The ropes came off and Frank angrily yanked his arms free, still festering, although his initial rage had subsided.

"So who are they?" Frank thumbed at the two grunts.

The one with the blonde crew cut spoke first. "Thomas Greene. Served with *40 Commando*, part of *3 Commando Brigade*. Nice to meet you, Frank." He flashed Frank a grin.

The dark-bearded one didn't look at Frank, choosing to check his equipment instead, as he spoke.

"Steve Piper. Also previous service with *3 Commando Brigade* and *21st Special Air Service Regiment, A Squadron*. Now at her Majesty's leisure. That's all I'm at liberty to say, mate."

Frank merely nodded. "And what about the third person, the woman?"

"Harriet? She's probably close to home now. Back to London and back to work in the morning. Just another employee at the company. You'll like her," Carl said.

"And what about the guns? Shooting at me like a bloody dog. Was that the icing on the cake for your little exercise?" Frank said sarcastically as he held a steady stare at the two men who had hunted him like an animal.

Piper took his sharpshooter rifle from his shoulder and took out the clip.

"This is a modified replica *LL129A1 rifle*, which is standard army issue. But the bullets are rubbers and if you were hit by one of these puppies, you'd certainly be hurt, but not killed."

"Well, the punch and kicking certainly felt real."

"Yeah, sorry about that. Realism was essential," said Greene.

"As I said, we needed to see you under pressure. You did very well, Frank." Carl returned to his chair. "You need to be prepared for live ops and I know you need another contract soon. The money would be handy, right?" Carl held out his arms in a gesture imploring Frank to trust and forgive him.

Frank rubbed his face and ran his hand through his thick black hair, the anger receding as he came to terms with the situation. Carl had a point and it certainly had given him another taste of real life-threatening danger, an adrenaline rush he hadn't experienced since Hong Kong. He thought of his partner and son and the hard time they were all having financially. The bills didn't pay themselves.

"Yes, mate, a contract would be helpful," he said finally.

Carl smiled in relief and held out his hand to shake Frank's, who ignored it. "Got something strong to drink, Carl?"

***

Piper and Greene cleaned up the cottage, erasing any trace that they had all been there as Frank sat in the passenger seat of the Land Rover, sipping bourbon from Carl's hip flask. The harsh liquid felt good in his throat as it slipped down.

"Listen, Frank, I..."

"Don't. No need. I know what you were doing." Frank paused, gazing at the misty haze that was building in the woods around them. "I guess it worked."

"I wouldn't have put you through that, mate. Came from above. Sorry." He turned to Frank. "You going to drink all that?"

Frank smiled and handed him the flask and they watched the two men load the last of their gear into a Mercedes cruiser.

"Those boys are good," said Frank, almost reluctantly.

"Yeah. Lots of experience."

"So is there something coming up?"

"Not yet. But I'm sure there will be." Carl gave a wave to Piper and Greene as they got into their hatchback and sped off down the track. "I'm sure there will be," he said again.

Chapter 12

Frank thought briefly about that exercise five years before as he stepped off the train at Hoxton station and made his way toward the rear cobbled lane towards his destination. It had been the beginning of another life. One he couldn't possibly have imagined he would end up living. Since then, he had been sent to many different locations around the globe and seen some horrors, things he never wanted to see again. Maria wanted him to quit and he couldn't blame her. There had to be an exit strategy soon but the money certainly helped ease the pain in the meantime.

He walked into the bar where Carl had suggested they meet. It was one of the new chain style pubs that seemed to be taking over anything that was slightly old or original. Frank hated them but Carl had arranged it and besides, it was near Shoreditch where Frank and his family had settled into a flat they'd bought several years earlier. The money Maria had received from her father's will after his horrific suicide had helped with the purchase, of course, but there were still hefty mortgage payments to contend with. In fact, with the galloping house prices heading ever skyward, they wouldn't have been able to buy anywhere without it.

"Frank!"

Frank turned to see Carl in a secluded corner of the pub, his round face and short red hair shrouded by bands of light streaming in from the window. It amused Frank that this ordinary looking man, a friend from his school days, had managed to get into Oxford University and gone on to join the world famous intelligence agency. It amused him but it didn't surprise him.

After the Hong Kong episode, Frank had been at a loose end and Carl had kindly promised to see if he could help him out. Old schoolmates always looked out for each other. After all, who else would?

Then just a few days ago came word of a joint set-up between MI6 and GCHQ outside of the normal apparatus: to nurture closer ties between the two organisations. Who or what was driving 'Ghost 13', Frank and Carl did not know but it opened up opportunities for both of them.

Frank had completed a security screening process years before and began his field surveillance training. There was a lot of equipment to get to grips with: encrypted radios, secure scrambler phones, recording systems such as *livebait* and *keepnet* that allowed for comparison of different signals. Learning how this equipment worked was no stroll in the park but Frank persevered. Then there were the Honeywell computer systems that kept GCHQ in step with the National Security Agency in the U.S. There were rows and rows of them in Cheltenham, providing acres of data.

Frank took to it easily, he had always been practical and clear thinking. Carl knew him better than anyone and had been pleased with his progress. After Frank had completed the technical training, it had been time for field training that involved exercises in urban environments, tracking surveillance targets in fixed locations such as offices and houses through to mobile vehicle and street surveillance. Then there was the combat training, which Frank hadn't needed any persuading to do after his experience in Asia.

"Traffic give you hell?" Carl smiled broadly as if hoping that it had.

They shook hands and Frank planted himself into the grotesque patterned lilac seat that adorned every other chair and sofa in the establishment like a sickness.

"Not really. I took the train. That mine?" Frank said, gesturing to the pint of Guinness sat on the table.

"No, I thought I'd get as many in before I had to speak to you."

Frank sighed and took a long swig of the black stuff. It tasted good.

"So, how are Maria and the kids doing?"

"Fine, thanks for asking, Carl." Frank leaned back and looked around at the lunchtime crowd, a mix of pie-faced career alcoholics and old frizzy-haired dolly birds laughing loudly at some crude joke. A businessman sat far away from them, gulping down his lunch as if to get the hell out of there as fast as possible, for which Frank didn't blame him whatsoever.

"Couldn't you have chosen somewhere better than here?" asked Frank, turning back to Carl, who was already fishing around in his briefcase.

"I'm sorry, Frank. Got a four o'clock nearby that I cannot be late for. But it's all good for you, mate."

He slung a stapled sheet of papers onto the table and leaned forward, lowering his voice as he spoke. Frank picked up the papers and saw it was a contract.

"This one is a live operation that will start anytime soon. By that, I mean it could be twenty-four hours, so get yourself ready. I don't know too many details but it might be long haul."

Frank cast Carl a glance. "It's not one of your tricks again, is it? I'm not up for that."

Carl shook his head. "Absolutely not."

"So where is it?"

"Sorry, I have no idea but you'll be briefed at the last minute as usual."

Frank smiled thinly. Pie-face was telling another joke at the bar and the atmosphere suddenly seemed to grate on him.

"Anything else you can tell me? Will I have company? How hostile is the location?"

Carl gulped down the last third of his pint with astonishing speed.

"Ahh, all I can say is it's probably the biggest operation you've done to date."

"How do you know I'll do it, Carl?" said Frank, frowning as he tossed the contract back on the table.

Carl stood up and grabbed his briefcase and jacket off his chair before carefully sliding the papers back towards Frank.

"Because money makes the world go round. I'll see you soon, Frank."

***

Frank moved into the shadow of his lock-up garage and bent down, pulling up the edge of a thick rug that covered the centre of the space. He levered up the edge of the floor vinyl underneath and began to pull it up.

A year or so earlier, he had laid the flooring himself so as to stash certain items. Not foolproof by any means, but perhaps safe from the average thief. The passport that had cost him a fair penny was underneath the vinyl and wrapped in plastic.

Years earlier, Frank had made the decision to get a passport that was his very own, known to no one else, except for Jake Hale, of course. Jake was his friend from way back who operated in darker waters, creating all kinds of fake documents for shady underworld figures. The agency would give him a so-called 'legend', of course, including all the documents that make up an identity. But this was for his own insurance policy; personal use.

Frank knew his employers would be giving him a cover passport as they did for every job but he had made the decision from the beginning to have a back-up that was known to no one.

After five minutes, Frank had pocketed the passport, re-laid the vinyl flooring, and was heading through the calm night.

Chapter 13

Studio 31 had new occupants and was now fully equipped. Despite the sunshine outside, the large warehouse windows were shuttered tight and artificial lights lit the rooms.

Dan Griffin, or Griff as he was known, sat at the flickering monitors, the blue light forming reflected squares on his thick-rimmed glasses. He tapped onto the keyboard and a roll of data flowed down on the Honeywell computer screen, running through a list of flight manifests.

Griff had been Frank's guide during his training on getting to know and use the surveillance equipment and they had clicked. His intelligence, when it came to computers and networks, had helped him get snapped up by the company after he graduated in Computer Science. The only child of a Tunisian father and an English mother. Frank guessed he was barely out of his early twenties.

"This is a waste of time if we don't know what name she's travelling under. You want a drink?"

"No, thanks," said Frank, looking at the mess around Dan's desk. There were two large screens on Griff's desk and a pile of hard disk drives with numerous wires forming a spaghetti junction that flowed down under the floor, along with thick data cabling.

The young IT analyst rolled on his chair over to a fridge nearby and took out a can of cola. Frank noticed it was stacked with them as he leaned back in his chair with his hands behind his head. On a large board at the end of the bare bricked room, there was a world map with a few photographs of Sarah Edwards and a few scribbled notes. It painfully lacked any real progress.

"What would she have done? Had a false passport made, assumed an identity and then she would have disappeared...somewhere?" Frank was talking more to himself than anyone else.

***

Carl came into the operations room with a coffee and sat down in his space, near the wallboard and picked up the telephone to dial his superior, the Rottweiler. He heard the brusque Scottish accent grunt at the other end.

"Mr. Keller? It's Carl Paterson. I need access to Echelon to see if there's any matching on some voice data we have."

"Aye, well, I see what I can do. That's casting a grand net, don't you think?"

"It's the only net I have right now," Carl replied.

"Okay, well, send over the packets and I'll get the process started for ya, Carl."

"Thanks, Mr. Keller."

Echelon, set up by the five eyes alliance of the UK, U.S., Australia, Canada, and New Zealand was a signals intelligence (SIGINT) collection and analysis global network that intercepted private and commercial communications on behalf of the western powers. The surveillance powers of this vast network of spy stations that were capable of eavesdropping on telephones, faxes, and computers were becoming more and more central to the operations of the agency.

It would take hours, more likely days, for any results to the voice sample of Sarah Edwards' voice for matches to come back, if there were any at all.

***

Griff turned to Frank. His eyebrows rose slightly, looking pleased with himself.

"Hey, I managed to get a high score in Warworld. Took over that neighbouring town and grabbed all their resources. Just have to get my armies up to scratch and I can push west." Griff fired up one of his other screens to reveal the bird's eye view of the game and tiny figures moving around the landscape.

Frank shook his head. "I don't know where you get the time to play that crap. Last I looked, my village had been ransacked and I was down to two knights, one infantry unit, and a wood mill."

In the lunch breaks, Griff persuaded a reluctant Frank to take up a 'Massively Multi-player Online Role-Playing Game' or MMORPG. The object of the game, as Griff had explained, was to build your kingdom, establish a castle, build up your army, and conquer territory.

"Sounds like hours of fun. Do I get to destroy yours?" Frank had said, his face deadpan.

"You can try."

Dan showed him a pop-up box in the bottom tray of the game controls and then started typing. The message popped up on the laptop screen Frank had opened on the desk: "Your mama is so big, her ass don't fit in the Grand Canyon."

"Great, right, Frank? I can taunt you directly from anywhere. It's all about using strategy skills. You grow food, mine gold and metals, and consolidate your city. Then train and expand your armies and prepare to be destroyed, my friend," Griff grinned. "I host it on my own server so it's just me and my trusted mates playing," he had added enthusiastically.

Finally, Frank had relented, logged in on another terminal, and allowed Griff to give him the full training walkthrough.

"Hmm, and what do I get if I win?"

"No prizes, I'm afraid, it's just a laugh. Top players are shown on the board."

Frank had thought it a complete waste of time but had a go at building up his avatar and empire just to keep the geek happy. He struggled to make any headway against the other factions and it was turning into a disaster for Frank's online empire.

And now, sitting in Studio 31, Frank and Griff typed comments to each other on the games comm system, in-between snippets of conversation.

"Where would you go, Griff?" Frank typed.

"Anywhere away from you, brother."

Frank turned to him and spoke. "Be serious…"

"Okay, serious…She has a plan, right? She's got to be selling it. To who? Who's going to be in the market for buying our secret shit? Russians, Chinese…"

"Yes, all the usual suspects. North Korea, rogue terrorist groups. I know."

Carl stood up from his desk and walked over to them with a sheet of paper. "This is a list of aliases she has used over the years when on company business abroad."

Griff took the paper. There were three names.

"Only three?"

"She was never a field agent so she didn't need too many aliases. However, to protect our people, we always give them the option."

"Okay, I'll run them through the manifests. Highly unlikely she'd use any of these though," Griff muttered as he began typing.

"I know, I know," Carl replied as he walked back to his desk.

Frank stood up suddenly and threw on his jacket. "I'm taking off, I'll catch you later.

"Where you going?" Griff asked suspiciously.

"To see a little bird."

Chapter 14

Frank drove his black Saab 900 from the Limehouse Cut and slowly made his way along the A1203 before heading to the South side of the Thames through the Rotherhithe Tunnel. After another thirty minutes, he finally arrived at his destination and parked in a housing estate in Elephant and Castle. He walked along a concrete underpass and up the exterior steps to the fourth level before moving along to the end flat. The door was a steel monster, with a thin slit for an ill-disguised look out. Frank banged on the door and almost immediately, a pair of eyes peered out at him. The door creaked open and Frank stood looking up at the tall figure grinning a toothless smile.

"Hey, Frankie boy. How ya doin'?"

"Yeah, I'm good, thanks, Jake."

Jake Hale was over six foot, half-caste with a closely shaven head and stood in the doorway donning a red tracksuit. Ushering Frank into a gloomy corridor with a jerk of his head, he slammed the heavy door behind them, and they walked into a living room where a young Oriental guy was slumped on a sofa playing a 'shoot 'em up' video game. He threw a nonchalant nod at Frank and continued firing at a group of soldiers running through some war-torn streets.

The flat was sparsely furnished with decoration that was straight out the 1970s but it was obviously not a home. There was a pile of boxes along one wall and cut out paper, film, and cuttings strewn all over the bare floorboards.

Frank sat down at a table by the window that had panoramic views of South London as Jake went into the adjourning kitchen and returned with a bottle of Jack Daniels and two glasses.

"So what are you after, not another passport already?" he asked.

"I wanted to ask you something," Frank said.

Jake sat down and poured out the drinks. "Ask away, mate. Just as long as it's not about my sex life...you don't want to know about that."

"Really? Pretty wild, is it?"

"Ha...no. It's non-existent, mate."

Frank laughed. "My heart bleeds."

He reached into the inside pocket of his leather jacket and pulled out a photocopied sheet with the image of Sarah Edwards alone on the page and flung it onto the table top.

Jake glanced at it and then at Frank.

"I do have a girlfriend, mate, despite the sex life being crap."

Frank let out a snigger and shook his head in mock sympathy.

"No, I'm not matchmaking. I just need a name. Do you recognise her? Did you do a passport for her? It would be really helpful to me, mate. I'll be eternally grateful."

Jake shook his head and then pushed a glass of bourbon towards Frank. "Have you not heard of client confidentiality, bruv? It's when you don't go around blabbing out all the personal details of the people who pay you."

"Yeah, yeah...but I'll make it worth your while, Jake. Trust me, I will."

"You're offering your body? My missus might be giving me the cold shoulder at the moment but I'd rather keep wanking and crying, thanks."

Frank shook his head and laughed. "Please c'mon, Jake. It's just a name. Two words you have to utter. If it makes any difference, the word is she has betrayed this country."

Jake leaned his head slightly to the side and stared at Frank with concern. "She betrayed our queen?" The tone was sarcastic.

Frank nodded. "Full traitoress, mate. No holds barred."

"Shit."

Jake stood up slowly and grabbed the photograph of Edwards.

"Well, I'll give you a name for old time's sake but not for the queen." He turned to his associate, who was giving his enemies full lead.

"Mark, you remember this one? She came in for a passport a few months ago. Remember the alias she used?"

Mark looked up from the sofa and glanced at the picture.

"Hmmm, yeah, I remember her. The name?" He paused his video game and stood up, taking the paper from Jake for a closer look.

"Emily Jenkins." He handed back the paper and sat back down straight away.

Frank was standing by Jake, both men staring at the young man. "Are you sure?" asked Frank.

"As eggs." The game music kicked back on and the rapid firing of an M42 machine gun resumed.

Jake turned to Frank. "He's good at names. That's the name you want."

Frank nodded.

"Is that helpful?"

"Immensely helpful, thanks, mate."

Chapter 15

Rain hammered the wet tarmac, blown almost horizontal from a sharp easterly wind as Frank grabbed his bag from the back seat of his battered Saab. Across the other end of the car park, Frank could see the huge warehouse doors ajar and three figures moving around inside the bay area. He locked up the car and sprinted across the concrete cul de sac as the roar of a Boeing 777 engine cut through the darkness overhead, descending to the Gatwick airport strip metres away.

The cargo area lay just east of Brockley Wood on the outskirts of the vast International airport. Frank had been summoned for 1100 hours and had made good time. As he approached, he saw Carl Paterson with his unmistakable sandy hair, wearing a white trench coat wave at him, with two burly figures he assumed were part of his team.

He had no choice but to keep Maria out of the loop, as usual. It was made crystal clear that he would be royally fucked if he told a single soul anything about his work. The certainty of spending the rest of his days cleaning toilets at Her Majesty's pleasure kept him on track. Close family were allowed to know that it was intelligence-related and nothing more. The contract was watertight. She had understood but in recent years had not wanted him to do this kind of work; it didn't sit well with her. "Get a normal job. You don't have to do this," she had said. "Besides, you can't trust those bastards. The agencies and the government are carrying out their own screwed up agenda and certainly not to help us mere mortals."

Maybe she was right but the mortgage rates for the flat were still a struggle and he fully intended that his family would want for nothing in the years ahead.

"Frank. Great night for travelling, huh?" Frank shook Carl's outstretched hand and then noticed the other two men, who stood, staring at him. One of them, with a blonde crew cut, winked and blew a mock kiss.

"Oh, bloody great," said Frank, unable to mask his annoyance. "You didn't tell me I'd be going on an op with them, Carl." He jabbed a thumb towards the two men.

One of the men, sporting a black Mohawk and beard, dressed in khaki trousers and black jacket, jerked his head at Frank. "Nice to see you again, too, Mr. Bowen."

"You remember Piper and Greene then," Carl said, deadpan. "Look, I know you didn't get off to the best start but these guys are good. You'll be glad of that security, I'm sure," said Carl warily.

"Forget it! Count me out," Frank suddenly turned back to head for the doors.

"Hey, mate." Tom Greene appeared in front of him and had a hand on his chest, blocking his path and started pushing him back.

Frank remembered that thin smile now.

In one swift movement, he turned his body slightly and dragged Greene's arm forward, using his momentum to get behind Greene. Suddenly, he had his arm around the man's neck in a rear naked strangle, with his palm over his other bicep, gripping hard. Greene grabbed at Frank's forearm that held him like a vice and began pushing his chin down in an attempt to get air.

Frank knew he just needed to hold the position for ten seconds or so as he cut off blood flow from his heart to brain and the man would be unconscious.

"Frank!" Carl barked. The other man with the beard, moved closer, carefully assessing the situation.

Frank threw Greene forward, away from him, and stepped back, ready for a counter-attack but the blonde man just turned to face him, caressing his throat. His stone straight face morphed into his smile again as he stared at Frank. "Nice move."

"I've been practicing."

"Can we stop this macho bullshit?" Carl was already between them, turning from one man to the other. "Frank. A word."

Carl led Frank to a stack of crates, out of earshot from Piper and Greene.

"Look, I know you've have bad blood about that day but these are good men. They're professionals and they'll look out for you in the field. You have my word on that."

"Just making my mark, Carl. They won't respect me otherwise."

A brief glimpse of realisation passed Carl's face and he gently patted Frank's arm. "So you'll go? This is an important operation, probably the biggest one you're ever going to get a swing at."

Frank sighed and glanced at the two men.

"I hope I don't regret this."

"You won't. Now, let's do this."

They walked over to where Piper and Greene were waiting by an upturned crate that had doubled as a coffee table. Frank held his hand out to Greene as a peace offering.

Greene paused, glanced at Carl before shaking his hand, and then Frank walked up to Piper and shook his hand as well.

"Good. Now we're all best friends again, can we get on with the briefing?" said Carl, pulling out a batch of reports from his case and handing them around. The men looked down at a photograph of a dark-haired woman in her early 30s along with a description, work history, and family details.

"We've got a target at large having taken a batch of top secret information that is a major breach of National Security. For this operation, she has been codenamed: Pandora, because she is potentially going to release a shitload of secrets from the box. Thanks to Frank here, we know she is travelling under the name of 'Emily Jenkins'. Our intelligence is telling us she went to Panama. Your job is to find her, place her under surveillance, and keep an eye out to see who she meets or talks to. She has to be selling the information to someone, we need to know who. If someone turns up, the next step will be to apprehend Pandora and the contact and haul them back to Blighty."

Carl looked up at the men. "Any questions?"

"So when do we get paid?" asked Greene, spinning a knife around repeatedly in his palm.

"Any other questions?"

Chapter 16

Nigel Harrison dabbed his brow with a well-used handkerchief, quietly cursing the hot weather. He hated the sunshine and would do his utmost to avoid going out in its leery glare. The cool comfort of a darkened room and a flickering screen were more his idea of passing the time, whether it was for work or leisure. But this bloody office had big, wide windows and the fans simply moved the air around. Air conditioning was a luxury and unfortunately did not feature in the older buildings. Britain had never been equipped for heat waves and this one was in its second week. Rising temperatures always seemed to add to his anxiety, the feeling of being suffocated by the air itself.

He checked the office server status and idly typed in a config command to locate slowness in the network, his fingers skipping over the keyboard with ease but his mind was elsewhere. Guilt welled in his gut; the feeling that had grown for the previous few weeks was all down to what he was about to do.

***

A year earlier, Nigel had sat in the Golden Lion in Islington high street, nursing an overpriced pint, his eyes never leaving the front entrance. Thirsty punters came and went but the man he was meeting was late, or maybe he wasn't coming at all?

Part of him felt relief if this was the case. It was a normal enough request, a possible job opportunity through the University bulletin board followed by a short telephone conversation and the arranged drink. Something to do with civil rights or a political movement campaigning for radical change.

He had caught some of what the guy had said but he had been concentrating so hard on not saying the wrong thing that the details became a blur. An element of his own persona that he hated. Any situation that was out of his comfort zone and routine was enough to spark the anxiety. It was bloody annoying and Nigel vowed to overcome it. He was determined to force himself to make a go of whatever this chap was offering rather than slink back to the safety of home and the alluring glow of his computer screen. He yearned to be connected with a crowd, to be part of something exciting and it sounded like this John Rhodes might be offering it.

Nigel was amazed at how he had survived university. Being a social outcast had given him no choice but to focus one hundred percent on his studies, which paid off with a distinction in his IT and Computer Science degree.

A stout man with white hair, a short-sleeved pale shirt with a laptop bag over his shoulder entered the bar and looked around, his gaze settling on Nigel, who nervously held up a hand. The man came over and slung the bag down onto an empty chair.

"Nigel, hello. I'm really sorry I'm late."

"Oh, no problem at all, Mr. Rhodes."

Nigel quickly stood up, knocking the last of his pint onto the table surface. He cursed to himself, picked up the glass, and then held out his hand.

"Please call me John. Another drink, Nigel?"

"Oh, no, thanks. I can't drink too much."

Rhodes was soon back from the bar with an ale and eased himself into a dark wood chair. The pub crowd ebbed and flowed until it quietened down into a scene of low murmur and clinking glasses. Rhodes leaned forward as he spoke, his eyes sparkled with youthful enthusiasm as he explained his vision and the legacy that he was determined to build.

Nigel felt drawn to the man; he couldn't help but share his excitement as he explained the vision behind Liberatus, the idea of breaking from state dependency and moving to a more self-sufficient society.

"The news media group is one part," he explained. "For society to change, we need to inform the populace about what is going on—the mainstream media certainly isn't. We connect the dots for them and when they realise they have been lied to and deceived by those who purport to work in our best interests, support and action will follow."

Two and a half hours later, both men shook hands and Nigel Harrison agreed to help them build and run their computer systems for the newsgroup. The role was to take advantage of the growing popularity of the Internet and the communication opportunities that it offered as well as build an I.T. infrastructure for their operations. It was a challenge but a great opportunity and Nigel had needed very little persuasion.

***

Nigel glanced once again at the clock on the wall. Most had left the office, only Maria remained at the far end, her nose buried in a report. He longed for her to leave, which was not a feeling he was used to. At any other time, he would have killed to have this opportunity to be alone with her in the office. But not now. He needed to speak to John but couldn't afford for anyone to accidentally overhear his questions.

He fondled the plastic coffee cup, the remaining liquid having long lost any warmth and toyed with the idea of making another one as if to signal to her that he was going nowhere. And what if John left before? It needed to be now! They had been demanding information and making threats and he needed to give them something, anything. Nigel checked the company calendar again on his screen. It was still there in John's purple highlighted calendar, an appointment with a member of parliament for Braintree, but it didn't say where it was or who it was with?

Just as his anxiety seemed to peak to another level, Maria began to make the telltale signs of leaving, to his relief. She rustled papers together, locked them in a drawer, and then grabbed her bag, looking across at Nigel. She gave him a quick wave which he gladly returned.

"See you tomorrow."

"Yes, tomorrow it is," he returned, but they were just hollow words. He felt empty. He felt he was betraying himself.

"Don't work too late," she said, and then she was gone.

Nigel paused for a moment and then got up, walked over to John's office door, and rapped quietly on it with his knuckles, his head bowed slightly as he listened for a response.

"Hello?"

Pushing the door ajar, Nigel popped his head round to see John's expectant look from behind his monitor. His white hair seemed to catch the light of a lamp behind him, reminding Nigel of a saint from one of those paintings in a church.

"I'm sorry to disturb you, John. I'm just on my way home but wanted to update you. The server thing...," he paused deliberately and Rhodes waved him in.

"Come on in, Nigel." He stood up and stretched and reached for his mug, draining the last dregs of stewed tea.

Nigel moved into the room, clutching a batch of papers.

"There was a lot of resistance and slowness on some of the servers. Seems to be running okay now but I'll keep an eye on it." It was no lie that the servers had indeed been struggling. Because of John's insistence on keeping everything in-house and the demand on the website from an increasing number of visitors, it was a common problem.

John Rhodes nodded and returned his mug to the crowded desk. Papers were piled high on either side of his monitor and Nigel noticed some had found their way onto the floor. He had an urge to point out this unnatural order of things but he held his tongue.

"We'll get the extra power you need soon, Nigel. It's top of my list."

"Will you be in tomorrow?" Nigel asked as nonchalantly as he could muster. He needed the confirmation. A calendar entry could be changed or postponed and in that circumstance was rarely ever updated.

John looked around his desk as if noticing the mess for the first time.

"Erm, no, not tomorrow. I've got a meeting with an MP from Westminster, might be a useful contact to have. An old friend from years ago. That kind of thing."

Nigel shuffled his feet, his hands tightly gripping the papers he held. He could feel the sweat staining them but didn't dare look.

"And will you be coming in here first or straight there?" he asked. "It's just in case there are any issues."

John was looking around for something on his desk now, playing the patient boss.

"No...Oh, sorry, yes. I have to come here first and then off to the meeting late afternoon. But just speak to Marcus if anything comes up with the servers." He glanced up at Nigel with a questioning expression as if to ask if he needed anything else.

"Great, thanks, John. See you in the morning then," said Nigel.

There was a wave of relief as he turned to leave. Hopefully, it would be enough to satisfy them and keep them off his back.

Chapter 17

John Rhodes stood up and stretched his arms, the aching bones reminding him he had not left his desk since lunch.

He thought about the meeting and hoped it would open some doors, or at the very least, Leo might become an asset. The more contacts he made at government level, the more leverage he hoped Liberatus could pull when it came to their aims. Of course, he still caught up with some of the boys from his MI6 days but they never really told him anything. It was as if a distance was being created between them. Rhodes understood though. They knew he was writing a book, one that would open several cans of worms about the agency, and certainly couldn't associate with him anymore. John Rhodes gathered his laptop and made his way out of the office and into the buzzing hub of Soho.

****

Nigel Harrison lingered outside the red telephone box for a moment and then stepped inside. He barely noticed the stench of tobacco and piss that hung in the confined space and dialled the number he had memorised. After a few seconds, the ringtone kicked in and it seemed his heart beat louder inside his chest.

It had all started several months before after Nigel had set up the web server and things were beginning to feel good. He was being useful at last and the feeling of using his knowledge and skills for the cause made him feel valued and important, not to mention actually enjoying the job. Then the email came from a dead mailbox. He couldn't track it, despite his skills, but it didn't matter. The images were of young children, both male and female, no older than ten years old, stripped naked or semi-naked. The email simply read:

We found these on your computer, Nigel.

Then these were followed by much worse images. Children performing sexual acts, on grown men, obviously under duress – their faces were hidden from the camera. Clearly visible on a muscular arm was a London football club badge that was based barely a mile away. The frightened faces of the kids told their own sick story. Nigel had never seen anything like it and it made him physically shake. Some prankster? Someone who hated him?

After that, he clearly heard clicks on his phone line at home. There were also calls but on the rare occasion, he answered, there was just silence. The phone calls kept coming and Nigel, long since having stopped taking them, would just hide under the duvet in his bedroom, covering his ears, sometimes even shouting as if to drown out the tormentors. Eventually, he ripped out the phone line; something he hadn't wanted to do as his phone was an important link with his mother.

Then, one evening when walking home from the office, as he turned into a quiet side street near his flat, he noticed an unmarked black van parked ahead and sensed a presence behind him. He looked back and was physically assaulted with a fist to the face that threw him backwards onto the pavement. Hands grabbed him under his arms and a hood covered his head. Nigel tried to cry out but a hand covered his mouth and then he felt himself being bundled into the back of the van. He screamed under the stifling material, wondering how long he had to live. Why did they want him? Who were they? A swirl of questions dancing on his sick leaden fear so heavily, he pissed himself.

"You dirty fucking bastard," a gruff voice said.

They drove for around twenty minutes, although to Nigel, it seemed like a lifetime, with no end in sight. Blood seeped from his mouth and nose, making it almost impossible to breathe under the hood so that he had to gasp for air through his mouth. The buzzing in his head from the punch was only matched by the clasping grip of fear. It reached the point when he just wanted them to get it over with. To kill him and be done with it.

The van slowed down and seemed to take a sharp turn and then the vehicle stopped and the engine died. The sound of the back doors opening and then a steady commanding voice, which sounded slightly muffled and Nigel had to concentrate to hear the words.

"Nigel. We know who you are, where you live, what you do. Everything you do, we know about. Nod your head to show you understand me."

Nigel did as he was told, vigorously.

"The pictures of the kids," the voice continued. "They can be given to the police at any time and will be traced back to you, make no mistake."

Nigel suddenly felt his skin go ice cold, the sheen of sweat on his skin had soaked his entire shirt, and his trousers were still damp after his other accident. This was all connected to the pictures of the children? He had assumed it was a bully from years back who had tracked him down. This was obviously a lot more serious. Then he felt a kind of strange relief. They weren't going to kill him after all. Maybe there was a way out?

The voice started again.

"You will end up in prison, and either become some bitch for a nasty group of blokes inside, or you will be beaten to a pulp on a regular basis. They don't like kiddy fiddlers inside, Nigel. You will not be protected, believe me."

There was a sigh. "Or we will kill you right here."

Nigel's stomach turned.

"There is a third option though, Nigel. One where you can make all this go away."

***

Now Nigel clutched the phone, ready to give them the information that they had asked for: John Rhodes' major movements and appointments. They had also wanted technical information on the servers and after that, they kept coming back for more.

A low voice on the other end of the line asked for a reference number.

"HN3162," he said carefully.

A click followed and then another ring tone before a male voice answered.

"What is it?"

"Erm. Jonah is going to be travelling by car tomorrow morning. From the Soho square office to Braintree in Essex for a meeting," Nigel said.

"What time is he leaving?" asked the voice, almost a whisper now.

"About 10:30, I think, maybe a bit later."

"A meeting with who?"

"I...I don't know."

The line instantly disconnected.

Chapter 18

The day was another glorious one and John Rhodes was glad he had driven down to Braintree if it only meant getting out of the city for a few hours. Leo Smith, an adviser to the parliamentary committee of MPs, wanted to meet away from any prying eyes, which John understood perfectly. The two men had known each other since university and Rhodes had recently reached out with a phone call.

He pulled his Audi A4 into a narrow road that ended at Bocking Blackwater woods that dominated the south side of Blackwater River. There was a lone silver Jaguar parked in a small enclave, set against the trees behind. Smith got out of the car to greet him, dressed in a casual chequered shirt that looked somehow out of place on him. He was a tall lean man with little hair, baldness having taken a firm grip.

"Beautiful day, eh?" John said. Smith nodded, smiled thinly, and both men shook hands.

"Shall we take a walk?" Smith gestured to the woodland path.

"Lead on," John said.

Both men disappeared under the canopy of the woods, where it was considerably cooler. The chirping of birds darting from tree to tree seemed to intensify.

"I used to play here as a child, many years ago now," Smith started. He appeared more relaxed than he had been at the car. "Know this place like the back of my hand. Just like the area and the constituents here. They know me very well, which is why I'm always re-elected," he said with pride.

John nodded in agreement. "You're a respected man, Leo. Long may it continue."

Smith seemed to find that amusing and snorted a laugh.

"Seems like I've been playing this game for quite a while now; there's a point when you really do start looking forward to retiring."

"Hey, you're a long way from that! There's plenty more for you to do, I'm sure. In fact, that's why I wanted to see you."

"Oh?" There was alertness in his voice.

"Liberatus needs your help. We need eyes and ears in Parliament and possibly a mouthpiece."

"Listen, John, I know we go back a long way, which is why I agreed to meet, but there are things I can and cannot do. I understand what you're doing, but you're still an activist, John. I can't be seen associating with activism. Your paper has caused quite a stir. It gets a fair few backs up, shall we say."

"Who said anything about public association? I'm not asking for some joint press conference," said John.

Leo Smith stopped walking and looked at his companion.

"What is it you're asking exactly?"

John sighed. It had taken a lot to come here and do this. He needed allies in the establishment, otherwise, the inevitable conflict between the people and the elite governments might only go one way. He needed an information source.

"Do you believe in true freedom and liberty, Leo? Bullshit aside, do you think the populace has the right to freedom of speech, the right to make their own decisions for their own lives?"

Leo frowned as they began walking again.

"Yes, of course,"

"But if there was a major threat to that, and I mean an advanced, planned threat on a global scale, would that concern you in any way?"

"What are you getting at?"

John paused.

"Did you ever hear of a Major General Smedley D. Butler from the States, before the second world war? He was America's most decorated soldier, apparently."

Leo shook his head. He had not.

"Well, having helped pacify various countries in the service of corporations, Mexico, Honduras, he was approached by a group of powerful men, I'm talking high-level corporate CEOs and bankers who planned to overthrow Roosevelt and install a fascist government. But Butler was fed up with fighting for capitalist interests and blew the whistle on the plot in front of the congressional committee in 1934."

"Interesting story, John, but I still don't..."

John stopped, halting their stroll again.

"I'm not asking you to sacrifice your career or put your head above the parapet. Just to keep your ears to the ground, and keep me abreast of any information we can use."

"A sordid mole for your newspaper?" said Leo with a wry smile.

John shook his head. "No, more like a supporter of true liberty, that's under threat without anyone knowing it is."

Further down the path, a squirrel watched them approach and then made off around the base of an old oak tree. They were approaching a break in the trees, a view of rolling fields that stretched to the farthest point on the horizon.

"So, what am I looking for? Fascists?" Leo said, with more than a hint of sarcasm.

John gave him a look.

"They wouldn't call it that now. But, yes, a cross-over of corporate power and government structure is pretty much fascism in my book," stated John.

Leo paused and thought for a moment. "There is a multitude of corruption and scandal on a continuous basis at Westminster. There are secrets everywhere but if I don't know what I'm looking for, how can I help?"

They both faced the fields, admiring the view of middle England with the blue sky opening up overhead and not a cloud in sight.

"I believe there is a coup being planned in this country. It will start with mass surveillance, for which I am confident I will have evidence of very soon, and then they'll create a situation, a problem which only they can fix. Problem, reaction, solution. It may not happen soon, or even in the next ten years, but it will happen and my mission is to be prepared."

Leo turned to him. "Some might say you're being paranoid. We have a fully functioning democracy, the country is booming, it's the good times." John could sense he was playing devil's advocate now, perhaps as a way to think it through. The politician paused. "There is a shadow behind us all. You know it, I know it, and so does anyone with any kind of finger on the pulse but it's always been that way. Strings are pulled, the players play...why fight against the status quo?"

Rhodes let out a chuckle. "Why indeed?" He had already put his point across and wasn't going to flog a dead horse.

"For our friendship, I'll help in any way I can but I want a water-tight method of passing information over. It has to be completely safe from detection, otherwise, it's not going to happen."

***

It was dark by the time John Rhodes gunned into fifth gear onto the A120 dual carriageway toward Stansted airport, where he would join the M11 motorway back to London.

He was happy with the way the meeting had gone and figured Leo would be an extremely useful ally, with a wealth of contacts in the upper echelons of government.

The roads were quiet and he anticipated getting back in no time. A black Ford Mondeo powered past him on the lamp lit road and pulled ahead out of sight. John checked his speed, seeing a steady 60 miles per hour; he estimated the car must have been doing ninety-five at least and tutted out loud.

John put on the radio and pressed the button for one of his saved stations: the sound of jazz filled the car and instantly put him in a more relaxed frame of mind. He had picked up the bug from his father, Charlie Rhodes, who usually had one of the greats playing in the background: Bix Beiderbecke, Duke Ellington, Charlie Parker. That was the great thing about jazz music, his father always used to say, you can just play it in the background and get on with what you're doing. John and his family were based in Chicago before John had decided to move to England and go to university. Once an affluent family in the press and newspaper business, the Great Depression had virtually wiped them out.

After a few minutes, he rounded a curve in the road and caught a glimpse of a footbridge that went over both sides of the carriageway. Then on the deserted road, he saw the Mondeo again but it must have stopped or slowed down because he was coming up towards it very fast. Suddenly, he was being blinded by a brilliant strobe light that seemed to come from the top of the bridge and he couldn't see at all. His hands instinctively went up to protect his eyes while desperately trying to slow down by taking his foot off the accelerator. Another foot tried to depress the brake and hit it too hard. Already out of control, the car wheeled and turned. A rush of movement, as if spinning. Screeching. A bang and the light faded into blackness.

***

Two men clad in black fatigues made their way down the embankment to the road from the footbridge. The Mondeo screeched into reverse, backing up to the crashed Audi that had careened onto the mid-section steel divider and then flipped upside down onto the road. One of the men crouched down at the car and shone a micro torch through the cracked driver side window and saw the slumped bloodied figure of Rhodes, who hung upside down, harnessed by his seatbelt.

A radio crackled. "Traffic coming."

A distant glow from behind the bend.

"Let's go," one of the men said.

They jumped into the rear of the Mondeo and the car pulled off at high speed as if it were on a race circuit.

A blue family Ford rounded the bend in the road and slowed down at the sight of the flipped over Audi. The driver pulled into the lay-by as soon as he could.

The rear lights of a vehicle faded up ahead in the darkness.

Chapter 19

As the British Airways flight from Gatwick began its descent towards Aeropuerto Internacional de Tocumen, International Airport of Panama City, the captain announced in Spanish that the temperature was a steady ninety degrees Fahrenheit with a light south easterly wind and welcomed the passengers to Panama. The city ran twenty kilometres along the Pacific coast from the famous Canal to the ruins of the Panama Viejo.

Frank glanced across at Piper, who looked every bit a tourist in his colourful shirt and slacks. The three men had not communicated or even exchanged glances on the flight. They had each assumed identities along with the corresponding passports provided by their operations head, Carl Paterson. Frank was currently Keith Feldman, an IT contractor visiting on a tourist visa. Piper and Greene had similar stories and IDs.

The name Sarah Edwards had used, Emily Jenkins, had come up eventually. At least Griff had something to work with and there was the name on the manifest for a Virgin flight to Panama, the day after she had disappeared. Frank didn't reveal to anyone how he had received the information, that would have been against his own interests. Never reveal your sources. Carl understood and it was the lead they needed.

The passengers disembarked and streamed into the arrivals

terminal and towards customs. Frank enjoyed the heat against his skin, a welcome relief from the recycled air conditioning on the flight.

"State your business in Panama, Señor."

"Pleasure," replied Frank.

The olive clad immigration officer asked a few more questions and Frank stuck to the story he was told to. The grey-bearded man glanced at him and then back at his passport photo.

"Have a pleasant stay, Mr. Feldman." He handed Frank the passport.

When they were all through customs, the three men continued to keep their distance and wandered through to the small airport arrivals area. They independently arrived at the outside taxi zone and were approached by a stocky Afro-Caribbean man who blended in with the other locals by sporting a dirty football shirt, knee-length shorts, and flip-flops.

"Taxi, gentlemen? My name is Dante Brull and I could take you all into the city if you please. Central express is the only service you can trust, believe me," he said, signalling to the men that he was their contact. Piper and Greene pretended to have a discussion and made a show of inviting Frank to join them.

Frank and the other men knew Brull's appearance was deceptive. He was a powerful and well-connected individual who had connections with numerous police departments, intelligence agencies, and even drug cartels in Central and South America. From the little information they had read, they also were aware that MI6 had employed his services since the mid-80s and he was deemed a valuable asset.

The minibus moved slowly with the other traffic exiting the airport and headed south towards the Corredor Sur freeway and Panama City. Frank watched the landscape flash by; palm trees, crumbling stone buildings, and old men sat at tables, killing time. The skyscrapers of the modern metropolis were already in view.

Twenty minutes later, the vehicle bumped up a track in the Calidonia district, views of the La Bahía de Panamá behind them. The car pulled in front of a ground floor garage of a condo, the doors automatically opening from a key fob Brull had in his hand. Looking up at the stone white building, Frank could just make out the bottom of a balcony.

Once inside the garage with the door closing behind them, they exited the vehicle and Brull led them through an interior fire door and up concrete steps into the condo living quarters. The large room they walked into was a living and dining room combination and had a pleasantly decorated finish; two leather sofas, a coffee table, a dining table in the corner. A photograph on canvas of the Panama skyline hung on the wall over an old unused fireplace.

"Anyone else have access to this property?" asked Piper.

"No, very secure. I rented the entire building," he answered.

Steve Piper sat down at the dining table, his fingers already typing into his palm phone, sending an encrypted message to Cronus, Carl Paterson's codename in London to say they had arrived. Frank put his holdall down onto the floor and wandered to the kitchen area, checking the fridge first and cupboards. It was all well stocked.

Brull put a set of keys down on the table.

"I only have two sets. I show you the alarm system."

"Did you get any weapons?"

Brull nodded and walked over to the kitchen sink. He opened up a wooden door and pulled out a briefcase and brought it back to the dining table.

"One Glock 17 for each man," Brull said as he opened it up, revealing the weapons and ammunition.

"Is that it?" Greene was standing, staring down at the contents, clearly disappointed.

"Better than a slap in the face with a wet kipper," Frank said, picking up one of the weapons and pressing the small eject button on the side to release the magazine.

"What the hell does that mean?" Greene sneered and took a pistol himself.

"It means be grateful for what you receive, mate."

After checking the condo, their weapons and their location on the map, Brull cooked up rice and pinto beans. Bare basics. There was no time for culinary cook-offs. The four men hunched around the table, scooping up their food in silence. After finishing up, they cleared the table and Piper laid out a map of Panama. The men stood sipping coffee and studied the city layout.

Piper passed a photocopied piece of paper with Pandora's details to Brull.

"This is who we're looking for. She arrived at Panama City airport three days ago, then disappeared," said Piper.

"What are we doing?" asked Frank.

"We're sitting tight and wait for Cronus and London to find other traces of Pandora," he replied.

"So basically sit on our arses while the trail gets colder?"

Piper gave Frank an exasperated look. "What are you saying, Frank?"

"Maybe we should get busy looking. Check the airport CCTV Start making enquiries at all the transport hubs, the stations. See if Brull has any..."

"Hey, Sherlock. You're talking about an unknown amount of man-hours." Thomas Greene had dismantled his Glock to check the parts and now his narrowed eyes were looking up at Frank. "Let London locate the target and then we'll take things from there. We're not getting paid to run around this shit hole."

Frank sighed as if disappointed at a child who had stolen sweets. "I'm sure we'd all love to kick back and sip piña coladas, mate, but with every minute, this woman is getting further and further away and the trail gets colder. We're the ones on the ground who can do something." He turned to Piper.

"We need to be on this now, otherwise leads go cold, and witnesses forget what they've seen. We should at least try."

Greene clicked the magazine back into the pistol with a slap of his palm.

Piper nodded and looked back at the map.

"Let's go over what we have then."

"You think she left already Panama?" Brull asked.

"I know I would have," Greene interjected.

Brull nodded sagely. "I have some resources here, a few contacts with the police and others but..."

"We want to be careful not to alert any police to the situation. We don't know who else might be looking for her," said Frank. "I suggest we split up the tasks. Ask around where she might have used transport. The bus or train station, the airport. Someone must have seen her."

Brull folded up the piece of paper with the Pandora details. "I also have underworld contacts. She may have changed passports, no?"

Greene turned to him. "Alert the bloody underworld as well? What's wrong with you?"

"Not if we have a decent cover story. She's a common thief, a missing person. Maybe she's a friend who needs help. Why don't you try using your brains?" Frank uttered the words with quiet annoyance.

Greene slammed his coffee mug on the table top and faced Piper. "Alright! Whatever you want to do. I'd rather be hoofing around out there in the bloody heat than be stuck in here with him." He jabbed a thumb in Frank's direction.

"Good. I'll go with Brull and you two lovebirds could maybe try and get access to the airport footage?" Frank said, eager to leave.

"Yeah, we'll do that. Now, why don't you go on your merry way?" Greene hardly held the contempt from his voice.

Chapter 20

Sarah Edwards glanced at her digital watch once again and drained a glass of soda water. The evening was turning to night and would, no doubt, be another restless one. She had been living in the hotel room for nearly a month now, rarely leaving the confines of her four walls or the hotel grounds as she played the waiting game.

Where was her contact? They were supposed to rendezvous with her a week ago and no messages had been sent whatsoever. This was deeply worrying. What worried her, even more, was that everything she was risking might well be for nothing.

The ceiling fan spun listlessly at low speed, barely keeping the humidity at bay but apart from complaining again, she would have to live with it.

She had chosen the small, discreet hotel long before disappearing to Cuba: the central courtyard restaurant meant she could occasionally dine away from her room and still be out of sight from the main road that linked up with the San Pedro harbour port road. There was also a secluded back exit to an alleyway, shadowed by towering tenant buildings, where a constant rotation of clothes drying hung overhead.

The plan had gone well so far and she was sure that every precaution had been taken. The assumed identity of Emily Jenkins to Panama and then she dumped that for a new one before heading to Cuba. She was determined not to underestimate the intelligence services, whether it was the British, Americans, Russians, or Chinese. She prayed the trail would die there or at least long enough for her to find permanent shelter.

She was under no illusions that any number of agencies would happily kill her for the information. It was important to be watchful, resourceful, and not trip up. That would be a costly mistake that would ensure she would become history. A tough time waited ahead of her, that much she was certain of, but it was the right course of action. This data would be the first step to exposing the lies and corruption in the establishment she had grown to despise so strongly. She felt her cause was completely justified when she had seen the details of black operations, undisclosed holding sites, and destabilisation projects on the agency files.

The thought of moving to a different hotel had crossed her mind more than once but if she did, she might lose the connection with the contact and it would all be for nothing. It had been agreed that any direct contact via telephone or email was out of the question but now she was torn with a dilemma. Send a message and risk the net falling over her head or stay put and risk them finding her anyway? Yes, moving on might be a good idea. She decided to give it a few more days.

Footsteps grew louder on the terrace walkway outside her room and Sarah tensed up for a moment until the footfall faded and only the sound of the ceiling fan remained.

Get a grip, Sarah.

She cradled the empty glass, still thirsty, and padded over to the fridge, which was empty. Just then, the lamp flickered and died leaving her in darkness. She gasped inwardly despite knowing that it must be a power cut, the third since she had arrived, but it spiked her adrenaline nevertheless. She peered out of the blinds and noticed all the rooms had been affected. That made her breathe slightly easier but she still didn't like it. She walked over to the bed and lay down, listening to the ceiling fan gradually slowing to a halt and felt the oppressive, thick air on her skin.

After what seemed like at least an hour, but was probably only 20 minutes, Sarah reached for the phone by the bed and dialled reception.

"Buenos Dias. Reception."

"Hi. I know it's difficult to say but do you know when the power will return?" she asked in Spanish.

"It's hard to say, madam. We are trying to contact the electrical system's headquarters for more information but haven't managed to get through yet. Do you want me to let you know if I hear anything?"

Sarah paused. "No, it's alright. Mucho gracias."

She replaced the telephone receiver, unaware of the homing beacon she had just planted on herself.

Chapter 21

At the Ghost 13 operations room in London, Carl felt the buzzing of his mobile in his inside jacket pocket and saw a withheld number message display on the screen.

"Carl Paterson?"

"Yes?"

"This is David Devlin. You know who I am. From now on, you report to me directly. Any update, any single item of information you learn, must be reported directly to me. Do you understand?"

Carl hesitated. "Right, I thought Keller..."

"Forget Keller. Is your phone encrypted?"

"Yes."

"Good. I will give you a phone number to call me on. Any updates on the Pandora situation must be relayed to me directly," he said, the tone deadly serious.

"Okay, will do," Carl said curtly, bristling at the tone.

Devlin gave him a number and then asked him to repeat it before disconnecting. Carl stared at his phone screen, frowning for a moment, and tossed the phone on top of the mound of paperwork on his desk.

He opened his drawer where a pile of chocolate bars were hidden and grabbed one, ripping off the top of the wrapping.

Carl had no idea what the Director of GCHQ was doing but he

obviously had a vested interest in this operation. Perhaps his head must be on the chopping block over the leak? Either way, it didn't make much difference to Carl who he reported to. If the head honcho wanted a direct line, then the head honcho would get it.

***

Across the far side of the expansive space, Griff rolled his chair over to the fridge and grabbed another can of cola before returning to the slow progress bar on his screen. The voice recognition software was scanning through the Echelon satellite data from the previous few days in the Central America area, Sarah Edwards' last reported sighting.

The software was trying to match the voice of Sarah Edwards with an audio sample that GCHQ had of her voice on file from her recruitment process. Griff knew that the voice traffic was being routed to high-speed Voice Recognition computers using a program called "Oratory."

It was a literal needle in a very mountainous haystack but if there was a match, then the scan would find it. Carl's figure drifted across Griff's peripheral vision in the background as his eyelids grew heavy from the workload. Everyone had been pulling long hours since the operation launch and it had been a good twenty-six hours since he had slept.

A beep from the computer jerked Griff from his drifting stupor. The screen proclaimed a near match. Quickly reviving, he tapped a key to check the results and reveal the location. The GPS coordinates took a few seconds to adjust and then he was staring at a line of text displaying the words "Havana, Cuba".

"Carl! Think I've got something."

Carl came over to the screen and was soon joined by Harry, the communications officer. Griff opened a window of the audio and played it. A male voice came from the speaker.

"Buenos Dias. Reception."

A woman's voice: "Hi. I know it's difficult to say but do you know when the power will return?"

The male voice returned and then the line went particularly bad.

A snippet of the female voice returned.

"...Mucho gracias."

The line was crackly and intermittently, there were gaps of silence but words could be made out, sometimes clearly, sometimes not.

"Eighty-three percent. It's not a ringing endorsement," muttered Carl, looking unconvinced.

Griff turned to look at him, frowning as if he was questioning his expertise.

"It's a close enough match, considering the quality," said Griff.

"How did Echelon pick up an internal telephone transmission? Vortex can only pick up regional communications through ground-based microwave towers, right?"

Griff shrugged and adjusted his glasses. Carl was referring to a spy satellite named 'Vortex' that intercepted communications.

"Yeah, that's right. The power cut must have re-routed the transmission externally to the towers and then Vortex picked it up."

Carl nodded and then stood back up.

"Thanks, Griff. I need to run this by people upstairs."

Griff swung round in his chair to face Carl. "What for?"

Now Carl frowned and spoke slowly. "Because that's the way it is..."

Carl walked into a private room set away from the main operations space and dialled David Devlin's number.

Chapter 22

Frank and Brull drove south in a black Toyota towards the older part of Panama City, Casco Viejo. Frank sat in the front, watching the streets blur by. It was a modern hub of activity, punctuated by the car horns of impatient drivers. As they headed south, the buildings became more dilapidated with boarded-up ruins, interspersed with terraced colonial gems. An urban slum, fighting to restore its once great place in the history of the city.

As they drove deeper, the spectre of poverty and crime was suddenly all around them.

"Sure you're cool with this guy?" asked Frank, as he brushed a hand across the bulk of the Glock tucked inside his jacket pocket.

"I know him for some years. It's okay. If he asks, just say you're a friend of mine looking for your girlfriend."

Frank nodded. "Yeah, makes sense."

Brull pulled up outside a two-storey condo that looked freshly painted; bright white against a turquoise blue sky and a view of Panama Bay completed the backdrop. Outside, sitting around a table playing cards, were three young men, all sporting dark shades. Their heads turned at the sight of Frank and Brull pulling up opposite.

Both men got out of the car and slowly strolled across the road towards them. One of the men stood up, his hand clearly reaching for an unseen weapon behind his belt.

Brull jerked his hand at him nonchalantly.

"We here to see Palacio. It's Dante."

Narrow eyes checked out Frank and Brull, looking them up and down.

"It's okay. Palacio knows him." said a fat man in Spanish who was at the table.

After a pat down, their pistols removed and kept aside, they were escorted into a reception room, where a short, squat man with curly black hair was slumped on a sofa, talking on an oversized satellite phone. He gestured with a plump hand for them to take a seat on the sofa opposite and continued bellowing obscenities in Spanish to the unfortunate person at the other end. Frank looked around at the clean, whitewashed interior. A piece of modern art adorned the wall behind the fat man, looking out of place in the sparse condo.

Palacio threw the phone down next to him and fixed two small eyes on the visitors. "So, what can I do for you, Brull?"

Brull pulled the print out from his inside pocket and handed it over to Palacio.

"My friend here, Mr. Feldman..." Frank nodded at the Panamanian. "Is looking for his girlfriend who went missing in this part of the world. She may have tried to leave covertly."

Piggy eyes scanned the photograph and then focused on Frank. The fat man smiled and for a moment, reminded Frank of a shark. "Are you sure she didn't find another man to satisfy her, Mr. Feldman?"

Frank made himself look irritated for a second and then grinned back, nodding his head slowly as if realising it was a joke.

"She is a loyal woman. I fear she might be in danger," he said.

The fat man's smile faded and he sighed, folded up the print and put it into his shirt pocket.

"I will make inquiries. Call me back in twenty-four hours," he said with a finality that indicated the meeting was over.

Both men got up and shook hands with Palacio before heading back to the vehicle.

"Do you think we'll get anything out of him?" he asked Brull.

"If anyone can find out, he can. He supplies assumed identities for many different groups, including some of the South American cartels."

Frank smiled. "Nice."

"You work many places, Frank?"

Frank gazed out at the tall stacked skyscrapers lining the horizon against a setting sun as they headed north.

"Not too many. The Balkans, Asia, Europe. Ever been to Europe?"

"Ahh, yes, many times. I like London, yes. But Paris and France is my favourite. I would love to retire there one day."

"France, huh? I didn't have you down as a Frenchie. Nice wine and cheese though."

"I like the pace. Very slow. And French women, too!" Brull said, laughing.

Frank smiled. "I won't argue with you about that. So, no family then?" he asked.

Brull shook his head. "No. There's no wife or children. That's on my list for one day in the future. But in our business, a quiet retirement is a distant dream. A very dangerous dream."

Frank nodded and paused. "Yeah, you could be right there, mate."

As the cityscape drifted by, Frank thought about Maria and the children. He missed them. Would he ever get more time with them? Would he even get to retirement himself? These thoughts always crept up again and again, something he usually tried hard to block out when working. Focus and discipline could be affected.

He tried to put himself in Pandora's shoes again. Where would he head to in her situation? There was any number of countries to disappear to in the region. To the north lay the central Americas: Nicaragua, Honduras and Guatemala. South America? Colombia, Ecuador, and Brazil? Across the Caribbean lay Cuba and Puerto Rico. Panama must have been a change-over point for Pandora before disappearing somewhere else. Somewhere near? But where?

***

Less than an hour later, Brull had dropped Frank off at the safe house and gone on some errands and now he stood in the condo, watching the endless ships and boats travel across Panama Bay in the far distance. The heavy afternoon was turning to evening and the sound of gabbling locals drifted through the balcony window

"She's not in any of these that I can see but it's a needle in a bloody haystack." Piper turned away from the screen of endless airport CCTV photos, his fists cupped together against his forehead. Greene also had his head buried in footage from the airport.

"Anything from Cronus in London?" asked Frank.

"No. If they had anything, I'm sure they'd be sending frantic messages," said Piper.

After their visit to the Panamanian gangster in Casco Viejo, Brull and Frank had dropped into a police station. They spoke to a police contact of Brull's telling the same story: a woman Mr. Feldman deeply cared about had disappeared. Could discreet inquiries be made? The die was now cast and all they could do now was scan CCTV footage, drink coffee, and moan about the heat.

Chapter 23

Frank opened his laptop to check for messages and instantly received a notification from his WarWorld game from Griff. He started the game and opened the comms console window to find Griff was online.

He read the message on the screen.

"Ordered not to pass to you as not deemed reliable by Cronus. Eighty-three percent voice match. Good fit in my book. File attached. It's from Havana; a Hotel Castro. This line is secure as houses for your info."

Frank smiled at the screen. Good old Griff. This back channel via the game was proving to be invaluable. But why was Carl holding off with this information? That made little sense.

Three hours later, Frank drained the mug of bitter coffee as he stood with Piper and Greene around the dining table and a spread out map of Havana.

"I don't want to get Griff in trouble over this so don't mention Havana," Frank said.

"It's bullshit. They haven't mentioned anything about Havana. So it can't be confirmed," Piper said.

"This is a member of our team, a bloody good one, telling us that Pandora is in Havana."

"..And Cronus. Why isn't he giving us this intel?" asked Greene.

Frank shook his head. Admittedly, he was confused by that little matter. "I don't know. He must have his reasons."

The loop of the recording continued to play in the background like a soundtrack to their thoughts. Snippets of a woman's voice none of them had heard before but someone they had to find as soon as possible.

"I'll go and request updates from London and see what they say first," Piper said and walked away to one of the back rooms.

Ten minutes later, he returned.

"Well, investigations in London are still ongoing. There's an order to make inquiries here in Panama."

"No mention of this Echelon match or Havana?" asked Frank.

Piper shook his head.

"No, no mention whatsoever."

Frank leaned over the table. "Maybe we're not being ordered but we are going to go to Havana. Our contract says "all actions deemed necessary to track down Pandora." If they're withholding information, then that's their problem, not ours."

At that moment, they heard footsteps walking slowly up from the car garage. The men shifted subtly, hands moving towards their Glocks simultaneously. The door opened and it was Brull, looking back at them in surprise, holding his hands up in mock surrender. Everyone laughed with relief.

Brull sat down at the table and accepted a coffee from Frank.

"Any news?"

"Nothing from our friends in the police," Brull said and paused. "But Palacio said a contact gave her a fake passport in the name of Helena Lopez. I had to pay him $2,000."

Piper, Greene and Frank all looked at each other with smiles on their faces for the first time since arriving.

"That's great work, Brull," said Frank. "Piper can get you

reimbursement, I'm sure."

Piper slapped Brull on the shoulder, clearly pleased.

"If not, I'll pay you myself. That info is gold."

"So now we have a name and an address. What are we waiting for?" asked Frank.

"Let's call the hotel. Confirm that a Helena Lopez is booked in first," said Piper. Everyone nodded in agreement and Piper went off to make the call.

***

Frank wondered again on why London had not passed on the information as the flight from Panama touched down at José Martí International Airport in Havana early the following morning. Clearly, Griff had thought it was credible enough to go on. What else did they have? Apart from her new assumed name that Brull's gangster contact had found out.

After Piper had confirmed that their target was staying at the hotel, Brull had gone on ahead to Cuba to set up a safe house, so they wouldn't be messing around when they arrived. He was proving a very useful asset to the team.

Piper, Greene, and Frank hired a Jeep Grand Cherokee 4x4 and headed into Havana along the main autopista as a new day broke over the city. The safe house was a small, detached, run-down building just south of the busy enclave of Havana port in a commercial district, set behind a row of palms that ran along the main road.

They drove around the back of the building into a lane and pulled up into a carport that had stone walls on either side. Inside, the décor was spartan. Peeling walls, a table and chairs, and an American fridge. It was a far cry from the condo in Panama. The windows were shuttered and closed to keep the light out and the rooms felt cool; a slight smell of damp lingered in the air. Greene immediately switched on the ceiling fan and turned to Brull, acknowledging a good job, without words.

"Did you manage to get us any equipment?"

"Si. It is all there as arranged," said Brull, leading them to a black box.

Piper checked the contents and took out several Glock pistols and handed one to Greene. Also inside was some of the surveillance equipment Frank would need to do his job, a selection of listening devices and wiring.

Frank leaned down and opened his suitcase. Taking out the piles of shirts, shorts, maps, and other typical tourist items, he placed the equipment inside. Then Frank shut the case and stood up.

Piper gestured to Frank with a grunt. "Okay, good luck. We'll be speaking real soon."

Chapter 24

Harry tore off a piece of paper from the incoming printer feed and walked over to Carl's desk. "Message from Ghost 13."

It was the usual rows of numbers associated with the One Time Pad code.

"Okay, thanks, Harry. Leave this with me."

When Harry returned to his desk, Carl began to decode the numbers, writing out the message and cursed quietly at what he read.

CRONUS EYES ONLY: CREDIBLE INFORMATION LEADING US TO HAVANA. DETAILS TO FOLLOW. HAD TO ACT QUICKLY. WILL CONTACT AGAIN.

He fed the paper through a shredder next to his desk and leaned back in the leather chair and thought for a moment. They had exceeded their authority and he'd bet his house that Frank was behind it. The others, though good men, were just grunts. What had they found out? Perhaps they were right and the voice data match might be correct?

He quick dialled a number and soon the voice of David Devlin answered.

"It's Carl. Ghost 13 is headed to Havana, based on some credible leads. Just letting you know."

There was a pause. "Did you order them there?"

"I asked them to make inquiries. Makes sense as they're on the ground already. They obviously found something. Together with the Echelon data, it's the closest we have to Pandora's whereabouts."

"No more surprises. I don't want any more actions without a direct order from us, Carl. We need to keep a firm grip on this."

"I understand but they do have carte blanch to do what is necessary to find Pandora," Carl said, determined to hold his ground. He was feeling that this operation was being steered too strongly away from his own hand.

"Nevertheless. Keep it tight and remind your team who pays their wages."

Carl sighed. "Right you are, sir."

Chapter 25

Frank glanced through the car window at the passing streets of Havana. Everything here seemed touched by the sun; even the most broken down buildings have an air of majesty about them. A beautiful place for tourists, not so much for enemies of the state.

Brull tightened his grip on the wheel and turned to face Frank. "You ready for this, amigo?" Frank paused as if to ask himself the same question. He couldn't turn back now. The question remained unanswered and hung in the air as the Toyota headed along the coastal road of San Pedro, the expanse of the wide blue sea on their right. Hued shapes of cranes and ships stood silently in the distance as they passed a group of tourists and locals boarding a ferry at one of the terminals.

Frank reviewed his documentation once again. Tourist ID, passport, and driver's license, all in the name of Keith Feldman. It was more than enough to solidify the truthfulness of his false identity. Thanks to Brull, they now had Pandora's hotel and room number. She would be lying low, waiting for whatever her next move was. That was the big question they all asked themselves. What was her next move?

Brull pulled the vehicle up on the kerb and pointed one finger up the busy street. "The hotel is just there on the corner. Best that you get out here and walk."

Frank nodded. "Thanks, mate. I'll be seeing you."

He got out of the car and walked up the road with his suitcase. Brull's Toyota roared by and turned at the junction ahead. Frank checked into the hotel as he might into a winter resort, filled with optimism for a much-enjoyed visit to Havana and infecting the receptionist with his jokes.

A young bellboy escorted Frank to his room, who asked the usual questions of any tourist. What was England like? What football team did he support? He tipped him five dollars and walked into the stark room, whitewashed with a simple picture of the Havana cityscape adorning the wall. Frank could only imagine the target's room was similar, maybe even an exact duplicate.

His imagined best-case scenario had him sneaking in under the cover of darkness but it was more likely he'd have to take any opportunity. Frank opened the suitcase and contemplated the fact that Pandora rarely left her room, according to Brull's sources. Bugging her room in that respect was tricky but if she was to eat, she had no choice but to leave, even for a brief moment. And if all the rooms are as similar as he hoped, a ten-minute window was all that would be needed.

Frank peered vigilantly from the glass window through two shutters. She had probably already had breakfast but chances were, she'd leave again before long. As the hands on Bowen's Nite MX10 watch drifted by, his attentiveness to the outside world only escalated.

Frank stared through the window across at Sarah Edward's room on the fourth level opposite. The rooms were arranged around an inner courtyard that housed the outside section of the quiet restaurant below; parasols sporting the Havana Club logo spread out, sheltering the guests from the sunlight.

Suddenly, he had a visual on Edwards, scurrying from her room.

The trembling in her fingers and finicky gestures told him all he needed to know about her state of mind. She looked scared. Frank shut the blinds a little tighter, just enough to watch her work at the lock with the key. She struggled with it, eventually exclaiming something unintelligible, and walked away frustrated. He watched her descend the steps and quickly moved out through his door. She was headed to the bar area. Now was the time.

Frank moved quickly, picking the lock expertly before slipping into her room with his small bag of gear. He looked around. Anywhere that was already covered up by furniture deserved a bug. He slipped listening devices behind the painting on the wall and behind the headstand on the bed. Next, he moved to the en-suite bathroom and found a gap behind the cabinet. It was trickier to get this one in place but it needed to be there, in case she made calls from in there on a mobile.

Frank double-checked that nothing looked out of place and carefully peeked through the blinds to check whether the coast was clear. On the opposite side, down a level, a cleaning woman hovered outside a room before disappearing inside, dragging a cart behind her. As soon as the door closed again, Frank walked casually out back to his room around the walkway.

Once inside, Frank dragged the desk and manoeuvred the chair to face the door and set up the Honeywell laptop. He didn't want any hotel staff seeing the screen. It was time to check the equipment and he began the pinging process, making sure each bug was active. After seeing all was in order, Frank felt a wave of relief that he didn't have to go back to her room to fix anything. He listened in for a while, adjusting the volume slightly on the recording software; the laptop screen displayed a flat audio line, telling him that was no noise in her room until a slam of the door on her return caused a spike on the screen. Everything seemed to be up and running smoothly.

She seemed so young. What had motivated her to do what she was doing? Did this nervous, stressed woman realise what she was getting into exactly? She must have her reasons for throwing herself into the abyss and must surely know her life would never be the same again? The information she held. It must be about the money; selling it to the highest bidder and then she must have some kind of exit plan.

Frank checked the fridge and was relieved to find some alcoholic miniatures and grabbed a couple of rums and a can of cola. He poured the contents into a glass and took a glug. It felt good.

Nothing much happened until she called room service for tea and a snack around 11:20 AM. For the first time, the voice confirmed that this was really her. There was no doubt in his mind that it was the same woman. Frank felt a wave of triumph, not to mention relief.

He padded across the marble tiled floor to turn up the ceiling fan, cursing the humidity, then looked through the window blind from where he could see the coming and going of the occasional guest and waiter in the courtyard restaurant below. Nothing seemed unusual or out of place. A couple of hours passed.

Again, Frank wondered at her motivation. She must have known she was risking everything. Known that she would not be able to contact her family, her friends. Probably never see them again. And then he thought of Maria and the boys and realised he couldn't wait to see them again. Every harsh word he had ever said to them now seemed cruel, uncalled for. Distance had grown between himself and his family and he had allowed it to happen.

Chapter 26

Viktor Kozel, or Alexei Demenok as his passport named him, smiled. The payment had been made. It amazed him how digits could transcend space itself from one secret bank account to another. Another step towards retirement from the game, a game that had become old.

But Kozel had no regrets. He had lived his life the way it had been dealt to him. It began in the Russian army and then he helped with the muscle end of the KGB, making sure prisoners talked when they had to. He was an expert in various torture methods but had always yearned to make good money. Dabbling in arms smuggling to criminal elements, two years before the Soviet Union collapsed, got him into trouble and he was thrown into a high-security prison near the Siberian city of Krasnoyarsk.

A twist of fate came and Kozel met and became friends with Vyacheslav Ivankov, a high level and 'made Vor' or thief, marked by the eight-pointed star tattoos on each of his shoulders with the single eye in the centre. It was in the grim, red-bricked prison that Kozel himself got his gang tattoos, the barbed wire covering his neck and throat just one of them.

By 1991, the top thieves of the Soviet Union planned for a post-communist Russia and when the time came, they were ready to pounce on and feed off the state infrastructure. Ivankov and Kozel were released, helped by the corruption of the day, and walked into a violence fuelled mafia war that looked like something out of 1930s Chicago. Russia became the most violent country on earth during that time. *Great days.*

The Russian disconnected the satellite phone and walked back down to the lower basement of the unused factory, where old machinery stood like rusting hulks from a by-gone age. Faded Russian writing engraved onto the metal pointed to better times for the Cuban republic when Soviet goods flowed freely into the country. They made Kozel feel at home although he was glad to be out of the sub-zero temperatures of Moscow and hoped for more contracts like this one.

His men were in the process of unpacking the equipment that had been brought into the country in unmarked crates. Several computers, cables, and a power generator had been the first to be set up and now Yuri Tarasenko, a tough Ukrainian with a blonde crew cut and angular features, was checking the weapons from another crate.

"How is our package?" Viktor boomed. His companion grinned wolfishly, holding up the formidable Bizon sub-machine gun, a weapon chambered for the standard Russian 9×18mm Makarov pistol cartridge that was also capable of firing high-impulse armour-piercing rounds.

"Looking very good. Everything is here."

Viktor looked down along the table that held the range of weapons, occasionally picking one up to check the clips. The Marquis had delivered as promised and genuinely impressed by the strings he must have pulled to get this order.

"These ones will need cleaning again," he said, gesturing to the culprit machine guns and shooting a glare at his giant employee, Leonid Dustkin. Viktor had employed the big man ever since his foray into crime after the good old KGB days had come to an end.

Leonid nodded his bald head slowly. "No problem, Viktor."

Suddenly, Viktor slapped the big man around the face, as quick as a viper strike, leaving the man stunned. Dustkin felt his scarred cheek with one massive hand, fear in his eyes as he looked down at his boots. The other two men glanced over but continued their work, keeping their heads down.

"No names. How many times do I have to say?"

Leonid Duskin stroked his cheek and nodded, looking like a scolded cat. "Of course. No real names...Alexei!"

"That's better. Now clean up these guns." He then turned to the other two men. "We must be more careful!" With that, the short stocky Russian walked along the basement floor, his boots echoing through the huge space, up to an open metal laptop placed on a workbench. It was attached to a printer that kicked into life and a series of numbers printed out on a sheet of highly flammable nitrocellulose paper.

Viktor studied it for a moment and translated the numbers into letters from his issued codebook or one-time pad, carefully re-checking each number until he had a series of indistinguishable letters. He translated the ciphertext and an address of a hotel in Havana revealed itself, followed by a warning:

ROGUE TEAM IN PLAY. MARQUIS

Chapter 27

"Havana Club, por favor."

The barman poured the golden rum into a crystal glass and placed it on the dark wooden bar in front of Frank.

"Gracias."

The barman moved away, leaving Frank gazing at the Che Guevara iconic image in a frame on the wall. He thought about the life story of this Argentinian revolutionary who had become a hero to the Cuban people. His meeting with Castro and subsequent involvement in the revolution before travelling to ignite further revolution abroad; firstly in Congo-Kinshasa and then in Bolivia, both ventures ending unsuccessfully. The latter especially as he was captured and executed by CIA backed Bolivian government troops. He wondered about Sarah again. Did she really realise what she was involved in?

Just then, Frank's mobile buzzed in his pocket. It was Brull.

"Frank. I have a very reliable source saying that there is a Russian group in Havana looking for Pandora. They are dangerous and they may know about the hotel."

"Do you know who they are?" Frank was watching the view through the sliding doors that led out into the inside courtyard.

"No, I do not know."

"They might be the buyers," Frank said.

"That is a possibility but my contact said there was a consignment of arms delivered just outside Havana...Why would they need so much weapons?" Brull asked.

There was a pause.

"You're right. That sounds more like a snatch squad."

Can you get the target out of there? Get her here? Sorry to ask this of you, Frank."

"What do I say to her?"

Just then, the line disconnected and Frank looked at the screen and cursed. Suddenly, the situation seemed to have escalated. His gaze drifted to the other hotel guests as they chatted and drank expressos under the parasols in the courtyard. A Caucasian woman wearing sunglasses with tied back black hair moved through the tables in his direction. Frank glanced away and then back again, realisation turning in his mind. She came up to the bar, standing just a few feet away and removed her sunglasses. It was Pandora, or Sarah Edwards, looking for bar service.

They caught each other's eye and Frank, not knowing in that moment what else to do, nodded an acknowledgement. He cursed himself silently. There was a sudden glimpse of suspicion and defiance in her eyes and Frank stopped himself short of saying anything at that moment as his mind raced. How should he deal with this? Play it right, otherwise, he'd lose her and the moment would be gone.

She ordered sparkling water to be delivered to her room and complained that her room phone was not working properly. It was all a big inconvenience and could they do something about it? There was a promise to look into it as soon as possible by the barman, who then moved off to get her order.

"Do you speak English?" Frank heard himself say.

She looked at him again, her eyes full of sudden fear, the defiance gone.

"Que?"

Frank asked again in Spanish.

"No, por favor discúlpeme," she replied and started to walk off.

Frank couldn't let her go. He might not get another chance.

"Your water. Don't you want it?" She stopped and turned around, checking him out with clear suspicion.

Then Frank slowly stood up from the bar stool. "Sarah, I really need to talk to you."

Chapter 28

"I think you are in immediate danger. Either from kidnapping or death or probably both."

Sarah studied Frank, her brown eyes searching his for clues. She wasn't sure whether to be scared, angry, or what, but she was wary. Was this some kind of trap? Her gut instinct said no but she had to be careful. The stakes were too high.

Sarah laughed easily, as if from nowhere.

"Who are you exactly?"

Frank leaned forward, closer to her, his voice quietening.

"That doesn't matter. I was hired by a British intelligence agency to bug your room and monitor your movements. I wasn't privy to what you did in detail exactly. But there are a group of Russians looking for you. They know you are at this hotel."

"Which agency are you with?" she asked.

"Does it matter? Take a wild guess."

"I'm just trying to ascertain the facts. You could be anyone."

Something caught his eye. Through the double doors, he had a view of the reception area and beyond that, the main street. He frowned and stood up to move closer for a better look and confirm what he thought he saw. A large man with a bald head was talking to the receptionist; he turned his head momentarily and caught sight of Frank. Frank could see up to the upper levels and the staircase, where another man dressed in a suit was rapping his fist on one of the doors. Frank instantly knew the Russians were here.

"We have to leave now." He turned back to Sarah, who was looking at him, a mixture of fear and confusion in her eyes. He grabbed her arm and began to lead her to the back of the bar.

"What are you doing?"

He maneuvered her around so she was facing the sliding doors along with the sight of a seven-foot bald thug striding towards them through the patio garden. The situation persuaded her to follow his lead.

They ran through a half-empty restaurant and rushed towards a metal door that led into the kitchens. Two Cuban chefs looked up at them in surprise and started gesturing to them to get out. One stepped towards Frank as if to block his path but received a shove that threw him against a fridge door. Pulling Sarah by the hand, they both pushed through. The other chef stopped, held his hands up and stood back, clearly not wanting any trouble. Just as they reached the back exit door, there was a loud "thunk" sound against the wall, less than a metre away from Frank. A gunshot!

The sound of plates smashing onto the tiled floor exploded behind them. They burst out of the exit door and Frank slammed it shut behind them before grabbing Sarah's hand again. Running hard down an alleyway, they both saw the main road that ran along the front of the hotel ahead.

Turning left on the main road, they ran past crumbling store-fronts, darting around people as they strolled at a casual pace. There was a skeleton structure of rusty scaffolding sprawled over the pavement that forced them onto the road. Frank stole a glance behind him and saw the man come out of the alleyway onto the road. He looked around and spotting them, gave chase. A chorus of angry car horns blared and then they darted back under a line of arched pillars that kept them out of sight from their pursuer. An intersection ahead gave them options. From his brief analysis of the city map, Frank knew the best place to lose the Russian was in the narrow alleyways and cobbled streets of Old Havana.

Turning to Sarah, who was a few paces behind, he shouted, "Left here. You okay?"

Sarah nodded but looked out of breath already.

Passing under the long shadows of colonial buildings and a line of still palms, they ran, zig-zagging around a large woman selling fruit from a cart. Busy sounds of chatter and traffic increased until they reached the busier narrow streets, where tourists were taking a stroll, looking for somewhere to eat or admiring the architecture.

Heading into the Plaza de San Francisco, out of sight from the tail, passing under the arched canopies of the 17th-century buildings, they kept close to the stone wall. The murmur of afternoon diners drifted across the square. A sudden sound of flapping wings broke as a flock of pigeons scattered, and the Basilica bell tower chimed. The distance to the next exit road was too far. Their pursuer would turn the corner and see them without a doubt.

The sound of feet running behind them echoed across the Plaza.

Turning at another street, they headed back in the same direction they had come. Rapid salsa beats drifted from a few streets away and Frank wished that he was with Maria, sipping tequilas and snacking on tapas, instead of running from this bastard. He stopped and beckoned to Sarah to duck into a large doorway adorned with crumbling pillars.

They breathed heavily and Frank gestured for Sarah to crouch down behind him. If he came past, Frank could ambush him from their position.

The street was almost empty apart from a scavenging dog, ripping apart a bin sack, and the distant cry of a child. Harsh shadows from the surrounding buildings diced up the cobbled road but no footfall seemed to follow, that Frank could hear. They waited several minutes then moved silently down the avenue.

***

They walked in silence and then Frank hailed a taxi and they slumped into the back seats of an old, spacious 1950's Pontiac.

"Ave de Mexico Cristina," he said to the driver, who nodded and pulled out into the road with a crunch of the gears.

"Was that FSB?" Sarah asked quietly after a pause. She was referring to the Russian intelligence service, re-moulded from the old KGB.

"I don't know, probably," he said, glancing through the rear window.

"And what's your name?"

"Frank."

"MI6?"

"Something like that."

"So this is a trap and you're reeling me in?"

Frank shook his head. "That would've been a good plan. Wish I thought of that."

Sarah laughed with a heavy tone of sarcasm. "So, where are you taking me, Mr. MI6?"

"Away from the Russians."

"How did you find me?"

Frank let out a chuckle. "I can't go giving away those kinds of secrets, Sarah."

She paused and watched the city blur past for a while. "Do you want to know why I'm doing what I'm doing, Frank?"

"I can guess, but go ahead."

She told Frank about Operation Oculus. The tentacles of the globalist surveillance plan of all online activity, the massive piping of data. Stage one of something even Orwell could not envisage. The entire western world will be watched and monitored.

"Not only is it totally illegal, but it will also set a precedent for what will come."

"Why come to Cuba? Why not straight to Moscow?"

He saw cold anger in her eyes.

"Are you saying this is about trading secrets? Selling the information? You are so far off the mark!"

Frank kind of shrugged, as if to say 'How the hell would I know?' Sarah stared out of the window and seemed to let her anger dissipate.

"Going to Moscow would be like going into lion's den, there's no way of knowing what would happen or where I would end up. This is not about being some kind of traitor or double agent, Frank. It's about exposing what's going on in our agencies."

"Look, I'm in no position to argue the rights and wrongs of what our governments are up to," said Frank.

"This goes above governments, way beyond."

"What do you mean, above governments?" Frank's eyes focused on her. Sarah sighed.

"The shadow behind the governments, the Cabal. A power that no ordinary citizen has any idea of."

Frank snorted with derision and leaned back in his seat, barely able to hide his scepticism. "What? Like a conspiracy? You sound like my partner."

"Do you really think they haven't penetrated organisations like MI6 or the CIA? That those organisations aren't knowingly or otherwise carrying out a hidden agenda?"

Frank shook his head. "All I know is I work with good people, mostly. We're protecting our interests, the interests of the UK."

"What are those interests? Really? You really think they give a shit about you? That they would think twice about throwing you overboard to protect their interests? That's their agenda; to compartmentalise, so no one can see the big picture or suss out what all the other moving parts are doing!"

Frank smiled to himself. She really did remind him of Maria. But she had a point there. Trust was a rare commodity.

"They will use everything in their power to discredit anyone who opposes them," she continued. "They'll label me as a terrorist or a conspirator, probably already have. And they'll probably come after you, too, Frank, when they find out you've helped me."

Chapter 29

Frank knocked in three rapid beats on the red door to the safe house and waited.

"How can I help?" It was a reply from behind the door in Spanish.

"It's me, Feldman," he replied, using his alias name.

Several locks were unbolted until the door opened a fraction and Piper stood holding a gun pointed towards him. He glared at him and then looked at Sarah before gesturing for them both to enter.

"Come on, get off the street."

Piper re-bolted the door and turned around, putting the safety back on his weapon. They stood alone in the small front room where the blinds on the two front windows were shut tight and a lamp in the corner cast a dim glow.

Piper looked at Sarah and grinned.

"So you're the cause of all the trouble?"

She looked at him with a frown, clearly not willing to join in with any banter.

"So anymore on this Russian crew?" Frank asked.

Piper shook his head. "I'm going to radio it in. This is a change of situation."

He began to turn and walk towards the rear of the house.

Suddenly, at that moment, glass on both front windows simultaneously shattered in a hail of machine gun fire. Frank, Sarah, and

Piper instinctively hurled themselves to the ground. The gunfire continued relentlessly, peppering chunks of plaster out of the opposite wall, glass fragments spraying in every direction.

After a few seconds, there was a pause in the sudden explosion of violence that had been unleashed.

Piper shouted towards the back of the house. "Green, Brull! Incoming at the front!"

They heard Green shout from the back room. "You got a weapon?"

"Yep, a pistol. How's the car looking?"

"All good so far, seems clear," shouted Greene.

The gunfire started again, hammering into the walls and it seemed to shake the whole building.

The shooting stopped again. "They'll be getting ready to storm in soon," said Piper. He gave Frank his Glock and pulled an exact same model from his belt.

"Were you followed?"

"God, no. We lost someone in a Plaza."

Piper shook his head, "They must have followed you. Doesn't matter now. We have to get out of here and find another safe house and call this in."

Frank could already hear Greene attempting to contact Cronus, Carl Paterson, their controller in London.

"Forget it," shouted Piper. "Check the back and the car. We need to roll."

Piper turned to Frank. "Come on, let's give these bastards some kind of response."

Frank turned to Sarah, who was crouched in a fetal position, her arms around her head. "Stay here."

They crawled along the floor and cocked their pistols, leaning against the wall under the window.

"You take a look, I'll cover," Piper said. Frank nodded. Piper held his weapon up, pointing it outwards and blasted off a couple of rounds. As he did so, Frank quickly peeked through the window and then fell back down in a crouch.

"I saw an MPV. Four men from what I can see. They have heavy armour."

"All clear," shouted Greene from the rear door.

"It could be a trap," said Frank. "Why would they not cover the rear of the house?"

"We can't stay here. They'll burn us out or worse. We just have to take our chances."

"What about the equipment?" Frank shouted over another volley of bullets that peppered the back wall, showering clouds of plaster dust across the room.

"Nothing we can do. Get the girl out of here!"

Frank gestured to Sarah and crawled on their hands and knees into a wide hall that led to a back room and the rear of the property. Piper stayed in the front.

Brull knelt by the back door, holding up his Glock pistol at the ready. Greene was backing up the Land Rover to the door and Brull quickly opened the rear tailgate, throwing in a black canvas bag before jumping into the back seat.

Gunfire erupted once again, quickly followed by a shuddering blast at the front door that could only be a grenade. Frank held his ears as the loud ringing jolted through his head. Dust belched throughout the entire downstairs floor. Then Piper appeared in the hallway, coughing and holding his mouth, manoeuvring on his hands and knees.

Frank saw Piper talking to him but no words came through, only a shrill tone in his ears. He gestured towards the car and pushed Frank toward it before turning back to face the front rooms, his weapon aimed in front of him. Frank, pistol still in hand, moved towards the vehicle and saw Greene at the wheel, his face turning back towards him, waving his hand. What was he trying to tell him? Frank wondered if he had forgotten something and then he realised in a microsecond Greene was trying to stop him from coming nearer the vehicle.

Then his face caved in; a spray of red lashed out from Greene's head, which lolled to the side, lifeless within a single moment. The shock awakened Frank's senses as he heard the shot, dull but precise and caught a glimpse of the shooter, crouched behind the far wall, his weapon swinging round towards him.

Instinctively ducking, Frank dropped to one knee, firing off a volley of shots towards the culprit from the rear door of the house. Crouching, he eased behind the Land Rover, out of view, breathing hard. He checked his pistol chamber. Shit. Low on ammo and the clips were in the bags in the vehicle. There was one shot left.

Sarah and Piper were crouching in the doorway, watching him intently. He held a hand up to them, indicating he was okay.

He needed to get the vehicle started and ready to get the hell out of there. He carefully re-opened the driver door as far as it would go until touching the stone wall behind him and Greene's body slumped against it, heavy and lifeless. A waft of sickly blood hit his throat as he pulled at the body slowly and carefully, inch by inch through the gap until Green was horizontal on the dusty ground. Frank tried not to look at the hole in his head where the spraying blood had ceased and brain matter covered his shirt.

Piper gestured at driving with his hands to Frank, who nodded and then crawled aside the driver's seat, positioning himself; ready to jump in. He kept aim at the far wall through the passenger window as an eerie quietness fell, punctuated by the sound of dogs barking in the distant street alleys at the avalanche of noise that entered their lazy world. Frank saw a head quickly pop up from behind the wall to check the situation, perhaps thinking they were dead or wounded. He adjusted his aim a few centimetres to the right and calmly pulled the trigger; squeezing as if at a duck shoot. The head suddenly fell back behind the wall without a sound.

Piper saw Frank's shot hit the target and realising it was a chance, shouted and grabbed Sarah's hand. "Go! Go!"

Sarah dived into the rear, next to a terrified Brull and Piper dived into the front passenger seat. Frank jumped in and fired up the engine, which turned lazily and refused to fire as if it wanted to hang around and watch their deaths.

The sweat on Frank's palms smeared the steering wheel like grease. A huge bang threw a shock wave from behind them, quickly followed by another. To Frank, they sounded like stun grenades, designed to produce a blinding flash of light and extremely loud noise. Frank tried again and the engine revved. In his peripheral vision, another head appeared over the wall and a hail of bullets smacked into the passenger side of the vehicle.

The Jeep almost leapfrogged out of the yard and Frank span the wheel hard to the right onto the back lane, away from their pursuers, a huge cloud of dust following in their wake. Piper was groaning in pain.

"Shit!"

"What is it? You hit?"

Piper nodded, sweat pouring from his nose and chin.

"I'm good," he said. But Frank knew he was lying.

Chapter 30

Frank jerked hard on the wheel, turning up onto the sidewalk. The whistling sound of bullets cutting through the air had long fallen behind them, but the tension of the moment hung thick within the vehicle, mixed in with the scent of blood pooling through Piper's shirt.

In the rear mirror, Frank spotted the black MPV's headlights with a cloud of dust in its wake, speeding to catch them. As the vehicle reached an intersection of the Paseo de Marti, he turned a sharp right onto it and pressed harder on the gas, heading south. As their vehicle easily cruised past the occasional old 1950's Buick or Russian made Lada, a distant screech told Frank their pursuers were only a block behind.

Frank killed the car lights and looked hard for a way off the main road, which was now feeling increasingly exposed. The MPV lights were behind them, gaining fast. Just ahead, Frank spotted the taillights of a large truck and overtook, before ducking in front of it, out of sight of the Russians. The truck driver flashed his lights at them but Frank ignored it.

"Keep heading north. We head to 'El Tunel'," Brull said. He was referring to "El Tunel de la Habana" that connected each side of Havana Port under the sea, a major feat of Cuban engineering and pride for the Cubans after it had been completed in 1958.

Frank glanced at Piper, who did not look good at all and was barely conscious, blood pooling through his shirt. Right now, there was little they could do for him.

"Brull. See if that Med Kit is in the black bag. We need to stem the bleeding!"

"After the tunnel, I know a place we can hide for a bit," said Brull, as he leaned back, grabbing the bag. He began to rife around inside and pulled out a medical box.

Just then, another dark MPV swerved onto the road a few metres behind them, causing an echoing screech that made them all jump in their seats.

It raced forward, drawing up beside them along the left-hand side. The windows were tinted black, no faces visible behind the glass. Suddenly, the pursuing vehicle rammed violently into the side of the Jeep, against Frank's door. They all were thrown hard against their seatbelts.

"Where the hell did that come from?" Sarah shouted.

"Shit...they have two cars. Must have been trying to head us off...hold on."

Frank spotted a right turn, changed down the gears, depressing the brake pedal slightly before swinging the wheel hard. The Jeep skidded and fishtailed across the asphalt and then Frank floored the accelerator hard, causing a cloud of smoke to appear behind them before they shot down the side street. A few evening strollers turned their heads and stared at them in alarm. Frank raised his eyes to the mirror and saw their pursuers had overshot the turning. There was a glimpse of the vehicle reversing into view.

Brull leaned forward with a bandage and began helping Piper to get it on his wound, who groaned in pain.

"Hold it tight...stop the bleeding," Brull urged.

Frank veered at the first left so they were heading in parallel with the Paseo de Marti towards the entrance of the Port.

"How far now, amigo?"

"Not far...ten minutes."

The Jeep sped along the largely empty roads and up ahead, they caught sight of the shimmering moonlight reflected off the sea.

Frank moved Piper's hand back over the bandage, pressing it hard. "Hold it tight, Steve, tighter!" He managed a faint smile and did as Frank said. It was obvious to Frank that weakness was seizing control.

They headed around a large maze of a roundabout that circled around the Parque Martires del 71 that led to the tunnel entrance. The headlights from the MPV appeared behind them on a curve for a moment, gaining on them fast as they went under a number of flyovers before hitting the harsh yellow light of the tunnel. It was a narrow, two-lane road with a white tiled wall that separated them from the opposite side.

"Policía!"

Brull pointed to the white Lada ahead of them.

It was too late. Frank would have to shoot past them and they'd soon have cops on their trail as well.

Well, if it was going to happen anyway...

"Hold on. Got an idea, gonna try to clip his wing."

Before anyone else could object Frank had sped alongside the police car so his front left fender was parallel to their rear wheel. He slammed the police car, sending it spinning on the asphalt, control clearly lost. As it barrelled in a 180-degree motion, Frank slowed to avoid broadsiding it and then slipped on past the Lada. Once again, he floored the accelerator to pick up speed.

Frank checked his wing mirror and noted with satisfaction that it had come to a standstill across the two lanes, blocking the path for the Russian pursuers. They wouldn't be stuck there for long though.

It was another neat little trick he'd learned from Sam Keane, his trainer, called the 'pursuit intervention technique' used to stop a vehicle pursuit. At speeds over seventy mph, it would only have needed a tap on the opposing car's fender but he had needed to slow down to match the police car's speed. As it was, he had to use much more force and a scraping sound told him he must have damaged the Jeep's wheel arch.

"We'll have police looking for us now. We need to get there quick…" muttered Brull, a hint of annoyance in his voice.

"I know, I know," Frank replied, his eyes fixed on the rearview mirror.

They came out of the tunnel under blue archways and sped up the carriageway, which curved around to the right. As they came around the bend, Frank saw a line of toll booths ahead. He breathed out and tensed, preparing to smash through them.

"Don't worry, they are empty at this time," said Brull. Frank nodded and gave a sigh of relief. "Good."

The Jeep sped past the unmanned booths and continued east along the carriageway.

"Next right," said Brull.

"Piper? How are you doing?"

In the faint yellow of the street lights that flew by, Piper's face was looking paler by the second.

"Fine," Piper moaned from the passenger seat, head bobbing and hand resting lightly over his gut. "Hurts like hell."

"I bet it does," said Frank. "We're gonna get you patched up as soon as we can, mate, okay?" Piper mumbled an acknowledgement.

"Brull, tell me where the hell we're going?"

Brull gave instructions and within seconds, they were hurtling down a side road.

"Another left," Brull commanded.

The Jeep swerved into another side road and Frank picked up speed again.

"We'll need medical help. Know any doctors, Brull?"

"Yes, there is someone. I will call now."

Brull fished around for his phone.

"What about the hospital?" asked Sarah.

"First place those guys will look, I imagine. They didn't exactly look like they wanted to negotiate."

Frank turned to Piper again and pressed his hand to keep the pressure on.

Gradually, the environment became less industrial and increasingly populated by dilapidated structures. Roads were emptied of any meaningful populace. They had entered a place where the reins had been returned to nature, but not enough that the buildings were entirely out of use. Many still belonged to family stores or were still used as industrial storage facilities, the latter of which provided the perfect cover for covert operations.

Brull gave detailed instructions on the roundabout, discreet roads leading up to the building, a worn out, tannish building with limestone-crusted windows and a hand-painted "no vacancy" sign. Four doors led, presumably, into the large storage blocks.

"Drive around," Brull instructed, pointing towards the upcoming street. Around on the other side, the building more resembled a traditional store with a single, metal door.

Frank eased onto the brakes and brought the Jeep to a halt in front of the building.

"Stay here." Brull hopped out of the back and turned back to Frank. "Get him out. Hurry!"

Frank doubled over to the passenger side and helped his comrade out and towards the building door, assisted by Sarah.

"Brull, can you grab that Med Kit?"

"Si, Si. I'll get it," he replied and opened the vehicle back door to retrieve it. He then moved quickly to open the building door and followed them inside, closing it securely behind them before running ahead to clear the surface of a metal gurney. All three hauled the now near unconscious Piper on top of it.

Frank carefully pried Piper's bloodied hands away from the wound in the side of his stomach and ripped his shirt open to a sea of dark blood.

Brull ripped bandages and prepared a patch. He met Frank's eyes and nodded, the sweat glistening on both men as Piper groaned.

"Stay with us, mate," said Frank urgently. He could barely keep the fear out of his voice.

Brull pressed the dressing over the wound and carefully wrapped a strip of bandage over his stomach and around his back, pulling it tight with each wrap.

"Okay, that'll have to do for now," Brull nodded and Frank pinned it through.

"I'll go look out for that doctor."

Frank nodded. "Stay hidden though." Brull jogged to the front doorway and stepped outside.

Piper stared glassy-eyed at Frank and moved his lips but no sound came out.

Frank leaned closer. "Say again, mate?"

"Pro...protocol. You have to call this in..." He gasped for air, struggling to speak.

Frank leaned even closer so their faces were inches apart. Piper's eyes closed.

"Piper?"

Frank slapped his face and the dark eyes opened again.

"A doctor's on the way. We're gonna fix you up, mate, okay?"

Piper managed a smile. "You think so? I think I'm out this

time...Frank...I.."

His eyes stared straight ahead, staring past Frank at nothing.

"Piper?" Frank felt his pulse and feeling nothing, checked his heartbeat. It confirmed his worst fear.

Frank slammed his hand down on the table in anger and turned away.

"Shit!"

He booted an old tin can on the floor. A flood of anger raced through him. He could have saved him. Maybe they could have pulled in somewhere along the way, hidden, and tried to make a better job on the wound.

Sarah came over and rested a hand on his shoulder as if knowing his thoughts.

"You did all you could, Frank. We were chased all the way."

The door opened and Brull stepped inside, looking expectantly at Frank and Sarah, his eyes moving to Piper's still form on the table.

"How is your amigo?"

Frank slumped down onto the concrete floor and leaned against the bare brick wall, staring straight ahead. A sudden rush of anxiety coursed through his veins, the feeling of being in over his head cast a deep shadow over his thoughts. He saw the faces of Maria, Joe, and Zak for a second in his mind. One mistake and he'd never see them again. A sick feeling overwhelmed his stomach.

"Dead. You might have to cancel your doctor," he said finally.

Brull cursed in Spanish and went over to Piper's body, needing to confirm the news with his own eyes.

They hadn't deserved to die; despite his differences with them, he respected their professionalism. Professionals with a lot of experience had been ruthlessly taken out and outwitted. But by whom? And why?

He took the Glock, quickly released the magazine, and then

slammed it back in. He repeated the action four times as if testing himself. He knew he would need to take more lives to survive this.

"You got a cigarette?"

Brull nodded and threw Frank his pack and lighter. It had been 3 years since he'd lugged on one. *It had been a bad day though,* he thought as he sparked the lighter and inhaled. *A very bad day.*

"What's the next move, Frank?"

Frank threw back the cigarette pack, followed by the lighter and Brull pulled one out for himself.

"I dunno. Get out of the country. Sarah, I'm afraid you'll have to come with me. It's way too dangerous here."

"And you don't think it's dangerous back home? I'll be thrown in prison, or worse!"

Frank shook his head. "Just bear with me. I need to communicate with home, somehow." He looked at his mobile phone and thought for a moment.

"Damn. My laptop is at the hotel."

Brull inhaled sharply. "They will definitely be watching it."

"Who do you think "they" are?"

Brull shrugged as he exhaled grey smoke. "Your guess as good as mine," he said quietly.

Frank started to dial a number on his mobile. "I'm calling Carl. Fuck protocol."

He paced around the space, listening hard, and then cut the call and tried again. After several attempts, he put the phone back in his pocket.

"Impossible to get a connection. We'll need a phone box. You can cancel the doctor but can you arrange to get his body to a morgue?...And there's Greene at the safe house, too."

Brull nodded, flicking ash onto the floor.

Frank walked over to Piper's still corpse on top of the table and began to go through his pockets, making sure there was nothing incriminating. He paused and looked at his still face, now at peace.

"I hate leaving him here."

Chapter 31

Carl made his way up the metal stairs and keyed in a combination at the main door of Studio 31. It was just before 11pm and had been quiet on the roads, so he had arrived quickly after his pager alert. He stepped into the main reception and moved into a corridor before stopping at one of the steel doors. He typed in another sequence of numbers onto the pad before they hissed open and Carl stepped through.

Harry, the comms operator, looked up from his screen and grunted a greeting. He had been there all night and looked it. There was a pile of plastic cups and cans littered all over the table and the remnants of continuous grazing including crisp packets, wrappings, and screwed up burger foil.

"Jesus Christ, Harry, this place looks like a bomb hit it," said Carl, glancing around with an unimpressed glare.

"Sorry, boss. I'll clean it up. It was another quiet one. There's still been no word from Ghost 13."

Carl contemplated this for a second. The team in Cuba; Frank, the others. An operation that David Devlin had taken a personal interest in. He wasn't going to be happy with this latest report.

"Nothing at all? Is the surveillance feed still active? Anything going on there?"

Harry shook his head. There had been no developments he said and began to play the last section of activity on the audio feed; the sound of footsteps leaving the room.

"That was 20:23 hours Havana time. She hasn't returned since."

"That sounds to me like she's packed up and left."

"That's why I thought I'd better call you, sir."

"Yes, rightly so, Harry." Carl sat down and waved at Harry to stop the audio.

"I put a request in with Echelon for any activity in Havana in the last twelve hours, especially the police radio traffic. Should be coming through any time now," said Harry, draining a mug of coffee.

Carl was leaning over Harry's desk, frowning at his monitor. The feeling that something had gone wrong gnawed away at him, like an incoming swarm of wasps, quiet at first, growing louder. He'd worked with Piper and Greene many times and Frank on a handful of missions since his recruitment. Things may have screwed up in the past but there had never been a complete communication breakdown.

Several hours later, a beeping sound alerted both men to the encrypted file that had just appeared on the local server. Harry downloaded the file and opened it via the encryption software as was the process. The data package contained several documents and audio files. After ten minutes of scrolling through the docs, they found a report from the Policía Nacional Revolucionaria transmitters of extensive gunfire in the neighbourhood of Rodriguez Este, exactly where the team had been stationed. The report was at 1:30 am, dated several days after the team's arrival. It could not have been a coincidence.

Carl and Harry kept looking but they found no other references to the incident.

"This doesn't sound good," muttered Carl.

"What do we do?" asked Harry.

"Just keep looking through that lot and call me if you find anything more. I'll have to let upstairs know."

Carl's mind raced as he dialled the number for Devlin. Had his friend, Frank, been caught up in all that gunfire? Hard to know; hopefully he was at the hotel but it didn't seem likely. So what the hell was going on?

Just then, Carl's mobile began buzzing furiously. Another unidentified number.

"Hello?"

"Mr. Cronus...this is Mr. Feldman."

Carl stood up and began to walk to the private room. It was Frank, obviously on an unsecured line.

"Mr. Feldman? It's good to hear from you. I hope you're well? How's business over there?"

"Not so great. Mr. Pegasus and Mr. Aquila are permanently out of the deal. There seems to be a rival business in town."

Carl caught his own breath. Piper and Greene dead? His worst fear from moments earlier had manifested itself.

After a long pause, he spoke. "That's very unfortunate, Mr. Feldman. Are you able to wire or email me further information?"

For a moment, the line went bad and Carl could only hear a transatlantic hiss of noise.

"The telephone equipment is bad here. I'm unable to find or use it right now," Frank said.

Was he referring to the telephone line? No, he meant his laptop, probably lost or destroyed in what had clearly been some kind of ambush. Which was why he had to use a standard phone line. That could complicate things, especially if the Cuban authorities got hold of it. All fingers would point to British agents operating inside Cuba. It would cause an absolute shit storm.

"You'll need to get that phone back if you can. The company wouldn't be happy, especially with all those numbers on it."

"Okay, I'll try. Also, I think we need to leave the country, Mr. Cronus."

Carl paused, trying to think things out. It was getting complicated.

"Can you hang in there and see if Mr. Libre can find you a safe bed for the night? And see if you can sort out the telephone situation. What about Pandora?"

There was a pause and suddenly the line went dead.

***

David Devlin sipped his scotch, wrapped in a black silk dressing gown, his feet warmed in sheepskin lined leather slippers. In front of him was a perfect view of the Thames from his penthouse apartment. Behind the dark jagged shapes of the skyline, the glow of the city at night could be seen, rising and fading into the black sky. He leaned forward, opened his laptop and ran a message from Cuba, a table of six letters in seven columns of which there was a long list of rows. This data file was the input that he ran the encryption process on, generating the ciphertext output that translated the message into something he could understand.

It was a message from Kobra, leading the Russian team.

TO MARQUIS. UNKNOWN MAN AND PANDORA PURSUED WITH-OUT SUCCESS. VISITED G13 +1 DOWN BUT OTHERS ESCAPED. PANDORA WITH THEM. AWAIT INSTRUCTIONS.

Devlin exhaled heavily and downed the last of his scotch before banging the crystal glass onto the coffee table.

Bloody idiots! What was he paying them for? They had lost them even after he had given them the safe house address on a silver platter.

The GCHQ Director tossed the laptop aside and then stood looking over the city of London, watching a tugboat make its way down the river. The pink dawn sky was turning to a clear blue, the seagulls circled both sides of the water eagerly scouting for food.

Interesting that one of the Ghost 13 team had helped the whistle-blower though. It kept them all in the same neat package. Kept things simple. He just needed to find them.

Just then, his mobile chirped. It was Carl Paterson updating him. They had heard from one of the team who had confirmed that two were dead. Devlin already knew but acted with shock. Was there anything they could do? Pull them out was the suggestion. Perhaps. "Let me think about that," Devlin had replied. "Keep me posted on where they go and I'll look at options. Try and confirm what is happening with Pandora. Where is she?"

Carl said he would and the call ended.

Devlin felt himself breathe easier. It sounded like he could get their location soon enough and then things would be back on track. He sat back down with his laptop, logging into his MI6 profile. He tried to find any Ghost 13 files. Nothing existed. Then he remembered that Keller had been instructed to keep it off all official databases, for now at least. Probably wise considering the box of secrets Pandora had opened. The entire system and all procedures would need a massive overhaul when this whole gang fuck was over with.

Bowen. The name suddenly came into his mind. Overheard from a discussion, one that probably shouldn't have taken place but did anyway. Was it with Keller or the time he met Carl Paterson? No matter, as he remembered now. Frank Bowen. He was 'Auditor', the surveillance man.

Devlin dialled the number for Keller.

"Keller. Tell me about Frank Bowen."

Chapter 32

Brull pulled over several hundred yards away from the hotel on the opposite side to see the front entrance. The early morning sun cast sharp shadows across the street, an occasional taxi or scooter hurtled by, and birds scavenged at a heap of rubbish on the sidewalk. From their vantage point, they could see a group of men play cards on a table down a side street. A boy of around nine or ten raced a bicycle up and down past the card players.

"What are the chances of police having been here?" Frank asked. He was thinking about the chase through the kitchens and the gunshot. The hotel would surely have called the police.

Brull laughed. "It is early. There'll be no police here. But maybe in an hour, they come."

They watched as a trio of tourists came out of the hotel entrance and milled around, looking at a map. There was a couple in their 50s and a tall, heavyset, blonde man in a pale blue shirt. A member of the front desk, a young male, stepped out behind them and appeared to give them directions.

"Can we go past, slowly, and park around the side?" Frank asked.

Brull nodded and fired up the engine and the car cruised past the tourists who were glancing and nodding as the hotel man pointed down the street. The blonde man glanced at the car briefly before returning his attention back to a map.

"Was that one of them?" Sarah asked.

Brull turned into a narrow road on the same block.

Frank shook his head. "Can't be sure, I never really got a good look at any of them. Apart from the shooter behind the wall, I think he was dark-haired," said Frank.

Before heading to the hotel, they had stopped in a store for new clothes. Frank had bought another plain shirt, a Panama hat, and large shades. Sarah bought a demure sunhat, a t-shirt, and jeans. Anyone glancing at them would automatically think they were Average Joe tourists.

"Are you sure you should do this? Maybe too dangerous," stated Brull as he stopped in sight of the hotel rear entrance and switched off the engine.

Frank sighed. "I have to try and get my laptop back. It could be damaging to the company if it fell into the wrong hands. Trust me, I'd much rather leave it but I have to try."

"And if something happens to you? What do we do?" she asked.

Frank looked at Brull.

"You can go on your merry way, I guess. But we can't protect you. I take it you have a plan to disappear somewhere?"

"I had disappeared until you found me. But, yes, Frank, I can look after myself. I would like to check if there are any messages at reception though."

Frank shook his head. "Not going to happen. Too risky. Let me go in first." He turned to Brull. "Can I borrow your lighter?"

Brull nodded, looking at him quizzically but handed it over.

He stepped out of the car and walked toward the rear entrance, a metal gate that led into a small courtyard garden and a doorway, just around the corner from the kitchens. Frank inhaled and stepped inside the hotel and a long corridor with guest rooms. Turning left, away from where he knew the kitchen and bar were, Frank padded along to the front area of the hotel, his eyes scanning the walls and ceilings as he went. A maid came out of one of the rooms with towels and smiled at Frank before heading in the opposite direction. He came to another external door that led out into the inner courtyard. It was breakfast time and most of the guests were enjoying their first coffee of the day.

Frank scanned the faces looking for anything out of place; a Spanish looking couple, an elderly man in his 60s and two European looking women were left in the courtyard. There were no signs of any police. Frank continued down the corridor; ahead were double internal doors to the bar and restaurant and just before was a fire alarm on the ceiling. Frank peeked through the doors and checked the bar; only a barman cleaning tables. He closed them again and took out Brull's lighter, lit it, and held it up to the fire alarm sensor.

Within seconds, a loud wailing sound echoed through the corridors and Frank immediately rushed to the courtyard, making his way across to the metal steps that ascended the different levels. There were shouts from several hotel staff and the remaining tourists looked around in confusion, looking for guidance. Within a minute, Frank was on the fourth level and approaching his room; he glanced down and saw staff rounding up any stray guests, showing them to the exit through the reception area. Then he caught sight of the tall blonde man in the pale blue shirt who had been outside the front and was now walking towards the steps Frank had just climbed. A concierge approached him, pointing towards the front of the hotel and then got a punch in the gut for his trouble. The man crumpled to the floor.

Definitely one of the Russians.

Frank quickly unlocked his room door, went inside and looked around, his heart sinking as his eyes rested on the empty space on the table where he had left the laptop. Taken. Either by the authorities, the hotel staff, or more likely the Russian. The suitcase he had brought with the surveillance equipment was also gone. No use hanging around. He slipped out of the door and looked down at the lower levels and the courtyard. There was no sign of blonde guy but it wasn't easy to see from that angle. Frank walked around the opposite direction so he could see the steps better, keeping close to the wall and then he locked eyes with the Russian who was looking back up from two levels down. Shit!

He started to bolt, running fast along the terrace and then up the third flight of steps. Frank looked around mind racing. One of the rooms? He tried a few doors. Locked.

Just a metre above, he could see the edge of the terracotta tiles of the roof, under which flower pots hung on chains from the gutters. At the end of the walkway were black painted railings. He eased himself slowly onto the railing so he was standing on it, steadying himself with his hands on the roof edge. On the other side was an eighty-foot drop onto the side street. One slip and he was dead. The men were still playing cards and now seemed to be arguing.

Frank hauled his body upwards until he was bent forward on his stomach, the top half of him now on the roof. A running footfall on the metal steps got closer and from his position, he could see the Russian appear along the walkway, looking around for him and clearly puzzled by his disappearance. Frank edged forward, inch by inch on his stomach until his whole body was flat on the angled part of the roof. A piece of tile broke loose under his weight and slipped down onto the street below.

Shit! He must have heard it.

The angled side of the roof flattened out at the top and Frank eased himself onto his hands and knees, slowly moving across to the other side. Behind him, the sound of scraping from the railings. The Russian was on his tail, moving quicker without the fear of making noise.

On the high roof, the skyline of Havana made an impressive view, a blue sky overhead without a cloud in sight. Frank jogged across the flat section, past a large ventilation box that pumped out air from below, until he was on the far side of the building.

Peering over, he could see another angled section of tiled roof and the street below where Brull and Sarah waited in the car. He moved along the edge, looking for a way off.

A glimpse of a window balcony.

Glancing back, he saw the Russian's blonde head bopping up and down as he climbed up to the flat section.

Frank crouched and moved onto the tiles, crab fashion, moving slowly to where he would be above the balcony.

Running footsteps.

The Russian was at the edge of the flat further along and looked down at Frank, a wolfish grin appearing on his angled face. He turned around and eased down onto the tiles, copying Frank's crouch style and began to move towards him. Frank was easing himself over the edge, looking down at the balcony below his feet. It was a twelve-foot drop but it only stood a few metres out. The Russian was right on him. It was fight or drop time.

A boot stomp-kicked Frank's left hand and he grimaced in pain. He began to swing himself away from the building to gain momentum so he could land in the right place and not risk falling back over the balcony.

"I hope you can fly," taunted the Russian as he continued to kick and grind at this hand and fingers. Lifting his foot for a second to slam a boot down hard gave Frank the chance. Letting go, he dropped, holding his body as upright as possible. His feet slammed onto the balcony and he fell back against the railing with the impact, hands desperately grabbing the top of the metal rails to hold himself.

A tile smashed by his right foot as the soles of Russian boots appeared over the side, directly above him. Frank reached down for a plant pot and banged it against the window, cracking and weakening the glass, and then elbowed the rest with hard but directed jerks. When there was enough space, he reached in with his hand and unlocked the window and hauled it upwards. The Russian had maneuvered so he was directly above him and dropped just as Frank scrambled into the hotel room. He heard the slam of boots behind him but didn't look, running hard and fast across the room and out into the corridor. The alarm had stopped but the hallways were still empty of any guests or staff as Frank bolted down the stairwell to the ground floor. At last, he reached the rear entrance where he had first entered the hotel and ran onto the street towards the car, which Brull had sensibly turned around engine idling.

Frank jumped into the passenger seat.

"Go! Go!"

Brull did as asked and screeched off towards the main street ahead of them.

Frank turned around to see the blonde Russian sprint onto the road through the rear window. He came to a stop and spat on the ground as he watched the vehicle speed off.

Sarah was staring back at Frank, wide-eyed.

"Whose bloody idea was it to get the laptop back, huh?" Frank asked, flashing her a cheeky grin.

Sarah sighed, frowning at him.

"That'll be your great idea," she replied.

Chapter 33

They drove back towards Centro Habana on Zanja, a long freeway that cut through the heart of the city taking them east to Calzada de Zapata in Vedado. There was an odd architectural mix of crumbling pillared mansions and ugly pancake stacked 1950's high rises that housed the city's population.

The vehicle headed into a labyrinth of Cuadras, neat one hundred metre blocks that made the grid layout straightforward to follow, street signs in the form of small stone blocks placed at every corner.

Brull nodded as he swung into yet another turning. "This one, it is Calle twenty."

"This place is a maze," Frank muttered as they pulled into an avenue, looking much like the others with compact, brightly painted houses nestled behind a row of palms. The car slowed and pulled over, the engine idling, as they both looked at the house Brull had specified.

"Stay here and I'll take a look," said Brull. It was quiet, barely anyone around in the midday haze. A lone dog rummaged around a group of bins, tugging at a black bag with its teeth. Brull got out of the vehicle and strolled across the dusty avenue and then disappeared into the house. After a few minutes, he returned and leaned into the passenger window.

"All clear," he said, glancing down the street.

Frank turned off the engine and then took the Glock out of his backpack. He checked it briefly and then tucked it into his belt under his shirt, then got out of the car with his backpack.

"Let's go, Sarah."

They went inside the house that had small sparsely furnished rooms with crumbling walls and the usual ill repair Frank was beginning to become accustomed to.

"It's okay, all safe here," Brull said.

"Let me look around," said Frank. He walked through to a central living area that had a large dining table and led to a hallway towards the rear. He passed a spiral staircase that led upstairs and carried on walking to a modest kitchen that had the bare basics. At the back was a small courtyard surrounded by high brick walls, and a metal table and chairs, rusting from lack of use. He then carefully moved up the staircase to see two sparsely furnished rooms. When he came back downstairs, Brull and Sarah were sitting at the table. Frank joined them and slumped down with a sigh of relief.

"So what is this place?" he asked.

"It belongs to a relative. They are away and only I have the key," said Brull.

Sarah was looking at Frank with narrowed eyes.

"I really appreciate you helping me but I'm not going back Frank," she said evenly.

Frank sighed and avoided her gaze, studying an old cross that was nailed onto the whitewashed wall instead.

"It's a bit dangerous with that gang running around out there."

"Maybe I should take my chances."

Frank looked at her with an expression of concern etched on his face.

"Why don't you wait until morning and then decide?" he asked.

"We eat and rest for now," Brull interjected.

Sarah, her face pale with exhaustion, seemed to think for a moment and reluctantly nodded.

Frank placed his palms flat down on the table top and stood up. "Good. Right now, I need to update Cronus on where we are and try and find some kind of exit to this situation. It's getting out of hand."

"I'll take you to a phone box. Maybe you can get permission to go home."

Frank nodded and thought of home. That was one place he yearned to be right now.

Chapter 34

Frank was quiet as Dante Brull served up a stew that had been cooking for over an hour. He had contacted Carl Paterson in London, updated him that they were in another location, and was told to sit tight and wait. Frank had then reluctantly told him that Pandora was with him, something that hadn't gone down too well. But what the hell was he supposed to have done when another group had crashed the party? She had to be protected and if he had to choose again, he would have played it the same way. As he had grown closer to Sarah, he wondered what would become of her. She was a good person. Sure, she had an agenda but fundamentally, she wasn't that far away from his own moral compass.

Sarah poured water into mugs and laid out bowls on the wooden table and they all sat down.

"This smells really good, Dante," Sarah said after dipping a piece of bread into the stew; she was looking at Frank.

"It is if I might say. My mother showed me to cook this dish, God rest her soul. It is Potaje de Frijoles Blancos, white bean stew. "

Frank didn't wait to be asked and dived right in, shovelling the stew into his mouth and the mixture of beans, beef, peppers, and cumin tasted incredible.

"So, your family. I take it your mother is no longer with us?" asked Sarah. Brull crossed his chest and pointed upwards.

"She is in God's hands now, along with my father."

Sarah nodded solemnly and then glanced at Frank again. "Everything okay, Frank?"

He looked up from his food. "Yes. Just thinking. Wondering why they want us to stay here."

"They re-think probably. Making new plans," Brull said, shrugging.

A gust of wind slammed one of the window shutters at the rear of the small house, causing their heads to turn.

"Weather reports a hurricane coming in tonight. But nothing serious, as we should only get the tail of it, but it will still be choppy," said Brull.

Just as he was standing up to deal with the shutter, the light dimmed and then cut out completely, leaving them in darkness, apart from a faint residue of light that penetrated through the windows from outside.

"What's going on?" Sarah's voice.

"Ah, another power cut," Brull replied and he soon had a flame from his lighter to guide him. "It's happening more and more in Cuba. I get the gas lamp."

Frank stopped eating and stood up. "I don't like it...are you sure it's not just us?"

They both walked to the front and Brull glanced out through the blind.

"No, everywhere is out. Just a normal blackout. I check the fuse box."

"Are there any other ways in here besides the front and back doors?"

"Only windows."

"Let's get them all closed and bolted up tight," Frank said. "It might be an idea to have someone stay awake through the night."

Brull checked the front road, which was quiet, and closed up the window shutters outside and locked the windows. Frank headed to the rear courtyard and closed up the two windows at the back, before looking up at the high wall towering over the property at the end of the courtyard. He heard the sound of neighbours talking as they moved chairs and loose items back inside their house. The rumour of the hurricane had spread.

Brull volunteered to take the first shift on staying awake. "You will need sleep, more than me. I will wake you at 4."

Frank and Sarah bedded down on roll-out mattresses in the small room upstairs while Brull cleaned up before returning to the table to sip coffee and smoke cigarettes. The wind was increasing outside as if angered and its powerful gusts slammed the cuadras. Brull fished around in a cupboard and found what he was looking for, a fresh bottle of rum to perk up his coffee.

***

Viktor Kozel scanned the row of casas through his night vision binoculars. The chaos of the hurricane would give his men perfect cover for the infiltration of the house. Although, it might also be a hindrance. He put down the binoculars and turned to the other three men in the back of the MPV. "20 minutes and then we go."

There was a collective groan. The men had been cooped up in the vehicle for 3 hours now and were keen to get moving.

The palms on the street were alive and swaying like demented dancers, the gusts played havoc with trash bins and debris flew across the air.

"It getting worse. Maybe we should hold off," said the bald Leonid Duskin from the back of the vehicle. Tarasenko and Glukhov both turned and glared at him. They didn't want to hang back for another few hours or even minutes.

"We have one chance to get them. There was a big fuck up last time, remember? So, definitely no room for failure now!" Kozel rasped. He hated it when his crew got itchy feet and whined. Duskin dolefully clasped his huge hands together and peered back out of the window.

Kozel sighed heavily and looked at his watch. They had been there long enough. He turned to the blonde Taransenko and the smaller, wily Glukhov and nodded.

***

The two men slid out of the rear doors and walked as best they could in the screeching wind, heading back along the block, parallel to the street where their targets were holed up. Their figures moved slowly against the force that nature threw against them, their dark clothes flapping violently. The tall figure of Taransenko suddenly ducked as a piece of corrugated iron roof flew past him.

"This is crazy!" he shouted to his comrade. Glukhov didn't answer but gave his comrade a look of understanding. Both men bent their heads and headed for the alleyway, which gave them some respite from the storm. The noise level was quieter there and they moved quickly down the narrow rubbish-strewn alley, counting the houses behind a high brick wall until they reached the target.

Tarasenko squatted down with his back against the wall and gave Glukhov a foot up with his clasped hands, grunting at the weight. Glukhov leveraged himself up. Tarasenko then changed position to support him with his shoulders as his comrade peeked over the wall to check the situation.

The howling wind tore away at loose window shutters and there was the occasional smash or thud of objects crashing into each other.

Seeing it was all clear, Glukhov eased himself onto the top of the wall and reached down a hand to pull up his comrade. They both eased themselves down into the small courtyard on the far side and crouched in the shadows, assessing the rear door and window to the house.

***

The Ford MPV rocked gently, buffered by the rasping tail of the hurricane as Viktor Kozel and Leonid Duskin sat in the front, smoking. They watched the palms lined down the road swaying and bending more and more erratically and shifted uncomfortably in their leather seats.

"Getting worse, I think," mumbled Dustin. Just then, the phone in Kozel's hand vibrated.

"They're in the back. Time to move."

The two men clambered out of the vehicle. Duskin's side was receiving the full brunt of the wind and he struggled to close the door for a moment, and then threw a backpack over his shoulder. Soon, the two figures were slowly making their way down the street.

***

Brull was sitting at the table, having drained his second glass of neat rum, and shook his head to revive himself. It had been a long time since he had caught any sleep. The wind, coming in waves, made the whole house creak and groan, reminding Brull of an old ship. Window shutters rattled continuously, especially the door in the kitchen at the back of the house. Brull's eyelids flickered. The food, rum, and lack of sleep all catching up on him.

Some small part of his brain was alerted to a noise that cut through the howling wind and rattling shutters, a sound like a footstep, barely audible from the kitchen. He slowly swivelled his torso around to the bookshelf and his hand found the Glock, where he had left it. Brull checked the weapon and slowly stood up.

The dancing shadows from the gas lamp made Brull more anxious and then they faded into blackness as Brull paced slowly down the carpeted hallway. He had been at the house long enough to know to avoid a small table that had a large vase placed on it. The back door that had been rattling was silent now and Brull felt the rush of outside air from the kitchen, which died in a moment. A hand grabbed his mouth and he felt a knee slam into the small of his back, sending shock waves of pain throughout his body. In the flash of his final thoughts, Brull realised they were already in the house. He had failed to be ready and on guard. He had let in the enemy. Then a hunter's knife opened his throat, sending warm blood streaming down his chest and his body, held by the unseen figure, he rapidly weakened and slumped into oblivion.

***

Frank stood on a tube station platform under a bluish hue of light as if in a hospital or laboratory. The service lift dinged at the end of the floor, a green light announcing its arrival.

Footsteps echoed from the blackness of the tunnel against a backdrop of hissing wind. Frank stood facing the blackness, feet apart as the steps grew nearer. Then a light, no, two lights. The train was coming, distant but getting nearer. The figure appeared, walking in the middle of the tracks, the same side as the train. Frank shouted and as he did so, he saw it was Greene. Thomas Greene, his colleague in Ghost 13. The lights were brighter now, the whoosh of the wind rushed the platform.

Frank shouted to warn Greene, who hadn't seemed to have noticed the train. He just looked at Frank and then made a signal to him with his hands, as if trying to tell him something, for him to back away and move back.

"Greene! Get off the tracks...Train!"

Suddenly, Greene's head seemed to pop in a spray of red mist as if blasted from an unseen vantage point. There followed a violent banging sound as the train slammed into his body and into the station.

Frank sat up, his deep sleep ended by the banging window shutter that had worked loose in the wind. He rolled out from under the sheet on the makeshift bedroll and padded over to the window. He glanced into the darkness outside that seemed to boil with the chaos of the hurricane and pulled the shutters together and closed the latch.

"Surprised you could sleep at all with that racket," came Sarah's voice from the bed. Frank returned to the bedroll on the floor. "Yeah, must have been dog-tired. You get any shut-eye?"

"Not much. I think this is more than a tailwind."

There was a distant clank and thud from somewhere. It was hard to tell. The wind sounded like a freight train and was getting louder and more violent.

Frank looked at his watch and tutted. "4:30. Damn, Brull should have woken me." He jumped up and pulled on his jeans and shirt.

"If you feel the need to make tea, I wouldn't say no," she said. Frank could sense her smirking in the gloom.

"Sure thing, madam. Peeled grapes with that?"

"Yep."

Frank descended the stairs that circled down to the centre of the casa.

Chapter 35

Only flickering shadows from the gas lamp greeted Frank as he stepped onto the tiled floor. The table was empty, apart from the overloaded ashtray and a bottle of Havana Club. Frank cursed Brull for not waking him up, but now he was suddenly concerned.

Where the hell had he gone?

And then he noticed Brull's Glock was missing from the top of the bookshelf and the chair he had sat in was pulled back as if an imprint of some earlier scene. He wasn't in the toilet as that was upstairs and he would surely have heard him. Perhaps he was checking the back courtyard?

As Frank moved across the room, he caught a glimpse of some kind of shape on the hallway floor. As he edged closer, a wisp of light from the lamp behind him revealed Brull's lifeless body, his eyes staring into the abyss. Frank froze, suddenly fully aware that he was in danger. As soon as that thought crossed his mind, an arm had him by the throat, crushing his larynx and his ability to breathe. He ground his chin down to try and give himself leverage but his vision was tunnelling, the oxygen to his brain dissipating fast.

Suddenly, the pressure lifted from his neck and he could breathe. A cold piece of familiar steel pushed against his skull, indicating the game was over.

"Do not move or you will be dead meat," whispered a gruff,

accented voice in his ear. He felt the presence of another figure nearby and then saw a figure with some kind of goggles on. Night vision goggles.

"Okay," he said. The figure in front of him removed his goggles and shone a torchlight onto his face.

Frank squinted against the blinding torch, making his irises contract suddenly. He held a hand up to shield the light.

"Where is the woman?"

Frank shook his head, wishing he had been more careful. There was light to see now and he looked down onto Brull's body. It made him feel sick inside. He had liked Brull and grown to trust him and now the poor bastard was dead.

"Did you have to kill him?"

The taller figure pushed him back into the large living room. "Just get your hands above head."

They moved back into the room and Frank stood, his hands on his head, back against the assailant.

"What do you want?" Frank asked.

He noticed the smaller of the men begin to creep up the stairwell, his pistol held out in front of him.

"Don't hurt her!" he rasped.

"Shut up," the masked figure growled and nudged a steel pistol against his cranium.

Minutes later, Sarah was standing in the middle of the room and they were both waiting, staring at the men. The taller one was the same man who had chased Frank across the rooftops at the hotel.

One of the intruder's phones buzzed and he walked to the front door and let in a stocky man with a Mohawk and a black goatee beard, dressed in a tight dark tee shirt and military fatigue trousers. The man studied Frank and Sarah for a moment before speaking to the others in what Frank recognised as Russian.

The assailant Frank had rumbled with moments earlier took out a roll of duct tape, turned Frank around, ordering him to put his hands behind his back, and wrapped the tape around his wrists. He then did the same to Sarah before taping both their mouths.

A thought came into Frank's mind. Something his old trainer, Sam Keane, had shown him. He buried the thought for now and looked over at the men. Who were they? It was the same crew that had ambushed them, he was certain of that. Russian secret service, the FSB? It seemed plausible.

Suddenly, their heads were covered with black hoods and they were led outside via the front door, where Frank felt the angry winds that continued to sweep through the city. They were pushed and bundled into the back of a vehicle and ordered to lie down and keep quiet.

Frank heard the engine start and felt the vehicle reversing fast to the end of the road and then away onto the main roads. After twenty minutes, he guessed they must be leaving the city and wondered about their fate.

Chapter 36

The two burly men pushed Frank and Sarah through the warehouse door, shouting in Russian. Their hoods were taken off and Frank saw they were in a huge, dilapidated space. Lengths of rusted chains hung from pulleys on rails that crisscrossed along the entire area. Frank's eyes darted along the boarded up windows, desperately looking for clues to a possible escape route. The windows looked well secured with metal sheets bolted onto them. Only a gap in the warehouse roof, letting in the early dawn light, at least thirty feet above them offered any hope and that looked like an extreme long shot. He glanced at Sarah, who was clearly frightened and tried to give her a reassuring look whilst struggling to hold his own uncertainty at bay.

The taller blonde thug took the duct tape off their mouths and commanded Sarah to lie on a pair of wooden planks that had been set on the ground by an old piece of machinery in the centre of the warehouse. She refused and he swung and punched her in the stomach. Sarah recoiled and bent double, gasping for air.

"Hey! You bastard..." Frank lurched forward but was grabbed by his arms from behind.

The bald man with a scar pushed her down onto the planks and proceeded to tie her hands and feet with rope before tipping the planks upward so her feet were higher up than her head. The other man then placed bricks underneath to prop them up.

A sound of footsteps echoed up towards the roof space, growing louder and Frank looked and saw the man with a black goatee beard and Mohawk from earlier coming in behind them. Frank noticed he had an arrogant swagger and as he came closer, he saw the tentacles of barbed wire tattooed on his throat for the first time. He held up a closed laptop and gave Frank a little wave with it.

"Have you missed this, Mr. Bowen?"

Frank stayed tight-lipped and just stared at the Russian, who was assessing him with his dark, cold eyes.

"We could use the information on this. Your employer. MI6, isn't it?"

He broke into a wolf-like smile at his continued silence and threw the laptop across to the blonde Russian, who caught it haphazardly. He balanced it upright on the shelving of a nearby machine and folded his arms.

"So, my friends. We have searched you from head to foot as well as your hotel room and found nothing. Where are the documents?" the one with the mohawk asked.

Sarah took a deep breath, seemingly digging deep for a stronger resolve.

Viktor clicked his fingers and the scar-faced henchman walked a few metres to a bucket and pulled out a damp cloth before placing it over Sarah's face. She seemed to know what was coming and took a deep breath before it covered her.

"What are you doing?" Frank protested.

He suddenly got a sharp kick in the small of his back from the other man standing behind him, throwing Frank onto his hands and knees. He grunted in pain and spat onto the dusty concrete floor.

Viktor spoke in Russian to the large, scar-faced one, who pulled him back onto his feet. Frank stared hard at the man in front of him, who smiled and took a piece of folded paper from his pocket. He opened it up and held it in front of Frank's face.

"Take a close look. You see who this is? You recognise?"

Frank blinked at the grainy photograph on the fax, momentarily disbelieving the image in front of him. It was Maria and Joe, both blindfolded. They each held a separate side of *The Times* newspaper. Conveniently placed underneath the image was a zoom shot of the newspaper's date: November 14th. A few days ago.

A sickening feeling in Frank's stomach overwhelmed him and he closed his eyes, trying to contain the rage that overcame him.

"You fucking bastard!" he mouthed quietly.

Viktor sucked in air through his teeth and stared impassively at Frank.

"Your girlfriend and son are in our hands. Think carefully about that. They are a long way from here and their lives are now up to you. Now, tell me, where are the documents?"

Frank wondered: *Why only Joe? Had they missed baby Zak?* He must be with the babysitter or one of Maria's friends. Thank god for that at least. He glanced at Sarah on the bench, attempting to breathe through the face cloth.

"How can I be sure you'd let them go?" Frank asked bitterly.

Viktor laughed, a low guttural sound that carried through the huge, open space.

"You don't. You have no cards to play at all."

Frank said nothing, his mind a whirlwind of questions, mixed with pain and anger. How had they found them? A tracking device? Someone in Liberatus? Carl knew where they were...and who else in Ghost 13? He knew the Russian was right. His options were zero, but he still couldn't give them the answer they wanted. Only Sarah could. He glanced down at her covered face, sinking and rising quickly as the mould of her mouth in the cloth desperately tried to suck in air.

Just then, goatee took a pager from his pocket, which beeped, and stared at it for a second, frowning. He looked up at the scarred thug still holding Frank.

He rasped in Russian and Frank suddenly felt hands grab his arms, pulling him to his feet followed by another shove in the shoulder for good measure.

Viktor began striding across the floor, away from them back towards the main entrance door from where he had come.

Frank caught a glimpse of the short stocky one pulling over a hose that snaked its way back into the depths of the warehouse towards Sarah. A glugging sound welled within its tube and suddenly, a stream of water burst free. The other man switched on a radio that rested on the old machine behind them and loud pop music began to blare out.

Sarah was already struggling to breathe, her lungs crying out for air when the water hit her face. It was a matter of seconds before she felt panic well up inside her, her mouth gulping for precious air but there was none. She felt like she was suffocating, her muscles burning, contracting with every second. Just as she felt like she had reached her last possible breath, the water stopped and the cloth came off. She gulped in oxygen, her face reddened by the near-asphyxiation, and then choked as phlegm caught in her throat.

"Where are the documents?" the Russian voice asked again.

"I don't know. Please stop," she pleaded.

"You don't know? You have the documents before. Where are they?"

Sarah choked and breathed in, a nasty wheezing sound that carried up into the roof space.

As Frank was pushed towards a door at the back of the warehouse, he turned his head to try and see what was happening.

"Let her go...she knows nothing!" he shouted, trying to buy time if nothing else.

The Russian grabbed Frank by the scruff of his neck and shoved him against a metal door, his body hitting it hard, causing a shockwave throughout his body.

He then pressed his Glock pistol hard against the side of Frank's head, causing him to freeze. The pain already replaced with a feeling of imminent death but surprisingly, he felt no fear, only concern for Sarah. His family. Frank felt his heart race hard in his chest.

"Keep your mouth shut, unless you tell me information. Under-stand?" the Russian growled.

Frank breathed hard through his nose, his face pushed against the door.

"Yes...I understand."

The man pulled the weapon away and shoved open the heavy door, which revealed a corridor leading to other rooms. Frank was pushed into the first room that had once been an office. Water dripped from a crack in the ceiling onto a large desk. An old filing cabinet lay flat on its side on the ground and a scattering of papers and files that had been pulled from the drawers lay discarded next to it. Frank felt another shove against his back. The Russian then grabbed his shoulder, turning Frank to face him and then punched him hard in the stomach. Frank grunted loudly in pain as he doubled up and reeled backwards.

Scarface laughed, a low, repeating staccato sound.

Getting into the spirit of the occasion, he grabbed Frank again and threw a massive right hook across his jaw. Frank fell backwards against the cabinet and crashed down onto the hard ground with a thud. A dull blackness circled, threatening his conscious state, and then the large hands grabbed him by the shirt collar and hauled him back up onto his feet. The laugh came again but muffled this time.

Frank forced himself to focus, his vision blurring. The thug was grinning ear to ear and his breath stank of stale coffee.

"You having plenty of fun, clever guy?"

***

Through the pain around his jaw and stomach, Frank knew one thing for certain: he had to get out of there. Not just away from this maniac but because Maria and Joe were in real danger. He had no idea how he would find them but there had to be a way.

Scarface turned his back on Frank momentarily, looking around for something. Some rope to replace the duct tape perhaps. Frank didn't care. It was the moment he had been waiting for, the little trick Sam Keane, his old trainer, had shown him years before. Without further hesitation, Frank quickly raised his bonded hands above his head. He pulled down with as much force as he could, pulling his arms apart, using all his strength, and as he did so, the duct tape broke with a snap, freeing his hands.

He lunged a thrust kick with his heel against the back of the Russian's right knee with all his force. Crumbling onto his knees, the big guy yelped in agony. Pivoting quickly, he threw a roundhouse kick at the Russian's upper arm in an attempt to make him drop the pistol. The Russian hunched up at the impact but stubbornly held on.

Continuing his momentum, Frank jumped forward, thrusting his knee into the centre of the Russian's back. The thug fell forward, hitting the ground hard with a thump and Frank immediately grabbed the hand holding the weapon, smashing it up and down, crushing his knuckles onto the concrete.

The Russian, still strong despite the blows, began pushing himself upwards with his knees and left hand, attempting to roll Frank off. Quickly realising the danger, Frank grabbed the back of his skull and smacked it hard repeatedly against the concrete floor.

The man groaned woefully and a puddle of dark red blood pooled from his nose, soaking the floor. Frank was now able to disarm the Russian, peeling each finger off the barrel of the gun. Even half unconscious, the big man didn't want to release the weapon. Frank smacked his head again for good measure and was finally able to pull it free from his clutching hand.

Frank stood up, breathing heavily, his senses of his surroundings slowly coming back to him as the adrenaline left his system. Hearing a rasp and scuffle, Frank turned, surprised to see the Russian slowly pushing himself onto all fours, mumbling and swearing in his native tongue. This guy was one mean mother.

Reaching down, Frank cupped his head and drove his knee hard into the big man's jaw with a sickening crack. Scarface hit the ground, finally out for the count.

Frank, unsteady on his feet, checked the chamber in the Glock before wiping spittle from his lips. He tucked it into his belt and went back into the corridor. He slowly opened the door to the warehouse and was met with Cuban Salsa beats from the radio. Then a shout. Sarah's voice.

"Get off me!"

What the hell were the bastards doing?

Frank slipped out the door, moving slowly behind a large piece of nearby machinery that ran parallel down the length of the warehouse. He needed to surprise them as they could easily gun him down if they saw him, even just a few feet away.

Frank kept low and glanced quickly around the edge of the rusty bulk. One of the men had his back to him but the other was on the far side of Sarah and would see him coming from this position. He doubled back and then moved towards the men from his original position.

The blonde man was pulling her jeans down and had them around her knees, taunting her as he did so.

"Priyatnogo appyetita! Enjoy it, bitch."

Frank heard her gasps and sobs, which only steeled him further for what he had to do. He let emotion evaporate off his body as he crept quickly across the wide, open space between them while being careful not to kick an empty can or stupidly trip on the numerous bricks strewn on the ground. He was scurrying now, closing the space. The pistol was aimed high in front of him; the weapons training he had received gave him the technical know-how but didn't stop his sweaty palms or his thundering heartbeat.

Ten feet away and the tinny sound of their radio increased. The smaller thug threw the cloth back over Sarah's face, while the blonde one had pulled her jeans off and was forcing her legs apart, whilst trying to undo his own trousers. Sarah kicked and struggled.

"Okay, bitch...you like Russian?"

Seven feet. Their backs to him.

Frank gripped the pistol harder, checking the safety catch was off.

Five feet.

The blonde thug said something to his associate, who followed his order and held one of her legs, attempting to restrain her. Frank noticed the other had his weapon tucked into the back of his belt. Good.

Three feet.

The man with the dark hair sensed a presence behind him and his face began to turn but before he could react, his body was pushed forward with the force of a direct head shot from Frank's weapon. The other thug turned at the sound of gunfire, hand already moving behind for his piece. Frank swung his pistol around to aim at his head and fired again. A hole ripped violently into his forehead, his facial expression held a look of surprise as his body slumped down onto the floor with his associate.

Both down. The leader would be fully alerted and there was no way to know if there were others in the building.

Frank quickly put the weapon down and removed the cloth that covered Sarah's face. She sucked in air hard, her eyes wide with shock as she focused on Frank. He quickly switched off the radio and began untying the rope as he spoke softly.

"Sarah, it's okay. Everything's alright. They're not going to hurt you anymore." Sarah nodded. Frank glanced towards the front of the warehouse. No sign of any back up yet. The rope was tight and he was wasting valuable time. Finally, he got her hand free and he moved onto the other one.

A slight noise from the far end, boots carefully creeping up metal steps. Frank looked across the floor and then, for the first time, saw the top of the stairwell leading down to some basement. A glimpse of the familiar black hair as the other Russian quickly glanced over the floor towards Frank and fired a shot that whizzed past and shattered something behind him.

Frank returned a shot. The bullet ricocheted, causing sparks on a metal wall plate and the head quickly ducked down. The sound of descending footsteps as the Russian retreated.

Frank saw that the noise had been his laptop, now lying shattered all over the floor in pieces. Shit! He returned to grappling with the knot in the rope and got it free. He helped her get off the planks and supported her weight as she moved onto her feet.

"Can you lie low here?" he asked, hating to leave her. She nodded, relieved to have some time to recover. She glanced at the bodies on the floor. "No problem." Then she looked at him. "Please, be careful, Frank."

"I will."

Frank moved behind another hulk of machinery, his pistol aimed squarely at the stairwell.

Chapter 37

Moving forward slowly, Frank kept his eyes fixed on where he had seen the Russian. His thoughts were a mix of self-preservation and keeping the last man alive for questioning. Suddenly, the Russian appeared in a flash of movement, firing a volley of shots in his direction. Frank dived to the hard floor, barrel rolled behind a crate, and returned fire.

A shout from the Russian just before bolting out of the entrance door told him he had hit the target but he instantly regretted firing. He needed him alive. There was a dull sound of a car engine gunning into action outside. Frank, rising to his feet, moved quickly towards the door, following the Russian's footsteps. He just caught a glance of a black MPV vehicle banking hard down the dusty driveway and then turning left on a road that was a few metres from the warehouse.

Frank kicked a stone on the ground in frustration.

"Shit!"

The only connection to his family's fate was now speeding off into the Cuban sunset.

He saw there was a second vehicle behind him and tried the doors. They were locked.

Frank stepped back into the warehouse.

Check that the basement is clear and get Sarah.

Standing at the top of the metal steps, he heard a creak of aged metal, like a groan from the depths of some vast submarine. He crouched down as low as he possibly could and quickly glanced below the edge of the basement ceiling. It looked clear. He descended on his hands and feet like a crab, step by step, carefully manoeuvring himself so he was ready to either fire his weapon or retreat back up the stairwell. The air was damp and musty. The dimmed light made it hard to see anything but shapes and Frank felt too exposed for his liking. He saw a crate at the bottom of the stairs and made his move, jumping three steps at a time. The hard metal shot pain into his feet like shock waves but in seconds, he was where he wanted to be, behind the cover of the huge container.

Listening hard, there was a dripping sound and the same random creaking from the back of the basement. He chanced a look, his eyes already adjusting to the low light and noticed a workbench against a partitioned wall, with new equipment stacked on top that looked out of place alongside the old rusted machine parts. Frank moved silently further into the open space towards the sound, stopping dead at intervals until he found the source, a wooden door that was catching an air flow from an air vent in the wall.

Satisfied there were no other Russians hiding, he returned back up the steps and towards the rear of the warehouse where Sarah was waiting, her body turned away from the dead bodies, her head in her hands as she sobbed quietly.

Frank bent down and put a hand on her shoulder.

"It's okay. There's no one left now, we're getting out of here really soon. I just need to check on a few things." Sarah nodded.

Frank went to the back office and checked the still unconscious Russian. He hunted around, found some rope, and tied up his ankles and wrists before coming back out into the warehouse.

"Just got to check these guys," he said as Sarah hauled herself up from the floor.

He searched the pockets and it wasn't long before he had a compact Nokia phone in his hand and was scrolling through a small list of numbers, each with a name in Russian. There was also a book of matches with a logo of a tiger on the front, a bar called 'Stripes', which Frank quickly pocketed. He rang one of the names on the phone, the number was dead. The second one rang from the pocket of the first man he had killed. A third mobile number, which had been phoned the most according to the log, named 'кобра', began ringing.

Then there was the sound of a click as it was answered and silence at the other end. Frank could hear the humming of a car engine in the background.

"How's your wound?" Frank asked, almost sounding sympathetic.

"Fuck you."

"Let's start afresh, huh, comrade?" Frank said.

"You've killed my comrades, for that, you will pay," the voice said, quiet but venomously. Frank didn't doubt for a second that he meant it.

"Sure, but that's the business we're in, isn't it, Cobra? Is that your code name?"

Frank knew little Russian but 'кобра' was one word he did know.

"You can call me your fucking death knell, Frank."

"Okay, Cobra. I want to do a deal. My family, you know who's holding them and you want the information we have."

Humouring him probably wasn't ideal after catching him with a bullet going out the door but he had to keep him talking.

"That information your employer wants, I know how to get it now." Frank glanced at Sarah as he said it.

The voice came back. "Keep that phone, I call you back."

"Wait!"

The line went dead.

Frank held back the urge to throw the phone onto the floor in frustration but his white knuckles held firm and he dropped his head.

It was risky. They could easily trace that phone but it was the only option right now. He'd ditch it as soon as he could but now, it was the thinnest of threads to the kidnappers and his family.

They both walked down the steps to the basement, Frank, realising she was still shaken from the ordeal, comforted her with a hand on her shoulder.

Frank returned to the workbench and flipped on a lamp that hung on a string of wires and looked over a modern Cuban-made shortwave radio. He saw a Ford embossed key lob and immediately pocketed it. His foot tapped a metal bin underneath and he picked it up to check the contents. Remnants of blackened crispy paper that had been burned. Something familiar. A small triangle of white paper that had not blackened caught his eye. Distinct handwritten numerals, a clear '4' and then another number that he couldn't make out.

"What's that?" Sarah asked.

"A piece of nitrocellulose paper. It's the same communication method we use." He handed it to her.

Sarah studied it. "Yes, it's nitrocellulose alright, from a one-time code pad."

Frank began to get the distinct feeling that nothing was as it seemed when it came to his Russian friends. He assumed they were FSB, Federal Security Service of the Russian Federation, the intelligence agency re-born from the KGB but now, he wasn't so sure.

"Are you going straight back to England? Your family."

Frank nodded. "I need to find them and work out what the hell is going on."

Sarah leaned against the worktop. "Of course. Thanks for saving me from those animals, Frank."

"No problem."

"Listen, the information on the drive, the cause of all this shit, you'll need some kind of negotiating position. I heard you say it yourself on the phone. I want you to have it," she said, looking at him with renewed determination. Frank returned it with a sideways glance.

"What? After all you've just been through to keep it safe, you'd really give it to me, just like that?"

Sarah fixed Frank with a genuine stare.

"Look, this data is too important to fall into the wrong hands. As long as they think you have it, it will buy you a few precious days of keeping your family alive. You know as well as I do, your family is just a loose end waiting to be tied up, a bargaining tool to get you to do their bidding, and as soon as they are no longer of use, it's over for them. This is your only chance to save them."

Frank looked at her with admiration.

"Wow, that's good of you. Thanks, Sarah. You were pretty good at keeping its location quiet, you must have hidden it someplace well."

"It's down the coast towards Matanzas," she said, rubbing her arms, as if cold.

"How far exactly?"

"A couple of hours' drive."

Frank thought for a moment and shook his head. "How's it going to work? They'd know that copies might exist. Handing over a thumb drive isn't going to help my cause."

"No, it's encrypted. It can't be copied that easily, unless it's accessed and if it is, then a log file is created. Frank, you need that file to bring them down. We go there, get it, and you can take it back with you as long as you get it to my contacts in London who can make it public but give yourself a few days to find your family first. I can give you their details."

Frank nodded. "Right. What if they don't believe I have it?"

"They will. Get an email address and send them a screenshot, so they know you're not bluffing. I'll give you the encryption code."

Frank thought for a moment.

"Okay, let's get out of here...we can talk on the way."

Chapter 38

The room was dark apart from small cracks of light around the edges of the chipboard that had been hammered against the window frame. The gloom made it hard for Maria to see but when their eyes adjusted, there was nothing to focus on anyway. A lone bed, with sheets, a blanket, and a sidelight placed on the carpeted floor was all she could make out. She held her arm around Joe and they sat on the floor, leaning against the wall.

"What do they want, Mum?" Joe's voice broke the silence.

"I really don't know, Joe, but don't worry, we'll get out of this."

"I'm not worried," he said, almost as an act of bravado for his mother. Maria couldn't help smiling in the gloom, despite their grim situation. That was typical Joe, always the brave one.

"I know you're not, but it's okay to be afraid sometimes."

"I'm not afraid!"

He pulled away from her and stood up, sighing loudly, clearly agitated. They had been in that room for at least a week and it soon dawned on them both that this was not going to be a short visit. Maria also guessed there was a high chance their lives were at risk, despite their kidnapper assuring them that this was just a bartering move.

Just then, the door unlocked and the tall man with cropped black hair appeared, the light casting his frame in darkness.

"What do you want?" Maria asked coldly.

The man took a couple of steps inside, his eyes fixed on Joe.

"Your boy. How old is he?" Maria could see that he was grinning, a wide sickening grin and in one horrifying moment, realised what he was saying.

"Joe. Come here," she said calmly but firmly, holding out her hand and gesturing for him to move. Joe did as he was told and walked over to his mother and she put her arm around him, her eyes fiery orbs that radiated hate towards the Russian.

"You fucking dare touch him," she said, her voice low and venomous.

Just then, a shout came from downstairs and the man slowly moved out of the room, locking up behind him.

***

Several days earlier, the morning had begun as usual. Maria's friend, Lisa, had dropped by to take Zak to nursery and Joe, who should have been at school, had complained of feeling feverish and was to stay home.

"I hope you're not just going to play your video games all day, Joe."

Joe groaned from behind his door, "Noooo."

Lisa had just left with a car full of three-year-olds and Maria genuinely felt sorry for her. She grabbed her bag and glanced at herself in the hallway full-length mirror and then the buzzer blared through the apartment for the second time that morning. It could only be Lisa. Did she leave something? Maria glanced around the kitchen and on the work surfaces to check. There was nothing she could see. She descended the stairs and opened the door, frowning at the visitor on the step.

"Hello, Maria," said Nigel Harrison.

"Nigel. What are you doing here?"

"Can I come in? It's really important." He looked scared.

Maria felt perplexed and slightly put out but something in his demeanour told her to roll with it.

"To be honest, I was on my way to the office. Can it wait?"

"No, I'm afraid not. It's John. He's dead."

Maria leaned her arm against the wall as she struggled to take in those words.

"Dead?"

"Yes. A car accident. Look, I'm sorry to have to tell you like this. That's why I came."

"Yes, of course, Nigel. I'm sorry, I didn't realise. Please come in. Shut the door behind you." she said, her shock displacing any previous irritation she felt. She turned and slowly walked back up the stairs as Nigel loitered in the doorway.

On not hearing his footfall, she turned back staring at him quizzically.

Nigel's eyes were wet as they looked up at her, almost pleading for her forgiveness, and then a shadow appeared next to him. A giant hand shoved him aside and a tall man with black short hair in a leather jacket appeared. He proceeded to point a small handgun at Maria, whose mouth fell open in shock.

"Stay there, bitch," he said, in a heavy accent. He sounded Russian.

The large man climbed the steps towards her and Maria dared not move. She would be dead in a second.

"Okay," he nodded, indicating for her to continue back into the flat and shoved her in the back.

"Nigel! Come here. Close door!" he commanded without looking back. Nigel dutifully shuffled in and Maria heard the lock click.

"Anyone else in the house? Do not lie."

Maria closed her eyes, wishing she did not have to say the words. Maybe Joe had heard and had hidden or he could find a way out. It was possible and she couldn't think straight.

Maria stared at his beady eyes that seemed to drill into her soul. She shook her head.

"No, it's just me," she said loudly, hoping Joe would hear and get the message if he hadn't already.

The intruder glared at Nigel and jerked his head. "Go look!"

Nigel shuffled off, as ordered, towards the living room. There was a stillness in the house, just the sound of footsteps moving to the bedroom.

Maria assessed the situation, stealing glances at the intruder, wondering what the hell was going on, her stomach sick with worry. What had she done?

Nigel returned, his watery eyes glancing at Maria.

"It's clear," he said.

"Clear? You sure," the big Russian growled.

"Yes, I'm sure."

"Okay. We take this bitch and go."

Maria began to feel the relief as they headed to the apartment door. She had done it. Joe was safe and would call the police.

Then a sound, like a knock. Maria's stomach tightened.

"What was that?" the intruder boomed. He grabbed Nigel by the arm and slapped Maria across the face with the outside of his massive hand.

"I told you, bitch. Do not lie!"

Maria let out a sob and tried to grab his arm as he marched back to the bedroom.

"Please, don't hurt him!"

He kicked the door down and walked in, breathing heavily as he looked around at Joe's bedroom. Posters of a rock band adorned the walls, typical of any kid's bedroom. A large wardrobe stood in the corner. The Russian opened the doors to find nothing but hanging shirts and football kit stuffed into carrier bags at the bottom.

Maria appeared in the doorway, Nigel behind her, eyes wide with fear as she looked around. Had he got out?

"Please," she mumbled.

He turned his attention to the single bed and with one hand, uplifted it, smashing it against the wall. The wide eyes of a boy stared up at him. The intruder bent down and grabbed him by the arm, forcing him to stand up.

"Up! Bastard, up!"

Joe struggled initially and then seemed to think better of it when he saw the man's gun in his other hand.

"Don't hurt him, you fucking bastard!" Maria screamed.

He shoved Joe towards Maria, who grabbed him with both arms and pointed the pistol at them both.

"Out...out!"

Maria and Joe went into the hallway where Nigel waited. The Russian bore his dark eyes into Nigel and spoke quietly, "I deal with you later."

"What do you want? Where are you taking us?" Maria demanded.

He glared back at both Maria and Joe.

"We're going on a little trip."

Chapter 39

It was mid-morning as Frank and Sarah headed out of the closed down industrial estate and onto the main Via Blanca coastal road. Soon, they were cruising along palm tree-lined fields with spectacular mountainous backdrops heading south. They had driven the Russian's black MPV to the nearest town and then spent an hour or so looking for a car garage, where they swapped it for an older, less conspicuous Chevrolet. The garage owner was delighted with the deal.

Sarah leaned against the window as they continued on the coastal road south and watched a group of school children in bright white shirts running along the road, their satchels bumping behind them. There was an endless trail of destruction from the hurricane. Roofs ripped from their joists, and trees uprooted and thrown aside like a rag doll from a bull.

"So why did you choose all the way down here to hide this thumb drive? You could have hid it anywhere."

"I gave it to someone I trust with my life. Someone I would never betray, even if it meant my death."

"You can definitely trust this person?"

"Yes, totally. I met her in my gap year when I took off around Central America for a few months. It was a low time for me but she became a good friend when I was over here before. But she has no idea what is in that key fob anyway."

Frank acknowledged with a slow nod of the head.

"Better that way," he said.

After twenty minutes of driving along the pot-holed road, Sarah directed Frank off along a maze of dusty back roads that came to an immaculate, small, single story house, painted bright blue with red tiled roof set against a line of trees. In a field beyond it, oxen grazed and the landscape seemed to stretch forever. It was one of the most tranquil scenes Frank had ever set eyes on, as if plucked straight from a picture postcard.

Frank pulled up, switched off the engine, and they both got out of the vehicle and went to the house.

A woman in her 50s with white, fuzzy hair and dark skin opened the door and shrieked with delight at her visitor crying, "Hola! Hola!" and wrapped her large arms around Sarah.

"Mi bella consorte!"

They stepped into the small modest but clean hovel and the woman gestured for them to sit at a wooden table in the centre of the main room. It was cool inside, a welcome relief from the rising temperature of the day.

"This is Frank," Sarah said and the woman smiled broadly at him. "Si, Si. Frank. Soy Vanesa."

Frank smiled and took the seat offered to him, glad of the rest. Vanesa disappeared into the back and returned with a jug of lemon water and snacks before she and Sarah caught up, chatting in Spanish. It was to this background ambience that Frank's eyes grew heavy and he was soon escorted to a more comfortable chair by Vanesa, who continually beamed at him, gesturing that she understood his tiredness.

He took the opportunity to grab some sleep, wondering how Maria and Joe were doing as he drifted off. Work out a plan and get back to

England. But that was the problem, there wasn't much of a bloody plan. He had no idea where to start. Yes, there was the key fob and Sarah's suggested idea, a faint hope maybe. Keep the Russians talking...make them follow his rules but he would only have 2 or 3 days to find Maria and Joe. How the hell was he going to do that? Any more time and they would track down the information. They weren't amateurs after all.

These thoughts drifted through Frank's mind as he drifted off. Less than an hour later, a clunk of a plate woke him up and he saw food being laid out by Sarah and Vanesa. Frank sat down at the table and tucked into the rice and black beans with a healthy dose of fiery sauce.

After eating, as Vanesa cleared away the dishes, Frank took Sarah outside.

"Sarah, this is all very nice and I needed the rest but I have to get home."

Sarah flicked a wisp of dark hair behind her ear, her expression was one of understanding and a vague hint of sadness.

"Yes, of course, you do. I'm so sorry. I'll get the thumb drive." Sarah went and spoke to their host and returned, handing over the key fob that she had brought from England.

"You'll do the right thing with it, won't you?" she said.

Frank stared at her. "You're not coming with me?"

Sarah sighed. "You know I can't go back to England. Not at the moment. Maybe some sunny day," she smiled. "But I want to tell you where my parents are. If you ever get a chance, let them know I'm well and that I'm alive."

"They found you before, they'll find you again."

"Not if you do the right thing with this. Once this is out, they're not going to be interested in me anymore," Sarah said.

Frank exhaled slowly and cast a long glance across the fields.

"I hope you stay lucky, Sarah, I really do."

She laughed easily. "I think you had something to do with my luck, Frank. Without you stepping in, I'd either be dead or hooded in some godforsaken pit – instead of here," She swung an arm out and gestured at the landscape.

"By the way, you'll need some money." She pulled out a wad of notes.

"No, I can't, you'll need it."

"I have plenty. I've been planning this for months, Frank. You have no access to money, right? Not without setting off some major alarm bells," she jerked her head, emphasising her point.

Frank thanked her and took the money. As he pocketed the cash, he found the book of matches he's taken off one of the dead Russians. It was a lap-dancing bar in London, according to the inside front. Had the team been in London before Cuba?

Sarah saw Frank frowning and smiled.

"You better get going, Sherlock. Find your family. There's one other thing I want you to do for me when you get back, Frank."

***

After leaving Sarah at her friend's house, Frank drove the vehicle back to Havana, dumped it, and found an Internet-connected computer in a hotel near the airport and proceeded to log into WarWorld, browsing through the remnants of a destroyed empire but Frank was not logging on to play games. He searched for other players online and found Griff's username, thankfully online, and nudged him via the chat terminal.

Frank read Griff's first message: *What the hell's going on out there? I heard the team got hit.*

Yes. Ambushed by bears. Can we keep this between us?

Sure, bro, no problem.

My partner and kid have been kidnapped. Russian connection. Highly possible that they're in London. Can you make enquiries?

Shit. Sorry to hear, Frank, but where the hell do I start?

CCTV around Shoreditch. That's where we live.

Will see what I can do.

Thanks, Griff. I'll send you a detailed description of the main guy.

Frank described the Russian with the goatee, a mohawk, and the prominent neck tattoo, who was becoming a major pain in Frank's life and sent it across the network.

It's a start, thanks, replied Griff.

That's the best I can do for now. I take it you can get an image of Maria and Joe OK?

Yeah, probably.

Also, there's a bar called Stripes...can you check it out? There might be CCTV on the same road?

Wilko Bravo

OK, thanks, I owe you. Over and out.

Frank logged off and then went in search of the next flight to London. He was in luck and saw a flight that took off in 3 hours. He walked over to the British Airways desk and used the passport that his old friend, Jake Hale, had made for him and paid in cash.

After taking the tickets, he found a quiet corner and took out the phone that he had taken from the dead Russian and dialled the number again.

"I thought I tell you to wait?" the familiar voice said.

"I'm fed up of waiting. What's going on? I want my family back!" Frank tried to keep the anger at bay but he was struggling with the concept.

"Do you have the thumb drive?"

"I'm working on that – where are you going to want delivery?"

"How do I know you're not lying, Frank?"

"Give me an email and I'll send you a screenshot of the first few pages when I get it. That'll be your proof."

There was a pause.

"Okay. We want delivery in London. Probably in a few days. You wait my call or text. Don't phone this number again."

"Use text from now on, it'll be wiser," said Frank. A thought had come to him. "Voice calls could be monitored easier," he added.

It was a lie. Both text and voice calls could be picked up but Frank didn't want any UK style ring tones sounding if the Russian decided to ring him in England. It would give away his location.

The Russian paused. "I text you email, save image in drafts folder. Then we know you're serious."

The call ended. Despite not being a religious man, Frank prayed that somehow he would be able to track down and save Maria and Joe in the narrow timeframe he had. If only Griff could work his magic.

Frank dared not even begin to imagine living his life without them. If he lost them...Frank shook the possibility out of his thoughts. It would not happen. It must not happen.

Chapter 40

After touching down at Heathrow, Frank went through the maze of a busy passport control, where no one looked twice at his details and soon found himself in the public area of the airport, gripping his holdall bag. He checked his Russian mobile phone and saw a text message with an obscure email address and login details.

Making his way out of the airport, he immediately began looking for an Internet café. After thirty minutes of looking, he found one, bought a coffee, and made his way to a computer at the back. He went online, logging into the WarWorld game and found Griff's avatar online as usual.

Frank began to type him a message:

Hey, G, am back in the UK. Did you find anything out for me?

There was a pause as Griff began to type and Frank watched the flashing cursor indicate a message was coming.

There might be something worth looking at. I think you should see it.

Did you tell anyone? Frank answered.

Nope, are you crazy? We need to meet with this.

Frank paused. It was entirely possible that Griff had been turned and was now ordered to keep track of Frank and reel him in. But he didn't believe that, not for one second.

Can we meet at that place where you took me for that cheap lunch when I was training?

Griff agreed to meet in two hours' time. Frank said goodbye and logged off before slipping the thumb drive out of the key fob and plugging it into the computer. A password prompt came up and Frank typed in the series of letters and numbers that Sarah had given him. The parent folder appeared on screen. He clicked through to the 'Oculus' folder and opened the document that booted up a PowerPoint programme and the title page appeared. Frank screenshot it with the 'print screen' button on the keyboard and then logged into the email, pasted the image into a new message and saved it to drafts.

He logged out again, wiped the browser cache, and grabbed the thumb drive out of the slot.

Several hours later, Frank, well out of sight, watched Griff stroll into the café. Frank had taken care to alter his appearance but he wasn't too worried. He figured anyone looking for him would be in Cuba, not London.

Griff seemed nonchalant enough. Frank could see him behind the glass, walking up to the counter to speak to a woman before sitting down at one of the tables set against the wall. Frank waited for several minutes more and looked around, both ends of the street. There was no sign that there were any suspicious vehicles or anyone looking around. He strolled across with a confident gait, moving between the cars and stepped into the café.

He passed Griff, who was too busy studying his phone to notice him and ordered a mug of tea and a bacon sandwich. Slipping into a chair opposite Griff, he put down his mug of tea, surprising the young lad, who hardly recognised the man he had helped train in technology and surveillance equipment. Frank was bearded now and wore a hat pulled over his head.

Griff adjusted his geek style specs.

"Jesus, you look like you've taken a beating out there."

"It wasn't the holiday I was expecting."

"Hmm, no, I did warn you about that crazy beach life." Griff paused and looked solemn. "I'm sorry about your team. So any more details on what happened out there?"

Frank sighed and watched the street carefully. Rain had started to patter against the window, hard and grey.

"As I said, it all went to shit. An ambush at the safe house. A Russian mob. Greene got hit and Piper died of his wounds later on. We must have been sold out somehow. Who knew about the safe house? The only ones were the agents on the ground and you boys here in London." Frank put on an air of accusation in his voice.

Griff shook his head and held up his hands. "Not me, man."

Frank continued. "I know, Griff. Just messing with you. When Brull found me and Sarah a new safe house, it somehow got compromised again. Our Russian friends turned up, murdered Brull, and then took myself and Sarah to their charming warehouse, for questioning." Frank spoke, the venom hardly hidden from his voice.

"You were with the whistleblower?"

Frank sighed. "Yes. Didn't Carl tell you?"

"And the files she took?"

"Never mind that now, did you get me any information? I need to find where the hell Maria and my kid are," Frank said, his patience at breaking point.

Griff nodded, sensing the deep concern in Frank and pulled out a large envelope from his inside jacket pocket. "I looked at a lot of C.C.T.V footage around Stripes, the gentlemen's bar. I was able to dismiss plenty of possibles from the way you described the guy but men with black goatee beards and mohawks seem to be 'in' at the moment so it was a nightmare."

Griff handed over the printouts to Frank.

"So, any possibles in here?" he asked, tearing it open and fishing out a batch of printouts.

Griff shrugged and leaned back in his chair. "You tell me, buddy. Take a look."

They were distracted momentarily by the café owner as she shouted out numbers and navigated herself around the tables, carrying cooked breakfasts, three at a time.

Frank thumbed through the various grainy photos of men matching the description coming out of the bar but they didn't immediately see any that looked like the Russian bastard he had encountered in Cuba.

Frank shook his head in frustration.

"No dice?" asked Griff.

Frank shuffled through the papers again.

"No, not…"

One of the prints was a possibility the second time he looked at it, but it was far from clear. A man in the street outside the Stripes bar, his face half turned, slightly obscured by another figure in front of him. There was a familiarity about the shape of the cheekbone. It was possible.

"When was this taken?" he asked.

"About twenty-four hours ago."

"Can you get more from this camera at around this time?"

"Well, yes, I can get the film but I'm breaking a million protocols here."

Frank stuffed the print out into his jacket pocket.

"Join the club. Just find out who he is if you can. I'll go visit this bar. Hey, Griff, thanks for this. I owe you one."

Griff nodded. "That makes me feel all warm and fuzzy inside. I hope you realise all the sneaking around I'm still gonna have to do?"

The waitress appeared and put down a plate of fish and chips in front of Griff and a bacon sandwich cut in half in front of Frank.

"There you go, loves," she said. Her mouth was arranged in a permanent droop where she probably would have had a cigarette fixed in place had it not been for the smoking ban.

Frank grabbed one half of his sandwich and took a bite as he slid a mobile phone across the table. "So we can communicate without having to go on that stupid game."

He got up to leave, finishing the sandwich in a few bites as Griff put the phone in his pocket.

"What are you calling a stupid game? Are you not eating that other half?" Griff asked, his hand already swooping towards Frank's plate.

"Go for it. I've got to go, my partner and kid are being held by a posse of maniacs, remember? See if you can get that film as soon as you can. I'm going to take a look around at that market."

Griff looked up. "And the gold, Frank? The information Pandora took? You didn't say whether you got it?"

Frank simply winked at him and then walked out of the café.

Chapter 41

Less than an hour later, Frank stood sheltered under a tree from the continuous rain opposite the house where Maria's friend, Rosie lived at Barnes Bridge. The autumn golden brown leaves scattered on the ground, an impressionist picture as if taken through a blurred camera lens. A policeman stood outside, draped in a waterproof overcoat, standing stoically on guard. The kidnapping had obviously been reported and someone had the sense to make the call that maybe Frank's other family members were at risk.

He wondered what his sons would end up doing with their lives. Would he even see them grow up at all? The spectre of death had hung over him more than once in recent months and then he steeled himself. He had to survive, for their sakes at least, and he had to keep alive to get Maria and Joe free from whatever psychopathic gang were holding them.

How had it come to this? Watching from under the shelter of a tree, hoping to catch a glimpse of his youngest son. Approaching them was too risky; they may be under surveillance but he just wanted to see that Zak was okay with his own eyes. He zipped up his jacket as the rain came down in sheets as the creeping realisation that he needed help gnawed away at him. But knowing who to trust was impossible.

There was Carl who had recruited him into this mess. What was he hiding? Did he have a hand in the turning events? Frank shook that thought from his mind. He didn't believe Carl was involved in the kidnapping for a second, yet that didn't stop the growing frustration that he had not properly protected his family.

The door slowly opened and Rosie struggled with a pram down the steps, holding a child in one arm, followed by other tiny figures. He realised as she put down the child that it was Zak. There was a flood of relief as his instinct that Zak was out of harm's way was confirmed.

Just then, the Russian mobile buzzed a text message and Frank read the screen.

Are you in the UK yet?

Frank began to type:

About to leave Cuba. Problems with flights.

Frank needed to buy time, whether the Russian believed him or not. He began to walk to the tube station away from the house.

After a minute or so, another text came through.

Employer is happy to negotiate. You bring product, agree not to distribute, and your family will be safe.

Frank replied, *They'd better be...I will come after you and never stop if any harm comes to them.*

Immediately, a return text came through.

Don't threaten me, Frank. Just be ready when I tell you the meeting place. You make sure you deliver.

Chapter 42

Frank came up the steps of Tottenham Court road station and walked east along Oxford Street, skirting the border of Soho.

The crowds had thinned out now that it was after lunchtime but it was still busy by any smaller city's standards. He kept his head down, hands in pockets, and hunched his shoulders in case the ever-increasing number of surveillance cameras picked him up.

After several minutes' walk, he turned left and crossed Soho square to an address he had memorised and took a step up to the newly painted black door of one of the red-bricked Georgian houses that had been converted into offices. After a short exchange of words, he was buzzed in and came into a plush reception room where he was greeted by a casually dressed receptionist who offered him a seat and a coffee.

"Mr. Brady won't be too much longer," she said, giving him a broad smile before going out to get his refreshment.

After five minutes, Frank had drained his coffee cup; the warm liquid felt good on his throat after being in the cold outside. A tall black man, dressed in a white shirt and jeans, appeared in the doorway behind the reception desk. He wore wire thin steel spectacle frames and had the demeanour of a man in charge as he cast an intrigued eye over the dishevelled visitor in front of him.

"Hello there. I'm Marcus Brady. How can I help you?"

Frank placed his cup down on the glass table and stood up to greet the man.

"I'm a friend of Sarah Edwards," he said quietly. Brady looked at him, surprised for a moment, and then nodded in acknowledgement.

"Please, come this way."

The two men sat down in Brady's office in low set chairs that were arranged around a coffee table in the middle of the room, packed with shelves of box files that seemed to bow under their weight. Above a disused fireplace, a framed print of the *Liberatus* front page adorned the wall.

"Our most recent edition," said Marcus, noticing Frank was looking at it. The headline ran: British M.P. Jailed for Perjury.

"We exposed that bastard a few weeks ago. He had been involved in high-level corruption in the government, had links to a CIA think-tank, and was involved in a Middle East arms scandal. Eventually, some of the national newspapers picked it up and one thing led to another. It's what our mission here at Liberatus is, to hound the corrupt." he smiled.

"Sounds like a worthy cause," said Frank.

"It is. John Rhodes, who was the founding father of our group, was involved in a car crash a few weeks ago. Which leads me to how Sarah Edwards fits into all of this."

Frank held up his hand. "Before we get onto Sarah, I want to talk about Maria."

"Maria?"

"Maria Chapman."

"Maria Chapman? Why, yes, she's employed as a researcher here but she stopped coming into work a while ago. I don't know why. Do you know her?"

"Maria is my partner. We have two children, Joe and Zak."

Marcus smiled broadly. "Ah yes, she talked about them a lot. How are they doing?"

Frank paused again, hoping he was doing the right thing.

"Maria and Joe have been kidnapped. I was away, on a job. That's when it happened," Frank said, studying Brady's face intently.

Brady leaned forward now, frowning with concern.

"Kidnapped? When, how?"

Frank related the story, leaving out the parts he thought he shouldn't know. The initial mission, the change of plan for Edwards, and then an unknown Russian crew crashing the party.

It didn't matter now. He just wanted his family back. He didn't give a shit about all the bullshit politics and games they played anymore. Sarah Edwards had assured him he could trust Brady and that he would be able to help find them. That's all that mattered now.

Brady leaned back in his chair, nodding his head silently at Frank's breakdown of events.

After he had finished, Frank leaned forward.

"I have something very important for you," said Frank quietly. "Something Sarah wanted you to have."

He fumbled in his inside pocket and brought out the thumb drive. He paused, holding it in his hands, and then handed it to Brady.

"You need to sit on this for three days to give me a chance to find my family. Then I'm either dead and it can be released or I succeed and it should go public anyway."

Marcus looked at him for a moment and nodded. "Sure, three days," he repeated.

Brady played with the key fob in his fingers.

"Such a small thing for so much trouble," he said. "John was supposed to go to Cuba to meet her. It had all been arranged but then, the accident..."

"He was the contact she had arranged to meet?" asked Frank.

"Yes. Unfortunately, it all went wrong." Brady said, looking at Frank, his eyes betraying a genuine sadness. "But Maria and Joe kidnapped? Jesus. Yeah, I will help you any way I can, you can count on it," he added.

Frank nodded. "Thanks, Marcus, that's very much appreciated."

He stood up and made his way to the door. "I'm afraid the bad news from Cuba is that Sarah is dead, in case you were wondering."

"Dead? What happened?"

"I don't know exactly, that's the information I got. Sorry, I can't tell you anymore. Needless to say, she would be happy that you got the information. I'll catch up with you later."

Frank left Marcus Brady staring at the door as he closed it behind him.

Chapter 43

Grey clouds swirled overhead, casting a dark shadow over the city and then the rain came again in torrents. Frank kept to the side streets as best he could making his way inland from the embankment, past Covent Garden, and then north-east and to the place where the kidnapper was last sighted. It was all he had to go on and hope slipped away like rainwater that streamed down the street drains.

He found the Stripes bar and knocked hard on the door but there was no answer. Frank glanced at this watch. Probably too early. He strolled down the street, looking for somewhere to grab a coffee and found himself standing across the road from Smithfield market and remembered seeing a café in there once. Sure enough, it was still there and he bought a takeaway Americano and strolled around the stalls. Wholesale meat traders were selling their finest cuts of every type of meat and poultry in the Victorian Grade II listed-covered market building. Customers were flooding inside to purchase their supplies for restaurants and cafés across London.

It seemed to Frank that the Russians must have been based in a house around there somewhere. If they had been to the club before Cuba and the photo was the man who called himself 'Kobra' then they must have returned to the same area and re-visited the lap dancing club. It must be worth flashing the photo of the Russian around?

Frank immediately started to ask traders if they had seen him, showing them the C.C.T.V photo of Viktor Kozel. After several shook their heads, he walked over to the trader, a bald, obese man in his 40s and nodded a greeting.

"Hi, mate. What can I get ya?" he asked, barely looking up from the lamb cutlets he had been stacking on a plastic tray.

"I'm looking for this man. Have you seen him?"

The trader looked up at the photo Frank held out in front of him, then cast a suspicious eye at Frank.

"Why? Who's asking?"

Frank fixed him with a level stare; there was no time for games.

"It's really important I find him. We know he was here a few days ago. This image was captured on a camera nearby."

The trader raised his eyebrows slightly. Anyone with access to those cameras was probably worth keeping sweet.

"Well, I don't remember the man. We got shed loads of people coming through here every day. My memory's not so good anyway."

He gestured with a burly forearm at a stall opposite him. "Ask Steve, he's got a memory for faces. Eyes of a hawk and memory of an elephant, that Steve."

The ruddy-faced vendor called Steve looked closely at the kidnapper's photo as if the cogs were turning in his mind. He looked up at Frank and nodded. "Yeah, I think I saw him, mate, couldn't miss a guy like that. Russian or Slovak. Something like that."

"Anything you can remember about him? Anything at all? Which direction he went afterwards?"

The trader shook his head. "Couldn't tell you, mate. He bought produce a couple of times, that's all I can say."

Frank gave him his new mobile number. "Do me a favour, if he turns up again, discreetly send a text." Frank slipped a Fifty-pound note to him along with the number and gave the man a knowing look. The trader smiled, more eager to help as he took the note. "Sure thing, pal. I won't ask any questions."

Frank circled the market, keeping his eyes open and head down. It seemed logical that the house Maria and Joe were kept in was close by if the man had been buying food from the market. Again, it was a loose lead but it was all he had.

***

The following morning around 5:15, Frank's mobile buzzed and he read the message. He jumped out of bed, threw his clothes on as quickly as he could, and then drove over towards Smithfield.

Frank watched the crowds jostling and pushing to get a look at the produce on sale. Deep frustration was growing by the second. The morning calm had made way to a Saturday bustle along with a rise in noise level, which the high metal roof dispersed, making it sound like a cattle market.

The text was from the butcher claiming the man was wandering around the market again. He watched the heads; wives, farmers, office workers, a glimpse of dark hair. A Mohawk.

Familiarity caught Frank in a blink of an eye, and then he was gone. He moved forward through the crowd, seeing if he could get confirmation of what he'd thought he'd seen. Was it him?

A glimpse again, making his way to the far exit. The head turned slightly to look around and Frank immediately saw it was the Russian or 'Kobra' as he had called himself. Frank quickened his pace, pushing through the faces that glared disapprovingly. This was a fine thread, a one chance throw of the dice.

Frank stepped out onto the street outside the east exit, glancing to the back of the Russian, who was walking fast, carrying a plastic bag of what Frank assumed to be meat just purchased. Kobra tossed a cigarette butt into the gutter and zipped his jacket against the cold.

Frank kept within a few metres, gambling there were enough bodies around to give him cover. At a crossing, the Russian stopped at the lights and Frank saw, just in time, a large dark glass frontage opposite, the reflection almost giving him away. Frank knew he looked different but it was not worth the risk. He stopped at a greengrocer and pretended to be interested in the fruit on display. Cobra moved across the road heading northwards, dodging vehicles, and Frank moved off again, determined not to lose him.

For around ten minutes, Frank kept close enough to the Russian before there was a sudden surge of people exiting a tube station that forced Frank to slow down, and he lost sight of him. Frank shoved people aside to get through quickly but on getting through the throng, he suddenly had no visual on his target.

Frantically scanning the line of shop entrances that ran along the high street looking for a glimpse, he saw nothing. Shit! Maybe he should have stuck closer and risked being seen?

As he checked the crowds on the opposite side, he saw a glimpse of the familiar rake of black hair, moving away from him down a side street.

Frank made up for lost ground and closed the gap, keeping ten metres back or so on the opposite side of the road. He noticed his target was on a mobile phone but Frank was too far away to hear anything. It was a residential street, with detached houses that looked more and more dilapidated the further they walked. Most of the houses had metal sheds or carports next to them, washing lines strung across fences, rusty caravans that had long since seen the freedom of a road.

The Russian swivelled around to glance behind himself briefly as he fished out a bunch of keys and stepped into the forecourt of an anonymous-looking house. Frank debated stopping, hiding, and watching but decided against it and moved casually down the road. Kobra disappeared through the front door. Frank clocked the number and took in as much information as he could with a brief glance. The windows at the front were boarded up and there was a driveway at the side that leads to the rear of the property.

Now he was convinced that this was Maria and Joe were being kept.

Frank did a circular appraisal of the surrounding roads around Prince Street, taking mental notes of anything that might prove useful. He walked down the street directly parallel to the road he was targeting, looking for a way around the rear of the house. There was a wall with a wooden door that Frank guessed led to the gardens and he checked that he wasn't being watched before jumping up and having a quick look.

Briefly, Frank could see a row of gardens that buffered back to back behind the houses. It was a potential route in except he would easily be seen by any curtain twitchers who chose to glance out the back unless it was at night. He couldn't risk any calls to the police; it could blow the whole fragile situation and potentially risk Maria and Joe's lives.

He jumped back down onto the ground and walked along the street, taking in anything that could be useful, assessing the situation. Then he came across a derelict house that had its windows boarded up with metal sheeting. He calculated it wouldn't be far off opposite the target house at the back. The front garden had an old sofa that had long since seen its sell-by date, its leather cover ripped open, spewing mounds of fibre filling. Around it lay piles of rubbish, black bags, and planks of wood that looked to have been ripped out of the house itself. There was a mound of worn burnt carpet that had been cut up and discarded.

Glancing up and down the street he could see it was still quiet and ducked down the pathway to check the front door. It had been secured by a sheet of metal and Frank could see it would be no easy task getting in that way. Alongside the exterior wall of the house was a narrow pathway that had a wooden doorway that had been bolted shut. Along the top of the door frame, a roll of barbed wire acted as the only deterrent. Frank barged the door with his shoulder to check how secure it was. It stood firm against his weight, without any hint of give. He took off his backpack and rummaged around for a few seconds before pulling out the wire clippers and putting them in his inside jacket pocket. Frank then replaced the bag on his back. Somewhere in the distance from a nearby open window, he heard the sound of clanking dinner plates and a slamming of cupboard doors.

After one more glance back to the road, Frank reached up and grabbed the top of the frame, hauling himself up using all his strength. Reaching up with his leg, he managed to get a foot on the round door handle for leverage. With his body leaning against the outside wall, he carefully untangled the barbed wire and took out the wire cutters. Carefully and methodically he clipped away at the wire, pushing sections down over the other side until he had enough space to get through. He replaced the Clippers in his pocket and pushed his body up on top of the frame and leapt down on the other side into the backyard.

At the rear there was another mountain of crap that had been ripped out of the house; an old olive green bathroom suite from a bygone era of style lay in a heap; mounds of plasterboard and more rubbish sacks.

The sun had disappeared behind the houses as evening drew in, casting the gardens in shadow. Fences either side that gave him privacy from the immediate neighbours and a low brick wall at the end backed onto other gardens for the houses on Prince Street. He had a good, clear view of the house where his family was being held. There wasn't time for a detailed reccy, he needed to make sure he would not be seen. There would be too much of a risk of police being called by nosey neighbours.

The rear windows and door of the old house were boarded up with metal sheeting in the same way the front was, except Frank noticed one of the ground floor windows had been forced open, revealing the smallest of gaps that would barely fit a child through. He had a quick look inside and listened carefully for any sounds and then eased back the loose section of metal sheeting to get a better look. It would make a perfect lookout to put eyes on the target house.

He peered into the darkness and just saw an empty room. There was a smell of damp, a few empty beer bottles strewn over the floor.

It would do just fine.

Chapter 44

The black BMW 5 series headed south out of central London on the A24, past Morden and Wimbledon towards Epsom. Marcus Brady was at the wheel, looking smart in his dark cotton shirt and Matt Fulford, the *Liberatus News* journalist, slumped next to him in an old Ramones T-shirt and jeans as he flipped through the CDs from the glove box.

"What's this? Dire Straits?"

"This ain't my car, nothing to do with me," Brady replied curtly.

"Yeah, of course. Diana Ross, Whitney Houston...think I'll pass on the muzak then."

"Diana Ross is the soul queen, have some respect," said Brady.

Matt sighed and put the CDs back in their place and glanced out at the rows of semi-detached Tudor style houses, set back from the road.

"So, you think these precautions are needed?"

"Most definitely. This is a serious business we're in and it's only going to get a lot worse. They're almost certainly watching the office now."

Brady had taken as many measures as he could to make sure they weren't being followed or bugged. He had a bit of help from Frank Bowen after their meeting; just some pointers but it had really helped. They both dumped their phones for new ones and Brady eventually persuaded Matt to let the business buy him a new laptop. No conversations of their plans to anyone, in the office or on any phone line.

They had taken separate tubes to Stockwell station and after both doing extended detours to shake off any tails, ended up in Brixton market, along the Atlantic road, to a section of fabric and carpet shops nestled in behind the rusting blue pillars, underneath the railway line. Brady arrived first, gripping the hand of the small stocky shop owner before giving him a bear hug.

"Still flogging these old rat rugs, Merv?" he jibbed, glancing around the cramped space that was filled to the brim with textiles and carpet rolls. Merv grinned and let out a low, staccato laugh. He was one of the early Jamaican immigrants to Britain in the 1950s and had been the 'go-to carpet king' ever since. The two men had known each other for a long time. As they chatted about the old days, Matt Fulford had no idea whether he was being followed or had succeeded in alluding any potential tails, he was virtually lost himself and just as he was silently cursing Marcus, he spotted the carpet shop. He strolled over, his large holdall bag containing his most essential needs slung over his shoulders.

Matt shook hands with Merv and then his eyes settled on Brady expectantly.

"We better be going, Merv. So, the wheels?"

Merv handed Marcus the keys to his beloved beemer and suddenly grabbed his arm, holding his stare for a moment, his eyes deadly serious. "Take care of my baby, won't you, Marcus?" he said. Both men suddenly burst out laughing and Brady slapped him on the shoulder. "Your baby gonna be alright, I drive safe, ya know."

"Alrigh'...I see you,"

Matt and Marcus slipped out the back of the shop, walked several paces up the street, and into the waiting car. When the doors slammed shut, Marcus asked, in a low voice, "You definitely weren't followed?"

Matt leaned his head back against the leather headrest, his eyes slid towards his boss.

"I have little or no idea. I did exactly like you said but...I have little or no idea."

"Come on, Matt. Tell me you weren't followed, please."

"I wasn't followed...," Matt said dryly.

Marcus sighed and pulled out, glancing in the rearview mirror. "Okay, well, we're gonna have to make sure."

"So you and the carpet man go back some?" asked Matt.

"He's a brother. I trust him more than my real brother," Marcus said.

"And this place we're going to...how do you know it's safe?"

"No one knows about this place, no one at the office. It's not owned by John...it's another one of my connections. They own it and usually rent it out. Just happens to be vacant at the moment. So you can focus on the story."

Marcus did another detour, heading west before doing a U-turn and heading back in the opposite direction the way Bowen had suggested. He checked his rearview mirror for tails and saw none.

As they approached Epsom and the houses became a lot smarter, all thatched roofed and barn style, surrounded by neat gardens. The car turned down along a narrow lane, slowed for a horse rider to go past and continued down the winding road that skirted scattered woodland.

The house was comfortable, cosy even, but sparsely furnished. A fireplace dominated the main room, which lay central in the cottage, off of which was a kitchen, bathroom, and a bedroom, and two rooms up above. A detailed painting of a crowded Epsom race day adorned the wall.

"I'll pick you up in a few days, just get the story done. There's a phone box back along the lane if you need anything but don't use it unless you have to and don't under any circumstances phone the office or me. Just the number I gave you. Merv will then contact me. There's plenty of food here so you shouldn't need anything."

Matt nodded, trying not to look bored. Marcus had gone through the spiel several times already. After his boss had left, Matt found himself a modest pasta meal, sipping a glass of water as he leafed through his notebook. Mopping up his plate with bread, he dumped the dishes in the sink and put the coffee on. It would be a long night and caffeine would be the cornerstone of his strategy.

Plugging in his Toshiba Satellite laptop to the mains, the young journalist navigated to the encrypted folder and keyed in the password to access the files.

Fulford read carefully, taking shorthand notes as he skimmed the classified files on the monitor. There were thousands of pages of information that outlined hundreds of secret covert operations. It would be impossible to cover everything, even within a series of news stories. He would need to find the gems to make the maximum impact. He was certain that after these went public, there would be a major shitstorm erupting that the mainstream media would find impossible to ignore.

Matt shook his head silently as he read some of the paragraphs with a mixture of shock at the lengths the intelligence apparatus had gone and were planning to go to increase their power but also a rising sense of excitement at the impact this story would surely have. GCHQ had been pushing ahead with a plan to listen in on every man, woman, and child in the United Kingdom. It felt good to him to fight back, to give the people some ammunition, and to blow this wide open.

He took out yellow post-it notes from his work bag and scribbled down main points and stuck them on the far side of the table in a sequence. When he had a first draft, it would need to be run past the company's legal advisors before publication to make sure no lives were inadvertently endangered.

The scale of the programme was planned to be ever increasing with a target of ten gigabytes per second of data for each cable that fed into the Bude GCHQ station in Cornwall, within the next ten years. In theory, the report claimed, this would give them a capacity of more than twenty-one petabytes a day, which was the equivalent of sending all the books in the British Library every twenty-four hours. It seemed astonishing. Matt doubted the Liberatus ADSL connection could even get six megabits per second, a drop in the ocean compared to what was proposed here.

Intercept probes attached to transatlantic fibre-optic cables would glean useful information from this data, which included phone calls, emails, or any electronic communications. The Internet surveillance involved planning a duplication of all the web data, hived off onto a separate network, stored, and ready to analyse with the co-operation of the phone companies.

There was plenty of crap to wade through: protocols, footnotes, and references to files that were not in the files.

After reading for around forty-five minutes, he decided to focus on the surveillance that affected people now rather than historical operations. The story would have more traction with the public if it affected them directly – their rights to privacy and the very core of civil liberties were threatened. Effectively, the British intelligence agencies were forming a system where they could spy on everyone, every day, without any kind of permission.

Matt wrote late into the night, only stopping to help himself to more coffee from the ever steaming cafeteria. He liked to hit a story head on, break the back of it over a few sleepless nights, and then mop up afterwards. The key, as Marcus Brady had explained, was to move fast and get the story out there. Once out, nothing and no one could reel it back into any dark corner from where it had come. They would be too busy denying and counter-claiming and although the storm would make it difficult for everyone involved, it was a lot less dangerous than it was now. This brief prelude was like crawling through the web of a spider as it waited to attack.

They had certainly weaved hard and fast these last few years, in the dark corners of central intelligence agencies. And he was under no illusion that lives were at stake, very likely his, for one. Matt leaned back in his chair, wondering what their reaction would be.

Brand him and the *Liberatus* as traitors? Almost certainly. Attempt to murder him like they tried with John Rhodes? The thought made him shudder; he was scared and not afraid to admit it to himself.

Chapter 45

Carl drummed his fingers on the desk as he leafed through a series of papers on Frank Bowen. He was sitting in a corner communications room at Studio 31 on the Limehouse Cut Canal; his desk lamp seeming the dominant light in a sea of darkness. Several screens lit up his face, making him appear, if anyone were to look, like a sculpture deep set with heavy shadows. Whispers and crackles seeped from the audio feed on his computer, revealing that Frank was approaching Blackfriars Bridge.

Carl was certain that his friend, now black flagged by his superiors, was the figure in the covertly taken grainy black and white photos on his screen. The MI5 crew keeping tabs on the *Liberatus* offices in Soho square had reckoned it was Bowen and they were right. A worrying development. What the hell was he doing there? Surely not selling them the information they had been chasing? That would put Frank in traitor territory. Selling out the company was a big no-no.

Funny how things worked out. All that time and investment wasted. It had been a few years since Frank had joined the company. They'd had a good steady run within MI6 in the last few years. A few hairy moments, for sure. At times, Carl had thought he had lost him. Frank was good, he had talent, but why had he turned against his paymasters? Against him? Deep down, he knew where

Frank was coming from. The blanket term, "in the interests of national security" had been taken to the limit and used to justify some eyebrow-raising actions, as Carl had seen for himself. These thoughts had to be cast from his mind. Well, they were bringing him in now. Questions needed to be asked.

Suddenly eager to shake that direction of thought from his mind, Carl focused on the other cogs in the wheel. Operation Whisper Hunt, the centre of his troubled mind. His first Ghost 13 op had turned into one big screw up; a major flapping turkey with bells on. One minute surveillance was on the target and everything was fine, then comms went dark and on the other side, Brull, Greene, and Piper all turn up dead! Killed by Russians apparently. It was an extremely hostile act by the FSB, to say the least. Acting like that could start hot wars. It didn't make much sense.

And now the whistleblower herself was holed up with Frank. To say it had gone tits up was an understatement.

Carl knew he shouldn't give himself a hard time. It was the business he was in. Things inevitably went wrong, despite the detailed planning. Greene and Piper were his men, good men who had been taken out purposely and expertly. He had worked with them for years. He would find out exactly what the hell happened over there, starting with his old friend, Frank Bowen.

Chapter 46

Frank walked quickly down Black Friars Lane, high office blocks loomed either side as a milieu of suited workers stood outside one of the buildings, smoking and chatting. Blackfriars Bridge was just ahead and then he would head south of the river to East Dulwich, which was a hike that he really didn't want to make but he needed to get some stashed equipment.

Weapons were needed and luckily, he had the foresight to put a few tools away that no one else knew about. It had been way back in 1991 before he had set off travelling to Goa that he'd seen Carl's lock-up garage. On his return to the UK, he always thought it would be a good idea to get his own and so he had. Setting it up in secret, he had a backup stash site he was relieved to be able to count on now.

He quickened his pace, even more, wanting to get back as quickly as possible. The prospect of losing his family through one error of judgement loomed larger than ever. This operation had to kick off as soon as possible and Frank steeled himself to focus. He had no idea what Maria and Joe were going through, whether they were in immediate danger or what?

He turned onto the main carriageway of Queen Victoria Street and went under a railway bridge. The stream of traffic, the expanse of the Thames and the skyscrapers on the far side of the river beckoned just ahead. A man with a green hiking jacket and laptop bag over his shoulder weaved through the traffic across to Frank's side.

A young couple, taking in the sights, took photos of the Thames. A gust of wind broke across the bridge, causing a loose coke can to freewheel across the tarmac.

Frank suddenly felt exposed on the bridge; he should have found another way across the river. Why didn't he take the bloody tube? Soon, he was on the other side but the man in the green coat ahead of him had stopped and was looking in his bag for something. A black Mercedes with tinted windows travelling towards the bridge seemed to be driving the slowest possible speed. Frank's senses felt like a cascade of pins.

He suddenly turned right at the steps that led down to the riverbank and jumped down them as fast as he could. On the path he turned right again underneath the bridge, trying to be as unpredictable as possible. Racing past a couple who stepped out of his way, he quickly glanced back. A stocky man with a shaven head and squat-like features reached the bottom of the steps on the other side of the bridge and started to run after him. The path opened up into a wider walkway, the shimmering cityscape of central London across the water beyond and red brick office blocks on his immediate right. Another brief look and he saw his pursuer was keeping pace with him but hardly gaining.

Ahead, the man wearing the green hiking jacket who had been on the bridge stood directly in front of him, holding his hand inside his laptop bag. He shook his head at Frank as if to say the chase was over.

Frank came to a resigned stop after catching sight of his weapon in the bag. The thug came up behind him, his face all puckered skin and scars, red from the exercise as he pointed a handgun that was partially hidden by a suit jacket over his arm directly at Frank.

"Frank Bowen. You're to come with us," he said. He had a trace of a northern English accent.

Frank let out a sigh and levelled his gaze onto the man speaking. "I take it I can't speak to a lawyer?"

The thug waved his gun impatiently. "Just come with us to the car or there'll be consequences."

There was no point in playing games. It was bad timing but he knew who they were. His old employers had tracked him down. They took Frank back along the path in silence and then back up the steps where the parked Mercedes waited. He was ushered into the rear seat, followed by the thug and then the man wearing the green hiking jacket got in the other side, closing Frank in.

The bald thug pulled out a black hood. "I'm putting this on you."

"Is there really any need?" Frank started to protest but no discussion followed as he shoved the hood over Frank's head without a word and then jammed his pistol into his chest, to emphasise the situation.

After an hour's drive, he was bundled out of the car and through a series of doors, then down endless concrete steps before the hood came off. He was in a room with no windows. The walls were stark and grey; old concrete, some underground place, but still in London. Steel mesh surrounding him, tied into the walls. After an hour of being on his own in the room, a man entered and offered him a drink. Frank held up his cuffed wrists that bit savagely into his skin.

"Can you get these off me please?"

The young man shook his head.

"Sorry, but I can get you a drink?"

"Coffee."

Another hour. There must be a connection. He thought through everything in his mind trying to make sense of the broken pieces. Russians in Cuba, doing the bidding of whom? FSB or some other entity? They were desperate for the information Sarah had taken. The Russians would be interested in GCHQ secrets but something didn't fit.

The other pieces. The One Time Code evidence in the warehouse, the same paper his side used. And most of all, their safe houses in Havana blown. Not once but twice. Someone here at Ghost 13 must be feeding the Russians the info.

Someone.

The door clanked open again and a tall woman with dark hair tied back into a bun, and a shorter, gruff man stepped in and sat down opposite him.

The questioning began. Simple questions at first. His name. His role. School. Names of friends. But Frank knew they were just getting rolling.

"What is your given codename?"

"Auditor."

"What happened to Piper and Greene?"

"They were killed. We were ambushed at the safe house. Greene got hit and Piper died later from his wounds."

"Why did you communicate and then take off with Pandora when in Cuba?"

"A group of Russians turned up. There wasn't time to follow protocol. She might have been killed and then we'd all have lost."

"What happened to Piper and Greene?"

"I already told you."

"Tell us again in detail. Indulge us, Frank."

He told them. The chance meeting with Pandora and then the word that the Russians were in the hotel. There was no time except to grab her and take off. Then once again, he described the ambush, the shooting, and how Piper lost his fight to live.

Didn't Frank realise he was going against protocol by communicating with the surveillance target? Yes, he did. That they could lock him up and throw away the key?

"Where's my family?" Frank demanded. They didn't know. He explained the photograph, the Russians showing Maria and his boy bound and gagged and imprisoned somewhere.

They didn't know anything about it but they assured him that the police were working the case.

Frank wasn't convinced he could trust the police to carry out a safe rescue mission of his family but now he was incarcerated, he might not have much choice.

"I need to see Carl Paterson, my superior."

After another hour, they took a break and Frank was left in the room alone again. He just wanted Maria and Joe safe. Fuck what his employers would do to him, it didn't matter now.

Another few hours passed. Was it day or night? The cuffs were killing him. How the hell had he got into this mess? He wouldn't do this again, ever. No more bullshit from that bastard, Carl.

On that thought, Carl walked into the holding room and slammed a briefcase down next to the table. He took out a batch of keys and undid Frank's cuffs before sitting down opposite him.

"Thanks. So what the hell's going on? Maria and Joe...they've been kidnapped. You need to get me out of me, Carl!"

Carl sighed and swept imaginary dust off the top of the table with his hand.

"Frank, you're in serious shit. You had a job to do; put a target under surveillance. Instead, you approached that target and disappeared with her and then your team was seriously compromised. I need to know what happened."

"Compromised, Carl? We were ambushed, pure and simple. Piper, Greene, and Brull all died out there. The same group who have my partner and child, here in London. Thanks for looking out for them, by the way. Look, I know where they are. You could help me!" Frank was shouting now.

Carl ignored him and stuck to the subject.

"You took off with a traitor to the group. Where is she, Frank?"

"You mean you don't know? She's dead, Carl."

"Can you prove that?"

"What do you want, her head in a bag? Gruesome pictures? I just heard she was dead."

"How?"

"Shot by that Russian mob."

"Maria works for *Liberatus News*, whose owner, John Rhodes, also runs a sister activist group under the same name. Did you know that?"

"No, I didn't," he lied. "But whatever that's about, I'm sure she knew what she was doing. She's a smart woman. So is working for a cause illegal now?" he said, tightly.

"I'm sure she didn't have illegal intentions, Frank, but I'm telling you that Liberatus are showing up on intelligence radars. I know MI5 are taking a keen interest in the group."

Carl stared at him unblinkingly as if waiting for a response. Frank shrugged.

"They're nothing to do with me," he said, lowering his head and closing his eyes as if to rest them, if only for a second.

"Are you sure? Maybe you killed the team, took the information, and sold it to someone, like Liberatus?" Carl had lowered his voice to an accusing whisper and he stared down at him.

Frank looked up, a veneer of contempt on his face.

"You actually believe that?"

Carl pulled up his briefcase that was standing against the table leg and opened it up, bringing out a manilla folder before snapping the briefcase closed. He nonchalantly emptied out a batch of photographs onto the table. Frank glanced down at the pictures that showed him entering and leaving the *Liberatus* newspaper office in Soho square. Frank silently cursed his mistake, wondering whether he jeopardised his chance to find Maria and Joe but he breathed evenly, his facial expression giving nothing away.

"Their offices are under surveillance by a team from MI5. Our contacts there knew we were keeping an eye out for you, so they passed on the information."

"Why are you telling me all this shit, Carl? I thought the key to intelligence was to never let on anything you didn't have to?"

Carl grimaced for a moment and adjusted himself in his chair as if biding time.

"I want to help you, as a friend," he said.

"Help me get Maria and Joe back, that's all I want. Then you can throw me in prison or whatever you're going to do afterwards, I don't give a shit."

Carl closed his eyes for a second as if regretting something.

"I'm really sorry about them, I will look into it, see what I can find out. The police are on it. But this whole operation has been a screw up from beginning to end, as you know. And you were right in the middle of it."

"You have to help me," said Frank, quietly but determinedly. He was growing anxious. Time was ticking.

Carl paused and rummaged around in his pocket. He threw a packet of cigarettes onto the table.

"Go ahead," he offered.

"I gave up."

"Well, I never said this before but you have an addictive personality, Frank. Always have. So, given the circumstances, I thought I'd offer."

Frank shook his head and pushed the packet away.

Carl exhaled slowly and stood up to leave the room. After a minute, he returned with the shaven-headed thug who had been in the car on the bridge. Frank groaned inwardly and prepared himself for the beating that was surely coming. The thug had a black hood in his hand.

"Stand up, Frank."

"Friendship over then, is it, Carl?" Frank snorted in contempt.

"Shut up. You're going to be hooded and cuffed again, temporarily."

He did as Carl asked, getting to his feet slowly.

"I need to find Maria and Joe, Carl. They're in danger, do you understand me? One last favour?'

Before the hood went over his head, Frank caught Carl's eye. He nodded ever so subtly and then his world went black.

Chapter 47

Frank had been in the back of a van travelling fast for around thirty minutes before it slowed down and traversed a few corners before pulling over. A hand grabbed his forearm and he heard the side door slide open before a shove in his back forced him out of the vehicle. A shock wave of pain shot through his body as he hit the hard pavement. A screech of tyres and the sound of the van engine receded.

Frank pulled off the hood and gasped in much needed fresh air. He rolled onto his side and groaned out loud, holding his shin that had taken the brunt of the fall.

No time to piss around, Frank.

He sat upright and looked around, discovering he was on a pavement that ran along a council estate car park. A boy around nine or ten years old, holding a skateboard, stared at him in awe, obviously having just witnessed the scene.

"Hey, where am I?" Frank asked. The kid seemed frozen, transfixed on the haggard figure pulling himself to his feet and then brushing himself down.

"It's okay, just tell me where I am."

"Camberwell," the boy spoke rapidly in a South London accent and then threw down his board and lunged his right foot on before skating off into the estate.

"Camberwell? That's good," Frank whispered to himself and he began to hobble towards a main road to get his bearings. He kept his eyes peeled in case he was being watched but it didn't matter anymore. Maria and Joe, they were all that mattered. Did Carl know where he was heading? He had let him go. The friendship was possibly still on then. The past still mattered, it seemed, even in the murky grey world they lived in. Had Carl defied his bosses? If so, he had done him a huge favour.

A bus got him closer to Dulwich and then cutting through a park, he came to a maze of council house complexes, red-bricked and packed tightly like cubicles. Eventually, he turned a corner where a line of lock-up garages stood and pulled out a bunch of keys, unlocked the padlock, and the secondary locks on the doors.

Slipping into the darkness, he flipped a switch that sparked a flickering lone light bulb into life. Frank shut the doors behind him and carefully looked around his garage, looking for signs of entry. The dust was still on the floor as he remembered. He was sure it was safe. The garage had not been mentioned to anyone, including Maria. The paperwork for the rental had been done through a fake name with no connection with his employers, or ex-employers as was now the case.

After looking at surfaces on the wooden table, and the shelves and chairs, Frank immediately checked for the SIG Pro SP 2009 pistol in the sofa lining. He felt around for several seconds, unable to find it. Just as he was beginning to think that maybe the lock-up garage had been compromised, the tips of his fingers brushed the familiar steel of the weapon. His fingers clasped around the butt and he slowly ripped the masking tape that secured it to the inside back of the sofa and pulled it free.

Frank soon found the 9mm bullets case alongside it and placed both items on a table top. He painstakingly took the weapon apart, cleaning each piece before putting it back together and loading it. After finishing with his weapon check, Frank gathered up equipment into a haversack. Small binoculars that he had used in the woodland exercise so many years ago, a couple of listening devices that could easily be hidden or attached on the underside of any table or chair. They transmitted to a notepad device, similar to what he had used in Havana. A pen torch with a powerful battery life and a hunter's knife in a pouch.

Finally, he strapped a concealed knife holster to his ankle and secured the Gerber fixed blade in place. After triple checking everything and grabbing a wad of pound notes from a hiding hole under the floor, Frank slipped out of the garage, locking the door behind him and disappeared into the evening gloom, determined to save his family.

Or die trying.

Chapter 48

The Golden Lion was one of those old forgotten London pubs that no one except local old men and traders from the market went to. The wallpaper had a flowery pattern that had faded over the decades and the upholstered seats seemed to melt into the walls in the dim light. Frank glanced around as he walked in. Three men touching 60 sat at the dark wooden bar nursing their ales, checking him out for a moment before continuing their chat about the football game on the television behind the bar. A few more solitary figures near the back, avidly read their newspapers.

Frank ordered a lime and soda and sat down in an alcove seat, facing the door.

After ten minutes, Griff walked in and after spotting Frank, made a beeline for his table. He slipped in and propped his laptop bag next to him.

"Hi, Frank. How're you doing? Nice place."

"Yeah, you can't beat a bit of spit and sawdust," he said grimly. There was sarcasm and no smile but he was genuinely glad to see the young techie again. He had always liked him, trusted his judgement, and admired the fact that he had a wise head on young shoulders.

"So what do you have for me, Griffy?"

Griff slipped a photograph to Frank and spoke low to him, relaying from memory while his eyes moved around the bar, settling on the

3 old guys watching the game.

"The man you thought might be the one? His name is Viktor Kozel, uses the codename Kobra. He entered the UK two months ago, we picked it up as he was on a Russian organised crime list. Usually, it would have been passed onto the Met crime unit but because he also had KGB connections, MI6 took an interest."

Frank looked over the clearer image of Viktor Kozel. Now that he had seen the Russian with his own eyes, it was merely confirmation of what he now already knew, but the background information finally answered some questions.

"So who's his sugar daddy?"

Griff shook his head and then pointed out other photos of associates in the folder.

Frank glanced over them, recognising the faces from Havana.

"Any idea who hired these charmers?"

"No idea."

"I think I found the house where they are but I might need you to help me with something," Frank said.

Griff shifted his gaze back to Frank again. "Help? As in what? Am I not helping already?"

"I don't want to go into the house without you nearby. I might need a distraction, an extra pair of eyes, someone to call it in if things go south."

Griff looked worried. "Frank, I'm a techie, not some kind of action man. Don't make me do something crazy!"

Frank smiled at his concern. "Relax, mate. I'm not going to ask you to go into the house. Just be nearby, keep an eye out. Watch my back."

Griff shook his head defiantly. "Fuck no!"

Frank continued in a low, calm voice. "Please, Griff. Just keep watch for me, just in case. You'll be well away from any action.

My kid, he's only eight years old and most likely terrified. I don't know how they're being treated, what they're being threatened with…Believe me, I just want to get up right now and go in all guns blazing. But that's hardly gonna save them…"

Griff held his hands over his forehead for a moment. "Ah, Jesus!"

Frank took a lug of his lime and soda, the ice cubes rattling in the glass.

"First thing is to get eyes on the place. I need to do a reccy. See what I can see. We may need to cause a distraction at the front of the house to help me sneak in the back."

Griff had taken off his glasses and was cleaning the lenses with his shirt.

"Do you have an RP?" Griff was referring to a reconnaissance point.

"I do. A derelict building looking across the gardens towards the back of the house."

"And who's in the target house exactly?"

"I don't know how many are holding Maria and Joe. There could be hundreds of those bastards all heavily armed and itching for a fight but I very much doubt it. I reckon three at the most."

Frank could almost sense the fear radiating from Griff.

"It's okay, bud. I won't put you in any danger. I promise you."

Griff looked unconvinced.

Chapter 49

The Secret Mass Surveillance Plan

18th August 1999

by Matt Fulford.

Although the technology would take at least another decade to reach the levels capable of this amount of data surveillance, the intelligence seems to be a statement of intent by the powers in Government to create a state reminiscent of George Orwell's novel, *1984*.

GCHQ and MI6 are at the centre of a plan to put the UK population under mass surveillance. The story has been uncovered thanks to the covert efforts of an unnamed whistleblower named only as 'Pandora'.

Not since a seminal investigation into GCHQ in Time Out revealing its very existence in 1976 has there been a more shocking story focused on the intelligence community.

The top-secret documents received by Liberatus reveal a myriad of covert plots, the bulk of which relate directly to a plan to access streams of data including emails, phone calls, and information from the increasingly popular Internet. The plan, codenamed 'Oculus', involved tapping into the cables and the communications they carry that run from the Atlantic and through the Bude GCHQ station.

Full details inside...

Chapter 50

Viktor Kozel took the call and heard the familiar rasping voice, altered by disguise software that made it sound like the man was speaking inside a tin bathtub.

"We're closing down 'Whisper Hunt' as there's been a leak. You know what you need to do. Please acknowledge."

There was a pause on the line before Viktor uttered a simple "Okay" and the Marquis disconnected. The kidnapper stood looking at his phone for a moment and swore to himself, before glancing at his watch. He would have to deal with this personally to ensure it was done right. It wasn't quite so much killing the woman, she knew what she was into, but having to pop the boy as well? That would be harder to wipe from his memory. He must be getting too old for this job.

It would have to be a couple of shots apiece, with a big fire to cover up the whole scene. Forensics could be paid off, pressure applied, and it would just be another tragedy in London hardly warranting a write up in the papers.

He ran through a mental checklist of the items needed as he climbed the stairs to the upper landing and then went up the spiral staircase that led to the secured room. After unlocking the door, he glanced in and saw them huddled in the corner of the sparse room wrapped in the duvet he had given them earlier. The heating had stopped working and the nights had been getting colder.

He felt bad having to kill them both but that was the order. Frank Bowen and the whistleblower had slipped through his fingers. That incident had been very unfortunate and Viktor surmised he would have to watch his back. The Marquis had expressed his dissatisfaction that he had lost them but that was all and the Russian was certain he'd want to punish him for that screw-up.

Now his gang had been wiped out and he was stuck with that paedophile, Yegor, who had to be brought in for the kidnapping.

No, he would finish the job, shoot the kid first and then Frank's bitch. After that, it would be a case of hunting down Frank Bowen for revenge, which was the least he could do for his fallen comrades. The second payments from the Marquis weren't going to happen now. At least he still had some of the money that should have gone to his men.

When this whole mess was over, he would go back to Mother Russia and work for the Chinese or his old employers. No more western intelligence agencies, they couldn't be trusted.

He took out his phone and began to type in a message to Bowen and then he pressed the send button. Was he already back in the UK? Most probably. And if he had any tradecraft skills left, he would be close to finding them. There wasn't much time.

Viktor studied the pathetic figures in the room and almost felt sorry for them. They were victims in a world they did not belong to. A world of spies, power-mad men, and covert plots. It was not his problem though, he had his orders. It was what he was been paid for. For now, though, he would give them one last meal. He had a heart after all.

"Do you want to eat? Food?" he asked gruffly.

Maria looked up at him with a fierce hatred Viktor had grown used to. If it had not been for Joe, she would probably have refused, but for his sake, she had been playing it calm and cool.

"Yes," she managed and the Russian closed the door behind him.

Chapter 51

Frank and Griff arrived at the derelict house and scrambled over the door frame to the rear. Griff struggled and was not being particularly quiet about it but they were soon in the backyard. Frank took out a pair of pliers from his backpack and began unbolting the metal sheeting that he had peered through earlier. After removing all four bolts on one side, he was able to peel it back, opening up just enough space for them both to squeeze through.

Once inside, they checked the whole house to make sure they wouldn't get any nasty surprises. Apart from random debris and the smell of piss on the top floor, it wasn't in that bad a state. A few licks of paint, new windows, doors, kitchen, and bathroom and it would be perfectly habitable. It seemed such a waste.

They set up in the rear room that was probably once a dining area, making sure they were able to get a good view of the target house from their position. Some of the plasterboard had been ripped away from the walls and electrical wires hung from the ceiling.

Frank scanned the immediate area through his binoculars before focusing on the target house. As he had seen at the front door, most of the rear windows were all blanketed with curtains, pulled tightly closed.

On the ground floor, there was an extension that was probably the kitchen with a side rear door. Frank raised his night vision binoculars to the upper part of the house again and inspected a small skylight window built into the roof. It was shut tight and along the edge of the blackout blind, he noticed a faint light. Whether it was from a lamp or a stairs hallway light, Frank couldn't be sure. He took the glasses away from his eyes, passed them to Griff and assessed the gardens. It would only be a few metres to get across to the house. That wasn't the difficult part.

"Okay, you get a good view of the rear of the house from here. Just keep an eye out and text me if you see anything at all."

"No problem, Frank. That I can do!" Griff peered through the binoculars.

"Just like a real stake-out, huh? Bit of fieldwork beats staring at a screen all day, huh?"

"Hmm, I dunno. I like the comfort of the flickering screen. I'm in a warm place and there's all the Doritos and Cokes I could ever want. This place is dark, cold, and damp."

Frank felt the vibration of his Russian phone in his pocket. He whipped it out and saw it was a text message. The words on the screen chilled him to the bone.

"Seen the news, Frank? You fucked us and leaked the information...this little game is over for your family."

Chapter 52

Frank had immediately tried to call the Russian back but only a disconnected, dead tone could be heard. Now he hung his head, taking shallow breathes as the danger hit home. They could be already dead…if not, then their time was very close. Brady had already published? It was too early! He couldn't believe what was happening.

"Frank?"

Griff was looking at him with concern. He was holding the night vision binoculars in his hand after looking over the target building.

"Give me those," he demanded and Griff quickly handed them over.

Frank scanned the terrace and once again stopped at the target house. It was quiet and most of the neighbours seemed to have gone to their beds.

"They're in immediate danger. I can't wait any longer," he said, rummaging around in his bag before pulling out the SIG Pro SP 2009 he had brought from the lock-up garage. He started to load up the chamber from the bullet case, his hand clearly shaking.

"Be careful. Just see if there's a way in there first. Don't make any stupid mistakes, Frank. You're angry now but that could cost you," reasoned Griff in a level voice. Frank nodded impatiently. He knew the geek was right but there was no time anymore. He put the safety catch on the SIG Pro, tucked it into his belt, and checked his watch. 22:35 hours. Ideally, he needed to wait another few hours or so but that was never going to happen.

"Just keep your eyes on the house for me, could you, mate?"

"Sure, Frank. And if I see anything that you need to know about?"

"Text my phone."

He took the compact Nokia out of his pocket and double checked it was on silent. The last thing he wanted was some stupid ringtone blasting out as he crept up the stairs. Frank checked the hunter's knife in a pouch was securely attached to his belt on his rear and the ankle holster with the smaller knife was tightly fastened.

A minute later, Frank moved through the gardens in the darkness, pausing every few yards to check he hadn't been seen. Razor focused, nothing else in the world mattered now. He slipped over the last fence into the target's garden, checking every step before crouching against the wall.

As expected, the back door was well secured but Frank thought he could get the kitchen window open. He began working away at the handle, probing a piece of looped wire into the key lock to try to get some leverage. Suddenly a light went on behind the blind and Frank froze. He heard the noises of someone about to prepare food, the clanking of saucepans and then the low tone of voices. Two men speaking in Russian.

Frank lowered his hand from the lock and crouched back down with his back against the wall, his head turned to the kitchen window, listening carefully just to see if he could pick up any clues or information. His eyes rested on an old black bin that had been dumped in the garden. Across the gardens, he could see the dark shape of the derelict building set back in the row of houses. There was no sign that Griff was watching from the small gap in the bottom window. A light went off in one of the neighbouring rooms.

Suddenly, there was a clank of an unlocking back door and then a light squealing sound as it opened. Frank kept dead still but positioned himself to pounce up if needed. If they came out into the garden and looked directly to their left, he might well be seen, at which point, he would need to attack.

Instead, a bag of rubbish was thrown from the doorway towards the main collection of plastic bins in the garden. Whoever was doing the deed obviously didn't fancy coming out into the night. The bag clanked with the sound of glass and tins just several yards from where Frank was crouching. The door slammed shut again and he waited for the sound of the lock but it didn't come. Then he heard more clanking in the kitchen as if dinner was being served. There was a way in.

Frank took out his mobile and began texting Griff a simple message.

It was twenty minutes before the kitchen light dimmed and he chanced a quick look through the window. He could see through the kitchen doorway that led to a living room where the flicker of a television set lit the hallway in between. He checked his Nite MX10; it was just after 23:00. He had no idea if these guys would be going to bed, or whether one of them would be staying up to keep an eye out. He had to assume Maria and Joe were still alive, otherwise, they would surely have cleared out long ago? The thought also crossed his mind that it could be a trap. Lure him in, take him out. Perhaps they would be satisfied with his head only and let Joe and Maria go?

Move now or wait? There was no alternative. Was there another way? Something else he could have done?

Frank realised he was already losing his focus, the feeling of impatience overwhelming him now. Just to see their faces again; to know they were safe. It seemed right to go now; it was his instinct telling him.

He went through the plan in his head. Work out how many hostiles were in the house without detection and then find the room Maria and Joe were in as quickly as possible. Try to extract them without confrontation.

Without further hesitation, he moved around the corner towards the back door and slowly turned the handle, easing the door open by a few millimetres, listening hard for that squeak.

A sudden sound of rapid gunfire and an explosion burst from a television that spiked Frank's guard for a moment. He eased the door open further, taking full advantage of the noise cover, and slipped through the gap, closing the door behind himself. He moved slowly to the kitchen doorway, pausing for a moment. He moved a step to see if he could see more of the living room, which had an open door and clocked a pair of feet in socks crossed over each other. No shoes, obviously, they were not expecting any change in routine or surprises.

Frank moved carefully across the doorway and along a hallway that led to the stairs. Luckily, the floor was covered in thick carpet, which kept the sound down and he reached the steps and began climbing.

The television action scene suddenly came to a halt and there was a silence. Frank froze on the first few steps. The louder sound of an advert came on, blasting the advantage of a premium pet food. Voices of two men speaking in Russian began. Frank guessed they were discussing the film and then more worryingly, there was the sound of movement. Someone was hauling their ass out of the sofa and a shadow moved across the wall. A tall figure went into the hallway, obscured by shadow and went into the kitchen, flicking on the light.

Frank continued to move, slowly but surely until he was near the top. There was a door directly in front of him, which he had guessed from his earlier surveillance was the bathroom. A hallway ran back parallel to the stairs with several closed doors.

He was aware and ready in case anyone suddenly sprang out of one of the rooms, but his instinct told him there were only two in the house.

Behind the first door was indeed the bathroom. He assessed it for possible exit routes and checked the window. The drop outside was around thirty feet, probably okay for him but probably too far a drop for Maria and Joe.

Back in the hallway, moving back towards the front of the house, he spotted two doors and then spiral stairs leading to the top. Each room on the mid-level was empty. One had a distinct smell of tobacco with an unmade bed and a pile of unwashed clothes. The window was facing the rear with tightly closed curtains. He slowly moved the curtain open by about a centimetre but saw very little in the darkness.

In the second room, it appeared cleaner but still lived in and Frank crept across the carpet to check the window, again, slowly edging the curtain open. The window looked out onto the street and Frank decided he preferred getting out via the rear and left the room. The sound of the television receded as Frank crept up the spiral staircase leading to the attic level. When he reached the top, there was a single door, reinforced with a metal frame and panels that, even in the gloom, looked like it was a formidable obstacle. He pressed his ear against it and focused hard on any sign of movement. There was none that he could hear.

A sound of footsteps arriving at the landing below made Frank hold his breath and then he heard them slowly climb the metal spiral staircase towards him. Frank moved back into the alcove and crouched, making himself still in the shadow opposite the door.

A figure appeared, easily six and a half feet tall with short black hair and carrying a tray with a metallic pot of what smelled like stew. He bent his considerable bulk down to place the pot on the ground as he searched for his keys.

Frank went through the options in his head, quickly assessing how to overcome this piece of shit. The knife was one but the guy was big and if he got it wrong, it would make him yell out. It had to be kept quiet, even with the television blaring on the ground floor. A clean cut on the vocal cords would be the only way but Frank would need to jump to get that high, could he really be that accurate?

Once the big man had his keys out, had unlocked and opened the door, Frank made his move. He pounced onto the man's back, his right arm gripping the kidnapper's throat in a rear naked strangle. Both men fell into the room, spilling the stew pot and Frank kept squeezing his bicep and forearm as hard as he could against the Russian's carotid arteries. He croaked like a frog, bucking and struggling, reaching for Frank and trying to pull him off. With the blood pressure dropping from his head, his body began to shut down from lack of oxygen. After ten long seconds, the bulk of the kidnapper suddenly relaxed as he fell unconscious, his chest rising and falling as he breathed heavily.

Frank rolled onto the floor and looked up to see the shocked faces of Maria and Joe staring back at him. He got to his feet and went over to them. For a moment, it seemed like they weren't going to acknowledge it was him as if he was an intruder and then their faces changed to relief.

"Frank?"

He leaned down and put his arms around them both.

"Is he dead?" Maria added.

"He'll live, but you have to do exactly as I say, okay? How many are in the house, do you know?"

"I think it was just two. All we've ever seen is this man and another with the mohawk."

"That'll be my friend, Viktor," said Frank. He wasn't smiling.

"What's the plan?" asked Maria. Frank noticed a calm but determined expression fall over her face, one that he hadn't seen since they were on the run from a Chinese assassin in Asia.

Frank looked at his Nite MX10 watch. "We get out of here, just wait."

Frank grabbed the man's keys and began to go through them, looking for the one to their door. He searched his pockets but there was no weapon.

"Right, okay. We need to get down a level and get out the back across the gardens. Be as quiet as you can. I'll check first."

Frank locked the big man in the room while Maria and Joe waited just outside it and then paused at the top of the landing, listening intently. He signalled them to stay put and descended the spiral stairwell, careful to be light-footed. There was still the faint drone of the television on the ground floor but no other sound.

Suddenly, a figure appeared in the hallway below. Where the hell had he come from? It was Kozel the Kobra.

"Yegor?" the Russian shouted upwards and immediately began to climb the spiral stairs. Frank reached for his gun but it was gone! There was no time. Frank had the height advantage and the fact he hadn't seen him yet.

He dived head first. The Russian, instinctively sensing the danger, curled up, bracing for the impact. Their bodies collided and fell heavily into the hallway, Frank's weight driving through the Russian before he rolled clear. Both men quickly jumped up, facing each other. Frank's eyes darted to his opponent's right hand and the blade he held within it.

"Why don't you have a go, Frank?" baited the Russian. "All that pent-up steam, waiting to be released."

Frank already with his right arm slightly behind him moved slowly, freeing the knife from the holster.

"Where are your friends, Viktor Kozel?"

The faintest hint of surprise flashed across his eyes at his real name being mentioned and then he smiled and nodded.

"Very good, Frank."

"Oh, yeah, they're just corpses in a Cuban warehouse now, already burning in hell, aren't they?" said Frank with as much bitter venom in his voice as possible. The knife eased slowly out of the pouch and Frank held it inversely in his palm. There was a rush of anger in the Russian's eyes before he moved forward suddenly, slashing out with his blade at Frank's chest. Jumping backwards, Frank kept clear of the attack and as the knife passed by, Frank drove his hidden blade across the Russian's forearm. The strike was deep. Victor looked surprised and stood backwards quickly. The blood was running freely from the wound, down his hand and dripping off his fingers, where it quickly pooled on the floor. He still held his weapon tight; these Russians were something else.

Kozel, enraged, struck out with his injured knife hand. Frank held up both hands instinctively, blocking with his own knife but the impact came from the Russian's shoulder in his chest as he level dropped and ran at him. Frank was thrown against the hard wall, the wind driven from his lungs. Dropping his knife onto the ground with a clang, he slumped to the floor, winded and gasping for breath.

Viktor grabbed his shoulders, thrusting a knee into Frank's chest. The impact felt like a cattle truck slamming against his lungs. He coughed and choked, hardly finding the air he so badly needed. Catching sight of the blade on the floor Frank grabbed it with his left hand but the Russian quickly stamped down, crushing his knuckles with his boot. Frank grimaced as the boot dragged the blade away from him and kicked it out of reach.

"Looks like I'll be getting sweet revenge for my comrades, Frank. Then I'll have the pleasure of blowing out the brains of your family. No one will ever avenge them, never."

Frank lifted his head up and glared at the kidnapper. His right hand slowly slipped out the blade he had packed on his ankle at the lockup. His eyes looked beyond the Russian at the spiral stairs behind him. "Maria," he whispered.

Viktor turned to the empty stairwell. It was just enough of a distraction. Frank lunged with the knife, stabbing the Russian just below the groin in his inside leg and with a violent twist, turned the blade before pulling it back out. Blood spewed from the injury; Frank had hit the femoral artery.

Instantly, Frank reached over and grabbed the Russian's knife hand. Lunging forward, Frank wrapped his arm around Viktor's calf and drove his weight into his leg. The blood streamed onto Frank as he brought him crashing to the floor. Kozel cried out in agony, his hands desperately trying to grab at Frank's head but the strength was draining out of him, second by second.

At that moment, Maria did actually appear, her face transfixed with horror as she saw the father of her child covered in blood.

Frank held his hand up as if to say he was okay. "It's all right, his blood!" he managed to gasp before standing up, stepping back from the Russian who was now attempting to hold his wound, breathing in short gasps, eyes wide with fear. Maria and Frank watched him, transfixed as his life ebbed away and then the gasping stopped, his eyes staring straight ahead.

Frank leaned over the body to check his pulse and nodded at Maria, confirming what he already knew.

"Better get a towel to cover him," he said and Maria came back from the hallway bathroom and threw it over the body as best she could. "It's all right, Joe," she shouted.

Soon, a light footfall came down the staircase and the boy stood looking at the Russian man in fascination.

"Everything's okay, Joe," Maria held out her hand for him but Joe stood as if fixed to the spot looking at the covered corpse.

"Yes, everything's okay – you're safe now," Frank added.

Joe nodded and went to his father. He held the SIG pistol in his hand and held it out for his father.

"It was on the floor. When you were fighting...," he said.

Frank took the weapon and put back in his belt. He ruffled Joe's hair and held him close against him.

"Good man. Jesus, thank God you're alright, Joe."

It hit him in that moment how close he came to losing him.

"I'm all good, Dad," Joe said. He leaned down and gave his son a hug and then he held his shoulders, facing him.

"You're the bravest kid I have ever known and I mean that. Now you have to do exactly as I say and we're going to get out of here, okay?"

Joe looked at his mother and back at his dad before nodding, his face fixed and calm, as if he had every confidence that he was now safe.

"I need to check the coast is clear and then let's get out of here." Maria and Joe nodded as they moved along to the top of the stairs as Frank descended to the ground floor.

Soon enough, he was ushering them across the gardens to safety where Griff waited for them.

Chapter 53

Nigel Harrison had already made the decision, but he still tidied up around the flat, putting items back in place and tearing up old letters. The sink needed cleaning, it hadn't been done for a while and then once he had started spraying bleach cleaner and scrubbing, the cooker and the other kitchen surfaces beckoned. It took his churning mind off the inevitable and distracted him, if only for a while.

A gust of wind rattled the kitchen window and for a second, Nigel wondered if he should change his mind but then dismissed his own cowardice. Because that was what it was. *Looking for loopholes already, Nigel? Trying to find a way out?* No, he was determined to see it through now. No excuses.

It was the method that concerned him. Slitting his wrists didn't sound appealing – he couldn't imagine how anyone could do that? Although they say that you just drift away into the oblivion, don't they?

A bullet in the head? Quick, certainly. Probably the fastest method. It would be over before he knew it, just a squeeze of the trigger. But it could go wrong. A bullet in the wrong place might leave him alive but paralysed or a dribbling vegetable. There would be no control after that. He'd be strapped to a wheelchair, fed by a nurse for the rest of his life. Besides, getting a gun would not be straightforward.

Hanging by rope? It would be easier to arrange, but he couldn't stand the idea of the strangulation. The gripping, tight squeeze on the throat made him feel uneasy.

No, it would be an overdose of pills, already purchased over the previous few weeks from separate pharmacies to avoid any suspicion and then squirrelled away until he was sure he had enough to do the job.

He thought about how he had let down John Rhodes, a man who had given him an opportunity that no one else would ever have given him. And the prospect of being framed for the child porn still hung over him like a guillotine – that was not something he was willing to live with, never in a million years. They would never stop, he knew that now. He was owned by them and he believed every single word when they told him that they would find him, no matter where he ran.

The faces of Maria and her son, Joe, appeared in his mind. He had helped seal their fate, leading the wolves to their door. What a creep. Now they were almost certainly rotting in a hole somewhere if they were still alive.

And Mother.

He wanted to join her in death, escaping the blanketing remorse, guilt, and hopelessness that had been smothering him since this whole bloody episode had begun.

Nigel switched off the electricity at the mains and went into the dark bedroom.

Chapter 54

Frank was sitting down at the dining table in the house at Barnes Bridge as a gentle patter of light rain mottled the window that faced the narrow stretch of the Thames. He put down the mug of tea he was cradling and cracked his knuckles; still brooding after reeling from anger at the timing of the *Liberatus* revelations. He had told Marcus to hold off for three days, hadn't he? It had very nearly put Maria and Joe on a collision course with death and he hadn't brought himself to tell Maria about that.

He needed to speak to Marcus Brady.

Laughter from the children running around the house echoed through the corridor as Maria finished a phone call on her Nokia mobile and turned to the breakfast bar to finish the sandwiches she was making. Rosie was somewhere in another part of the house, giving Frank and Maria some space.

The radio was on in the background and they both heard the familiar pips of the news.

"Can you turn it up a bit?" Frank asked. Maria turned up the volume and they both listened.

A parliamentary investigative enquiry has been announced, to be headed by Leo Smith, M.P. for Braintree, into the 'Pandora revelations' on the recent GCHQ spying scandal. Smith promised a thorough investigation into the matter but would not comment on whether GCHQ

Director, David Devlin, should resign.

This follows several mainstream newspapers picking up the story amid calls for the resignation of the top brass at GCHQ and MI6 by privacy campaigners. Public demonstrations have also been adding to the pressure and Smith added that it "threw open the question whether GCHQ had violated human rights legislation."

In other news...

Frank nodded and Maria switched off the radio.

"So, John Rhodes nearly died in a car accident. He's at St. Thomas' Hospital in intensive care and I'd really like to go and see him, Frank."

"It's not safe," he said, almost monotone.

"The Russians who kidnapped us are all dead, aren't they?"

"I just think we should be careful." He softened his voice, appreciating that she was alive and with him, pottering around the kitchen. It could have been so different.

"And while we're over there, I want to check on Nigel Harrison. He was used by them but I don't believe for a second he was overtly on their side," she continued.

"For God's sake!" Frank was exasperated. "We can't go hairing around London right now."

Maria turned to him.

"When is it ever going to be over? We need to take control. The story. This Pandora thing is going to press right now. The heat will be too much. They can't act once it's out."

"You don't know that!"

Maria was determined. Frank knew she wouldn't back down and exhaled slowly with exasperation. He was turning events over in his mind, trying to make sense out of it all. He had to admit to himself that it would be good to hear exactly what had happened from Rhodes.

"How is Rhodes? Is he conscious?" he asked, more calmly now.

"I spoke to Marcus. He's in and out of consciousness. Many broken bones but he'll survive." she said quietly. "He is very lucky to be alive apparently."

Frank thought for a moment, his eyes wandering back out at the rain.

"I'd like to speak with Marcus. And Nigel Harrison, the guy who you worked with who turned up with one of the Russians. You think he was forced into it?"

Maria came and placed the plate of finished sandwiches on the dining table and sat down opposite Frank, who grabbed one and began to wolf it down hungrily.

"Yes, he was scared, I could tell. They had something on him. He even said John was dead to get access to our flat. An odd man, but really completely harmless. He..." She stopped and shook her head, unable to fathom what had happened. She looked at Frank, her eyes telling him she wanted to do this.

"If we go, is it safe here? Leaving the kids?" he asked.

"You took care of the Russians, Frank, remember?"

It wasn't them he was worried about. It was whoever had hired them and lay waiting behind the curtain.

***

A woman, looking harassed with life in general, opened the main door of the flats just as Frank and Maria were looking for Nigel's name on the buzzers without success.

"Nigel Harrison? Do you know which flat he's in?" Maria asked quickly before she walked on. The woman, in her 50s with tightly permed hair, glanced at them and jolted her head.

"Top floor, luv. Number nine. He's a bit of a funny one. Go see for yourself." She held the door for them and they nodded their thanks and climbed the stairs to the top floor, their footfalls silent on the thick carpet. It was a well-maintained house that still held the faint smell of paint. They stopped at the dark pine door of Flat nine and Maria rapped it with her knuckles and then pressed her ear against it, listening carefully. She looked concerned.

"Can you kick it down?"

Frank looked puzzled and glanced around. "Kick it down? He's obviously out, Maria."

She knocked again. "Nigel? It's Maria. Are you in there?"

She took out her mobile and pressed it to her ear. Within a few seconds, they both heard the gentle chirping of a ring tone from inside the flat.

No answer.

Then they heard footsteps slowly coming up the stairs and an Indian man in his 50s appeared, ashen faced with swept back grey hair. He was fumbling through a huge bunch of keys before looking up to see the couple standing on the landing.

"Can I help you? I'm the landlord."

"Yes. We're looking for Nigel Harrison, a bit worried about him. I'm a work colleague," said Maria. "He hasn't been seen for a quite a while."

The landlord knocked on the door and continued to rummage through his keys.

"We've been knocking for a minute or so," said Frank.

The landlord unlocked the door and they entered the flat. "Hello?" their voices asked.

No answer.

Frank checked the bathroom, which was the first off the hallway and the others went into the main living room that had a kitchenette partition inside. He then went through the door opposite and saw what looked like a body lying on the bed in the gloomy room.

"Nigel?"

He went over to the window and pulled up the blind, flooding the room with much needed light. A vomit trail came from the mouth and a dried pool of it had conjuled onto the bed sheet.

"In here!" he shouted to the others before checking on Harrison but Frank already knew he was dead. He checked his pulse, two fingers on his wrist, and could feel nothing. The skin was cold.

Maria and the landlord came into the bedroom, concern etched on their faces. Frank caught Maria's eye and shook his head. He double-checked the pulse and then stepped back.

"I'm really sorry but he's passed on."

Chapter 55

Maria was shocked but remained calm as Frank drove to the hospital. They had waited for an ambulance to confirm what they already knew and then slipped away before there were any awkward questions. Frank was still feeling exposed and concerned about what lay ahead.

They walked into the busy reception at St. Thomas' Hospital and asked a stressed looking young woman behind the desk where John Rhodes was. She tapped on the keyboard and narrowed her eyes at the screen. She looked up at them. "Are you relatives?"

"Work colleague."

She smiled thinly and gestured towards a row of red plastic seats. "Could you wait and I'll get the doctor."

"Is something wrong?"

"The doctor will explain further," she replied quickly and then looked back down at her monitor.

"That doesn't sound good," Maria said quietly to Frank.

They sat down, Maria holding onto Frank's hand tightly. The day was taking a very unreal turn for her. Then a petite nurse in her mid-30s with her hair tied into a bun appeared before them.

"Mr. Bowen and Ms. Chapman. You're associates of John Rhodes, I believe?"

"Er, yes, that is correct," said Maria.

"Please come with me," she said and began to walk along a corridor, towards the back of the hospital. They followed her through double doors and into another stark walkway bleached by light from florescent tubes on the ceiling until they were at a fire exit, which she pushed open.

Frank and Maria looked at her quizzically.

"What's going on?" asked Frank, clearly wary.

"It's okay, Marcus is out here," the nurse said.

They walked along an enclosed path and then turned into a car park where they immediately saw Marcus, standing in front of a dark BMW.

"Marcus, what the hell is going on?" asked Maria.

"I'm taking you to see John. We'll come back and get your car later if that's alright?"

They weren't really in a position to argue and the thought of getting some answers prevented them asking anymore. Frank glared at him, another thought at the forefront of his mind.

They all got into the vehicle, Frank in the front passenger seat and Maria behind as the nurse returned to the hospital.

Frank turned to Marcus.

"So what the fuck happened to our agreement?" he said, his voice low and menacing.

"Frank?" Maria said in surprise from behind them.

Frank ignored her and continued staring hard at Marcus. "Three days! Not two. Fucking three!"

Marcus shook his head in realisation. "Oh, shit...I'm sorry. There were complications...a lot of pressure. We got raided..."

Maria grabbed at Frank's shoulder and shook it.

"Frank! Explain what's going on."

Frank turned his head slightly.

"They published before I was ready to get you out. We agreed to wait three days. It's a miracle everything turned out okay but the Russians were going to kill you and Joe after your crowd…" He threw a hand up toward Marcus. "…was so hell-bent on publishing!"

Marcus turned back to face Maria.

"Maria, I'm so sorry. The police raided our offices, tearing the place apart, looking for the information. Our staff were harassed and followed. We had to get to get it out there."

Maria shook her head as if to dismiss the apology.

"Maria? They were going to kill you and Joe, because of this bloody story!" Frank shouted, turning fully to face her.

"I think they were going to kill us anyway, Frank."

Frank, fighting himself to keep his temper from exploding, turned to look out of the window. *They were safe, that was all that mattered,* he kept telling himself, over and over. *They were safe.*

"Can we fucking go?" he said.

Thirty minutes later, after a silent journey, Marcus, Frank, and Maria were standing next to a bed upstairs at the Epsom cottage where Marcus explained, Fulford had hidden himself during the writing of the GCHQ revelations for the Liberatus news outlets.

She had been taken aback by John Rhode's appearance. He looked thinner, a dark purple and yellow bruise covered his cheekbone and eye, and a bandage was wrapped around his forehead. His eyes were closed and he was perfectly still, the gentle rise of his chest, monitored by a heart rate machine next to his bed, the only clue that he was still alive.

"So they let him out? Has he been conscious?"

Another nurse with short blonde hair and an officious manner came into the room, looking at the visitors with slight disapproval.

"Yes, he has been awake a few times. Karen here says it's just a case of careful nursing, nutrition, and plenty of time, isn't that right, Karen?"

The nurse nodded and pushed past Frank to check on the monitor and drip.

"It's one step at a time at this stage. He needs complete rest and no distractions," she said, making space around the bed so the visitors had to step back as she began to replace the drip.

Marcus looked at Frank and Maria and gestured silently with a nod of the head to leave and they climbed down the creaky stairs to the living room.

There was a copy of *Liberatus News* on the dining table and Maria picked it up. The headline of the small tabloid-sized newspaper read: 'The Secret Spy Programme Revealed.' Maria started reading the cover and then opened it up and spread it out on the tabletop. It was extensive coverage that dominated the paper's contents.

"You and Matt did a great job," Maria said, attempting to disperse the tension between Frank and Marcus.

Marcus nodded but he was looking at Frank. "It's just the tip of the iceberg. It'll run for some time. There's a lot more to come out yet though," He paused before adding, "Thanks to Sarah."

Maria looked up from the paper at Marcus and then turned to Frank questioningly. "Sarah?" There was a pause as both men realised she had not yet been privy to Sarah Edwards' involvement.

"She was the whistleblower who started all this trouble," Frank gestured once again with his hand at the spread out newspaper. "She revealed the secrets and was the one I had to track in Cuba." Maria glared at him for a moment before Marcus slowly sat down with them at the table, picking up the thread.

"Sarah Edwards is the unnamed source for the stories we're running. She was part of our group, Liberatus. She has been with us from the beginning and John was supposed to meet her in Cuba but..."

"...he had an accident." Frank finished the sentence.

"Where is she now then?"

"Safe…," Frank said. "But she wanted the authorities and anyone else to think she was dead. It was her request."

Marcus looked at Frank in surprise and then his face changed to realisation.

"Ahh, you didn't trust me," he said.

"I did," said Frank. "But not your offices. Anyone could have been listening."

Chapter 56

It was early evening when they heard the noise from upstairs, like a thud. The nurse had driven to Epsom to get some supplies as Frank, Maria, and Marcus drank tea in the room below.

"He's awake?" asked Maria to no one in particular. Frank and Marcus were already standing up. When they reached the room, John was reaching from his bed as he tried to stretch for a mug that had fallen off his table and onto the floor.

"Hey," said Maria. "How are you doing, John?" She instantly leaned over and picked up the mug with one hand and gently pushed back his arm. He slumped back onto the bed in relief and gave Maria a faint smile.

The others came in and gathered around the bed, pulling up chairs, Marcus nearest to him on the far side of the bed and Frank at the end.

"How are you feeling, John?" asked Marcus.

"Could be better," he wheezed. The voice was faint but it was obvious he was mentally intact and still his old self.

"Do you want anything?" asked Maria, who cast an eye over his drip.

John flapped a hand in dismissal, a mask of tiredness falling across his face.

"Tell me what is going on?" he asked, his voice so low, the others leaned in slightly to make out his words.

Marcus cleared his throat.

"They tried to kill you, John. You were in the car, driving back from Braintree in Essex. Do you remember?"

Rhodes shook his head.

"We got the information from your contact inside GCHQ. There's gold in those files and we've been flat out publishing as quickly as we can. Operation Oculus...a massive surveillance programme. There's other damaging revelations in there, too. We're causing big waves in the establishment. I'll give you the full details later but it's big." Marcus paused as if to reign in his enthusiasm.

John leaned his head and looked at Marcus, a grin appearing on his pale face.

"That's fantastic. Good work, Marcus. The girl?"

"She decided to stay in Cuba...for the time being. It's probably safer for now."

Rhodes turned to the window, to the view of a tree in the dusk light. "I hope we can help her one day," he said weakly.

Chapter 57

Liberatus News. 12th September

Shocking Oculus Files Reveal Covert Assassination Programme

Recent documents have revealed a secret assassination pro-gramme led by a group, as yet unnamed, associated with MI6. The documents, unrelated to the Oculus surveillance programme, detail how a small Cabal within the intelligence community unleashed what can only be described as a murder policy on deemed enemies and threats to their interests.

More inside...

13th September

Intel Chiefs Resign

Braithwaite and Devlin resign as agencies look to clean up acts amid mass political fallout following the breaking of the story, led by Liberatus.

Following the Oculus revelations, both heads of MI6 and GCHQ resigned yesterday as the political fallout intensified and further revelations also indicated that the planned data fishing was to be shared with America's National Security Agency, who is also thought to have a similar surveillance programme at an advanced stage.

More inside...

Chapter 58

Frank arrived at Hyde Park and speaker's corner and walked towards the gathered crowd as a young woman was getting into full swing with her speech. From what he could hear, she was on the topic of the recent revelations concerning surveillance and the intelligence services role in it. There were murmurs of approval from the listeners as anger poured through her words.

Frank spotted the familiar reddish hair in the crowd and eased towards Carl.

"Enjoying the speech?"

"It's very topical and no one's talking about anything else at the moment," Carl replied.

Both men started to walk along the pathway towards Tyburn Brook and the Serpentine Lake in the centre of the Park, the pronounced voice fading behind them until only gusts of wind carried the odd word of the woman's speech.

"Everyone is safe then?" asked Carl.

"My family, you mean? Yes, they're safe."

"That's great, a relief."

Carl nodded and took out a stick of gum, offering one to Frank, who shook his head, before rolling one up and popping it into his mouth.

"Bad for your digestion," said Frank almost as an afterthought.

"So why did you release me?" he asked.

"Believe me, I'm in a world of trouble for doing so but thanks to your friends at Liberatus breaking this story it's turning into a huge political scandal. There's enough firefighting going on for them not to be focused on me right now. Devlin stood down and was then arrested, Braithwaite is probably next..." He paused. A group of children were shouting and laughing, running through the grass past them.

"I wanted you to have a chance of getting Maria and Joe back. Why do you think I had you dropped off in Camberwell? I knew you had a lock-up around there somewhere but I wasn't in a position to help you directly and I'm sorry about that. We're still friends after all."

"Are we? There isn't really such a thing in this business, is there?"

Carl thought about that for a second. "Maybe not."

"So, this is what I have discovered. Devlin used information that I gave to him to target your team. He was directing the mercenary Russians as a clean-up operation. He wanted the stolen information and Edwards destroyed."

It confirmed what Frank had long suspected although he had not realised the extent of Devlin's involvement.

Carl continued. "Devlin ordered them to leave Russian made equipment in the warehouse in Havana, just to throw up false scents. It would confuse the Cuban authorities, who would wonder what the hell their allies were up to. Devlin could then claim that their team had been intercepted by the Russians or an unknown entity. It wouldn't make him look very good, of course, but he didn't care. His main objective was to silence Edwards and get the data she took...or just destroy both."

"So the safe houses were comprised because you passed on the details directly to Devlin?" Frank interjected.

Carl avoided Frank's glaring stare and nodded slowly.

"There was no way I could know the top level of the company was compromised."

Frank shook his head in disbelief.

"Unbelievable! Unbelievable. Bloody hell, Carl."

Carl ploughed on. "To make it seem like a genuine Russian FSB mission, he had them wipe out your team and then kidnap Maria and your kid to bring you out of the woodwork."

"A big fucking mess," Frank spat.

They had reached a snack hut that stood next to the brook, water rushing by, and beyond in the haze stood the grey jutting buildings of London. They ordered a couple of coffees and strolled along the bank.

"The Rhodes crash, it was a warning," said Carl.

"A murder attempt, you mean."

"You know how this all works, Frank."

"Like Nigel Harrison."

Carl gave Frank a sideways glance. "Nigel Harrison?"

"He sold out Rhodes or gave some information about his movement. But he had been pressured, blackmailed. Do you know anything about that, Carl? I assume you know he committed suicide."

"No, I...didn't know that."

Frank had a feeling that Carl was lying, he had known him too long. At that moment, Frank wasn't sure if Carl was friend or foe.

"Did your people get to Harrison, did they try to kill Rhodes?"

Carl stopped walking and Frank turned to face him.

"My people? Frank, you need to choose which side of the line you're on because you're way over it right now. This is your ex-employers we're talking about; your allegiance to the government and the crown. Leaking those state secrets is treason!"

Frank jerked a finger at Carl's chest as he made a face of disgust.

"Our employer sent in a mercenary gang of Russians who ambushed and killed my colleagues. Our bloody employer then kidnapped my family. Why are you defending that? By the way, I think I have a case for a lawsuit, Carl."

Carl sniggered and shook his head.

"Look, I understand the shit you went through. You've forgotten that your contract forbids any legal action. But the treason...well, maybe they'll let it slide."

"An apology, then?"

Carl shook his head and pushed past him. Frank turned to follow. A couple passed them by and they stayed silent for a while. A family of ducks made their way past them towards an old man throwing bread in the water.

"Piper and Greene were my people, too, mate. I never met Brull but he was a major asset, a good operator."

Frank nodded. "I know, he was a legend. I liked him. We could've been friends."

"Now tell me honestly what happened out there and I'll tell you about Rhodes and Harrison but it has to stay between us, Frank."

Frank held out his arms in a defensive manner. "Sure, it can stay between us, but don't forget I saw Greene killed in front of my eyes and I tried to save Piper's life. I was the one who was there, Carl."

They continued to walk along the edge of the Serpentine Lake.

"We're getting nowhere. I answered all the questions about Cuba in your charming little basement room. Yes, I took off with Sarah; the circumstances changed slightly with the Russian mercenary team bouncing in. They wanted to kill me and Edwards. I was doing my best to save her," said Frank.

"And she's definitely dead?"

"What else do you want me to say? Like I told you at your interview, I heard from reliable sources that she was dead." Frank re-affirmed the lie. He didn't feel guilty about it at all. He was protecting her.

Carl seemed to accept it and blew on the stream from his black coffee for a moment, took a sip, and stared off across the park.

"It's ironic. At any other time, I'd be the one getting the boot but as Liberatus named Devlin, he had to step down. Prison is around the corner for him but I get to keep my job...for now."

Frank began to walk away, discarding his coffee cup. "I'm so glad for you. Goodbye, Carl."

"I helped you, Frank, remember? I released you and gave you a chance to save Maria and Joe. Don't forget that."

Frank Bowen kept walking past the trees, the milling crowd at speaker's corner, and disappeared into the thronging city.

It felt like the world was changing, darker elements taking an increasing hold and Frank wasn't sure if he could be a part of it any longer. He had a family that he nearly lost – he had to keep them safe. The question that hung over him as he walked through the city streets towards home: should he actually be on the other side of the line? Should he fight for those who railed against freedom, disguising themselves as the establishment?

Or should he join Liberatus?

III

Ghost Order

Prologue

(AUC) Autodefensas Unidas de Colombia base camp

Putumayo, Colombia

June 1999

Through the window, the rain cascaded down in continuous waves, battering the tin roof with its insistent drumming, pouring down onto the wooden steps.

Outside, a group of soldiers in deep green fatigues moved across the camp and hurried inside one of the long huts that made up part of the barracks, slamming the door behind them. A small bedraggled dog, having made the camp its home, scavenged around a pile of rubbish piled up at the side of a smaller hut. Under the torrential rain, a sodden flag of the Autodefensas Unidas de Colombia – representing the new umbrella organisation that brought together a large number of right-wing paramilitary groups – hung lifelessly on a pole fixed to the barracks hut wall.

To the agent present, it made no odds that this paramilitary group was connected to the cartels or the wealthy Colombian landowners or even that they were responsible for tens of thousands of deaths inside the country. He had a job to do; even if that meant aligning with the Devil. So be it.

He had been fully briefed on the backgrounds of the leaders he was addressing now; how they had amassed their fortunes through emerald smuggling, kidnapping, arms dealing, robbery and, of course, the default source of income for many cartels; drug trafficking.

Yes, it was clear who he was dealing with. No one needed to remind him how precarious the tightrope of influence was over the muddy waters of South America and he knew he had to be careful how he handled the upcoming meeting.

He drained his coffee mug with one long pull, put it down and reached in his shirt pocket for yet another cigarette.

Through the window, the agent could see a black 4X4 pull up. Two men in AUC uniform jumped out and hurried across to the hut where the agent waited.

The two Colombian paramilitary leaders entered and shook hands with the agent, formally introducing themselves according to the expected military protocol, even though everyone in the room knew who each other was.

Gustavo Bejarano, the leader of the AUC, a tall, gruff-looking man with pockmarked cheeks shook the agent's hand. His subordinate, answering to the name Moreno, was a stout figure wearing mirrored sunglasses, which the agent would later figure out was a permanent fixture of his appearance no matter what the weather. Both men looked like gangsters in their ill-fitting uniforms. The agent also knew from his file that Bejarano had once been a member of the Medellin drugs cartel and had built a significant power base in Colombia off the back of it. The leader of the cartel, Pablo Escobar, lured two of Bejarano's allies to the self-built La Catedral prison, accused them of betrayal, then murdered them both with his own hands. Bejarano had also been summoned on that day but strongly suspected he was in danger and didn't go. After that incident, Bejarano allied himself with the rival Cali cartel against Escobar and from then on, the drug lord's days were numbered.

"We welcome you to our base of operations," grunted Bejarano, glancing down at the empty coffee mug on the table along with an open map.

"Well, I see you've had your coffee, so what have you got for us?"

The agent leaned over the map and pointed to a spot marked with a red cross. It was the identified location of a FARC camp (Revolutionary Armed Forces of Colombia or Fuerzas Armadas Revolucionarias de Colombia in Spanish), the Marxist-driven force that had plagued Colombia since the sixties.

"Our surveillance has identified this base where Commander Jiménez is in hiding – a mile over the Ecuadorian border across the Putumayo river. I'll take point on the mission but leave the tactics to your excellent team," he continued, deliberately stroking their egos. "However," he said, pausing for emphasis, "I insist on going in with the first wave. I'm sure you're well aware of the high possibility of detection by the FARC camp as well as from the Ecuadorian authorities, so I'd suggest finding a point to land the teams at least five klicks away and we make the rest of the way on foot. The terrain isn't ideal, but the cover is good enough."

"And what happens to Jiménez?" asked Bejarano, studying the agent closely with his beady eyes.

"As per our arrangement. We need an interrogation window to get what we want from him. After that, he's all yours," the agent replied, knowing full well that would be a green light for Jiménez's death.

Moreno turned towards him, a flicker of a smile forming.

"So you know. We don't fuck about down here. We will drain the sea to kill the fish, my friend."

The agent nodded as if in agreement, but was not entirely sure of his meaning.

***

At dawn, two squads of six men moved silently through the jungle as they formed a dragnet around the FARC camp. As planned, two choppers had carried in the soldiers, dropping them off in an open clearing on the far side of the muddy Putumayo River, just inside the Ecuadorian border.

The agent, armed with standard-issue AK47 and dressed in AUC fatigues, tucked in just behind the main advance. When the camp was under a kilometre away he split off with a three-man squad of Moreno's men in a pincer movement towards Jiménez's supposed location at the East side of the camp.

They crouched down within sight of their target location – a long Nissen hut draped in camouflage nets. Behind it lay another cluster of smaller huts, all with the same netting. In the fresh morning air they heard the snuffling of pigs from some unseen stall and through the gaps between the buildings they caught a glimpse of an antenna dish.

The agent was concerned.

Too quiet.

Where the hell was everybody?

They didn't have to wait long for the fireworks to begin. The first contact came within minutes. Crackling gunfire ripped apart the peaceful dawn, causing a chorus of animal screams and howls at their rude awakening. The small arms fire from the AUC gunman, west of the camp, increased in intensity.

The thump of explosive force ripped through the trees then a fireball engulfed one of the outside perimeter huts. That was the RPG team unleashing hell and their signal to move.

The squad leader, followed by the two privates, moved quickly to the target hut, weapons focused on the shuttered windows. There was a loud crack as a boot broke down the door and the soldiers stormed inside. The agent followed them in, his pistol in front of him.

The paramilitaries cleared each area inside the sparse accommodation that consisted of two bedrooms, a living area, toilet and a kitchen.

Empty.

No one home.

The agent in frustration kicked an empty crate that careered across the floor.

"Whatever was happening here is gone, we fucking well missed it," he hissed.

One of the soldiers glanced around casually, almost as if their enemy's disappearance was entirely expected.

"All right. Go join your commander," the agent said, reluctantly, before pulling open a bag of clothes that was lying on the floorboards.

The soldiers left just as a staccato of small arms fire resumed in the background. Commander Bejarano's men were clearing out the last remnants of resistance and searching the camp.

The agent continued searching but found nothing except the evidence of a quick escape; strewn clothing, a broken radio, a coffee pot with still-dirty mugs placed on top of a makeshift table made from boxes and a section of flat wood. He reluctantly gave up and headed to the middle section of the camp to find Moreno.

The AUC soldiers had rounded up a small group of FARC survivors; all young, both male and female dressed in civilian clothes. Another three AUC men were stripping off the dark olive uniforms from the dead bodies of FARC guerrillas, leaving their corpses strewn on the ground dressed only in their underwear, limbs flailing in the mud. The agent counted ten men and four young women among the dead.

Another soldier came with a jerry can found amongst the camp supplies and placed it on the ground. Moreno looked up.

"No sign of our friend?"

"No, they must have had lookouts by the river," the agent replied.

Moreno let out a low, guttural laugh. "Si, that is most likely. Your gringo technology doesn't work so well out in this country. Perhaps you should leave the insurgent hunting to us."

The agent ignored him and glanced around the now-quiet camp. There were cables tied to tree branches that led to the satellite dish he glimpsed earlier creating some early warning system for their communications. As smoke drifted lazily through the camp from the earlier explosion, he followed their line with his eyes and saw the cables led directly into the hut he had just searched.

Another FARC prisoner, a bit older than the others, stumbled into the central circle of prisoners, shoved by an AUC soldier who had found him. Moreno gestured impatiently to the soldier, who pushed him into a line with the other prisoners, then gestured at the gasoline.

The agent watched as the first male prisoner was doused in gasoline, the liquid running freely over his hair, face and exposed body. The man sobbed and begged, evidently realising what was happening.

"Where is Commander Jiménez?" Moreno demanded.

The man shook his head, refusing to open his eyes. "Please! Please! I do not know!"

This is interesting, the agent thought, taking out his cigarettes. A small part of him wanted to stop this apparent insanity, this drift into evil. The prisoners were all so young.

Yet it was also intriguing. Would these "hard" tactics produce the information needed? How many of them would Moreno burn to get what he wanted? These were unfortunate circumstances, and this was war, he reasoned. Even so, the agent steeled himself to watch.

Moreno asked again.

"Palma Roja, they went to Palma Roja!" the man blubbered between rapid gasps.

"Bullshit," Moreno countered. He wore an expression of boredom as he fished out a box of windproof matches from his pocket.

The agent saw the match strike in Moreno's hand, the flicker of flame drew all eyes toward it like bees to honey.

There was a pause, the silence thick with tension.

We will drain the sea, to kill the fish.

Then, with a casual flick of fingers, the match flew through the air. A small, fragile dancing flame – almost dying – just before the fuel on the prisoner ignited it back into life.

Chapter 1

County Cork, Ireland

Frank Bowen headed up the winding lane, cutting through endless fields until he came to a crossroads and stopped to consult the map. He knew it was around here somewhere, but the fact that it was hard to find was a good thing.

He changed up a gear and drove the rented Audi A3 straight across, towards the grey sky opening up ahead. Fast-moving clouds painted a stark backdrop behind a row of silhouetted trees. At a fork in the road that he recognised from the map, Frank drove onto a narrow lane and followed the twisting uphill road for several miles. He was soon passing old houses and farms, with their tumbling stone walls and towering corrugated hay sheds dotted here and there, and then came to an open five-bar gate partly obscured by a group of trees.

This must be it.

He drove along the track, mostly unused judging by the long grass sprouting from the occasional crack in the road, until a farmhouse came into view. As he pulled into the courtyard a spectacular vista of a lush green rolling valley with a dark blue sea sparkling in the distance came into view. A green Ford Explorer was already parked up on the gravel and a young man, who Frank guessed was the estate agent, was speaking into his mobile. He gave Frank a wave of his hand and finished his call.

Frank parked up, exited his rental car and nodded at the man.

"Mr Hales. How're ya doing? Grand day for it?" he responded cheerfully.

Any day, it seemed, was a good day when it wasn't raining in Ireland.

Frank gave an easy smile, almost forgetting he'd used an alias. "As long as it's dry, Mr O'Farrell." He turned to the main house, looking up at the roof as if surveying it. "So this is the Manor House?" he quipped.

The young estate agent nodded, following Frank's gaze. "Aye, it was a farm for many years. It's a great property but, as I said, has been on the market for a while. Let me show you around inside first, so."

They toured the farmhouse. It had a large central kitchen with wood-burning stove and an impressive dining room, as well as a front living room. Upstairs were four spacious bedrooms and an attic that spanned across the top of the building. The curtains were faded as were the carpets and the walls showed evidence of scuff marks and scrapes. The air inside was musty and beams of dust-laden sunlight streamed through the windows, adding to the sense of neglect and abandonment.

However, Frank warmed to it straight away. It felt like home. They then walked down to a dimly lit basement, divided into two rooms. The stone walls were covered with dark soot, old rusty farm gear was scattered on the concrete ground, and old wood shelves creaked with tins of paint and boxes of forgotten tools.

They walked back outside. "It comes with around two acres of pastureland, including the cow shed over there," the young agent gestured at the curved roof. "You could take it down, I guess." They walked to a stone building that had presumably been used for wood storage, but was now simply piled high with discarded furniture and rusting appliances, junk the previous owners had seemingly thrown inside from the house.

A small patch of woodland stretched from one side of the property for a few hundred yards with a stone wall cutting across. "That's part of the property boundary, up to the wall," the agent explained with a sweeping hand.

"How come no one's been interested?" Frank asked, turning to O'Farrell who made a face as if the answer personally puzzled him. "Just one of those properties that doesn't get sufficient interest, so. There were some offers but they just fell through."

Frank looked around again. It was a contender and, due to the lack of offers, it was highly likely he could negotiate hard on a price reduction. He would, however, need to carefully consider his dwindling finances and personal situation before making any commitment.

Chapter 2

CIA Headquarters, Langley.

Brett Fallon, Head of Field Operations, tapped the screen, reading through the decrypted updates from one of his many HUMINT assets on the ground in South America. The continent had been his turf for a few years now, but he had taken over just as the significant action had wound down. The high-profile hunt for Pablo Escobar had ended with him being killed on a Medellín rooftop in 1993 after Fallon's section in the agency had become embroiled in an ongoing drugs war. Of course, the drug business hadn't ceased in the slightest. Other cartels had picked up the slack without a blip and Fallon certainly had his work cut out trying to stem the rising flood of drugs reaching the streets of American cities. However, as the media attention had shifted away from the drug war, budget allocations had been reduced even though the threat remained as high as ever.

His computer beeped. It was a reminder alarm for an urgent brief with the Deputy Executive Director, Kate Foster. He wondered what it was all about. Fallon himself reported directly to the Deputy Director for Operations, Greg Reinhart, a pay grade below Foster, so this was a rarity.

After another five minutes, he logged out of the terminal, shut everything down and headed off towards the East Wing, via the coffee station.

A shakeup, that's all it could be, he thought. The management and pen-pushers were moving personnel like chess pieces vying for some obscure organisational advantage and that – most likely – meant bad news for him and his current set-up.

He approached a ramped metal walkway that led to the SCIF (sensitive compartmented information facility) that kept listening electronic ears at bay in an encased "bubble", as it was nicknamed.

After swiping his pass key through the access portal, Fallon walked into the elongated meeting room where his superior and Foster stood talking at the far end in front of a large blank monitor screen affixed to the wall.

"Mr Fallon. Thanks for joining us," she said, gesturing to one of the chairs at the top of the table.

Fallon gave Reinhart a "what's going on?" look, which was ignored, and slipped into the chair. The superiors took their seats and Reinhart tapped a few keys on his laptop that booted the screen monitor into action, lighting up the blank screen with a Top Secret CIA emblem.

"Naturally, it goes without saying none of what we're discussing today leaves this room, Mr Fallon," said Foster.

"Naturally," Fallon replied.

Satisfied, Foster indicated to Reinhart to continue with a nod.

Reinhart pushed a file across the table to Fallon and gave him a moment to open it up.

"Some big changes are happening in the intelligence community," Foster began, fixing Fallon with her green eyes. "For some time we've been aware of the infrastructure being put into place for a new global agency: G13COMM. Reinhart will bring you up to speed." She turned to Reinhart, who clicked his mouse revealing a covertly taken photograph of a mousy looking man with reddish hair getting out of a car.

Reinhart cleared his throat. "This is Carl Paterson, head of a small, secretive set-up in Britain that started as an alliance between the British secret service and GCHQ while on the hunt for a whistleblower last year. The group is codenamed Ghost 13." Reinhart sipped his water, changing the slide to a photo of an older US military man with short white hair. "This is Colonel Dean Wexhall, originally attached to U.S. Army Special Operations. He is now detailed with running what is known as Operation Darkwood: the creation of a new agency – G13COMM – with intelligence and military capabilities that will swallow up the British operation, effectively merging them. Yes, Brett?"

Brett had leaned forward, opening his mouth to speak. "So Ghost 13 was originally a Brit creation and now it's set to expand under Wexhall?"

"Correct, except the agency is already up and running from what we understand," Foster clarified.

Brett nodded. He assumed they had an asset inside to have this up-to-date information.

"So, what is the mission for this new agency?"

"We don't know everything. There's a very tight lid on it, and this is pretty much all we can share with you at the moment."

Foster and Reinhart both fixed eyes on Fallon.

"You will need to hand over all your current operations to Lisa Graham and focus on uncovering as much detail on Darkwood and G13COMM as possible. I'm sure Graham will do an excellent job," said Foster.

"Wait a minute. I'm up to my eyes right now. I can't just abandon assets in the field—"

"You're not abandoning anyone," Reinhart interjected. "Graham has the skill set to take over your role."

Fallon shook his head. "She needs more time."

Reinhart and Foster exchanged glances.

"Then you will need to split roles. This is a priority. I'm sure I don't need to spell out that any rival intelligence group like G13COMM is going to be bleeding budget dollars away from us."

"You're saying the Agency is under threat from that tin-pot operation?" Fallon waved a hand at the screen, dismissively.

"That 'tin-pot operation' has some very powerful backers. We're not here to argue with you, Mr Fallon."

Fallon sighed. He was right. Someone was playing chess.

"Alright. What do you want me to do, exactly?"

Chapter 3

London

Below, the patched squares of green fields, snaking roads and dotted buildings spread far into the distance, fading on the horizon where the blue sky appeared. Sunlight glinted off the wing and Frank turned away to sip on his black coffee. The captain announced over the PA system that they were to be arriving at Heathrow airport in ten minutes and went through the usual monologue of resetting seats and tray tables.

Frank hardly heard any of it as his mind drifted back to how his life had changed in the last few months. The family he thought he was part of had been shattered when Maria asked for a separation.

Temporary, of course. See how it panned out.

It had knocked him off balance, shooting him between the eyes like so many of his adversaries had tried to do. Anger, hurt and betrayal all mixed into a cocktail of negative emotion had boiled up inside.

Then, after weeks of talking it through, he began to understand. The kidnapping of Joe and Maria must have percolated in her mind, giving her a different perspective of their relationship. The safety of their family was paramount to her and so she had dealt him the separation card. There was no way he could argue about being able to keep them safe in his line of work. Now he believed he was done with

"

all that. There had been a few short-term contracts in security work. Nothing too dangerous but the damage, it seemed, was already done.

He loved her still. How could he not? She was the mother of their children. The one woman he would kill for and, indeed, had killed for.

Frank made his way through the lines at immigration, picked up his gym bag and made his way out into the harsh New Year's air to flag down a taxi. The cab driver gave him a nod at his instruction and Frank stared out from the rear window, still lost in thought, as they weaved through the hectic London traffic towards Stoke Newington. After thirty minutes he exited the taxi outside his small flat located above a twenty-four-hour convenience shop. People went about their business at all hours on this busy road. An Asian man unloaded boxes of vegetables onto the pavement. In his peripheral vision he caught a glimpse of a figure throwing a cigarette butt onto the road before moving off. Out of habit, Frank took note; middle-aged, tall and dark-haired, wearing a black leather jacket and faded jeans who was looking his way.

Was there something in it? Or was he being paranoid?

Frank bought cigarettes from the shop, then came back out and caught another glimpse of the same man turning the corner. He took his time fishing out his keys, managed one more glance and noticed the figure had disappeared.

Frank unlocked the door to the apartment, edged past the bicycles parked in the hallway and climbed the stairs. Once through his door, he looked around the sparsely furnished flat, checking each room for any sign of tampering.

Satisfied everything seemed in order, he grabbed a ready meal from the fridge, placed it in the microwave and grabbed a bottle of Jack Daniels bourbon and a glass from the cupboard before slumping onto the ageing sofa. The TV sparked into life and he tossed the remote aside, wondering how he had ended up back in the single life. He should be in Islington with Maria and the kids in the house that they had bought after moving from the flat in Shoreditch.

Now here he was, back in bachelor mode; alone in a cold, spartan flat.

Perhaps his idea of starting a new life in Ireland was too much of a stretch? It was barely affordable with his meagre savings and Maria hadn't worked since the kidnapping episode a year before.

Yet the farmhouse had felt perfect. Isolated but calm.

A family could live there under the radar. It could be a lovely card to play; an olive branch to offer her.

Who was he kidding? She wanted this. He wasn't to blame. Perhaps it was karma from when he left Jodie all those years ago. He had been young – what a naive idiot. The beep told him that his prepackaged meal was ready so he grabbed his Bolognese and wolfed it down.

Although he barely admitted it to himself, a deep part of him missed the adrenaline rush of being in the field, taking risks and holding the cold steel of a weapon in his hand. Instead, he had the prospect of an early morning shift, merely walking around a warehouse checking that everything was in order while his thoughts stewed and swirled.

Frank tossed the empty plate and cutlery in the sink to fester and turned in for an early night, knowing that the turmoil in his mind would deny him sleep for hours despite his tiredness.

***

The following day Frank clocked in for his shift at a machinery warehouse further north in Woodford after as much sleep as he anticipated. Two hours at most. The work was mind-numbingly dull but it paid a few bills. Frank stepped into a small, claustrophobic office where another man sat slumped in a chair, a bank of CCTV monitors in front of him and the room reeking of takeaways and human sweat.

"Morning, Toby. Jesus, it stinks in here," said Frank, covering his mouth and nose with a glance of his palm.

"A New Year present for you, Frank," said the younger man, grabbing his phone and wallet from a side table and standing up with a sudden eagerness to leave. "You're too kind," said Frank with undisguised sarcasm.

"Oh yeah, the boss man said he wants a word with you this morning. Guess he'll pop by?" Toby added with a half shrug.

"Oh right, thanks, Toby," Frank replied, curiosity mildly piqued.

The young man typed in a code to the console panel and left the security office with a slam of the door, leaving Frank alone to get on with his routine. Coffee first, then login to check the night's logs and take a first of several walkabouts to check the integrity of various exits and entrances inside and outside of the warehouse complex. Fifteen minutes later his employer, Mr Parkinson, walked in. He nodded to Frank.

"Morning, Frank. How's it going?"

"Not bad, thanks. Not bad. Toby mentioned you wanted to see me?"

Parkinson nodded, his face serious. "Yes, I'll not beat about the bush, then," he muttered, hesitating for a moment. "Your contract – the company are re-structuring a few things. The short of it is, I—"

Frank held up his hand, unable to listen to anymore. "My contract isn't being renewed?"

Parkinson sighed. "That's it. I'm sorry, Frank."

Frank shrugged. "It's the way it goes. Not ideal, but I'll find something else."

He had guessed it might be something like that with his contract renewal a few weeks away. There was no doubt it was a harsh blow to him and his plans to restore his relationship with his family, despite his outward show of nonchalance to Parkinson.

During his shift he had spoken to Maria but didn't mention the work situation. Time was needed to sort that out. Then he had checked in on the kids; Joe and Zak. Baby Zoe was barely a year old and gurgled in the background. He would have some time to spend with them at the weekend, he said, and genuinely looked forward to it. It was Thursday.

After the shift finished, Frank decided to stop in the pub on the way back home, the pull of downing a pint was just too hard to resist.

He left his car parked on the street and began the short stroll to the pub. In an old Vauxhall Astra opposite, Frank caught a brief glimpse of a semi-familiar face. Was that the guy that he'd seen opposite his flat? He was making a call inside the vehicle and it was difficult to get a clear view.

Same man? Frank sneaked another look as he continued on his way but couldn't be sure. What he did know was his senses were on full alert.

The pub was busy with the after-work crowd of punters desperate for some escapism at the bottom of a glass. A television relayed the news, the sound turned down while the closed captioning rolled over the bottom of the screen and a murmur of conversations, laughter and shouts filled the air. Frank was sitting away from the bar in a booth, the paper spread out in front of him, nursing a Guinness with a bourbon chaser on the side. He had positioned himself so that he had an eye on the door that he scanned every time it opened. Another familiar figure walked in and Frank instinctively lifted the newspaper higher to conceal himself.

"Hello, Frank."

He peeked from behind the paper to see a familiar Afro-Caribbean face. The long dark coat, open at the buttons revealing a crisp suit and tie underneath. The epitome of a smart, hard-working businessman – maybe a debonair playboy or an aspiring entrepreneur, born to hustle. Except the face looking at him was worn and tired-looking. A stark contrast to the well-turned-out attire.

"Marcus? I thought it was you. This is a coincidence," Frank said evenly, knowing it wasn't.

Marcus gestured to the seat opposite. "May I?"

Frank nodded and folded up his paper as Marcus eased into a chair. Frank noticed the man in the black leather jacket entering the pub door before moving to the bar.

"How have you been keeping?" Marcus asked, keeping the conversation light.

Frank looked at him for a moment, pausing, wondering what this was all about.

"Well, it's been better. How goes the world of *Liberatus News*?

"Good. Yes, good."

Frank jerked his head at the man at the bar. "Who's your friend?"

Marcus glanced over and then caught Frank's level stare, a moment of embarrassment flashed across his face as if caught out with a hand in the piggy bank.

"Ah, you noticed."

Frank waited, taking a sip of his pint, forcing the explanation.

"He's security. A private detective hired by me."

"To follow me? What's that all about?"

Marcus shook his head. "Don't take it personally. I needed to make sure of your routine. And check no one was shadowing you."

"There's been no-one except your friend. He's been shadowing me." Frank sighed, not sure of what to make of it. He cut to the chase, draining the bourbon. "What's going on, Marcus?" he asked, catching Marcus looking at the drink.

"Don't judge," Frank snapped, slamming the glass on the table.

Marcus shook his head and leaned forward, resting his elbows on the dark wood table.

"There's no judgment here. You want another one?" gesturing at Frank's glass.

Frank gave him a withering look that told Marcus where to go.

"Look, I have a message from John. All I can say is," Marcus glanced around the pub, "he wants to talk to you, urgently."

Frank let out a snort of derision. "I don't owe him or you anything," he snapped.

Marcus studied Frank's face. "Look, I know I fucked up when it came to Pandora Red but lessons have been learned. You're needed, and you'll be well paid. At least hear me out?"

Frank leaned back and sipped his pint. "Not interested," he snapped.

Marcus kept his face impassive but Frank could tell he was reeling inside. He surely couldn't have thought it would have been that easy. After all that happened? It would be hard for Frank ever to forget. When Maria and Joe had been held captive by the criminal Viktor Kozel under the orders of David Devlin, the MI6 head at the time, Marcus Brady had royally screwed up. Frank had told Marcus to hold back the information from publication for three days to give him enough time to track down Maria and Joe to save them from execution. Yet *Liberatus News* had published the revelations about Operation Oculus – a massive surveillance programme a whole day early.

A mistake that had very nearly cost his family their lives.

Marcus Brady's pathetic justifications had been that "the police had raided their offices", "the staff and journalists harassed" and "they had been followed by the authorities".

The PI had moved from the bar to sit a table close to the front window and stole the occasional stealthy glance towards them.

"You can tell your man his job is done. It's not happening, Marcus. I'm trying to restart my life, away from all that shit." It was true, partly. On the one hand he wanted to look out for his family and be there for them. A steady, safe job could win Maria back. Convince her that his old yet brief life with the Dark State was over. On the other hand, there was the numbing mindlessness of a "safe job" just like the one he'd lost. He felt the pull of excitement associated with the very same world he just disavowed bubbling just under the surface and tried to dismiss it as a risk not worth taking.

Marcus placed his hands, palms down, on the table and dropped his head. "Alright. Your decision." He rose to stand, then buttoned up his coat.

"There's a time factor involved in this one. So if you change your mind, make sure you do it by Sunday." There was now a more authoritative tone in his voice as if he was no longer bothered by what Frank decided. He tossed down a business card in front of Frank.

"Just in case you lost my number," he said.

Then Marcus was gone with the PI quickly following him out of the door.

Chapter 4

After leaving the pub Frank headed over to the family house in Islington and slipped through the front door, immediately hearing the excited patter of feet. Zak appeared, peeping around the kitchen door, and Frank crouched, giving him a broad smile. "Hey, little man."

Zak's face broke into a delighted grin and he ran to his father who scooped him up with his hands, holding him high over his head. Frank screwed up his face in a mock grimace that always delighted the boy.

"Back here!" It was Maria shouting from behind the door. Frank carried his second son through the corridor to the back of the house. There was a screech as Frank entered the kitchen and Maria was comforting baby Zoe who was not happy about something.

"Oh, that doesn't sound good."

She gave him a knowing smile as she patted the baby on the back, rocking her to and fro.

"Another sleepless night. She's teething, I think," replied Maria.

Frank put Zak down who immediately scurried across to his toys that were piled up in the dining area of the extended kitchen.

"Where's Joe?"

"Football."

"Oh, right," he muttered, not hiding his disappointment. Maria gestured with a jutting of her head to a letter on the table. "That came through."

Frank picked it up and opened it. As he read it, his expression turned to a frown as he saw red lettering embedded in the text.

"What's this?" he asked even as he read the words from the mortgage company.

"Repossession threats," said Maria, with a hint of anger in her voice. Little Zoe had calmed and gurgled as Maria placed her in a baby recliner.

"Dammit. Payment of £3500 due immediately?" He read the rest of the letter.

"Well, they say if the arrears are paid, they will not go ahead with the repossession," said Frank hopefully. "Oh well, that's alright then," Maria muttered, sarcastically.

Frank sighed and put down the letter as Maria moved to the back of the kitchen to put on the kettle.

"Look, don't worry about this I'll find the money," he said, not entirely convinced. He had some cash put by, and his current employers still owed him a month's pay. But after that, he had no idea how to make ends meet. "Paying rent on my place doesn't help," he added, flatly.

"I know but I think this is for the best right now. I don't want to go over it all again." She slumped down opposite Frank, her face strained by conflicting emotions.

"I'm not going over anything again. Just pointing out some practicalities," he muttered. "Look, we'll sort something out. Don't worry."

Just then Frank's mobile chirped in his pocket. He fished it out and looked at the caller ID. It was from Ireland.

"Mr Hales. This is O'Farrell from Unicorn Estate Agents."

"Ah yes. Hello." Frank stood up and walked back to the corridor away from the kitchen.

"I'll cut straight to the chase. I'm afraid the owner has rejected your offer but he indicated that if you could stretch to fifty, he would be happy to talk." Frank felt his stomach turn and sighed.

"OK, thanks for letting me know. Like I said, that was my best offer. Leave it with me anyway but I think it'll be a struggle." It was true. He was stretching things to snapping point as it was. Perhaps this wasn't the best time to be attempting to buy property.

"Alright, so. I'm sorry 'bout that. They're digging their heels in on this one," O'Farrell muttered in a sympathetic tone.

"Keep me in the loop. Take care and thanks again for letting me know."

"Good luck, Mr Hales." Frank cut the connection and swore aloud – his dream had evaporated with that one call. It seemed that all his plans would have to be put on hold.

***

Frank stared at Marcus Brady's card.

The man very nearly put his family in their graves with his mistake of publishing the Oculus revelations early.

It was a good reason not to trust anything he said in Frank's book. And yet over the past twelve months, Frank's anger had dissipated. He would never forgive him entirely, but Brady had apologised, more than once. It was just a mistake, a human error. It wasn't as if they had to be best mates. John Rhodes he could respect but Brady – not so much.

Thinking back to that time brought Frank's thoughts around to Carl Paterson. He had never quite forgiven Carl for the way things had turned out after Cuba. The former MI6 man, now heading up Ghost 13, had been "economical with the truth" when it came to

"Whisper Hunt" and, to some degree, the kidnapping of Maria and their eldest, Joe.

Still, he had merely been playing his role. A job not envied by Frank in the slightest.

He glanced back toward the kitchen as Maria took some milk from the fridge and he saw her cast him a brief look. Unjudging and trusting.

There could be severe consequences if he made this decision.

It was a curious paradox. Would Maria hate him for going back into the world of shadows? It was likely.

Yet, if he did this. *If.*

Then there was a real possibility he could set them all up for life. Make them safe.

And he kept wondering whether he was behaving recklessly. Was he unconsciously rolling the dice to get back at Maria?

Yes, he had children to think about, but she would take care of them, of that there was no doubt. He did not dare analyse or speculate what could happen. A million different possibilities lay ahead.

But one thing was certain -- once again he would be a mere pawn to be manipulated by the serious players lording it from above; all with agendas in a world where deaths were just part of a numbers game. Influential figures in the shadows pulling strings from the comfort and safety of their old boys' club armchairs with the aroma of cognac and cigar smoke filling the air of their cloistered environment. With all that he faced he knew there was only one thing to do.

He walked into the front room, typing in Brady's number as he went and then closed the door behind him.

Chapter 5

Paris

Frank stepped inside the cafe that was tucked away alongside the train tracks running into Gare du Nord, the central Parisian railway station. It had been a quick journey from St Pancras, through the Channel Tunnel. Inside, the cafe had high ceilings with ornate fixings and a large tiled wall blocking the kitchen. The daily menu was scribbled incoherently on a blackboard and, behind the counter, the coffee machine hissed and gurgled.

A young woman standing behind the service counter gave him a warm smile and asked him what he wanted to eat.

Frank only ordered a black coffee before moving deeper into the cafe, with decorated walls of old black and white framed photographs depicting a bygone Paris. He scanned along the sofas and low seating placed along the walls, then recognised a tanned Rhodes with his white hair near the back in a circular booth.

It was quiet, and there was no-one within earshot.

Rhodes looked up and smiled at seeing him.

"Frank!"

"Good to see you, John."

They shook hands and Frank sat down.

"Bienvenue à Paris," Rhodes added in a mock French accent.

"You're based here now?" Frank asked.

Rhodes shook his head. "Good God, no. I move around a lot – you know that."

Frank nodded, getting just the vague answer he expected. He guessed after Rhodes became a target a year before, ending in a nasty car crash, that he'd keep the details light. The man had nearly died and had carefully kept a low profile since.

Yet judging by this request for Frank's services, Rhodes was far from being done with his passion; the fight for greater liberty against the rising global state.

"So, I'm glad to see you're looking well. Keeping busy?"

Rhodes smiled. "Always."

After a few minutes of small talk, Frank sipped on his coffee while Rhodes leaned forward, his face becoming serious.

"I'm sure Marcus didn't give you too much information but you have to understand this is a delicate one. The usual reasons for discretion apply, of course. You understand?"

Frank nodded.

"I'm building a network to work on behalf of the people, not the State," Rhodes continued, "Someone who has important information and contacts, wants closer ties, perhaps a deal. This asset, let's call him 'Nero', wants to bring in his own 'take' personally using his own method. Having said that, he's already sent some compelling samples of his merchandise. It looks like he's got pure 'glitter'. And that would be a massive coup for us."

"Glitter?"

Rhodes smiled ruefully. "Ah, an old intelligence term: 'information not yet understood or acquired.'"

Frank nodded while draining his coffee. "So, he's got intel for a media story that you are going to release?" he asked.

Rhodes shook his head. "No. Too early and too sensitive for that," he leaned back. "What I need you to do is rendezvous with Nero in Europe – he's currently somewhere outside the US sphere of influence – then escort him to another location, nearer my base of ops. I need him there, on my team." Anticipating Frank's response, he continued, "he could just fly over but we need to be careful. The authorities have increased the monitoring of all global transport manifests so, as a precaution, I need you to babysit him. It's imperative you get him over there safely."

Frank's face remained impassive but, inside, he had doubts.

"Can you tell me where?"

"Right now, no. But you'll get the destination soon enough. I would estimate it'll be around a month's mission time."

Rhodes took out a tablet from his bag and tapped on the screen, then handed it to Frank who looked down at a young man in his late twenties with dark hair, a trimmed beard and the pronounced cheekbones of Anglo-Asian descent.

"So accompany this guy somewhere, destination yet to be confirmed."

"Yep."

"Will there be other interested parties involved? I need to know this, John." He observed Rhodes as the old man shook his head.

"No, as long as we're careful. Just communicate the way I tell you, don't take any chances. I'll give you more details as soon as you're ready. You'll get a phone, a legend ID and cash. Nero will be travelling as Mark Simpson."

Frank nodded slowly, looking at the face again.

The money for the job would certainly help him get that farmhouse in Ireland, perhaps even get his family back together. But he sensed something was off. He had a lot of questions that needed answering.

Rhodes seemed to read his facial expression. "You'll get all the info you need soon. Just think of the money, Frank," Rhodes scribbled down a figure on a piece of paper, then slid it over to Frank, who glanced at it.

"It's pretty good 'Fuck you' money. You could do something good, maybe even buy property—"

Frank glanced at him sharply, wondering if he knew about Ireland. He didn't want anyone to know about that. Not just yet.

"Have you been in touch with Maria?"

Rhodes took the tablet back and tapped on the screen as he spoke. "Maria? No, I've had no contact with her at all. Why?"

Frank regarded him with interest. He seemed genuine enough.

"Just wondered. We've separated," Frank heard himself say. He wasn't sure why.

Rhode's face changed to concern and he looked at Frank with sympathetic eyes. "Oh God. I'm sorry, Frank. Really sorry. What—" he stopped himself and finished, "none of my damn business."

Frank waved a dismissive hand. "Not something I thought would happen either. But with this line of business—"

Rhodes held up his hand and nodded with understanding.

"I know, I know – I have a family too, as you know – it's difficult."

Frank glanced out towards the street and sighed. Deep down he had already made the decision and was now teetering on the edge of making the commitment.

So, let it begin.

Chapter 6

Carl Paterson had never felt so on edge. He downed a whiskey to calm his inner turmoil and leaned forward, feeling the amber liquid burn the back of his throat as he gestured to the flight attendant for another.

A new world order would see the end of intelligence institutions such as MI6, CIA and the rest, of that Carl had no doubt. It might take twenty years, maybe fifty? He simply didn't know. But his instinct was telling him it was coming and Carl wanted a legacy to reflect his true worth. It had been bloody hard work building up his enclave of power since being given the opportunity to head up the Ghost 13 estate. He had rapidly nurtured a small group of assets, scouts as he called them, and now he wanted to expand that as quickly as possible.

If there was any hint of truth in this rumour, all that he had built could be swept away in less than the blink of an eye. His network, his power, everything, which was why he was heading to the Buckley Air Force Base in Colorado to get clarification, under the guise of a fact-finding mission. G13COMM had already been set up in the US under Colonel Wexhall's command. The next item on the agenda was the take over of Carl's UK operation. What that might mean for Carl he had no idea.

Carl turned his gaze from the flood of endless cloud outside the aircraft to the dog-eared book laying on his fold-out table, the one he carried around in his briefcase along with his work files. It was a welcome distraction and he picked it up once again. It was an in-depth historical account that focused on the first secret agent network in England during the reign of Elizabeth I. In recent years he had turned to history as a conduit for knowledge.

History repeated itself, so the cliché said. But it was true.

The world of the Elizabethan court fascinated him and kept his mind occupied on those occasions when he needed to push his work worries out of his head.

He flipped open the book to his last read page.

Robert Cecil had inherited the spy network from his father, William Cecil, the man who had entrapped Elizabeth's sister, Mary Queen of Scots, and then ultimately condemned her to death for her plot to become Queen of England. Despite his intention to protect Elizabeth, it had got him banished from the court for his trouble. Robert, now first secretary to the queen, already having been brought up learning the spycraft and the extent of his father's extensive network, had spies everywhere. His rival for the queen's ear in the court, the Earl of Essex, was an athletic man with many victories in battle under his belt. This was a direct contrast to Robert, who was hunchbacked which gave him the demeanour of a crouched toad, and as such was nicknamed 'pigmy' by the queen.

One of Cecil's spies, Lopez, the queen's doctor, had been accused by Essex of plotting to poison the queen. Cecil had considered whether or not to stand up for one of his own but ultimately deemed it too dangerous to intervene on Lopez's behalf. Cecil's own future goal to become as the ears and eyes for the queen was at stake, and so he did not stand in the way of the doctor's execution despite knowing he was innocent.

Carl took a pause, sipped his drink and looked back out at the flat blanket of cloud. The sun rays were lighting up the top of them.

He did what had to be done. To protect his network. Smart.

Carl continued reading.

As Elizabeth came to the end of her life, it was apparent that there was no natural successor, except the Protestant King James of Scotland (The son of Mary Queen of Scots). Fearing James would hold the death of his mother against him, who had been condemned by Robert's father, the private secretary knew he had to tread very carefully indeed.

When Essex, having fallen out with the queen, attempted a coup with 200 men (backed by King James), it was Cecil's spy network that ensured it was crushed. Essex was executed on the 25th of February 1601. On hearing that the coup had been unsuccessful, King James approached Cecil, sounding him out on whether Cecil would act as James' eyes and ears in the queen's court.

This could easily have been a set-up in this era of intrigues and treasonous plots. It was a dangerous time for Cecil, so he took extra precautions and waited before giving a response to the Scottish monarch. When he did eventually reply he did so through a coded proxy by diplomatic cover so his direct contact would not implicate him. He told James to wait it out.

When Queen Elizabeth passed away on 24th March 1603, Cecil oversaw the succession of King James to the throne, while retaining his own power base.

Carl put down the book and sipped his whisky. It was a compelling parallel. In some ways, he saw himself as Cecil. A man who needed to be smart to survive, and keep an eye on the board pieces at all times.

His thoughts returned to his own situation.

Stay calm, Carl. Let's see what the wind smells like in Colorado and hope it doesn't smell like shit.

***

After around thirty minutes of waiting, Carl tossed his plastic coffee cup into the nearby bin and slumped back into the plastic and chrome chair, absolutely seething. The intermediate US official had kept him waiting as if he were some lowly civil servant. He could do without this bureaucratic posturing, but there would be no complaining on his part. Subtle shifts were happening in the global intelligence community, and Carl needed to step carefully to make sure he was still standing after the flux.

A major appeared finally.

"Mr Paterson. The colonel will see you now."

Carl stepped inside a sparsely furnished office and saw Wexhall in military fatigues behind his desk talking into a phone. Wexhall acknowledged him with a nod and Carl waited for the call to end, shifting his weight from one foot to another. He focused on a world map behind the colonel, wondering where on the globe he intended to stretch his tentacles.

He slammed the phone down.

"Mr Paterson. Please sit down."

Pleasantries over in a flash, the colonel cut to the chase.

"Listen, Carl. We all heard about what happened to your boys over in Cuba, the leaks and red faces. The boys at the top of the tree getting caught with their paws in the cookie jar."

Carl remained impassive, barely holding down a boiling frustration. This meeting was going exactly as he thought it would.

"It was regrettable. Impossible to predict that our top line could be compromised. Lessons have been learned."

Wexhall placed his elbows on the table, leaning forward.

"The fact that the head of MI6 was running his own show, bringing in assets isn't what bothers me about this. What bothers me, is he got caught."

Carl could feel himself shrinking in his seat and barely hid a flash of contempt on his face.

"The Ghost 13 Command is expanding whether you like it or not. Military and intelligence wings sitting outside of the power of individual governments. A more global approach. That means your little set-up will soon be coming under our umbrella. We need to work together, Carl."

"I understand the nature of the restructuring. I've seen the brief," said Carl sternly.

"So, my big question is – do I *really* need you? Can your network deliver? Can *you* deliver? I'm not sure I've seen anything that convinces me that's at all possible," Wexhall growled in a tone that matched Carl's.

Carl drummed his fingers on the side of the chair.

"Well, that clarifies things, but I have to warn you that any shakeups right now are going to have a direct effect on current operations," Carl warned, "We have assets in the field and rocking the boat right now could put lives at risk. It would be a problem."

Wexhall seemed to be thinking as he swung round in his chair to face the window.

"Y'know what would be useful, Carl? Little eyes and ears inside a certain 'group of interest' based over on your side of the pond." Wexhall shot Carl a glance and swung back round to face him. "What have you got on Liberatus?" he added the question, heavy with hidden meaning.

"They've been on our radar for a long time. The news media side has been a pain in the authorities' backside for many years. The founding CEO, John Rhodes, worked for our side once, but now we believe he's building a rogue intelligence network, so definitely a person of, or should I say a group of interest—" Carl paused, assessing if the colonel had anything to add but Wexhall said nothing, so he continued.

"His brother founded Goya Tech in Silicon Valley. They have some consumer tech products, they're behind some of the Internet's most progressive tools but have been putting out feelers regarding government contracts both here and in Europe."

Wexhall rested his head back on the chair rest, seemingly bored with the assessment. "So, Liberatus could be seen as a potential internal threat in your country," he said, sharply.

"We've crossed swords before now," replied Carl, his mind returning to the messy Operation Whisper Hunt, and the subsequent Liberatus exposure of the Oculus programme.

Wexhall straightened up. "So then, it might be seen as beneficial to both our interests to have an asset inside their organisation?"

"Right, I see where this is going."

"Then see it goes somewhere; deliver me something I can actually use, Paterson, otherwise you're out."

Chapter 7

Carl Paterson had to stay at the hotel near Denver airport for the flight back. He checked in and went to the restaurant, sitting alone in one of the corners, slowly destroying a rare filet mignon steak with methodical precision. A Cabernet Sauvignon complemented it perfectly. Foolish not to take advantage of a generous expense account. The perks associated with this job had been tremendous from the beginning. Even Percy Braithwaite, the man who had helped set up Ghost 13, had always made that clear: everything was off the record. No official salary, no pension. All that would be provided by means of employment by SIS (The Secret Intelligence Service) or MI6 as they were better known. If he wanted holidays, cars; it was all provided by the Service including access to the various plushly furnished apartments dotted around the country.

As he finished patting his mouth with an Irish linen napkin, he felt his phone vibrate in his pocket and decided to ignore it, nodding to the waiter to order the blueberry cheesecake and double cream instead. He would enjoy his meal first before fielding any calls. The meeting hadn't been a great experience. What was it Wexhall had said? "The Ghost 13 Command is happening whether you like it or not." That riled him but at least it confirmed where he stood. His place in the new order was threatened, absolutely no doubt about that.

Have to play it carefully, he thought. Make every move count. Think like Cecil.

After the coffee and cake been placed in front of him, Carl pulled out his phone and read an encrypted message with a wry smile. It was one of his operatives back in London with news of his old mate, Frank Bowen.

***

Frank buttoned up his jacket to keep out the biting harshness of the wind and jammed his hands back in his pockets as he hurried down the Edgware Road. Either side, the darkened buildings reminded him of cut-outs used in the backdrop of a theatre stage. Overhead, the sun struggled to break through a blanket of high cloud bleaching out the sky, completing the effect.

He had accepted the job with Rhodes and was about to step on stage. What new drama skulked behind the curtain exactly?

Gotta keep that shit out of your head. Focus on the job, Frank.

And he would have to sell it to Maria. Doing this kind of work was precisely why they had separated in the first place. Should he lie to her?

Frank crossed the street outside Paddington Green Police Station, weaving around the slow-moving traffic in the direction of the tube station. A siren faded against the background city hum.

Obviously he couldn't give her any details, or even say that it was working for Rhodes. She might even support that, having worked for him before. But he was still putting himself and his family on the line, no matter which way he could spin it.

No lying. Frank would be effectively lying to his kids in that sense too. Zoe and Zak were too young to be anything but accepting of what their dad told them. But Joe, he'd also ask questions.

Frank sensed rather than saw a black Chevrolet 4X4 pull onto the double yellow lines just a few yards ahead of him and focused on it. Then a familiar figure got out. Bald, squat with beady eyes that focused on Frank. The man was already moving towards him.

Carl Paterson's rottweiler.

Just then, strong hands grabbed his arms from both sides.

"Don't run anywhere, Frank." A gruff voice from his left.

He turned to see the culprit, long grey hair, unshaven with a smell of cigarettes and body odour. On his right, another big thug with close-cropped ginger hair wearing a grey bomber jacket.

"Hardly likely, is it?" he hissed.

They were pushing him towards the car while the bald one gestured to the open rear door of their 4x4.

"Carl just wants a friendly chat," he said, casually.

Right in front of the police station. Cheeky bastards!

***

Carl Paterson was waiting for Frank in Hyde Park. The place didn't evoke the rosiest of memories after their little dispute there but Frank guessed Carl was fond of it.

His rottweilers had searched him in the car and scanned for any concealed electrical devices before they drove up towards Marble Arch. At least he didn't have the phone that Rhodes had given him for their initial comms. He wondered if more thugs from the firm were breaking down his flat door at that very moment, slashing open his mattress and throwing his clothes onto the floor.

Bald thug and ginger lad walked with him across the park. The other man stayed in the vehicle.

Frank caught sight of Carl drinking out of a paper cup huddled against the outside bar of a permanent snack hut that had its back to

Serpentine Lake. Cold blasts came in off the water that cut through to the bone as grey clouds drifted overhead.

Baldy nodded in the direction of Carl.

"Have your chat. Don't be a prick and try anything stupid," his accent gruff and Northern.

Frank's recent conversions with Rhodes echoed in his mind as he approached Carl. The gravity of this didn't need underlining. He took a deep breath and sidled up next to his one-time good friend. It was just the business. The way of things, now. The days of them sharing their private thoughts over a pint seemed a long time ago.

"Well, Carl, you goin' to get me one?"

Carl glanced up and offered a thin smile, his features hagged, chin, unshaven.

"Of course. You still drinking it straight and black?"

"Thanks."

Carl added to the order and they took their drinks.

"Let's get out of this bloody cold, huh?" muttered Carl. Hunched like an old woman he started to scurry to a wooded section that offered a bit more shelter. There was a line of tables with the hardcore smokers braving the elements. They placed their paper cups on a vacant table but didn't bother to sit down.

"Well, I wasn't expecting to see you again," Frank said.

Carl was staring across the lake beyond Frank's shoulder and his eyes turned to him.

"I know. Neither was I. But such is life…"

"Look, it's all water under the bridge. Right? We both had our reasons to be angry. I don't want to rake over old grass again."

Carl nodded in agreement. "So, any guesses why you're here?"

"—because your merry pack of lap dogs dragged me off the street? Dunno, mate."

Carl's eyes seemed to grow colder, more focused.

"I know you're working for Rhodes and his little band of fucking ingrates."

So, he knows. Or was it a trick?

"Rhodes? Why would I want to go near him ¬– or any of that other again?"

"I don't know, Frank. You tell me. Why would you want to? Trust me, I know you've met up with him. I heard Paris is nicer in the spring. No idea why you'd want to go there this time of year."

Frank let out a long sigh. "You've been watching me?"

"Him. Naturally. "

Carl blew on the hot coffee and risked a sip, followed by a facial expression of regret.

"What do you want?"

Carl turned away from Frank and glanced over at his two men, who were now sitting on a bench a few metres away.

"I need eyes and ears, that's all. Just keep me in the loop. I don't know what he's asked you to do, but I can make life very difficult if you get my drift?" There was a subtle tone of threat, then became more upbeat. "But you'll be compensated. Something extra for the family."

Frank felt his temperature rise a fraction at the mention of Maria and the kids.

"What are you getting at?"

"Now, now don't be touchy. I'm doing you a favour. You remember the old place, huh? Come and see me.

The sooner, the better."

He gave Frank a friendly slap on the bicep and moved off.

"You're just a ladder man, Carl," Frank said, flatly. It was a derogatory term for anyone in the intelligence community that climbed the career ladder with a cold indifference to their colleagues.

Carl gave a snort of derision. "Good to see you again, Frank," he added before moving off around the shack.

Chapter 8

G13COMM, Buckley Air Force Base, Colorado.

Wexhall kneaded his football-shaped stress ball in a quick con-tinuous rhythm as if he were replicating his own heartbeat. A light rain pattered against the office window behind the drawn blinds providing background noise to his thoughts on the Brit – Carl Paterson.

The whole agency was now up and running, albeit in skeleton form. The next stage would be to establish satellites in Europe and naturally its namesake in London would be an important hub. But as Wexhall had stated so plainly, whether Carl Paterson would be "head honcho" over in Britain was very much in the balance.

Wexhall placed the stress ball aside and sipped his coffee. Perhaps it would be interesting to see how Carl operated, whether he would step up and be useful. After all, the man's position was in Wexhall's hands, and he knew it. Wexhall and his associates had worked damned hard to bring this about – there could be no weaknesses tolerated in the machine.

An incoming message on his console brought him back to the present. Wexhall stared at the notification as he ran the decryption and waited for the message to appear. It was from his CIA insider at Langley.

Possible Darkwood compromise. Recommended you check for leaks, no other info known.

Wexhall grimaced. This would put everything he had worked for in jeopardy. It was frustratingly brief but told him enough. He closed the window, stood up and left his office, heading down the long corridor inside the temporary unit. Inside another adjacent space a skeleton staff were sitting in front of a bank of screens. The blond-haired sergeant major came to the door of an internal private office and saluted him.

Wexhall went inside and closed the door.

"Sergeant Major Stark. Pull up everything on Operation Darkwood. I need an overview right now."

Stark returned to his sunken chair and began typing on his keyboard. The colonel pulled up a chair and sat down next to him.

The screen revealed the Ghost 13 emblem for a moment before it evaporated as he logged into a secure interface.

The sergeant major turned to face Wexhall. "What do you need, sir?"

Wexhall gestured to a file symbol at the top right of the panel.

"I want a list of everyone involved in 'Darkwood' or have ever seen eyes on any aspect of the plan above security clearance level two. Give me a print-out."

"That will be in the hundreds, sir."

"I know, just do it."

A series of page icons flashed on the screen as the section of that document was sent to print, and the process began with a quiet rapid humming from the printer. The colonel grabbed the sheets one by one as they spat out onto the metal tray. After he was satisfied he had them all, he turned to leave.

"Alright, sergeant major, shut it down. Thank you."

He returned to his own office and laid out the sheets of paper across his desk. Then he poured himself a coffee and stared down at the faces. These were all people involved in the setting up of infrastructure for the new covert agency. Any one of them could be the source. He would need to roll up his sleeves and carry out a thorough investigation.

***

Tech analysis had isolated a timeframe and location of the data breach. It whittled the list down considerably. A large amount of data had been transferred inside K-section on the date in question, and that had given Wexhall a red flag list of five names. These were trusted employees, carefully sourced to help implement the backbone of the G13COMM set-up. It was hard to believe anyone inside would compromise them, let alone the people on this list. Precautions had been taken backed up by high salaries, and of course harsh consequences for any disloyalty.

He picked up the phone, spoke for a few moments then left for the interrogation rooms.

***

Wexhall watched the woman's eyes dart over in his direction through the dark glass two-way mirror in the wall. She looked scared.

Rightly so.

She was hooked up to a lie detection machine and had been asked a seemingly endless list of questions. The young blonde interrogator glanced up from his file, his emotionless voice tinny through the sound system inside the observation box.

"Ms Gilmore, thank you for your time," he said. Wexhall smiled at that. As if she had any choice.

"You understand that in cases of security breach situations we need to make thorough investigations," Stark continued. "You may return to your post."

The woman smiled, relief evident on her face and she stood up, brushed her hands down the front of her skirt and left the claustrophobic, windowless room.

Wexhall depressed a button on the small panel next to the mirror.

"Thank you, sergeant major. We'll take a short break, then get the last name in." Stark acknowledged him with a nod and stood up, stretching his back.

The colonel remained in the small observation room alone, watching through the fishbowl mirror as Stark left to get a coffee. He took a seat at a small table, clutching the list in his bear-like hands and ran a pen through Ms Gilmore's name. The lie detector was the most accurate gauge of the truth available to them. The alternative method would have been of a more persuasive nature. But that method, Wexhall knew full well, would be extremely difficult to carry out on American citizens on home soil even if they were working inside military intelligence. The fact that it even crossed his mind crystallised to the colonel how desperate he was to plug this hole.

He would have to tread carefully and avoid stepping on any shards.

After a few minutes, Stark returned with a mug of coffee and glanced in Wexhall's direction, as if waiting for the order. He was the only one Wexhall could trust it seemed. A loyal, dependable and faithful soldier.

Wexhall leaned forward and depressed the microphone control. "Sergeant Major Stark. Let's get this-—" Wexhall glanced down at the last name on the list, "Bradley Meers in and see what he has to say."

Stark picked up the phone, spoke for a few moments and then

left the room. He returned with a short, thin man in his forties with a balding pate and unsure demeanour, apparently surprised and afraid of what might be coming. Wexhall recognised him as a member of the signals unit, those responsible for the integration of all the G13COMM systems at Buckley Air Force Base, Colorado. According to the file before him, Meers had worked for the NSA before being approached by one of Wexhall's staff to work on Operation Darkwood around six months ago. His login keycard had been recorded online at the exact time that the sensitive data had been copied to a remote device.

Wexhall leaned back, bristling with anticipation as he watched Stark hook up Meers to the lie detector and proceed with the questioning. He had left the best one to last in part to savour the moment; as if saving a cookie until after lunch.

Stark ran through a list of basic questions establishing his identity, age and address and other criteria, a monotonous routine he could blitz through in his sleep before getting to the matter in hand.

"You were here, working as normal on the third of January. Is that correct?" Stark asked evenly.

"Er, the third?" Meers wiped the back of his neck, glancing at the mirror like they all had, wondering what their fates might be. "Yeah, I was in, sure. I've never been off since I started, except weekends and the Christmas holiday of course."

"Between 12–14.30 on that date we have your login ID as online at the same time that there was a data breach. This corresponds with your access level – a grave offence, Mr Meers."

Meers clasped his fingers together on the table, fidgeting, eyes wide as he took in the accusatory tone of the questioning.

"No, that's absolutely not true. I have never breached any rules or done anything I wasn't supposed to be doing."

"Do you feel loyalty to your previous agency, the NSA, Mr Meers?"

"Well – I – they were my employer, just doing my job there, enjoyed it but no I don't consider—"

"So what we have here," Stark cut in, "is that you were logged onto the Ghost network, level five at the same time as this breach. How do you explain that?"

"As I said, I didn't do anything wrong – I can't explain," he trailed off, the anxious expression turning to a frown as he struggled to remember. "Wait. Let me think, that date is familiar actually. It was the first Monday after the holidays, right?"

Stark didn't even need to blink. "Correct."

Meers looked more confident as the memory returned. "Yeah, Monday, right. I remember because it was Susan Gilmore's birthday, from our team. You can check that. Someone had arranged a quick and dirty birthday cake with the kitchen staff. We arranged to meet in the canteen, but one of the other guys popped his head around the door and asked me to come with him. I was a bit rushed and I'm afraid to admit I may have left my key card on my desk. Stupid, I know." He looked at Stark, resigned.

In the observation room Wexhall crossed his arms as he watched, slowly shaking his head.

"That should have been reported, Mr Meers. You left the keycard for how long?"

"Ah, an hour I guess. At least an hour – yeah – maybe more."

"Was there anyone else around in K Section that you noticed when you left?"

Meers brushed his hand over the bald dome, screwing his face up for a moment. "I know Clara was at her desk, over by the windows. Then that Asian guy, didn't know him too well – Tom Lee – I think?"

"He was where when you left?" Stark asked in a monotone voice.

"Just milling around, at his desk by the windows where he usually works."

Stark nodded and glanced towards the mirror at Wexhall for a moment, then continued the questioning. The colonel could see the detection graph was steady. It was highly unlikely this idiot was lying.

Meers wouldn't see out the rest of his contract – Wexhall would make sure of that. He'd be lucky not to get buried in the desert.

But now they had a name.

The Clara woman had already been cleared, and that left the last suspect – Tom Lee.

Time to get to work.

Chapter 9

Studio 31, Limehouse Cut Canal

Frank parked up near the old grain warehouse, situated on the Limehouse Cut Basin, and the sight brought back mixed memories from only a year before. He buzzed the intercom access explaining his appointment. After walking up the circular metal steps, his footfall echoing up through the shaft-like space beneath him, Frank was met by a man he didn't know who offered coffee. Then he was ushered into a side room, sparsely furnished with a desk and a few chairs. An unused whiteboard was on the wall and a blind covered an internal window overlooking where Frank remembered the open-plan ops section was situated.

After a few minutes, Carl joined him, keeping it light with a handshake and a few small words of small talk before easing himself behind the desk.

"Any old faces still here?" Frank asked, gesturing towards the window behind the blind.

"Ah, well. Keller's gone, replaced by my new superior. Griff and Harry are still holding on by their fingernails."

Frank nodded, wondering if Carl's thoughts had drifted back to the Pandora operation and regretted asking.

"Coffee good?" Carl asked, flipping open a folder in front of him.

Frank took a sip and smacked his lips. "Hmm, actually not bad."

"One of my numerous shake-ups to this operation."

"Our enemies must be quaking in their boots," Frank quipped. Carl's smile weakened.

"I'll put you on the payroll, give you the protocols, codes, identity, all that jazz. You need to keep me informed with regular updates. Any further word from Rhodes?"

Frank shook his head. "No, should be any day now."

Carl glanced at him and shut the folder.

"Alright, Harry will take you through the protocols. A few of them have changed since you were with us before. Then that's it."

Frank drained his coffee and made his way to the door.

"And, Frank—" Frank turned back as Carl stood up. "Do some press-ups or something for Christ's sake – you look terribly out of shape for a field op."

***

The hazy mists that had clung to the hills and small ridges of the Mendip Hills in the West Country had receded as Frank and Sam trooped up the path.

It'll clear in an hour Sam had said, and he was right.

It was a few hours drive from London, but as Sam was based in Cheddar, a small town bordered with hills, Frank decided it was worth the trip. The area was rich with wild plateaus, gorges, and calming stretches of water scattered around its hills, interspersed with peaks and thick woods.

"We'll take a run, sweat out those toxins. Just follow my lead," Sam said before breaking into a leisurely unforced sprint.

Frank followed, his large backpack clunking with the rocks inside and basic supplies. Both men had their ankles wrapped up tight with bandages to keep the risks of any sprains or breakages to a minimum.

Frank focused on the ground, his heartbeat setting a regular rhythm. In his mind he pictured himself as a machine – his legs were pistons that propelled him across the ground. He smiled, remembering a comic from when he was a kid – the numbskulls: about a group of miniature characters inside someone's head, directing their actions from their pilot cockpit.

Stupid, but a classic.

After a few miles, Frank felt his lungs burning – the recent lapse into booze and the occasional smoke all coming back to haunt him. The backpack seemed to weigh more than ever, and he wanted nothing more than to stop and lie down on the soft, inviting grass.

"Keep going!" Sam shouted as if reading his mind from afar. "Just pain – push through it," he added, almost certainly with a smirk.

"Fuck," Frank winced and gritted his teeth, "you."

The crest of the hill with a clump of rocks beckoned nearer – their rest point.

When they arrived, Frank threw the backpack onto the ground with a clunk and joined it there, gasping and spitting, sucking down air in greedy gulps.

He looked up at Sam, who remained on his feet with a slowly shaking head, tutting.

"There's work to be done, I see. Huh, Frank?"

He was right. Lots of work to be done and this was just the beginning – just the bare bones.

***

Frank stretched his calves under the table. The gruelling week of training with Sam had put him in much better shape, physically and mentally. He wanted to savour the remaining time with Maria before he dropped the bombshell.

Rhodes had sent word – he was to leave in two days.

The added element of Carl crashing the party was a real pain, but Frank cast it out of mind, for now. Time to think wasn't a luxury he had right now.

Maria finished a phone call, grabbed a carton of juice from the fridge and held it up at Frank.

"No, I'm alright."

She sat down and rested her elbows on the table top, fixing green eyes on him that silently questioned him. Joe was at school, Zak was in afternoon nursery and the baby was asleep in the kitchen cot.

"I'm gonna be away for a while."

"Where are you going?"

Frank glanced out through the old sash window that looked out against a red brick neighbouring wall. A ginger cat casually strolled along the top before jumping down on the far side.

"I can't say—"

Maria stood up.

"Oh for fuck's sake!" she blurted out.

"It's a case of being able to help you and the kids out. You want to stay here, don't you?"

Maria had her hands on hips and looked away from him as if he had insulted her.

"You're putting yourself in danger again, aren't you?"

When he didn't answer, she stared back at him, shaking her head.

"Why would you want to do that? What about the children? You want them to be fatherless or something?"

"It's not like that at all. I wish I could say, I really do, and give you more details, but—"

"Is it for Carl?"

Frank focused on the juice carton, the logo depicting a very happy orange cartoon as if it had won the lottery. He wanted to close his eyes when saying it.

Lies, bloody lies.

"No, the other team and that's all I can say. No more," Frank rubbed his eyes, "I'll be back in about a month." he added.

She held her head down as if battered down by a cloak of disappointment, but the anger was gone as quick as it had manifested.

"The other team," she repeated slowly and began busying herself, picking up a stray bib that had fallen from the washing basket before clearing away dirty plates.

"What about Joe? You going to tell him you're off to Disneyland without him?"

Frank groaned out loud at the jibe. "It's work. He'll understand."

"And he'll be scared. It hasn't even been a year since he saw you deal with that Russian guy and take him out—"

"He didn't see me take him out."

"He heard it and saw the body under the towels. Look, he locks it up inside himself, won't talk about it, but all that must be affecting him."

Frank knew it was. How could it not be?

He stood up to leave.

"I never wanted any of that to happen—"

"And you saved us, of course. So we will always be in your debt, won't we?"

"You don't owe me anything." He stepped to the kitchen doorway.

"Frank—" she reached out her hand and held his arm. "Please don't go. I know we've had our shit to deal with and it's been difficult, but your children need a father."

He took her in his arms and they hugged.

"I know, I know," he whispered as he held Maria tight, nuzzling his face in her hair.

Chapter 10

Wexhall's office, just beyond the high fences that cordoned off the G13COMM area in the Colorado air base, overlooked a small road and the seemingly endless rows of barracks. The colonel adjusted the blinds and stared out for a few moments before taking a seat in his leather chair to go through the file on Lee.

His backlist included Blackwater, the private security company, specialising in corporate intelligence. No parents or family were known, but he had come highly recommended to G13COMM from every one of his employers.

They must have missed something. *Too clean.*

He picked up the phone and summoned Sergeant Major Stark.

Minutes later, Stark knocked and entered.

"Sergeant Major, change into civvies, take a specialist tactical team and go to Lee's house." Wexhall showed him the address on his screen which Stark memorised quickly. "See what you can find," the colonel continued, "in the unlikely event he stuck around, try to keep him alive."

"Sir!" Stark responded, snapping off a crisp salute before turning on his heels to leave.

Wexhall submitted Lee's details to various border agencies just in case he popped up on their radar. Then he launched the recently installed facial recognition software Face Glass with a few clicks.

He had managed to get early access to it from the military tech corporation, Cryostone. The biometric tool wouldn't roll out to the central intelligence and police agencies for years. Glitchy, for sure. Like a beta version of software thrown to the masses with a reluctant promise to fix the bugs later. Wexhall didn't care – he was determined to have fun with his new toy.

A photo of Tom Lee was loaded up, and Wexhall let it run – launching a fast-moving twin box next to the mugshot that flashed other faces with lightning speed.

He thought about Carl Paterson in London. Wexhall wondered whether to call on his services to help him out with all this? Carl's little operation was based nearer Europe – he had ears to the ground over there after all. Then Wexhall decided against it. Things might need to get nasty. It was his problem and his alone. Best keep it in the family and nip it in the bud.

***

Two teams.

Alpha one, a six-man unit, waited in the vehicle at the front of the single-storey condo in the leafy suburb of Thornton – their M-16's at the ready while the point man and breacher crouched by the rear doors. Stark waited with them, along for the ride. He was an efficient operator, and although fully trained in most military manoeuvres he would enter only once the house was deemed secure.

Around the corner, at a safe distance, were two more vans. The first held Alpha two, tasked with gaining access and securing the location with a waiting forensics team. The second held another, team Delta, acting as a comms centre.

"Alpha One Go! Alpha Two Go!" the crackle came across the comms from the command vehicle further down the street.

Simultaneously, a stream of heavily armed men clad in black fatigues and Kevlar helmets descended on the house in a snake – a single file to narrow the chances of being targeted. The teams moved on their objective with smooth efficiency, one moving to the rear of the building while the other took the front. There was a massive crunch as the first two men took care of the door breach with ruthless efficiency.

The point man went in first, stepping through the doorway into the hallway, a small kitchen visible at the end of the house. He stepped against the wall just outside the first left door to the living room that was shut firm. Another of the unit slowly opened it from the side. The point man, his M-9 sighted into the revealing space, quickly sliced the pie to the apex of the room to check for threats then moved to the left wall. He was followed by the other who covered the right with his M-16. To their right, an alcove connected to the dining room at the back.

Another two unit members peeled off to the right-hand side bedroom, mirroring the procedure.

"Front left, clear, Alpha Red proceeding to front back," came a voice through the comms.

A moment later. "Alpha Blue, front right, clear."

Another two men moved straight up the hallway to the kitchen in a crouch, weapons high, finding another empty space.

Moments later. "Alpha Green. Rear kitchen and bathroom clear."

A voice came through his earpiece, "House secure. No Tangos home. Over."

Stark holstered the sidearm he'd been holding while the tactical unit cleared the house, and picked up a small hard case box.

"Lionheart coming in. Forensics, meet me there," he replied and stepped out of the van into the cool breeze. Stark walked up the pathway and began to check each room carefully as the tactical unit prepared to leave. The team leader nodded to him as he entered the house.

"Are we done here?" he asked Stark.

"I'll take it from here, thanks, officer."

He walked through the rooms doing an initial scan, then placed the box down in the kitchen and called Wexhall on the mobile.

"Target has long gone, sir. I'll call in help from Forensics and see if we can find anything."

"Do that. Keep me posted."

Stark took out a pair of forensic gloves from the box and returned to the front living room. The house was sparsely furnished and devoid of any personal belongings, pictures or anything that gave a clue to Lee's character or lifestyle. He pulled on the gloves, stepped over to the sofa and crouched down beside it, running his steely gaze over the dark brown leather.

He spotted a small ripped section of plastic stuck out from one of the seams. It had probably been covered with a shrink-wrapped plastic sheet the whole time Lee had allegedly lived here to keep down on DNA leaks. He moved to a side cabinet and opened the drawers. Both empty.

Moving through the archway to the dining area, Stark saw a round glass table, with four chairs, neatly aligned as if they were in a showroom. Against the wall, a pine wood side cabinet contained just a stack of three plates. After making his way more thoroughly around the house, Stark had found nothing to take back to Wexhall.

"Sir?"

Stark turned to see two forensic investigators coming down the hallway.

"Give the whole place a good clean sweep and be quick about it."

The team set to work, unpacking their gear, while Stark went to check the outside perimeter.

***

From his peripheral vision Wexhall saw that the rapid movement on the screen had paused. He slid his chair closer.

"Sonofabitch," he muttered.

It was a match from security in Vienna airport. Wexhall scrolled through the details. Travelling under the name of Mark Simpson – the manifest had him on a flight to Las Palmas in the Canary Islands.

"Looking for a bit of sunshine are you, boy? What in the hell are you doing over there?" he said out loud.

Wexhall breathed out in satisfaction. They had a lead, at least.

Just then his phone buzzed. It was Stark.

"Tango left the building and he cleaned up well, but we found a print."

The fact that he had disappeared came as absolutely no surprise to Wexhall, but finding a single fingerprint might give them something. Was it fake? They had his biometric data on file including prints, taken during recruitment, so they'd soon find out.

"Alright. Bring it in and wrap it up."

Wexhall cut the call and stood up, pacing his office. It helped him think. He needed to check his assets in the field. He went to the wall safe, opened it up, retrieved a coded list and held it up to the light. The encrypted numbers, letters and symbols in columns indicated the different types of assets, their specialist skills, current locations and codenames. The colonel returned to his desk, typed into the decryption tool for a few minutes, then stared at the result. He had very few assets in the field. G13COMM were still in the process of putting together the infrastructure of the agency. His eyes settled on one –Elvira, currently based in East Europe, who could get there inside a day with any luck.

He checked some other options and decided on his original choice.

He calmly activated the Ghost Order that would relay a coded message via phone.

Wexhall felt a glimmer of satisfaction. At least now one highly trained asset would soon be closing in to plug the leak permanently.

Chapter 11

Bratislava, Slovakia.

Iskra Polyak codenamed 'Elvira', watched the snowflakes drift down from a bleak, dark sky to settle on the ledge of her sparse apartment window as she drained her espresso. Like a background ambience, the gentle hum of the fifty-year-old heating system had just kicked in. It was still dark outside, the yellow street lights revealing nothing more than the relentless snowfall. She was glad to be back in the warmth after her early run. Every spare moment she had outside of her work hours was used to hone her skills, keep herself in shape.

While she waited.

The small lean woman took a shower, then padded over to the kitchen alcove wrapped in a dressing gown and refilled her cup with more coffee. She found some eggs and began to whisk them up in a bowl. Methodically she chopped up some chorizo and onion, before adding a dash of spices, mixing them and pouring the yellow mixture into a butter heated pan.

As she began to eat the omelette she'd just made, her mobile phone started to vibrate on the worktop. Elvira picked it up and answered, listening to the short message, then ended the call.

Her wait was finally over.

It was a *Ghost Order*.

Elvira glanced at the clock: 3:48 AM.

She finished her food, washed up, dressed and began to go through the apartment, filling up a bin liner with anything she thought might compromise her identity or leave clues that might lead others to trail her – the bedsheets, items in the bathroom and cupboards. It didn't take long. Her wardrobe and clothes were kept to a minimum. Anything else in the apartment had come with the rental.

Her identity documents for her cover legend, Danika Klimer, had been kept in a waterproof bag and would now need to be ditched. It was just a case of wiping down any objects she touched often.

Less than an hour later she had dumped two bags in the bins in a quiet alley some way from her apartment, generously doused them in gasoline and left the burning trash behind her, smoke rising between the two buildings. She moved through the snow-caked streets, her fur-lined leather coat buttoned up tight, a white wool skull cap covering her dark hair and stepped onto a passing tram. She then watched the sparse streets rush by, figures in furry hats and heavy coats, heads bent down against the wind while making their way through the icy streets.

Her job, the bare old apartment, her identity – all fake – all make-believe. Would she miss Danika Klimer? She allowed herself a rare smile. How dull to have to clock into a deadly boring routine every day just for the privilege of paying a mountain of bills. No, she would not miss Danika or her job at the travel agency or the Slovakian capital that had been her sleeper station for almost a year now.

She exited the tram and headed toward the Nové Mesto district, turning off into a narrow road where grey housing blocks stood on either side. Apart from a dark figure crossing the deserted street, the neighbourhood had not woken up yet. That was good. Up ahead, she saw the trees from a little park, in the centre of the small housing estate, and turned in alongside, walking around its edge.

She glanced back at her previous route, then into the empty park and slipped through a gate in the metal railings. Crunching through the fresh snow, Elvira reached a clump of trees that sprawled across the middle of the location. She glanced at her watch. The drop should have been made thirty minutes ago. Elvira moved to the children's play area at the rear of the park, behind a concrete public toilet, her eyes alert for any danger, then she spotted the mark – a symbol sprayed onto the side of the toilet block.

Confirmation.

Entering the play area, she slipped into a gap behind the toilet block and a fence then crouched down behind a large wheelie bin at the far end and pulled out a small backpack that had been stuffed underneath. She moved off quickly, throwing the pack over her shoulder as she headed towards the train station.

Chapter 12

Las Palmas, Canary Islands

Frank strolled along the promenade on the Playa De Las Canteras in Las Palmas, Gran Canaria. It was a warm evening, with just the right amount of breeze from the Canarias sea to feel warm and balmy. A handful of tourists and locals alike took in the evening air. A group of joggers padded by while out on the beach a middle-aged couple waded hand in hand out into the sea where fishing boats bobbed around like corks in the distance.

He had flown into Las Palmas the previous day, checked into a small apartment that Rhodes had provided and then met up with him in a park where the older man gave him his legend identity and other details.

Rhodes had delivered everything as promised and now Frank would be travelling as Frank Milligan, just another lone traveller making his way around the globe. Rhodes had even given him a large backpack to complete the illusion and established the final destination – Colombia. Mr Milligan was a researcher for the British Environmental Agency taking a sabbatical year, following his dream to travel to South America. The legend package Rhodes had given him included a passport for Milligan along with a driving licence as well as covert communication instructions and codes.

Colombia. All Frank knew about the country was it had been a narco drugs hell in the 80s but was supposedly a lot "safer now". That morning he had read through a background brief on the situation there. The drug cartels had wielded great power across the country, their tentacles of influence reaching the highest levels of government and police. It was apparent corruption would still be rife. Paramilitaries, both left and right wing, had caused a civil conflict that had lasted decades. FARC, the *Revolutionary Armed Forces of Colombia*, were a communist group operating a war against the Government since 1964 that used a kidnap for ransom policy as one of their tactics. They were also knee deep in the drug trade.

Then there was the National Liberation Army (ELN), regarded as being more politically motivated than the FARC. It had been responsible for hundreds of kidnappings and destroying infrastructure such as oil pipelines.

Another growing force was the United Self-Defence Forces of Colombia (AUC) – a right-wing umbrella group formed by drug-traffickers and landowners to combat left-wing rebel kidnappings and extortion.

The AUC, its roots in the paramilitary armies built up by drug lords in the 1980s, found influence from the military and some political circles. However, critics had denounced it as little more than a drugs cartel. Mix in numerous criminal gangs or *Bacrims* as the government and Colombia called them, and it still made for a perilous place to be in. Frank consoled himself that they would not be going to any of those dubious regions with Medellín being the end destination.

Frank turned off the promenade into one of the side streets, thronging with crowds all dressed up for the carnival. A continuous cacophony completed the backdrop: whistles, drumming and brass music drifted up from the streets that spiked inland.

He knew the hotel name where Nero was staying under the name of Mark Simpson – Hotel Canteras – given to him by Rhodes and decided to take a discreet look; check out his new friend from a distance.

It would be easy to have a few beers, check out a club; he was essentially single again, after all. But no time for that. Frank shook away the thought before it took hold. He needed to check out this guy as a priority, make sure there were no nasty surprises to be found or anything that might jump out of the shadows and bite him on the arse. Information is power and the more he knew about Nero, the better.

Frank arrived at the hotel, set on a corner of a busy road that housed bars and restaurants where the customers were already filling up the outside tables. He found a seat with a view of the hotel entrance and the street he had just walked down. He carefully watched the crowd of pedestrians walk across his field of vision as they headed for the seafront promenade. Just taking it all in while keeping his eyes open for anything that registered on his radar.

A waiter appeared, and Frank ordered a beer. For a moment he wished he had a cigarette. His gaze drifted to the hotel entrance where a few guests came and went. After twenty minutes of nursing his beer, satisfied no one was following him, Frank strolled over to the Hotel Canteras and into the busy lobby. It was an old building that hinted at the grandesque with fine-looking chaise longues and stylish furniture placed in the common bar area. A crowd of guests pushed past him, laughing and joking in Spanish. Frank glanced around, then took a seat on a couch in the bar area that faced the reception desk and surveyed the scene while ostensibly flicking through the menu. It was just due diligence; see what he could see for his own piece of mind if nothing else. After ten minutes the reception area became busy again, and Frank made his way to the elevators for the rooftop bar.

No one gave him a second glance.

The rooftop bar was crowded with festival goers warming up for the night's festivities ahead. Plush booths with low tables lined the edges. A bar was set in the middle, stationed by a smartly attired steward who was rushed off his feet with the relentless demand for wine and cocktails. At one end steel steps led to an outdoor Jacuzzi that appeared to be closed for the night and a balcony overlooking the lights of Las Palmas. Frank moved slowly around the rooftop, peering across at the city lights while discreetly checking faces among the party-goers. He casually circled the entire terrace, occasionally stopping while looking into the hidden nooks.

No sign of Nero.

It was as likely he would just have stayed in his room or gone out somewhere else. Frank leaned over the circular metal railings, watching the moon's reflection across the bay. In the distance, high spindly cranes were dark silhouettes, barely visible against a darkening sky.

What the hell was he doing here? The question came to mind out of nowhere. There was a moment of regret before he remembered his goals and reasons.

His family.

It's always for the family.

Even if Maria disapproved, which she did, but he couldn't blame her for that.

Frank glanced around again and recognised the figure coming down the steps from an upper balcony.

It was Nero, dressed in a blue short-sleeved shirt, jeans and holding a beer from which he took an occasional sip.

Frank waited for a moment, turning back to the view, then casually moved to the bar as Nero headed to the double glass doors back into the building, toward the elevators. Frank shifted away from the bar and followed Nero through the doors.

Frank checked his watch as he stepped back onto the busy street, back into the carnival. Just past eight. He followed Nero, wading through the crowds. Distant batucada drums drifted in and out from up ahead, while revellers with painted faces, masks and an assortment of wigs moved by in a blur. Up ahead, Frank could see the carnival floats, the bare flesh of dancers in tropical bird costumes gyrating to the drums. Nero stopped at a makeshift stall and bought another beer, so Frank hung back on the opposite side, glancing around at the crowds while keeping an eye on Rhodes' new golden boy. Frank decided he would give it another twenty minutes, let Nero get on with his night then maybe even treat himself to a few hours to enjoy the carnival himself.

You're not on bloody holiday, Frank reminded himself, his professional training reprimanding him for entertaining such thinking.

A group of young women with feathered headpieces, linking arms, came down the street, singing loudly. A woman with blonde hair tied back in a ponytail, wearing a black T-shirt and backpack moved to the side of the road to let them pass. It was a young crowd, warming up for a long night of partying. The woman paused at a storefront and casually glanced over at Nero.

Frank's casual surveillance of his target seemed to have revealed a potential problem.

Nero moved off sipping his beer and nodding his head in time to the continuous drums, and the woman continued to shadow him, confirming Frank's suspicions.

Nero continued towards the *Parque de Santa Catalina*, all the roads leading to it seemed to create a bottleneck, where the crowds thickened considerably. The blonde followed. In the square, a giant Chinese dragon appeared, towering over the crowd, while a bleat of trumpets, drums and whistles punctured the atmosphere. Nero spoke to a few revellers outside one of the packed bars, accepting a few swigs of what looked like rum from the bottle. He seemed to be having a great time. Frank took a position by some benches, next to a group of party goers who were talking and laughing. He used them as cover to keep a subtle eye on both Nero and his new stalker.

Have to be careful here, Frank thought to himself. Be so easy to lose either one of them in this mayhem.

After ten minutes of socialising, Nero was on the move again, slowly making his way along the east side of the square before doubling back via a different street in the direction of the promenade. The blonde wasn't far behind, and Frank tried to keep them both in his sights at all times, but it was messy. There were too many people, and he found himself having to push through the bodies of tightly packed revellers to catch up.

It soon became clear Nero was returning to his hotel. Had enough partying perhaps? Through the packed crowd Frank saw that the woman had caught up and was speaking to him now, flicking her head back as she laughed at something.

Perhaps it was just his lucky night?

But something told Frank otherwise. She had tailed him for a fair distance, never letting him out of sight and had displayed all the signs of professional tradecraft.

What was he supposed to do? Call it in with Rhodes: 'Your man has a beautiful woman with him, and it looks like they are heading for his hotel room?'

Frank watched Nero and the blonde disappear through the doors of the hotel. As Frank walked in, he came up against a wall of carnival goers spilling out into the lobby from the packed bar. He spotted Nero at the reception desk waiting to talk to the desk clerk who was on the phone. His new friend loitered by the stairwell, seemingly keeping her face out of sight. Frank moved through the crowd, near enough to hear Nero order a bottle of bubbly to be delivered to his room, number 207, immediately. He then went to join the woman, and they disappeared up the stairwell, arm in arm.

What was her agenda, exactly?

There were two possibilities. Either it was just Nero's lucky night in which case what the hell was he doing here? The more likely one that Frank was increasingly convinced of was that this woman was a 'swallow' – a honey trap sent in to snare or even kill Nero. It was too much of a coincidence considering who he was.

***

Elvira walked through the door past an en-suite and built-in wardrobe either side and into the modest hotel room. She looked around, mentally taking notes of her surroundings, as was her habit. Large windows dominated the room, the curtains half shut, the hum of the carnival drifting up from the street. The double bed was made up with bedside tables and a wooden desk with the usual hotel paraphernalia on top.

"*Mi casa es su casa* – the drinks should be up soon. It's Ana, right?"

Elvira turned to him with a broad smile. "You forget already? Yes, it's Ana. Leon?" She had no doubt "Leon" was nowhere near his real name. He returned the smile, nodded and tossed his keycard onto the desk. Elvira slipped off her backpack and casually dropped it by the bed, running her other hand over the bedspread. "I do love good hotels. It's the little things like the soaps and shampoos in the bathroom, everything on call," she cooed.

"Not having to clean up after yourself?" he added with a wry smile.

She laughed and sat down on the side of the bed facing the window, gently bouncing on it as if testing the mattress.

"You don't stay in hotels much, then?" he asked, crouching down in front of the minibar before opening it up and peering inside.

"No," she sighed. "I am a budget traveller – hotels too expensive."

"Where are you staying?"

"Down near Parque San Telmo. I stay in Las Palmas for two or three days, then maybe travel to the other islands."

"You want a gin or something?" he asked, peering into the array of drinks in the room's minibar.

"Hmm, I wait for the bubbly stuff." She let out a long sigh and leaned back on the bed, spreading herself out.

He turned to glance at her and she gave him her most seductive look while patting the side of the bed. "Why don't you wait here?"

She was well aware she was no catwalk model but knew she had an undefined beauty that men always locked onto. Leon, or Tom as he wasn't revealing to her, stood up with a hint of galvanised lust in his eyes. He then moved across the room, glancing towards the door.

"Maybe we'd better wait—"

She let out a light giggle. "Of course, what kind of girl do you think I am?" The words came automatically, relayed so many times before. She was in the full flow of her act, a naïve travelling student, out for a good time, seeing some of the world before returning to "university in Latvia". Seduction was her speciality; she had been carefully trained in these matters. It should be straightforward: a few glasses of champagne when it arrived, give him a few tantalising glimpses of her body, a taste of her lips then retrieve her special powdered cigarettes from the bag when he was distracted. A secondary follow-up message to the Ghost Order had requested her to try and extract information by questioning, some torture techniques would almost certainly be required, then eliminate if necessary.

He stood next to her, running a hand through her dyed-blonde hair.

"Well, I had some thoughts on that."

There was a gentle tap at the door. "Room service," came an accented voice on the other side.

"Don't go anywhere," he said in a low murmur.

As the target went to the door, Elvira leaned over and quietly unzipped the pocket of her backpack. Scopolamine, the drug from Colombia that turned the hapless victim into a willing zombie accomplice. A few sprinkles of the odourless powder she had put in a few of the cigarettes should do the trick.

There was a pop as the champagne was corked at the door and a low murmur of conversation as "Leon" accepted the delivery.

"If you could just sign for it here, sir," she heard the hotel concierge say. She pulled out a small tablet canister and slipped it into her jeans front pocket, ready to administer, and placed the cigarettes on the side table.

"Thank you, that's very generous," the concierge said.

Nero returned to the room holding a silver tray, ice bucket with the bottle and placed it down on the desk, his back to her. She heard the fizz as the liquid hit the glass and he handed her one and held up his.

"Well, *salud*, Miss Ana." She took a sip as he gulped down a mouthful and let out a satisfied sigh. "Not bad stuff. Certainly not the first drink or the last—"

She placed her glass on the bedside table, picked up the Donskoy cigarettes and offered one to him. "You want?"

"No, I'm good, but you go ahead."

She nodded, keeping her expression unreadable and slowly took out a cigarette, then played with it, unlit, between her fingers. She would need to get the powder from the tablet canister into his drink or think of something else.

He sat down on the edge of the bed next to her, his eyes furtively checking her out, then he held up the glass again as if to toast.

"To – what's the next island you're visiting?"

She picked up the glass again and clinked his.

"Lanzarote or Arrecife, I'm not sure."

"Here's to Lanzarote or 'not sure,'" he repeated with a smile.

"So, how does this carnival compare to others, Ana?"

She shook her head, a dull pain now penetrating her skull.

"No, I haven't been to many other carnivals. Las Palmas is my...first."

She felt sick for a moment, drowsy.

"Maybe Rio would be worth putting on your itinerary, Ana?"

She ignored his words, trying to move to the far side of the bed. Something was wrong.

"Ana isn't your real name, is it? But then I'm no Leon," he said with a light chuckle.

She had screwed up, had been so fixated on getting him drugged that she had let her guard down. Her vision blacked out, the dizziness coming over her in waves, a cold sweat soaking her skin and her heart seemed to be pounding through her chest.

Fuck!

It was her last thought as she fell onto the floor, a void of blackness tunnelling her vision.

***

Frank had intercepted the concierge as he made his way through the long hallways of the ground floor of the hotel with the champagne for room 207. After dragging him into one of the restrooms he had knocked him out and thrown on his jacket and name badge.

Next, he took a small package from his backpack supplied by Rhodes and prepared a small sample of benzodiazepines, a central nervous system depressant in the form of tablets. Between his thumb and forefinger, Frank crushed one up into one of the champagne glasses.

Then he took a pen from the concierge's jacket and scribbled a note in clear capital letters on the order pad with the introduction code he was to give Nero on their first meeting alerting him to who Frank was, along with a warning that his visitor in his room was an immediate threat.

There could be no misunderstanding although there were un-doubtedly multiple things that could go wrong. What if the woman answered the door instead of him?

He'd have to deal with that problem if it came up. There was no time to think or plan and this was the best idea considering his resources.

Frank wheeled the trolley up to the elevator and headed up to the second floor, then continued to the room. Only a hotel guest passed by, barely glancing at him.

It was a big relief to see Nero open the door. Frank immediately held up the note along with a finger over his lips. Nero read it, frowning, then looked at Frank and nodded.

He understood.

"Good evening, sir. Your ordered beverage," Frank said in an accent. He gestured with a hand sign to one of the glasses, then pointed past the guest's shoulder into the room and made a sipping motion with his hand.

"If you'd just sign for the order, I'll open the bottle for you," Frank continued and did so with a loud "pop" and placed it back into the ice bucket.

He jabbed his finger again at the same glass, emphasising to use the correct one. Nero nodded again and gave a thumbs up.

"Thank you, sir, that's very generous," Frank said, before pointing at the floor to indicate he would wait.

Nero took the tray and stepped back inside. Frank waited outside, glancing up and down the corridor, ready to look busy with the notepad if anyone passed by.

After barely a few minutes the door opened, and Nero gestured him inside. Frank shut the door and walked in to see the woman lying on the floor, out cold.

"Did she bring a bag?" he asked. Nero pointed a finger at the far side of the bed. Frank picked it up and unzipped it before tossing out the contents: bottled water, a spare zip-up jacket and a small toolkit containing pliers but little else.

Frank held it up for Nero to see. "Not sure what she was gonna do with these, use them on your balls, maybe?" Frank said, grinning. His new acquaintance didn't smile back and glanced down at the girl again, forlornly.

Frank looked into the now-empty bag.

"Well, no phone, ID or anything that hints at her identity – help me get her back on the bed."

They placed the unconscious body on top of the bedspread.

"Are you sure she's some kind of agent?"

"I don't know what she was planning, but something wasn't right..." Frank began as he searched her jeans pocket. He immediately found the small pill capsule bottle and held them up, "Drugging you by the looks of it. Probably not to take advantage of you either." He pocketed the bottle and glanced at the Donskoy cigarette packet.

"Did she offer you a cigarette?"

"She did."

"They're probably drugged too. We'll take them with us."

Frank turned to Nero who was standing cross-armed, still looking stunned.

"So what do I call you – Nero?"

The young man shook his head, "Mark Simpson is fine," he said, holding out his hand.

"I'm Frank," he replied, shaking it.

"Alright, Frank. Thanks, by the way. Didn't think we'd meet like this."

"I take it you booked into the hotel under Mark Simpson?"

Nero looked regretful. "Yeah, yeah I did."

"OK, not ideal but maybe it won't matter. We should be off the island in a matter of hours." He glanced back at the woman. "She should be out for an hour at least, a couple at most. We need to leave ASAP."

"What about her?"

Frank glanced around the room. "Well, there's nothing we can tie her up with unless you've got something?"

"Like ropes?" Mark shook his head. "No, buddy."

"Best we can do is lock her in then, cut the phone line and take her stuff. Let's get started."

Chapter 13

Early the next morning Frank made his way to La Luz Port and took a while looking for the ship *Anita*. It was hard to miss; a colossal beast, the dark hull casting welcome shade across the dock. From the bridge to the bow, towering lift rigs hauled the deck containers into bays, stacking them into blocks that reminded Frank of the toy Lego bricks Joe used to love playing with. Straddle-carriers brought a constant stream of containers for loading. He watched the process for a while, keeping his eyes along the dock and sat down.

They had slipped out of the hotel and holed up at Frank's apartment for a few hours, then left individually and made their way to the dock. Frank messaged Rhodes with news of the 'new player in the game'. Rhodes had told him to stick to the plan. Frank didn't like it. Things were already going south, and they hadn't even left yet.

Ten minutes later, the figure of Nero appeared, looking every bit like a backpacker. He glanced in Frank's direction for a second but didn't acknowledge him and began to climb up the passenger gangway. Frank checked his watch. There were two and a half hours before the ship was due to leave but Frank was wary of hanging around too long. He got up, grabbed his bag and walked over to the gangway entrance. A squat, bearded crewman greeted him who mumbled something that Frank barely heard as he tried to get past the man.

"Ticket?" The man asked again, slightly louder in a heavy accent.

"Oh sorry, mate." Frank handed him the paper folder that Rhodes had given him. The crewman checked the details and gave him a friendly grin. "We don't have too many passengers. It's very rare."

"Well, I just hope I don't cause the ship to sink," Frank replied. The crewman laughed and held out his hand. "My name is Yuri, I'm the first mate on the ship, and I welcome you to the *Anita*."

Frank was shown to his quarters, deep in the belly of the ship. The crewman gave him a rapid rundown of the schedule, mealtimes and so forth and promised he would check in with him later that evening. It was surprisingly comfortable and clean, almost like a basic cruise cabin. He slumped his backpack down, took a shower and changed clothes, giving himself a short time to rest. He almost drifted off but was pulled back into consciousness by the ship's horn blasting from above. He peered out of the porthole as the dockside began to pass by slowly. They were setting sail.

He moved down the corridors, passing crew cabins to find his way up top to the deck. In the passageway exposed pipes laced the ceiling overhead, interspersed with thick hatch doors. After taking a few flights of metal steps, Frank came to an exterior door and stepped out onto the main deck, at the mid-section of the ship. He glanced back at the bridge castle, a white block structure dotted with a row of tiny windows where, Frank guessed, the captain spent most of his time. He strolled towards it, getting a feel for his bearings, passing the lifeboats before eventually coming to the stern behind the bridge.

A crewman dressed in a blue boiler suit walked by and nodded a silent greeting but, other than that, the ship seemed ghostly quiet. Then Frank saw Nero, leaning over the railings at the back of the boat, watching the port of Las Palmas shrink on the flat sea.

He leaned over next to him. "Goodbye, Las Palmas," Frank said. The younger man turned, appraising Frank with a glance, smiled and turned back to the view.

"Yeah indeed. I'll miss the sand sculptures. Any sign of our friend?"

"No, it seems clear. I'm just glad we're on our way," Frank replied. "Just so you know, I'm travelling under the name of Frank Milligan," he added.

"Milligan? Did you choose that name or was it given to you?"

"What difference does it make? We can swap real names later. Eaglecraft wants you at his RZ without any hiccups. So I hope we get along as it might be a long journey, mate."

Nero gave a quiet snort of derision. "Eaglecraft, nice. Assume he picked that one himself," Nero stood up straight, turning to Frank. "Why we couldn't just fly, I'll never know?"

"Did he not explain to you?" asked Frank with mild irritation. "It's longer but far more secure. Less airport security, a lot more under the radar."

"Sure," Nero said with finality.

"What cabin are you in?"

Nero sighed, "134."

"Alright. I'm just down the corridor: 102. We need to remember these things, just in case."

The young man nodded. "Yes, I understand...Mr Milligan."

"Good. Well, I'm gonna take a look around the ship. I'll catch you later."

The younger man nodded and returned his gaze to the port disappearing on the horizon.

Chapter 14

Elvira drifted back into consciousness with a sour taste in her mouth and a pounding headache. Before she even opened her eyes, she knew something was wrong. A deep feeling of unease had settled on her and on seeing the hotel room it all came back.

Shit!

She had fucked up and, worst of all, she had been played. Stupid!

With waves of nausea washing over her, she forced herself to sit up on the bed and glanced down to where her backpack had been. It was long gone. Luckily she hadn't anything in the bag that could compromise her, but it was still bad news. She glanced at the ice bucket and bottle neck sticking out in disgust with herself. The glasses were gone, naturally.

You're still alive, Iskra. Next time you won't be so lucky.

She patted her jeans pocket and knew that the tablet canister with the Scopolamine had been taken, then went to the bathroom, splashed cold water over her face and proceeded to search the room, just in case. Finding nothing, she slipped out and down to the lobby. The party crowds had long dispersed, but a policeman was speaking to one of the reception staff and a dishevelled concierge. She walked past and loitered by a table of newspapers just within earshot, pretending to read the headlines.

There were snippets of conversation in Spanish – the concierge had been knocked out by someone – no, he didn't see who it was; he was just on his way to deliver drinks to room 207. A Mr Simpson.

The policeman asked to see the room and at that Elvira left through the doors into the morning sun.

So, an imposter concierge that came with the drinks, the one she had not seen. Nero had help, that much was now certain. She tried to analyse why she had not been more alert, but all the intelligence had led her to believe he was an office boy without external help.

Not so.

She would report that, but not yet. She needed some lead as to why the seemingly straightforward objective had not been completed.

The target and his new accomplice would be leaving the island, somewhere. She had to find them.

Chapter 15

Frank headed below deck, past the lower stowage holds and along a walkway that ran alongside the crates in the lower 'tween decks. He came to a blue sign that labelled the decks alphabetically and looked for the mess hall where he could get a bite to eat. After negotiating another labyrinth of corridors and hatches, Frank came to a large room with several round tables, all immaculately laid out ready for the evening meal. A board on the wall displayed a menu which Frank studied before a cook's mate walked past.

"Hello," he chirped.

"Hi, I don't suppose I can grab a snack, like a sandwich or something? I haven't eaten for a while," Frank asked politely.

"No problem. I can fix you something. What would you like?"

"Anything: ham, cheese, I'm not fussy."

The cook nodded and disappeared through the metal door off the mess. After ten minutes he returned with a steak and onion sandwich on rye bread with a small side salad.

"Ah, you're a star. Thanks, mate."

The cook grinned. "My pleasure, let me know if you need anything else," he said as he returned to the kitchen.

A tall man with a shaved head and tattoos on his neck and arms entered the mess, glanced over at Frank, smiled and disappeared into the kitchen. Frank chewed his food, staring out across the vast ocean. After five minutes he heard a voice and looked to see the same man walking up to the table holding a plate and steak sandwich.

"I saw yours. It looked so good I thought I'd join you."

Frank smiled politely, but he wanted to be alone with his thoughts.

"Hi. No problem," Frank heard himself say.

The man sat down and extended a large hand.

"I'm Lukas. Second mate of the *Anita*." Frank detected a slight accent. Slavic, perhaps.

Frank shook it. "Frank Milligan, nomad of the seas."

Lukas laughed.

"So, how long have you been a seaman?" Frank asked.

"Over ten years. I was in the Russian navy before."

Frank paused for a moment before eating the last of his late lunch. A memory reared its ugly head: the Russian mob he had come up against less than a year before.

"I assume Russia is your home then?"

"Yes. St Petersburg. What brings you on the *Anita*? You're travelling?" the Russian asked.

Frank wiped his mouth with a paper napkin and leaned back, gazing back out of the window.

"Yes, a bit of a life change. Get away from England for a while."

"That's great. I'm very jealous. For me, life is just hard work. But I have a plan. I save my money and hope to make sailing trips around Panama and Colombia."

"Sounds like a nice plan," said Frank with genuine interest. Sailing had been a hobby he'd always promised himself but never got around to. Perhaps after this job.

Lukas finished his sandwich and stood up.

"Sorry, I have to go. Do you play Poker, Frank? The crew sometimes have a game – if you want to join?"

Frank held up a hand. "I'm fine, thanks for the offer."

"Alright, well, if you change your mind. The captain even likes to play on occasion."

Frank smiled as Lukas walked off.

"I'll bear that in mind, thanks."

Frank was wary. A reminder that although they might be heading to the middle of the Atlantic, he needed to stay alert. If they had tracked Nero to Las Palmas was it such a wild notion that they had people on the ship? Frank silently cursed Rhodes for not changing their route.

Chapter 16

Mid-Atlantic. Five days later.

The days and nights had merged into one, drifting by like the ship's journey across the vast expanse of the endless ocean surrounding them. Occasionally other ships appeared, mere specks in the far distance and the sunsets seemed to become more spectacular the closer they came to the Caribbean. Frank was surprised at how calm the crossing had been. There had been one or two rough nights but, overall, it was a case of getting used to the rolling movement and adapting to it. The wonder of the natural order of things certainly put things into perspective for Frank.

Frank and Nero were invited to the Officers' Recreation room to enjoy an aperitif before sharing another excellent dinner with the captain. The ship was due to dock at Antigua the following day. Captain Nicolae Petrescu was from Romania, a tall man with a typically rugged demeanour who seemed to enjoy the small talk with his only two passengers. They would be there for a few days, unloading around twenty containers, so the captain suggested Frank take a trip around the island. The rest of the officers hailed from Lithuania, Georgia and Bulgaria. The two passengers recited their stories, keeping to the script of their legends as the captain drained his wine glass.

"The crew sometimes have a game of Poker. Would you care to

join us?"

Nero shook his head immediately. "I'm gonna have an early night, don't feel too great, so I'll pass."

The captain smiled politely. "No problem, Mark." His gaze turned to Frank who felt like wheeling out a similar response. Still, perhaps it wouldn't be a bad idea to bond with the crew and captain.

"Sure, I'll try a few hands. Your first mate mentioned it – Lukas?"

The captain chuckled. "Ah yes. He already asked you? No surprise. He is an excellent player. You watch him carefully."

***

A few of the crewman, including Lukas, the captain and Yuri sat around a small table in the mess, cards and chips scattered across the table. Lukas put down shot glasses and a bottle of vodka. Frank groaned inwardly and shook his head.

"It's a ship tradition. Come on." The captain poured the clear liquid and put Frank's shot in front of him with a slam.

"Alright," Frank muttered reluctantly. He picked up his glass and toasted the captain's health.

Frank began his game well, winning a hand with style before the luck – and the money – began running dry. It seemed the other players always had one slightly better hand than him and their bluffs were top notch.

On throwing down his hand and once again declaring he was out of the game, Lukas began to push some chips over the table.

"Here. Have these—"

Frank shook his head. "No, Lukas, keep them. I should call it a night."

A brief expression of offence passed across the Russian's face, and he shoved the chips in front of Frank anyway, then nodded with finality and pointed at Frank's hand of cards face down on the table.

"You play – and drink."

Frank couldn't help but laugh out loud as he picked up his cards. There was no avoiding the directness of the Russian. Frank was beginning to feel at home with the crew.

After a few hours, just the captain, Lukas and Frank were left at the table, on top a scattering of cards, several empty bottles and a full ashtray. The men had stopped playing.

Frank slammed down his shot glass, having learned it to be the standard protocol and leaned over toward Lukas.

"You're not bad for a Russian," he murmured.

Lukas laughed. "Sounds like you had a bad experience with my countrymen, Frank."

"Yeah, you could say that—" He was thinking of the thugs who had kidnapped his wife and kid again. He shook his head and waved away the thoughts. "I'm stereotyping, sorry."

Nicolae, the captain, held up his hand. "Frank, don't apologise. I hate the Russians too." They all laughed.

There was a moment of silence.

"You have family, Frank?"

He nodded automatically, aware he was being unguarded but past caring. "I do, and hopefully they're tucked up at home, safe."

"So, you travel and leave them behind," said the captain. He quickly held up his palm. "I'm not judging; we all have to do what we do," he said, plainly. Both men looked at Frank as if understanding something unsaid. As if they knew who he really was.

Lukas stood up. "I'm done. Early shift tomorrow—" He slapped Frank on the shoulder.

"I think we're all done," smiled the captain, raising his glass at Frank before draining it.

***

The next morning, feeling worse for wear and still reeling from his bad run at the Poker, Frank checked on Nero, banging loudly on his door.

"Yeah? What is it?" Nero shouted.

"Just checking you're in there."

"Thanks. Yeah, I'm still here," came the unimpressed reply. Frank went to the canteen and grabbed a coffee before heading up on deck to watch the island of Antigua come into view. A deep blue sky stretched unending overhead, and gulls circled the ship as it slowly approached St John's Port.

Once docked, Frank leaned over a rail sipping the coffee, watching the activity below as local dockworkers secured the boat, followed by a few crew members from the *Anita* spilling onto the scorched concrete dockside from the ship's hull.

After a few minutes, a group of three travellers moved forward to board. Another two men, one with slick black hair, the other with a reddish crop, both in short-sleeved shirts and long shorts loitered farther back. They both cast their eyes up over the ship, their suitcases at their feet before pulling them toward the gangway. The crewman checked the traveller's tickets and let them on board. Frank appeared to watch the dockside gantry crane unloading the containers, but his attention focused on the two men.

Chapter 17

Frank hadn't bothered taking a trip around the island. It felt like he should stay on board, stay alert and keep an eye on Nero, who had taken ill. Something was spiking in his senses, and he wanted to follow his own lead. The ship set sail around 6.30PM and a half-hour later Frank rapped on Nero's door. "You eating?"

There was a pause followed by a light groan. He knocked again. "Mark?"

"I'm going to skip the dinner. Still feel like shit. You go ahead."

"Alright. I'll be back in an hour."

Frank walked up the stairs to the lower decks, looked up and down the empty corridor and then descended, lurching into the side of the stair rail from a roll of the ship. The weather seemed to be getting more stormy. When he went to the canteen, it was empty. No one around, not even the cook.

Frank opted for a sandwich and a plastic bottle of water from the vending machine. The big lunch he had indulged in still weighed on his stomach. He paused at one of the tables about to sit down, then thought better of it and headed back to the cabins.

When he arrived, he unlocked his door and was about to step inside but noticed Nero's door ajar further down the corridor. He quickly put his food and drink down and walked up to the door, then stopped and listened carefully.

Slowly, he pushed the door further ajar and looked into an empty cabin. He walked inside, "Mark?"

No answer.

Frank checked the en-suite bathroom. Wet towels were sprawled all over the floor, his wash bag was still there, and in the main cabin, his backpack and clothes were scattered over the bed.

He was gone.

Frank rushed down the corridor in the opposite direction from the canteen. The first thing to do was alert the captain and take it from there. He couldn't have got very far, thought Frank. We're on a ship, for God's sake.

Frank decided to check outside first. Nero sometimes went out there for a cigarette. He ran up the stairwells of the midship, up past the second and third decks and came to a hatch for outside.

The wind pressed against him like an unseen hand as he stepped through and he had to push hard on the door to get through. Outside the sun had long gone, plunging the ship into darkness apart from the sporadic deck lights. At the bridge castle, he saw figures through the windows. It seemed busy up there. He walked in that direction, looking across the cargo hatch covers to the other side, then noticed a figure at the bottom of the steps to the bridge. Nero or one of the crew? Frank couldn't quite make them out, but it looked like they were standing guard from their posture.

In the distant darkening sky there was a tiny flashing light from a plane. As he moved along the deck, there was movement in the bridge window, silhouettes across the stark light. Someone was shoving one of the crew, and he swore he saw the outline of a gun.

Frank stopped and slid into a dark alcove.

Something's up.

Nero was missing. New faces had just boarded. Frank's instinct was on full alert, and he didn't need to convince himself there was a situation developing here.

He moved stealthily along the deck, half crouched toward the figure at the bottom of the steps, now guarding access to the bridge. It looked like a crew member from the jumpsuit he wore, but the black greased back hair didn't look familiar. As the man glanced in his direction his face was clearly lit by one of the exterior lights – one of the new passengers he had seen on the dockside who had boarded at St John's. He had a handgun in his hand, casually holding it down by his side.

Frank stood there, frozen in the shadows, watching. He couldn't tackle the man from the front, there was too much distance, and the greaseball would easily have time to get a shot off. Frank reached into his pocket and pulled out a coin. He tossed it onto the deck the far side of the man with a metallic clank. The man turned to face the noise, his pistol rising, pointing at the unknown.

As soon as his back was turned, Frank moved forward in a half-crouch towards his assailant. When he reached him, Frank's left arm swiftly moved around the man's neck, dragging him back and off balance. He grabbed the arm with the weapon and yanked back hard. Greaseball's arms hyper-extended, his elbow pivoting on Frank's chest, the gun falling away from his grip.

As they stumbled backwards, Frank slipped, losing his grip on the arm and his assailant. Instinctively, he planted his feet for better grip on the deck, recovering his footing. Then, a jolt of pain across his face. Greaseball had thrown his head backwards, connecting squarely with Frank's nose. Eyes watering, he turned away. Immediately, a barrage of punches came raining in. Hands came up fast to block, but one connected with Frank's temple with a dull thud. His legs collapsed beneath him, sending him sprawling on the hard decking.

Frank was dazed, but he curled up into the foetal position, waiting for the world to stop turning. As the inevitable rain of kicks came in at him, Frank braced, many of the blows on his arms and legs.

Through one eye, Frank saw Greaseball raise his foot, about to stamp on his head. He rolled quickly, grabbing the assailant's supporting leg and driving all his weight through it.

Greaseball flipped backwards, his head bouncing off the deck.

Frank leapt up, sitting on top of him in a securing mount. Then he rained punches down with dull thumps, focusing all his hatred on that face until the assailant was out cold, his face bruised and broken like a beetroot on a bad day.

Frank crawled off the figure, breathing heavily and forced himself up onto his feet. He looked around and found the weapon, a Glock 13 near the bottom of the bridge steps, and checked the chamber.

All good, now he had a piece.

He pulled the unconscious guard down the deck to the lifeboat area and into a hidden nook then headed back, creeping up the bridge steps, the barrel of the Glock aimed straight ahead. The ship rolled as if a storm was rising. A buzzing that Frank only just became aware of grew louder.

There was a change in the light, in the pattern of shadows. Overhead, a helicopter suddenly came into view, a spotlight shining down onto the far side of the bridge castle. A figure in black appeared in the door and dropped down a line, before proceeding to fast rope down onto the deck. From his position, Frank could see another person appear at the helicopter door holding some sniper rifle. It was hard to make out, but Frank swore it was the woman they'd encountered in Las Palmas.

With a scurry of footsteps, Frank came to the bridge door. For the first time, he saw the situation inside. Nero, hands seemingly tied behind his back, was being held at gunpoint by another man, one of the recent embarked. Nicolae, the captain, was navigating the ship with a grim expression, evidently forced to carry out the gunman's bidding. The far exterior door opened and the masked abseiler entered, with a submachine gun at the ready and spoke a few words that Frank couldn't hear to his comrade.

Frank also realised for the first time that the ship had slowed right down to a crawl. The helicopter was now hovering to position itself in front of the bridge as if to land on the cargo bay.

They were taking Nero off the bloody ship.

Two targets and two friendlies inside the bridge. Too dangerous to go in shooting. All Frank could do was mix it up. It would alert them inside the bridge, but he had no choice. He moved back down the steps to a different position and got the helicopter in his sights and squeezed off a series of rounds aiming at the spotlight on the chopper.

The pilot, realising he was under attack, veered away quickly, the lights disappearing into the windswept darkness.

Frank moved back up the steps and glanced through the bridge-door window. The tall man with red hair that Frank had seen board earlier had a weapon to Nero's head and was pulling him out of the door on the far side, alerted by the shooting. The new arrival killed the lights inside the bridge, then began firing at the door Frank was behind, shattering the window. Frank took cover and heard the rush of footsteps on the far steps. He gingerly stood up and glanced through, where Nicolae had crouched down on the floor to hide. The others were gone.

"Nicolae!" Frank hissed. "Lock the doors! Quickly!"

The captain didn't hesitate to get back up and locked the far door, then rushed over to Frank.

"Who the hell are they?" he demanded.

"Don't know yet – barricade this the best you can, I'll be back."

Frank rushed down the steps quickly and jogged all the way around the back of the bridge tower, the massive ship funnel looming overhead. Stepping around the mooring gear, Frank kept close to the walls until he came to the other side and caught sight of the figures moving along the deck.

The helicopter was closing in again.

The only option was to cut off the assailant's escape.

First, he fired above the heads of the figures to get them to take cover.

Frank moved his aim at the dark shape of the chopper with both hands and continued firing, aiming more or less at the tank. *Pok! Pok! Pok!*

Then a flash of a muzzle from the 'copter door and a bullet hit a metal capstan drum right next to him with a pop.

The chopper billowed slightly, the bullets finding their mark. It swayed to the side and veered away from the ship, the side lights revealing a small column of smoke. Hopefully he'd done enough. Frank knew that despite how movies portrayed these events, tanks of fuel did not automatically explode when hit by bullets. It would have been nice if it had though, he thought.

On his haunches, Frank sensed the whizzing sound, followed by a close crack of metal hit near his body from the men on the deck. Time to move.

Frank duck-walked around a tube-like deck ventilator and kept his eye on them while the chopper now circled around the rear of the ship. The tone of the engine told Frank it was struggling, probably losing fuel fast. No doubt it had come from Antigua and could only now either land on the ship somehow or head home.

Now was the time to grab Nero. Frank stealthily moved up some steps to a walkway above where the assailants were. He half jogged a few metres, well away from the rails, so he was ahead of their position and lay low, peeping over to get eyes on them. Both assailants were heading in his direction, pushing at Nero and urging him forward as they scanned the dark sky. It seemed like they were desperately hoping the chopper would return to make their escape.

Frank slipped back out of sight, moving into the shadows. He heard them walk past, snippets of low whispers.

"Chopper went back. We're on our own"

"Fuckin' great. Where's the shooter gone?"

The abseiler jabbed a thumb over his shoulder. "Back there."

"Well, keep an eye on our six—"

The black figure of the abseiler dropped back and turned around to check his rear. Frank, crept forward, silently climbing over the railings.

The helicopter came into view above the containers that filled out the bulk of the ship, just for a few seconds then dived out of sight, the engine fading. It looked to Frank like they had aborted the mission and were leaving their buddies behind on the ship.

The abseiler came underneath Frank. He jumped down, just behind his footfall, driving his elbow into the back of his head with a well-aimed strike. The man stumbled forward, clearly dazed, there was a clunk as his gun hit the deck. Frank ran ahead, grabbing the abseiler around his neck. Pivoting, Frank turned to face Nero and the redhead who immediately raised his weapon.

Frank shrank back, using his hostage as a shield.

"Nowhere to go now your bird has gone. Give up, and I'll spare your life!" Frank shouted.

Red grabbed Nero by the collar, pressing his pistol into the base of his skull. Nero grimaced for a moment, staring at Frank, but his expression resolute.

"You want me to pull the trigger, buddy?" Red bellowed, "I'll happily splatter his brains across the deck right now. Let my associate go, then kneel down with your hands raised – you can go on your merry way, live your life."

"How stupid do you think I am?" countered Frank, "If you wanted him dead why go through all this bullshit trying to grab him? No, obviously want him alive, which means your threat is empty." Frank edged forward. "Now let him go and put your weapon down."

Red began backing off, slowly dragging Nero around the corner and out of view.

Frank almost didn't see it. A glint of a blade in the abseiler's hand.

The knife came at Frank's head, over his shoulder.

Instinctively Frank ducked down, the knife barely missing him. Not waiting for a second, Frank drove both of his knees into the back of his attacker's legs, pulling him backwards at the same time. As they fell, Frank rolled him, smashing his body onto the deck, face down ending up on top of him. Frank postured up, now straddling his attacker, and unloaded a continual assault of blows. Two connected with his cheekbone and Frank felt the abseiler stop struggling.

He pulled himself to his feet, plucked the knife from his hand and tucked it into his belt. He then dragged the barely conscious abseiler to the railings and hauled him overboard.

No time to fuck around.

He didn't want that one coming back into the game.

Frank was already moving down the deck as the body of his assailant hit the dark water with a massive splash.

Frank unclipped the magazine in his pistol to check his rounds, three bullets left, and then slammed it back in.

From what he could hear and see, the helicopter was long gone.

He made a quick assessment. Two assailants had been taken out by his own hand. Now there was just one he knew of with Nero. Could it have been a small infiltration team? The bigger questions of who they were would have to wait. Where had all the original crew gone? He had hardly seen anyone. Should he go back to the captain for more information? But Nero was the priority. He was supposed to have protected the asset, and now the poor bastard was being dragged around at gunpoint.

Got to sort this.

He moved fast, sprinting along the deck to catch up in the direction of the bow and almost stumbled into a body lying seemingly unconscious. He recognised the shaven head: Lukas.

He was lying half through the doorway of a hatch that was banging against his body with the rise and fall of the ship. Frank crouched over him and felt for his pulse. The poor guy was dead. Put up a fight and died for it. Frank didn't feel so sorry for putting abseiler guy overboard now.

Frank glanced through the porthole – the steps inside leading down into one of the cargo bays appeared empty. Squatting low, he opened it wider and listened. A shuffle of a footfall from the depths below.

Frank froze and narrowed his eyes, trying to make out something from the dark void. He moved slowly inside, descending one step at a time until he came to a walkway. Ahead, a mass of containers in an area the size of a football field. The black clouds moved through the gaps above.

A shot rang out and sparked off nearby metal. He crouched down quickly, locating the flash from the weapon from the centre of the containers.

Frank moved quicker, running down another set of steps until he was on the ground level of the bay and followed a narrow gap between the steel containers that towered high above like skyscrapers. Knowing they were twenty or so metres away, he moved quickly to close in. Above, a gap in the clouds revealed a half moon, bathing the containers in a soft light. Shadows shifted across the grid-like boxes, and Frank slowed down, inching around each corner.

He stopped and listened for any sounds that might give him a clue as to their position. His assailant was a professional and would have moved fast after firing.

Frank moved forward again, pieing the corners at each small cross-section where the bottom of the containers met. There was hardly any light in the deep bowels of the boat making Frank hesitant about moving forward.

It was like hunting blind.

A distant footfall echoed through the container corridors at the far end, toward the bridge tower at the back of the boat. Frank stalked the sound, step by step, then saw the figures climbing laddered rails that led to a higher walkway on the edge of the bay. Frank stealthily moved through the gaps until he had a more precise shot of the silhouettes which were now running overhead. He aimed at the figure, but just then Nero slowed as if trying to buy time. They were too close together. Then Red gave Nero a shove in the back, almost sending him sprawling before turning and firing a shot in Frank's direction. Frank ducked and began climbing up the ladder after them.

As he reached the top, Frank noticed the ship was turning around. The captain, now no longer under duress, must be trying to get back to St John's. That also meant he'd alert the authorities if he hadn't already, and serious questions would be asked. Frank slowed down, spotting them at one of the lifeboats at the bottom of the bridge tower. Red was making Nero prep the boat by pulling the levers to ready it for release to the writhing sea below.

Frank ducked into an alcove, trying to get a clear shot but Nero was in the way. Frank inched forward, keeping a straight aim in case a shooting opportunity arose. The assailant quickly turned, spotted him and fired off a shot, the bullet missing Frank by a whisker. He pressed in hard against a nook at the side of the walkway trying to figure out the best move.

Just then movement in his peripheral vision. Frank turned, but it was too late. What felt like a brick smacked into the side of his head. Frank hit the floor. It was Greaseball, standing over him wielding a bar.

Fuck. Should've dealt with him properly.

The man smiled down at him with evil menace through the bruises Frank had given him earlier and signalled his colleague, Red.

"Time you disappeared and let us get on with our job." He stepped forward, raised the steel bar, ready to swing it down on Frank's head. Already dizzy and reeling from the first blow, Frank gave an inward groan and then scissor-kicked the assailant's shin, trapping his ankles.

Greaseball grunted with pain just as Frank followed with a forward lunge, using his boot to kick his knee. There was a crack of bone followed by a shout of pain.

Frank grabbed the side of the railings and hauled himself up to his feet, the metallic taste of blood in his mouth. Throbbing pain shot through his skull. Greaseball recovered and somehow still clung to the bar, taking a final lunge at Frank with the last of his strength. Frank reacted with a sidestep, pivoted and pushed him, using his own momentum to send him over the railings. There was a cry of surprise. Then he disappeared into the inky ocean with a splash that quickly swallowed the bruised face. Whether he saved himself or drowned, Frank didn't care.

He refocused on Red who fired in Frank's direction again. Then the assailant shouted at Nero to get in the boat as he began to climb on board hesitantly. Frank dropped to his haunches and took a shot. Red spun around, his pistol dropping to the deck and slumped down to his knees. Frank moved in a scurry to reach him and kicked the weapon away, as Red remained on his knees, clutching his chest.

"Who are you?" Frank demanded.

The eyes looked up to him with resigned acceptability of death, and he smiled thinly.

"Who the hell sent you?" Frank repeated, with edgy impatience.

He slumped down onto his side, blood escaping his mouth as he began to bleed out, the pool expanding on the rusty metal floor. The eyes now staring sightlessly through the rails out to the black sea.

"Shit!" Frank shouted, then he stood up and went over to Nero and gestured for him to climb back out of the boat. He pulled off the gag from his mouth. Nero spluttered and swore.

"You alright, mate?"

"Alright? Sure, I'm having a great time." He looked down at the corpse near his feet. "I'm guessing you have no idea who they are?"

"No idea. Now, listen to me. The captain has turned around for Antigua. We need to be ready to get off this ship. The authorities will now get involved, and that's bad news all round."

Chapter 18

St. John's, Antigua

The *Anita* docked once again at St John's just as dawn broke over the small town. Frank and Nero stood ready for a quick exit from the ship.

The captain had been a stoic type, apparently no stranger to the sight of bodies or blood. As these guys had held him at gunpoint while trying to kidnap his passengers he wasn't overly concerned about their fate. However he had tried to convince Frank to check in with the local police.

"I can't do that, Nicolae," Frank had said, "for reasons I can't tell you." Frank turned away and glanced towards the town, then added, "For what it's worth, I'm sorry those bastards killed Lukas." Frank genuinely felt in any other situation they might have become good friends.

The captain had sighed, accepting the situation, then nodded once, as if to say, "I'll take it from here."

Frank gave him a brief salute, shook his hand and then disappeared down the gangway with Nero onto the dock.

Frank hated leaving the captain in the lurch, a man he'd shared those vodka-fuelled poker games with, but what else could he do?

The captain could have chosen to dump the remaining bodies and say no more about it. Frank had offered to help him do that. The question remained: Who had those men worked for? The captain agreed to keep quiet for the initial few hours to give Frank and Nero a head start. "I knew you moved in dark waters, my friend," the captain had told Frank.

Through the sticky mid-afternoon heat they walked through the tourist spot around Heritage Quay, catering hard for the daily cruise ship passengers who invaded on a regular basis. Eventually they got away from the crowd, where the brightly painted houses hailing from a colonial-era changed to shanty timbered concrete block houses.

Behind St John's cathedral they found a roadside cafe with stickers in the window that promised an Internet connection. Inside, a television was showing a baseball game, and two older local men played cards in the corner while drinking the local stout. The Caribbean cafe owner, apron slung over his shoulder, greeted them both with a broad smile.

"You want some fine rum, gentleman? You look thirsty to me," he said with typical Caribbean joviality.

Frank gave an easy laugh and waved him off.

"That would be great some other time."

They ordered bottles of cold water, spicy rice and chicken lunch and took refuge under the cooling downdraft of the ceiling fan.

Frank took out his small laptop and, using the agreed security protocol, sent an encrypted message to Carl Paterson with a simple update:

'En route with baggage.'

He was deliberately vague. Frank had no idea how their location had been compromised. There was a terrible sense of déjà vu, and Frank wondered if he could go through all this again.

When it came to Rhodes, there was no other option but to leave a message. He asked for a pay phone, and the cafe owner showed him one around the back. Frank dialled the number, a South American message service. When the automated female's voice came on, he waited for the beep.

"This is Milligan calling, a message for Eaglecraft. I collected the baggage as requested but there's a problem with shipping. It appears the tax man wanted more duty and tried to intercept the package. Had to change plans and now we are using a different courier service. Will contact you when able. Hoping to avoid having to paying any more import duty."

He ended the call, yearned for some time to think and figure out who he could trust. But it was probably the case that they needed to keep moving, get off the island to mainland Central America.

Was it Carl playing some game? Would his old friend hang him out to be killed? Frank couldn't believe that. Was Rhodes specifically someone he could trust? He said all the right things. Certainly, he was anti-establishment and a dedicated believer in his cause. But that could also mean he had his own agenda, and Frank knew only too well how far men would go to advance their own purposes.

The food arrived, and they both tucked in without hesitation.

Nero appeared calm, despite his recent trauma.

"What's going on? You make contact with Eaglecraft, then?" he asked.

"It's all in hand. I'm sure it's just a blip," Frank replied, unconvinced.

Nero looked up at him.

"A fucking blip? That infil team was more than a blip!"

"I know that. Any ideas who they were?"

Nero shook his head and ate a mouthful of chicken. "No idea. One was American, so maybe CIA? But some of the others had accents."

Frank nodded.

"The helicopter might be a clue. It must have come back here somewhere. Our options are: keep running and hiding, but the helicopter might give us some clues about what we're up against – if we can find it. This is a small island and there's only one airport so my guess is if it's anywhere, it's there."

Nero threw down his fork angrily. "You want to go chasing ghosts? I'm far more concerned about reaching safety. Experiencing the 'safe'" Nero made quote marks with his fingers, "'—passage' Eaglecraft promised so we do what we need to do. I'm not up for running about like a blue-assed fly around this island."

Frank simply raised his eyebrows at this outburst and calmly rounded up the last of the rice with his fork before replying.

"Listen, I understand your concern, mate. But while you're with me, we have to play by *my rules*. Okay? Besides, we'll have to head to the airport, anyway." He flashed Nero a sarcastic smile.

Chapter 19

Frank paid the bill and casually asked the cafe owner if he'd heard about a helicopter in trouble over the island. Unless it had crashed without anyone's knowledge, then the airport was the most logical place to try. The cafe owner then called them a cab.

As the taxi took them across toward V.C. Bird Airport, Frank got the same answer from the driver – a rumour about a helicopter trailing smoke as it flew – but not much else. They paid the driver and walked into the main building. It was a small airport, basic but functional. A group of three businessmen made their way out of the exit underneath large ceiling fans that made the temperature inside the building almost bearable. A large row of windows looked out across the single runway where heat shimmered off the Tarmac like a magician's illusion. A private jet took off running the full length of the runway to the edge of the coastline before climbing gracefully into the clear blue sky.

Frank headed for the departures ticket desks, while Nero took a seat and stared around at the small amount of airport activity. He asked what was available to South America, but the only flight running was to Panama City that evening. He booked two tickets under the identities Rhodes had given him and went back to Nero.

"We have our tickets and eight hours to kill," Frank said, looking around. "The steward said we could check in our bags early. Let's do that and find somewhere to keep out of sight. Then I might have a look around."

"All right, fine," said Nero, making it clear he didn't want to move anywhere.

With their bags checked in, they headed back out onto the road, walking back to a small hotel they had spotted on the way in. Then, slumping down on the most comfortable seats in the quiet bar they ordered a couple of cold beers. Frank gulped his down and stood up.

"You gonna stay here without getting grabbed this time?"

Nero slowly shook his head, his face impassive. "Don't worry, boss. Maybe you should leave me your weapon?"

"Nope," said Frank as he left the bar.

Frank walked back along the road, passing the main airport entrance again and continued until he reached a fence that separated the airstrip. There were several outbuildings built along the wall with mounds of earth and a few dormant diggers on either side. He continued walking past the last of the buildings and saw an inlet with two hangers inside the airport perimeter, where a small aircraft was visible in one of them. The other hangar had a steel-latticed pull-down door that hid the interior. From around the back of the plane came a figure of a maintenance worker. Frank stepped behind one of the concrete posts lining the fence and watched. The workman moved to the other hangar, pulled up the door a few feet and slid under inside.

Frank kept walking until he was at the end of the fence. Another large building marked the end of the airport where an eight-foot-high concrete wall stretched up to a pile of rocks. A loud roar passed overhead, and the incoming aircraft landed further up on the runway. Frank took a look around to check he was clear, jumped up and fluidly hauled himself over to the other side in a few swift moves. On the far side, he crouched, staying frozen for a moment, assessing the scene.

Across a stretch of open land that looked exposed were the hangars that appeared devoid of life. He looked back up the airfield towards the control tower, but the glinting dark glass told him little. There was a chance of being seen but how likely was it that busy controllers would stare out at this relatively quiet and distant corner?

Frank took a breath and walked casually toward the hangars as if he had every right to be there.

Goddamnit, don't get caught, it'll screw up everything.

He wondered if any of the assailants from the chopper were still around somewhere.

Got to be wary.

He reached the side of the first hangar. Now out of sight of the rest of the airport, he moved around behind the hangars and headed to the other side. As he came up to the shutter door, he heard some scraping noises. He crouched down and peeped round to look inside. There, on the back of a transport truck, stood a helicopter, almost certainly the one he'd encountered the night before. Black, with very few markings. A workman was busying himself at the back. Frank took out his pistol and slipped inside before hiding himself amongst a pile of boxes and engine parts. He waited for an opportune moment to edge closer to the chopper. Underneath and around the gas tank he could see the bullet holes that had come from his weapon.

A sudden sound of footfall from the rear of the hanger spiked his concentration, and he slipped back into the shadows as the young Caribbean approached. Frank needed information and decided to risk the potential consequences. When the young man walked by, Frank stepped out of his nook.

"Hey, buddy."

The young man turned with an expression of complete surprise.

"What tha hell—" His wide-eyed gaze went from Frank's face to his gun. Then he froze.

Frank held his Glock, steadily aiming the barrel at his chest and put a forefinger to his lips for a moment.

"Don't be afraid, I just need to ask a few questions," he said, reassuringly.

The man raised his hands unconsciously.

"Questions? Alright..."

"What's your name?"

"Vincent."

Frank jerked his head at the helicopter. "Alright, Vincent. This beast. Where'd it come from?"

"I–I don't know. It not normally based here. Some dudes come in it early yesterday. Tha's all I know, and that's the truth. I swear."

Frank nodded. It was unlikely he was lying.

"What'd they look like and how many?"

"Three men." Vincent then proceeded to describe the three Frank had encountered on the ship.

"Alright. I need to look inside, mate. Can you open the door? Remember, any quick moves or something I'm not expecting and my twitchy trigger finger will want to party, you understand?"

"You ain't gonna get no trouble from me, sir."

"Good. Open it."

Vincent proceeded to open the door and stood aside for Frank.

"Climb inside. The pilot seat. I don't want you running off." Vincent did as ordered and Frank started in the rear seats, running one hand down the side and underneath, looking for anything that might help him out. Nothing. Then he moved to the co-pilot seat and did the same. It had been cleaned thoroughly, and Frank knew there was nothing to be found here that could help him out.

"One last question – did you clean up the helicopter?"

The young guy nodded his head vigorously. "Yep! Vacuumed and scrubbed as ordered by the boss guy." He jerked a thumb over his shoulder towards the main airport building.

"Show me where you put the trash?"

The man looked at him, genuinely puzzled by this request and led Frank to the back of the hangar and gestured at a bin liner and the dormant vacuum.

"Jus' this...nuthin' but dust and shit."

Frank glanced to the main doors, then jerked his weapon at the vacuum.

"Just open it up. Let's see what's in there."

Another look but he obeyed and took out the bag from the vacuum and opened it up; thick wads of fluff and dust, as expected. Frank bent down and rummaged through it with his fingers and pulled out a cigarette butt; the brand still visible along the filter: Donskoy. The same brand the girl had smoked or at least partly laced, in Las Palmas, that packet now in his possession. Undoubtedly her on the helicopter. The question was: who was she working with?

***

Fifteen minutes later, Frank returned to the wall, climbed over and headed back to the hotel. He had led the man to the rear of the hangar and apologetically tied and gagged him after Vincent revealed his shift change was in a few hours. Then Frank slipped a fifty-dollar bill in his top chest pocket. He couldn't risk him raising the alarm before flying out of there.

He still needed to know what he was fighting against and who. The thought crossed his mind to update Carl but could he trust him? It seemed a stretch to suppose he had anything to do with all this. Even so.

No, he would leave Carl out of the loop, for now.

Back at the hotel, Nero was still waiting in the lobby bar, looking bored.

"I thought you took off. Find anything out?"

"Yeah, I found it in a hangar. Everyone else involved seems to be long gone. Hard to know. It looks like your date from Las Palmas was definitely on that chopper though."

Nero looked aggrieved at the suggestion she was his date, but said nothing.

"I have to make a call," Frank said and walked off to call Rhodes.

There was a booth near the small hotel entrance, and Frank watched as two elderly retirees shuffled out then, satisfied he was out of earshot from anyone, picked up the receiver and dialled the number.

It was the message service again.

"It's Mr Milligan about our transport again. There was a rogue package. One of the couriers; a female with dyed-blonde hair. I'll email more details, and I'll call back when I can."

After the call, they left the hotel and entered the main airport building, once again as separate passengers. Frank stayed wary, keeping an eye on the other passengers or anyone else milling around. It seemed to him danger was lurking around every corner.

Chapter 20

Their flight arrived at Tocumen International Airport in Panama City, and the two made their separate ways, according to protocol, passing through the endless hallways and immigration lines before meeting up just near the airport exit. At VC Airport, just before they left, Frank had found an area of wasteland and cleaned, then dismantled the handgun before burying it in the ground. He felt naked without a weapon but smuggling a pistol through airport security, no matter how lax, was too risky.

"What now?"

Frank looked around and gestured at the tourist information desk.

"We'll need a map."

They took seats in one of the numerous coffee bars, away from the main foot traffic and Frank opened up the map on the table.

His eyes went to the border region and the notorious Darien Gap, the 10,000-square-mile area between Panama and Colombia. Frank remembered his background briefing on the country. There were various reasons for a 60-mile gap in the Pan-American Highway in that region. The sheer natural barrier of a vast untamed rainforest made building a road very difficult, and combined with the political corruption that was rampant there was little chance of it happening anytime soon. Last but not least was the dangerous presence of narco drug gangs, FARC, the communist paramilitary force as well as right-wing guerrilla groups were all known to operate freely in the area.

No, best avoid that region by any means.

"We'll want to keep moving down the country towards the border."

"We have several options. Fly on from here. That's the most obvious – or we could disappear in Panama City for a while, take another way – a bus or something," Frank paused, gathering his thoughts. "I think we go to Albrook Airport for a plane to Puerto Obaldia. From there we can get a boat to Capurganá in Colombia. We need to keep away from major airports which means taking some longer routes. It's getting too dangerous now."

Nero looked resigned to some preordained fate for a moment, then nodded.

"Sure, buddy. And our friends? They still snappin' at our tails, you think?"

Frank looked around the airport at a constant stream of passengers walking towards the departure gates. "We have to be cautious. Keep your face down, away from cameras while we're here—"

Just then two armed policemen walked past. One looked in their direction. "Just look at the map," Frank whispered, and they both looked down. Nero pointed to an area on the map as if they were discussing plans. The cops seemed to take an age crossing the gap between the two pillars, both of them now actively scanning the cafe from behind mirrored sunglasses.

From Frank's peripheral vision he could see they were passing by before disappearing into the crowd.

"All right, panic stations over," Frank sighed.

He couldn't stop wondering who their pursuers were, who that blonde woman was? Had they lost them or were they being watched right now? The old uncertainty and twists of the game pulled at his stomach. All Frank and Nero could do was keep running, get to the RV.

"Let's get out of here," Frank said, folding up the map.

Nero insisted on buying a fresh pack of cigarettes before they made their way outside where Frank hailed a cab. The taxi snaked its way through the night traffic of Panama City and then dropped them off at Albrook Airport. A sea of faces greeted their gaze, backpackers, locals, entire families all filling the small terminal. While Nero got their tickets, Frank scanned the faces in the crowd for any sign of recognition from the previous flights and airports. A good surveillance set-up would rotate operatives, of course, but it was worth staying vigilant. His mind kept returning to wherever the hell this crew was from.

Got to get there. Keep this kid alive. Get the job done.

After an hour of waiting around, they walked out to the Panama Airways small, rotary-engined plane. When Frank got on board, he noted there were only twelve seats. He checked the faces of all the passengers, one by one. No recognition. Every person aboard was Latin American apart from them.

Frank hoped they served beer, he needed one, just to relax. It had been a testing few days but, to Frank's disappointment, there was no beverage service at all.

The propellers kicked into action and, within a few minutes, they were airborne, flying over the outskirts of Panama City, the relentless lush green vegetation rolling away below them. The flight was short and, just under an hour later, the wheels appeared back in place from under the wing ready for touchdown. For a moment Frank caught a glance of the Caribbean Sea sparkling in the distance, then it disappeared behind the hills of the jungle. Frank stared out of the window at a tiny village of Puerto Obaldia, in the Kuna Yala indigenous region of Panama, consisting of single and double-storey buildings in blocks with painted balconies. The plane skirted along the dusty runway and all he could see for a few minutes was a hut on the side of the airstrip and jungle.

Once the light craft had pulled to a halt, the passengers jumped out. The pilot handed out the luggage, and then each passenger walked off towards the immigration hut. There were only six passengers including Frank and Nero so by rights the queue should have gone down quickly, but this was a South American official bureaucratic chokepoint. Nothing would happen soon. Frank could see a few main streets of the town. Beyond it, the sea. On his other side were hills of jungle growth that rolled off into the distance. Frank immediately understood why this area was not accessible by land.

"Any idea when this boat goes?" Nero asked, lighting a cigarette.

"I have no idea. We'll have to ask once we get in there," Frank muttered, casting a stare to the front of the queue in the building. On that note, a passenger came out past them with his passport stamped.

After another five minutes they finally got to the Panamanian border guard, dressed in camos that were more akin to some special forces unit than border security detail. Frank noted his sidearm tucked into a holster on his belt, a SIG Sauer P226.

The man stared down at Frank's passport – his Milligan legend – and looked up at him for a moment. "You need photocopies. Two!" He stuck two fingers up, emphasising his point in a seemingly rude gesture.

Frank nodded, understanding, and fished them out of his wallet. Luckily he already been warned about this from the tourist desk and had had them both get copies of their passports before taking the plane.

The soldier slowly took them and placed them down on the table in front of him and took his time checking the details. Finally satisfied, he grabbed a stamp and pounded them like pieces of meat being tenderised before handing it back.

"Adios."

Finally free to get the boat, Frank and Nero began walking along the fence by the small runway that resembled a short strip of road. There was a shout from behind them. The soldier was at the door waving a piece of paper.

"You forgot something?" Nero asked Frank.

There was a moment when Frank felt his senses spike as if he knew something was about to happen. He'd experienced it before.

"Oh he wants me to take the paper, I thought that was for—" Frank began.

Just then a shot rang out from the trees behind them. Frank and Nero both instinctively hit the ground fast. There was a shout from the village as another volley of gunfire burst through the trees, raking the ground in front of them.

"Back to the hut, we're in the open here," Frank hissed. Both men took off at full speed towards the hut, keeping themselves low to create a small profile. At the cabin they could both see the body of the Panamanian guard on the ground. As more shots rang out, they dived on the floor. On their stomachs now, they both crawled forward; edging towards a slight indent in the ground that might give them a few inches of safety.

Frank risked a glance and saw a stream of men starting to move through the trees, heading in their direction. They moved with military precision, and now Frank realised this couldn't be a coincidence. No way.

They reached the hut, moving behind it, giving them some cover from the incoming fire. Ahead of them in the village, people scattered, heading for cover. Frank remembered the sidearm on the border guard, but it was right in the firing line.

Frank couldn't see a way out except for straight ahead into the town, using the immigration hut as protection for their backs. Before he could give Nero the signal to move, they heard a shout from behind.

"*No te muevas!*"

Frank didn't move as instructed. With a side glance, he could see olive green trousers and army boots come into view, an AK-47 barrel aiming at his head. Frank closed his eyes not wanting to imagine what lay ahead.

Chapter 21

There were six men that Frank could see. Three were behind them and three ahead, all armed. The paramilitary soldiers had considered blindfolding them but decided that would make their progress too slow. One soldier had searched the prisoners and taken their backpacks but, at Frank's insistence, left them with their cigarettes. Then the group slowly trekked up the snaking path that cut into the jungle.

Were these guerillas just in the area and decided to grab a few tourists? But then why just him and Nero? Unlikely. The coincidence was too great.

It seemed their attempt to avoid the radar had backfired spectacularly.

This squad of soldiers must have come here specifically to pick them both up. Initially, they both acted like scared tourists, begging to be let go or to pay them for their release. But all pleas were met with silence. Frank tried to listen in on any muttered conversations, but the guerillas were professional and kept interpersonal comms to a minimum.

The jungle grew thicker, a cluster of deep green foliage interspersed with long, spiralling palms towered overhead. The air was scented with a fresh, woody aroma combined with the occasional scent of Jasmine. A chorus of chirping crickets along with a light buzzing of insects and the occasional squawk of birds in the trees accompanied their journey.

Frank kept glancing at the direction of the sun, trying to get his bearings when he could see it through the canopy. It had been too many years since he had gone through basic training on navigating by the sun or stars, but now was the time to dig into the memory bank. He still had his watch and on spotting sun rays through the trees, subtly held it up so the hour hand pointed at the sun. The imaginary line sitting between the hour hand and the 12 o'clock mark marked out north to south, at least giving him a rough idea of their direction. Taking into consideration that they were still in the northern hemisphere and it was March, the sun would rise directly east, Frank concluded. So it appeared they were heading south-west. He also tried to mentally calculate the distance going by their rough speed and the time while keeping his eyes peeled for any opportunities. Right now they were surrounded, and any sudden moves would probably end their lives.

Finally, they stopped in a clearing and a soldier told them to sit down, so Frank and Nero took a seat leaning against a nearby rock.

"*Agua, Por Favor,*" Frank asked. They had not had any water since the kidnapping.

The squad leader, a man who looked in his mid-forties, gestured to one of the young soldiers who turned and fetched a metal water flask, then came back and handed it to Frank. He took a few swigs and gave it to Nero.

"What are we gonna do?" Nero whispered.

Frank looked over at one guerilla as he set down a radio transmitter and attempted to make contact. Frank supposed that it probably wasn't far off the mark that they were contacting their paymasters regarding their newly acquired treasure.

"Not sure. Nothing we can do right now."

"Just figured you'd have a plan."

"I'll think of a plan. Not much to work with right now."

The radio man began to speak low in Spanish and Frank strained to listen, looking down at his boots as if lost in thought. He could only catch snippets of words: '*carga adquirida cero quinientas horas*': Cargo acquired: 0500 hours.

The other soldiers were talking amongst themselves quietly, glancing over at their prisoners. One caught Frank's eye as he looked up and grinned eerily with tobacco-stained teeth. Frank wasn't sure who they were, but he guessed it was the AUC; the right-wing paramilitary group he had read about. Recalling his background notes on Colombia, he knew the militia had its roots in the 1980s when militias were established by drug lords to combat rebel kidnappings and extortion. In April 1997 the AUC was formed through a merger, orchestrated by the ACCU, an organisation of local right-wing militias.

If these guys were AUC then it would go some way to explain their current circumstances. The CIA most likely funded these guys and they were doing a little house cleaning for their sponsors.

After only ten minutes' rest, the two prisoners were ordered back to their feet. The terrain was getting steeper. There were points at which the men had to crawl on hands and knees, gripping tree roots that protruded out from the muddy ground. The rank smell of sweat and sounds of heavy breathing filled the air. Odd shouts in Spanish punctuated the silence as they navigated the trail. The hill finally levelled out, and the front guard hand-signalled to stop. A camp lay in a clearing ahead, where a bamboo hut protruded out from behind a clump of trees. The soldier on point continued, and the group entered another clearing. There were three small huts in the treeline, simple wooden constructs with bamboo roofs, draped with camo nets.

On one side was a cage, set apart from the huts, also made from wood with a solid floor and handles on either side for carrying. Frank sighed, knowing it was for them. It had just about enough space for three people. The door lay open.

"*Dentro!*" demanded the commander, jerking his pistol at them.

Frank fixed him a look and started to complain. The commander stepped forward and gave him a shove in the back.

"Get inside!"

Frank slowly got down on his hands and knees and crawled into the confined space. Nero followed, struggling into the cage and fell on his side. The door was slammed closed by one of the soldiers who proceeded to lean down and attach a hefty padlock. He leered down at them both as he got back up and walked away pulling a pack of cigarettes out of his chest pocket. Frank hauled himself into a sitting position. Leaning back against the tightly knit bamboo bars, he took a good look over the cage itself. He could see straight away that it wasn't particularly well made. That gave him a glimmer of hope in what had been a grim few hours. Perhaps it was just meant for just temporary imprisonment.

A guard sat himself down almost opposite, outside one of the huts, rested his AK on his lap and proceeded to sharpen a knife on a stone, while occasionally glancing over at them.

"Well, things are just getting better," Nero muttered.

"Shuddup."

"We should've tried escaping earlier, while we had a pissant's chance."

Frank couldn't have agreed more, but Nero's sniping was irritating him. He tried to think. It seemed like their captors were waiting either for further instructions or for a rendezvous to occur. If Frank's suspicions were correct, they either could wait until the exchange for an opportunity or attempt to escape now. He suspected that after the exchange escape would be almost impossible and the dark fate ahead probably involved torture, death or – most likely – both.

Next, he focused on the snippets of radio chatter he'd heard. Could a handover be happening at 0500 in the morning? The door opened from the main communal hut and, judging by the uniform, a commander wearing mirrored sunglasses who he hadn't seen before came out, glanced over at them before stepping into one of the nearby huts.

Frank looked around the clearing. Easily big enough for a chopper to land. That was what they must be planning.

That made sense.

"We've got to get out of here," Nero said suddenly, breaking the silence. He was staring over at the hut the commander had just entered. "They gonna kill us, I'm sure of it."

"Maybe. But wouldn't they have done it already?"

Before Nero could reply, one of the soldiers came over with a small plastic bottle of water and shoved it through a gap in the bars, with cooked rice wrapped in a dirty plastic carrier bag.

"Enjoy," he said in English and laughed.

"How long are you going to keep us here?" Frank asked with disdain.

"Maybe years for you," he said, with a smirk before walking off.

Nero ate some mouthfuls with his hands and handed it to Frank.

***

Darkness fell fast. Members of the guerrilla squad kept their camp mainly unlit, apart from inside one or two of the huts. Most of the men had gathered inside and, judging by the shouts and groans, it sounded like they were playing cards. Another soldier had come onto watch and sat opposite them, mainly smoking.

When he sensed the guard was distracted, Frank pressed the soles of his boots against the far side, testing for weaknesses. It was tied well and barely had any give. It would be pretty hard to kick through without a considerable amount of noise. His hands fell on the floor that had planked strips nailed to the structure.

Nero lay on his side in a foetal position.

"How did they bloody well find us?" The question came out of the blue. He tried to think back since the ship. It was possible they were tracked by someone at Antigua airport. Maybe seen at Panama airport through the security surveillance. If it had been when they had arrived in Panama, perhaps seen or picked up by a camera. Had Nero been flagged on facial recognition, or had their watchers just got lucky?

Then who had the power to then order a group of paramilitaries into position within an hour to pick them up from the runway at Obaldia? Was it connected to Rhodes? Had he sold them out for some reason that Frank had no knowledge of? The questions swirled around his brain, but he wasn't any closer to figuring it out.

Frank studied the guard, who was slumped in a relaxed position, his head leaning against a thick piece of wood that made the door frame of his hut. His head dropped slightly, and he righted himself quickly and looked over at the cage as if to check whether he was being watched. They both appeared asleep, and the guard relaxed again.

"I don't imagine these pricks are gonna play nice for long," said Nero. He shook the cage bars when the guard wasn't looking as if they might crumble at his touch but they remained firm.

Frank joined him in checking the seams and joints of the wooden cage. It seemed pretty solid, but he couldn't make any noise by kicking just yet.

Frank checked the boards they were sitting on. They appeared to be simply nailed to the main cage frame that made their enclosed prison.

"Dunno if we could roll it over, kick out the bottom," Frank muttered.

"Not with a guard watching," Nero replied, glaring at two of the soldiers chatting by one of their huts.

Frank sighed, feeling despondent. He felt angry at himself for letting this happen.

They had the cigarettes, of course, laced with Scopolamine aka "devil's breath". The soldier hadn't seen the harm in letting them keep them, bar the long-term health risks, Frank cynically mused to himself.

The lone guard sat opposite, a few metres away, sipping water. He got up and moved across the camp checking the perimeter. Frank used the opportunity to kick the bars with both feet. But there was no "give" if any movement at all.

He tried again. The bars remained firm.

Frank brought out the cigarettes, and Nero gave him a knowing glance.

"I can't smoke any of these myself – you have any normal ones?"

Nero fished around and brought out a pack he'd bought in Panama airport.

"Give me one, I'll offer him these," Frank's eyes darted to the Scopolamine laced pack.

When the guard returned, Frank had the cigarette Nero had given him in his mouth.

"*Señor*. Do you have a light? We don't have one."

The young guard paused, slowly walked over and crouched down, a plastic lighter in hand. Frank inhaled and made a show of exhaling with an expression of relief. He nodded his thanks, then held up the pack and offered the guard one, who fished one out.

"*Gracias*."

He stood up and walked back to his spot, then sat down on his seat, placing his rifle to his side while Frank and Nero surreptitiously watched his every move.

The soldier placed the cigarette in his mouth and finally lit it, leaning back to take in his first drag.

"How long does it take?" Nero asked.

"No idea, but I think it's fast. Just hope this works."

Nero's eyes, caught by a pale moon, focused on the guard. "Sure, hope so, buddy."

Frank didn't want to screw up. If he made a move too soon, the guard might suspect. The stupefying effect – if it worked – should make him compliant to any of their suggestions.

If it worked.

They waited for five minutes, long after the soldier had stubbed out the cigarette, while they agreed on a plan in low whispers.

"*Señor?*"

The guard leaned forward at Frank's voice, then stood up and walked over, slightly unsteady on his feet. He touched his throat for a moment, then bent down, smiling at them with dilated pupils.

So far, so good.

Frank smiled back and looked apprehensive.

"Erm, I need a crap, but—" He turned his head and looked at Nero. "I'd rather go out there than in here, if you understand me?"

Nero made a face, agreeing wholeheartedly.

The guard nodded serenely.

"*Si*, I understand."

He hesitated for a moment, then unlocked the cage door and opened it wide. Frank crawled out and hauled himself up, stretching out his back and legs. It felt fantastic after all the hours hunched up inside that cage. He checked the other huts, the soldiers still inside.

"*Gracias, mi amigo.*"

The drugged guard nodded benignly and turned to Nero as he crawled up to the cage door.

With a swift move, Frank grabbed the soldier around the mouth with one hand and secured his bicep around the throat with his other arm in a classic sleeper hold. The soldier kicked wildly but his strength had been weakened by the drug, and it was easy, like throwing a dog a bone. The soldier soon slumped into unconsciousness, and Frank dragged him into the cage then relocked the door.

"Let's go," Frank whispered.

Just then a voice from one of the huts got louder as if heading to the door, a shadow from the door crack shifted and a shaft of light danced across the grass.

They ran across to the treeline and disappeared into the thick jungle. A wind rustled the trees which Frank hoped would disguise any footfall. Being quiet wading through the foliage was impossible. They moved further and further from the camp, the half moon their only source of light. It would be impossible to navigate precisely, although Frank had an idea of the general direction they needed to go. That was back to Puerto Obaldia; the nearest place resembling civilisation. It had been too dangerous to retrieve their backpacks with their legend passports and gear, but at least there was nothing in them to give the paramilitaries any leverage.

Their boots sploshed through deep ponds of dirty water as they carefully navigated their way through dense reed beds and over moss-covered boulders. The further they got from their camp, the faster they dared to move. At that moment they both heard shouting. Their escape had been discovered. Distant torchlights cut through the thick foliage, barely penetrating it as their captors began their search.

"Keep moving," Frank hissed to the dark shape of Nero, who'd stopped to look around.

"Fuck, we're screwed," he replied.

"We're not screwed yet," Frank growled. He hoped he was right.

Chapter 22

Frank wiped the sweat from his forehead. The wind had dropped. Somewhere in the distance, Frank thought he heard the sound of flowing water. With that, he realised how thirsty he was and took another swig from the bottle they had been given earlier. He handed it to Nero. That, of course, was the other vital consideration. In escaping they had found themselves with no water, supplies or weapons. They had to get back to that airstrip.

The hill loomed overhead, and they continued to brush through the undergrowth, glimpses of moonlight casting the plant life with a faint hue. Nero had slipped and nearly fallen into an abyss of darkness but was surprisingly agile and unperturbed by their new situation. Frank let him lead for a while, occasionally hissing at him to change direction. He couldn't believe how fast things had gone downhill: lost, trying to find a way back to civilisation in the pitch blackness with only the whine of mosquitoes and pursuing paramilitaries for company.

They continued, making slow progress. Frank assumed their hunters would know parts of this jungle well, certainly better than them. That, with the darkness and the rough terrain, made stopping and waiting for the dawn light tempting. As if reading his thoughts, Nero stopped and turned.

"This is insane. We should find a hide and wait."

Frank paused. It was a risk but, he had to admit, thrashing around and burning up energy in the dark was not the answer.

"Alright. If we can find a spot."

They continued up the hill and then moved along it instead. Another glimpse of moonlight from behind the clouds gave Frank a better view of a narrow indent in the hill, surrounded by bushes and trees.

"This seems good. Should hide us from visual contact at least."

They crawled through the foliage and crouched down between the clump of trees, positioning themselves so they were facing in opposite directions.

Frank checked the ground with his hand for any hidden surprises before taking a position leaning up against one of the tree trunks. From his vantage point, he could see the direction they had just come, through the dark, jagged shapes of the plants and trees. Nero had a view ahead of them, just in case the guerrilla army somehow got around that way, although Frank couldn't imagine how they would.

They sat in silence, just the sound of crickets and high-pitched sawing sound of the mosquitoes. The damp air held the combined scent of soil, vegetation and wood. For the first time, Frank consciously breathed it in with deep inhales.

"You've got powerful people very keen to talk to you, haven't you, mate?" Frank whispered.

There was a silence as if Nero was contemplating his answer. He spoke in a severe low tone.

"—to be expected, buddy. What I have is critical information. The finer details on a global agency that will operate above all governments. They've got big plans for it."

Frank nodded in the dark to himself. He wondered if it was their situation and the very real possibility of death or re-capture that was helping Nero to open up.

"Is this US-led?" Frank asked.

"It's a global thing," he replied.

"Then whoever is trying to grab us is trying to protect their investments, their little secret. Why are you taking this to Eaglecraft?" It was apparent, but Frank was testing, probing.

"There are reasons that I can't go into. But, let's just say there's money on the table, always a great incentive. Then there's the morals of the whole thing. It's a risk. I always knew it wouldn't be easy, switching over to be with David against the Goliath."

To him, it seemed the money angle was believable, but being influenced by a pivoting moral compass? Frank wasn't so sure Mr Nero had a moral compass.

High above them, the dark sky had lightened to a predawn hue giving the dark shapes of plants and hanging vines around them the more familiar contour of detail. Frank was able to finally see down the hill they had come up. All around them was a wall of thick foliage he hoped they could find a way through. To the side of them was a sharp decline where the trees followed a slope down what sounded like a ravine with the distant sound of flowing water. They fell silent, and Frank was about to suggest it was light enough to move when he caught a noise, alien to the harmonised chirps of insects that belonged to the rainforest. It had come from the direction of their earlier climb.

Like the accidental click of metal against metal.

Frank reached round to touch Nero's shoulder, signalling silence. He slowly turned his head, acknowledging Frank, and looked in the same direction. Frank levelled out his breathing and narrowed his eyes, focusing down the hill. Then there was a repeat of the same faint sound, slightly nearer.

Frank, not keen to be caught off guard, carefully and quietly repositioned himself onto his haunches. Nero followed his lead. A group of palm leaves just ten feet away slowly parted. First he saw the barrel of the rifle, then the hand holding it and the green camo sleeve. The guerrilla moved through the leaves, half crouched, slowly swiping his barrel aim in an arc. Frank recognised him as one of the younger ones from the squad. The soldier was checking the ground, and Frank wondered how much of a trail they might have left. Had he seen their tracks? Was that the reason he'd come up the hill? In which case, it'd lead the guerrillas straight to them.

Frank turned to Nero and signalled to stay put with a jerk of his finger to the ground. He moved back around Nero behind the tree in a semi-circle and crouched. The soldier, still treading carefully in kitten-walk mode through the undergrowth, moved past him and towards Nero's hidden position. The others must be near, but he had to act now. Frank silently moved from the tree, now in touching distance from his back. A sudden rush and Frank leapt, throwing his right arm over the soldier's right shoulder and locking the guerrilla's throat with his forearm. With his other hand he covered the soldier 's mouth and squeezed hard, pulling him back off balance. They both fell onto the ground. Nero didn't hesitate and came out in front of them, grabbing the AK out of the guerrilla's hands and following it with a harsh kick in his groin. A low grunt of pain came from behind Frank's left palm.

His eyes stared wide as Frank crushed his larynx, depriving the man of essential oxygen. As his strength sapped, the soldier kicked and thrashed, flailing his arms, desperate to hold onto life. Frank held on hard as the soldier thrashed and attempted to wriggle free. The struggling slowly dissipated until he fell into unconsciousness and death.

Wasting no time, Frank proceeded to search him, taking his ammo belt holding spare magazines for the rifle, a knife from a holder around his chest. There was a grenade. Inside his backpack Frank briefly saw an assortment of useful stuff including a water bottle, a roll of wire and a medical kit. There was also a wallet filled with Colombian pesos over varying denominations.

"Great, we're in business," said Frank, standing up as Nero finished off checking the AK's curved magazine before slamming it back into place.

Frank held his hand out to take it. For just a fraction of a second, Nero hesitated, then handed it over.

"That guy got anything else?" the American asked, glancing down at the dead body.

"Nope," Frank replied, setting the weapon in high port position. He checked the direction the soldier had come.

"The others must be close."

"Any idea where the hell we are?"

Frank paused, looking across the sloping hill that ran down to the ravine.

"More or less," he replied before moving off.

Descending back down the hill, they occasionally stopped at intervals to listen, then continued along the route they had come. Frank intended to continue to find a reference to get back to that village. What that might be he had no idea. They reached a point where another route leading down to the ravine and deeper into the jungle looked possible. Frank held up a fist by his head, signalling Nero to stop, and both men crouched low. He had sensed something ahead and was right to be cautious. Through an opening in the thick foliage came the sight of three more guerrilla fighters, stalking through the green shade like wraiths of Death.

Chapter 23

Frank and Nero edged back down the rocky ravine, retracing their steps as their pursuers moved onto their position. Their route was steep and rocky. Mangled trees grew out of the hill at impossible angles but at least made good supports for holding onto. Below them, a muddy slide led to a clump of rocks. Through the gaps, Frank caught a glimpse of the river they had heard the previous evening.

On one particularly steep descent, Frank lost his footing and had to grab a nearby branch to stop himself falling.

Shit!

There was a crack from the broken tree limb as he did so and both men froze. Nero glared at Frank for his mistake. Frank gestured to keep moving, and they continued down the slope.

Then, from somewhere above them, they heard a noise followed by a burst of gunfire, shredding bark and plants just behind their position.

"Down!"

Frank scrambled through the mud behind a clump of trees. He turned to see Nero hugging the floor, his hands around his head. More shouts as the shooter called his mates.

"Hey, Nero!"

The young man looked up.

Frank gestured for him to get ready and brought up his AK gun, aiming the barrel up the hill in the direction of the enemy. He caught a glance of a soldier just as he stepped out from behind a palm tree.

A burst of fire from Frank's weapon peppered the palm, and the soldier quickly fell back to cover. Frank fired another burst as Nero crawled across the slippery hill towards him. He continued moving along the natural treeline that acted as a barrier and Frank followed. They edged downwards, aiming for the rock cluster and the water.

More rounds hit their original position.

When they reached the rocks and crouched down behind them, Frank peered over and heard the shuffling feet as runners approached. He waved his free hand for Nero to continue to the river and aimed the clump of trees. A barrel appeared, an arm of a cautious soldier. Frank squeezed the trigger in a three-round burst and heard a cry as the soldier spun back out of sight.

Time to move.

Nero was stumbling between boulders, and then disappeared. Frank turned and saw two more soldiers come around the corner. He fired, hitting one in the leg, and the man crumpled.

The other saw him and began to take aim.

A crackling burst from Frank's AK stitched a bloody pattern across his chest.

Both down.

Frank turned and ran between the boulders.

The narrow brown stream rushed past and Nero was sat there, resting on his haunches, waiting for him. Frank jerked his hand to indicate downstream and continued running. They found a clear path alongside the river and followed it. Frank checked their six, keeping his eyes around and ahead. There was no reason to doubt the enemy could come from anywhere.

Was it a pincer move? Some trap?

These guys knew the jungle, and they certainly weren't stupid.

They continued for twenty minutes in a southwest direction. Frank again held up a fist and then waved a flat hand downwards for them to assume cover. They crouched, catching their breath.

"All right," said Frank through ragged gasps. "I think we're way ahead of them. Got to be careful though. They're jungle fighters. Must know this place pretty well."

Nero nodded. Frank unshouldered the backpack he had taken from the young soldier and opened it up. "I'm sure I saw a map in here," Frank said, rummaging around.

"Ah, we got a compass too." He took a look at the basic army issue device. "All right—" he added, folding out the map.

"By my estimation, we should be around here," Frank pointed at a ridge on the map, "they're probably forming a dragnet along here," his finger tapped on the curving line of a river. "There's no way to get back to that village without taking a huge detour here," Frank pointed his finger along an area inland. "By the time we do that, we may as well keep heading south further into Colombia."

"Fuck," Nero muttered, as he held his head back, rubbing his neck and looking up at the canopies.

Frank folded up the map and started putting it and the compass away.

"I know, I don't like the idea either."

"What about water? What have we got?"

Frank pulled out a half-full plastic bottle and stared at it.

"No more than a litre. There should be a freshwater stream on the way, or we can hack into some bamboo trees, next time we see one. Just have to be frugal with what we've got, for now." They each took a swig and then continued moving at a steady pace, looking for a place to cross.

"This should lead to a larger river, according to the map," Frank said, tracing a path on the map. "We've got to be careful. There are still other dangers."

Nero cast his eyes around at the impossibly thick jungle.

"Dangers worse than those guys?"

"There are plenty of groups in this area; FARC use it, so do the drug cartels. The group that's after us is most likely AUC. Well, that's my guess. Plus there're the natives– keep your eyes wide, that's all I'm sayin'."

"Sounds like you know more than me. Just keep that weapon loaded."

They came to a clearing with a panoramic view of the valley and the river that looped through it like a brown snake sliding through thick grass. The terrain looked formidable, a vast untamed natural vista of endless green mounds that faded into the mist of the early morning. Frank closed his eyes for a second. This felt like his biggest challenge yet. It was precisely what he didn't want to do; head deeper into that unknown, running straight into the thick of it.

"Hey!" Nero pointed at a clump of bamboo trees just ahead. "I say we get some water from those."

Frank pulled out the knife, chose a section of the tree and began hacking a wedge into it. After a few minutes, as the clear liquid flowed out from the bark, Frank and Nero smiled and nodded at each other. A rare expression of relief. They weren't going to die of thirst – at least not yet. They gulped down the abundant water before filling their water bottle.

Just as they were about to move on, a distant noise caught their attention. It was a rapid whupping sound that faded in and out in the distance.

"Hear that?" he asked.

Nero looked up and around.

"Yeah, that's a chopper," he confirmed.

Chapter 24

The pulsating staccato of rotor blades grew louder, cutting through the dense overhead canopies. No doubt about what it was now. Certainly not anything that might be looking to rescue them. How nice would that be? Frank mused to himself.

No, they were being hunted.

"Come on! This way." Frank began fast walking along the ridge. They couldn't hide where they were for long with the guerrillas at their back, and the sound of the helicopter indicated it was getting closer, but it was difficult to locate with the surrounding rising valleys. Ahead, there was a brief stretch of open ground, then thick jungle that would make a good cover for them.

Frank glanced back to check Nero was following him and saw him stumbling. At the same moment, beyond his shoulder, a brown face in olive camos appeared in the treeline, raising his weapon. He fired and Nero grunted, spun around and pitched into the ground hitting some protruding rocks hard with a grunt.

"Hit!"

Frank jumped down onto the ground and pulled up his weapon, firing a round in the general direction of the guerrilla who immediately withdrew, calling for backup. He crawled back to Nero.

"Where?"

"Shoulder, I think."

"We can live with that," Frank said, trying to get eyes on the wound.

"I fucking can't, man. Jesus, it hurts like hell," he grunted. "Shit! Shit! Shit!" he hissed.

Frank studied the wound. "It looks like a graze, but we'll keep an eye on it."

He searched in his bag and found a basic trauma kit, pulled out a bandage and did a quick patch-up job.

"The bleeding doesn't look too bad. That'll have to do for now." Frank glanced towards their pursuers, then back the other way.

"Can you get to the treeline?"

Nero exhaled loudly. "Yeah sure. Just gimme a minute."

Distant shouts cut through the trees.

"We haven't got a minute. Keep your hand pressed on the wound and move, I'll cover."

Nero gritted his teeth as he forced himself into a crouch and ran, clutching his shoulder.

Frank took aim and looked for his target. He could see three of them spread out in different directions and fired short bursts, each time changing the direction of fire. They had dropped back into cover, and he had no idea if he'd hit anyone. Frank stayed low and followed Nero. As if from nowhere, a black helicopter appeared above the trees swooping across the valley.

"Down!" Frank shouted.

Nero was already under the trees, but Frank felt incredibly exposed as the blades whooped up ahead. The nose of the chopper tipped down exposing black-tinted windows. It turned to its side and hovered.

Running now, Frank focused on the trees. Nero had disappeared, swallowed by the thick jungle.

In the side doorway of the chopper, a woman in black swivelled a mounted machine gun around to her target.

Frank swerved his run, changing direction suddenly, his heart pounding.

This is insane. Too exposed!

Brakabrakabraka. The drill of 50mm rounds churned up the spot of his original trajectory. Chunks of debris flew through the air, raining on Frank's back.

Frank dived and rolled in the muddy ground, behind the cover of a cluster of rocks, and held his head in his hands. Swishing bullets whistled overhead, smashing fragments of rock through the air in all directions.

"Shit! Shit! Shit!" he shouted.

Brakabrakabraka. The firing continued for another ten seconds then halted.

The direction of the low whooping sound changed. They were circling to get a better shot. Frank wiped his brow and checked his magazine. From his haunches, he raised his height slowly, barrel pointing through a slit in the rocks. It hovered like an angry wasp, spitting bullets. On the ground, he caught a glimpse of the soldiers, who were trying to flank him. He fired a quick two rounds at the chopper, then bolted, skirting around them the rocks before heading to the mass of trees.

The throbbing of the chopper's engine grew nearer as it moved to get a clear line of fire on him before he hit the trees. Around ten metres stood between the rocks and the treeline. Behind him the deep cavernous drop.

Frank hurtled as fast as he could run across the gap. He heard the machine gun open up with its murderous staccato once again, just as he jumped head-first onto the jungle floor; a thick waist-high wildness.

Bark splintered and wood and shredded foliage sprayed in all directions as a wall of concentrated firepower seemed to rip the jungle apart with its deadly rain.

Frank crawled, using his elbows to pull himself along in a diagonal line, his head almost flat to the ground. His elbows, jabbing hard, felt raw.

He was dead. It was over.

Then the relentless drilling halted, and the engine changed tone as if gaining altitude.

Frank didn't stop moving. Crawling deeper and deeper to get as far away from that chopper. The ground sloped down into a ditch, and he rolled onto his side, gasping for air.

"Jesus, Jesus!" he gasped.

Frank closed his eyes and sucked in the much-needed air as a light mist rose from the ground. All his body wanted to do was stay put and rest, but he forced himself to move on. This was no time to dick around; he needed to find Nero. He rolled onto his hands and knees and looked back through the shredded jungle towards the ridgeline. Whole palm trees had been chopped in half. The machine gun had cut a wide arc like a scythe through butter. No doubt the guerrillas would be coming in to look for their bodies any minute.

Frank checked his magazine and reloaded from the bag, then looked around.

"Nero!" he hissed, trying not to shout.

A few yards behind him he heard a light groan, then he heard, "Over here!"

Frank crawled over to his position.

"Are you hit anywhere?" he asked.

"From that firepower? Don't think I'd be alive if I were. My shoulder hurts like hell, though. Need to fix it up, quick." Nero looked ghostly pale, the sheen of sweat appearing across his face. "I didn't think they wanted to kill us?" Nero added.

"Guess they do now," Frank replied. "C'mon, we'll patch it up further on but not here. The ground forces are still on us."

Frank checked behind them for any sign of the enemy and hauled Nero up to his feet by his upper arm. Ahead of them, through the constant dull green light, lay more thick trees, hanging vines ascending another hill. Frank felt the sweat almost rotting his clothes, now caked in green smears and mud.

"How long can we keep this up? Seriously. I'm dying."

"No bloody choice, mate," Frank muttered.

Nero stopped. "Hey. This is a clear route, right? There'll be no doubt we came this way. Can we do something with that grenade?"

"Like a trap? Yeah, I don't see why not?" Frank replied. He thought back to an earlier time with his mentor, Sam. A brief lesson on grenade traps. Lessons learned in the military. Simple stuff stemming back to the World Wars or the Viet Cong. Now they laid some pretty nasty traps in that jungle. They had wire and a grenade. It was worth a try to give their pursuers something to think about.

"There's wire in the bag."

"Alright. We need two stakes or something similar. Sticks will do, both sides of the path," Frank glanced around, "the grass is long enough here to hide the wire."

They found appropriate sticks and hammered them into the ground, opposite each other across the path. Frank took out the grenade, tying it to one of the sticks. Next was the tricky part. The safety pin was split with both the ends bent outwards through the fuse assembly and strike lever. Frank carefully closed down the split pin and then wiggled it almost out, so the slightest tug could remove it. Taking the wire, Frank secured one end to the pin and the other end to the far stick, stretching the wire out across the path.

When the trap was in place, they checked the wire was just below the grass line before moving off into the jungle.

Frank spat into a mesh of palm leaves as they edged through the cluster of undergrowth, both men only too aware they were leaving tracks for their pursuers.

We're against the ropes here.

Frank just hoped the ground would soon become less trackable.

They kept moving at as fast a pace as they could, navigating the clustered jungle foliage until they came to an impassable scattering of swamps, their flat surfaces mirroring the green hue of their surroundings. They moved around the edge of it and then the ground began to descend, the trees and vegetation at last becoming more sparse with rockier ground underfoot. It would be harder for the guerillas to track them now.

"Let's look at that wound now."

Nero stopped him with his hand.

"It's fine. I got it. You don't have to be my nursemaid, buddy."

Frank shrugged. "Whatever. Just tryin' to help."

"And it's appreciated, but I'd rather take it from here," Nero muttered as he pulled off the hastily applied bandage from earlier. They both looked at the patch of congealed blood where the bullet had sliced the flesh at the top of his humerus. "Like I said, a graze. Looks fine to me."

Nero acknowledged him with a nod.

Another hour and they came to a rocky trail that spiralled downwards into the same ravine they had encountered earlier, albeit farther south.

"Alright, we stick close to that river and we should be on course to get to a place called Ancandi, according to the map. Hopefully we can get supplies, maybe a ride out of here." After feeling safe enough to stop, Frank bandaged up Nero's wound with rags stripped from their own clothing. The overwhelming humidity made for the worst conditions for an injury, slowing down any healing. There was also a high risk of infection.

Afterwards, they ate the meagre rations from the backpack consisting of some plantain fruit, nuts and a bag of cooked rice. They drank more water, but the level was now dwindling in the bottle. Their situation was at crisis point. They needed freshwater fast – and not only that but they were just a few hours from darkness. There were now no bamboo trees in sight. Forcing themselves on, they hiked for over an hour, slowly descending their way down to the rocky trail.

For a brief moment, they both thought they heard the sound of the helicopter in the far distance, but it soon faded leaving the familiar jungle background track of crickets and howler monkeys. The wilderness around them seemed to be seeping into their pores, and sweat continued to soak their entire bodies. They continued stumbling across slippery rocks and past gnarled tree roots that protruded from the ground.

The sky had darkened when they reached the stream, but they barely noticed, dipping into its cool liquid haven before taking cautious mouthfuls. Frank filled their only water bottle and checked his ammo. Three rounds left. He hoped they wouldn't run into their friends again anytime soon.

He looked around their surroundings and found a spot where they could hide and rest with only one possible approach, in front of a wall of rocks. Not ideal, but it would have to do. Both of them needed at least a few hours' rest otherwise they would be falling over their feet. They took turns as the night sky descended, but the mosquitoes made rest fitful. Without any repellent, both of them were getting eaten alive. They covered themselves up as much as possible. Then Nero suggested they covered their exposed skin with mud from the river bank which kept the biting down to some bearable level.

As soon as it was light enough, Frank rechecked the map, as well as their bearing with the compass. If they were definitely in the location he thought they were, it meant a riverside village lay twenty klicks away. If all went well, they could be there before nightfall. Whether it was safe was another question.

They headed off again, transversing the stream and setting a steady pace, strengthened by the intake of water. Despite it being dawn, dark and foreboding clouds swirled overhead. The heavy *drip, drip, drip* began to patter on the plant leaves around them.

"Don't suppose you brought an umbrella?" Nero asked, barely managing a smile.

"Left it back at the hotel," Frank answered. Nero laughed then. "If we ever get out of this. Well, I might even buy you a lemonade."

Frank couldn't help snort. "Thanks, mate. That's given me the spur I need to get the hell out of here."

They walked in silence as the rain grew heavier, growing into a rumble as they came to a section of the jungle that stood in their way. Frank attempted to hack reeds and a mass of hanging vines aside with the butt of his rifle with little success.

"So, you worked for one of the British intelligence services, I understand," said Nero.

"Something Rhodes told you?" He didn't bother with codenames. They both knew who they were working for. The need for secrets and caution seemed like another world, far away.

"Don't worry. He didn't give you away. But I needed some assurance who was bringing me in and carried out due diligence. Can't be too careful, right?"

"Right." Frank concurred.

Moving off from the impasse of the jungle they came to a ridge and below, just as Frank had hoped for, they saw the village, a ramshackle mesh of stilted wooden houses and canoes tied up to the trees. Wooden steps descended into the river, a sloped small patch of mud like a dark beach hosted a row of motorboats. A few figures moved around and the unmistakable shouts from children who played on the riverbank.

Nero lightly slapped Frank's shoulder. "You saved us, buddy!"

Frank stared emotionless down at their apparent salvation. Something told him the danger was far from over.

Chapter 25

As the waves of torrential rain came down, the two men made their way towards the village. It wasn't a straightforward route and took more than an hour. The black mud stuck to their boots, forcing them to tread carefully or risk stumbling over in the quagmire. Finally, soaking wet and exhausted, they came to a more well-worn track, the first buildings of the village in sight.

"So, what's our story?" asked Nero.

"Just lost travellers. I think this place might be controlled by FARC so we have to be careful. I might have to hide the weapon."

"Sure."

It was a calculated risk, but Frank felt they had no choice. The need for supplies and help battled against the fear of danger. They found a sheltered nook under a rock and hid the AK-47, along with the camouflage backpack, before approaching. A child of around five saw them first, turned and ran back. A black man sheltering under a corrugated sheet that jutted out from one of the stilted houses waved and shouted. "Amigos!" A positive start. Frank waved back and they continued, seeking shelter from the downpour. A group of children ran up to them and followed their progress, pointing and laughing, apparently unconcerned about getting soaked in the rain.

"¿Dónde está la tienda?" Frank asked, looking for someplace to get help. One of the older boys tugged at Frank's arm and ran ahead, splashing through the puddles.

As they moved deeper into the town, passing clapboard houses on stilts, a few of the villagers turned and stared. Another man by the river tying a boat glanced up for a few seconds, then returned to his task. The boy scurried up to a door of one of the wooden houses, up the steps and inside, then turned and waved them in.

Frank and Nero trooped up the steps and into a dry goods store that appeared to cater for foolhardy jungle treks. An elderly woman, dark-skinned with jet-black hair, looked up at the strangers and smiled. The two men returned the greeting and stared up at tinned sardines, tuna, beans as well as packets of pasta, rice and coffee. They grabbed bottles of water, food they could consume easily like rice cakes and empanadas, along with bars of chocolate which they ate while picking out their supplies. The boy disappeared. Fish hooks and plastic tarp were also added to the pile. After stacking their new supplies and getting the price, Frank took off his belt that had become partly mouldy and unzipped a hidden section on the underside, fishing out carefully folded-up US dollars for payment.

He paid, then asked the woman if anyone could take them down the river in one of the canoes they'd spotted. She asked if they were migrants. More were flooding through, heading up to Panama to try and get to the USA.

"No, just backpackers on an adventure trail – we lost our way," he replied in Spanish, followed by a shrug as if to say, "idiot gringos".

She laughed. "The commander will come. They give permissions for travel here," she said. Frank paused, a tin of beans in his palm.

A commander. That didn't sound good.

"Who is the commander?"

"Señor Jiménez." She pointed and, as if summoned out of thin air, a rough-looking man stood in the doorway, dressed in green fatigues with a rifle slung over his shoulder. He strolled into the store, surveying the strangers. He was a short, squad figure with a shaved head.

"Buenos dias," Frank started, trying to keep it light.

The commander nodded but said nothing, circling around to look over their supplies.

"Where are you from?" he asked in English.

"I'm English, he's American," said Frank, thumbing at Nero, whose eyes darted between them. "We were trekking but got a bit lost." He glanced at the commander's jacket badge; the emblem with FARC-EP and an outline of Colombia backed up by the colours of yellow, blue and red and two rifles crossed. The uniform similar to the guerrilla fighters that had kidnapped them, but with a different dispersive pattern.

Frank understood enough from the background files on Colombia that FARC had fought a war with the Colombia state since 1948. Not only that, but the right-wing AUC was their sworn enemy.

The commander's eyes switched to the bloody patch breaking through from under Nero's ragged shirt. He looked up at Nero, awaiting explanation without a word.

"We were attacked by soldiers," Frank interjected.

The commander eyed Frank with sudden interest. Frank described them vaguely. "They had badges, ACU, something like that," he said, casually, deliberately getting their name wrong.

"AUC? Autodefensas Unidas de Colombia?" the commander asked, staring hard at Frank, his features darkening.

Frank nodded as if thinking about it. "Right. Sounds like them."

"You come with me. You can get your things, later," he said, almost as an order before walking outside. Frank and Nero gave each other a look as they followed him out into the continuing deluge. The commander walked only a few metres before stopping at another wooden house and gesturing them up a short ladder. They climbed up onto a flat layer of planks and an ample space. Another three soldiers, two of them female, sat cross-legged, their dark eyes assessing the gringos as they climbed inside. They were striking in their appearance: beautiful and so young but, in that instant, Frank could tell from their faces that they had seen horrors to last a lifetime. A number of sleeping bags were strewn around the floor along with army backpacks as if a whole squad of them were staying there.

The commander ordered one of the female soldiers to find the medical kit. Frank and Nero sat themselves down, cross-legged at the commander's gestures. The commander poured two tin mugs full of black coffee and handed it to his two guests, as it now appeared. They took them gratefully and gulped down the hot liquid.

"Muchos gracias," Frank said, wiping his lips.

"So you were attacked by AUC. Where?" he asked.

"North. Nearer the Panama border."

"It's strange they are operating up there."

Frank made a face as if he had no idea why either. "It was very scary. They saw us, we ran, and they shot my friend, but we managed to escape."

The commander appraised them both, impressed. "You were very lucky, señors. Very lucky." He poured himself a coffee. "You do know that you are in FARC territory now. You cannot travel here without permission." He spoke as if going through the motions.

Frank dropped his head slightly, "I know and we're very sorry. We didn't know where we were."

"If you survived an attack by those bastardos death squads, then you are welcome here." He then gestured to them both. "And your clothes – you can dry them out here."

The young soldier returned from rummaging around in one of the bags and gestured to Nero to remove his shirt.

The commander offered around cigarettes. Frank paused, then declined. Nero took one and grinned.

"Those bastards," the commander continued, warming to his theme, "they come here two years ago. The people, they run. One man, he stayed. They chopped off his head and played football with it." He spat on the wood beneath his feet. "Animals. All of them!"

Frank nodded gravely. "Animals."

"So, where will you go?" he asked.

Frank thought for a moment. What to reveal and what not to. He decided on the truth.

"With your permission, to the mouth of the Cacaricas would be good. From there we try to get across to Apartado or somewhere on that road, or down to Domingodo. We should've just taken a plane the whole way."

The commander smiled. "We see many gringos, also migrants all flow through here. Some go into the jungle and never leave. Never seen again," he said with an air of menace. He drained his coffee, then added, "Comrade Isaza can take you there in a piragua canoe when it stops raining." He gestured to the male soldier who had watched the conversation in silence.

Frank glanced out of the door space at the torrential rain and wondered when exactly that would be.

Chapter 26

Several days earlier, Wexhall felt he had been running a very tight ship and, despite the apparent setback of the mole running around loose, it could only be a matter of time before the situation was resolved. It had to be, surmised Wexhall. They had excellent people on the ground and were steps behind their prey.

The fingerprints found in Lee's house and the ones they had on file did not match. So either he used fake biometric prosthetics when he joined G13COMM or in his daily life. Was one his real print or both fake? So far nothing had come up on either, but these things took time.

Additionally, their monitoring systems that connected the G13COMM station with the satellite surveillance might of Echelon, the signals intelligence (SIGINT) collection and global analysis network, had pulled in some impressive results. The facial recognition system had flagged another sighting of Nero, at Panama airport. That, with access to the flight manifests brought up their identity legends on a plane from Albrook airport, giving Wexhall a specific destination: Puerto Obaldia, a tiny village with an airstrip close to the Caribbean coastal border with Colombia.

It seemed perfect. Elvira was in the Caribbean, so he issued another message ordering her to proceed to Panama.

Then he had pulled out some numbers in his black book. Apart from FARC, South America was a hotbed of militias and groups funded by various US interests. Wexhall had his own contacts and pulled out the details of an acquaintance; Colonel Moreno of the paramilitary and drug trafficking group Autodefensas Unidas de Colombia.

Now, though, Wexhall was looking at a situation that had drifted into dangerous waters. The targets had escaped and it sounded like his idea to connect Elvira with the AUC was not working out. They were ripping the jungle apart looking for them, but there was a genuine possibility they had lost the trail and the cap on his operation was potentially going to be blown wide open.

He needed a backup plan and knew just the man to help.

Dean Wexhall picked up his encrypted phone and dialled the number for Carl Paterson.

Chapter 27

The following day the young soldier, Comrade Miguel Isaza, with tattoos covering most of his neck and face, expertly guided the Piragua canoe, fitted with a small outboard engine, downstream. On either side of them, the jungle closed in like monstrous green walls, with trees arching over their route visibly shaking as Howler monkeys screeched in their direction.

Miguel explained in Spanish that they should look out for crocodiles, who had been known to tip canoes over when attacking. Both Frank and Nero looked into the dark muddy water with trepidation. Warming to his nature lesson, Miguel also claimed to have seen jaguars on the banks.

Frank and Nero exchanged glances once again, happy not to have encountered any – so far. They weren't out of the jungle yet, it seemed. Although they had new supplies, the decision was made to leave the AK and the bag where it was. There was no way to explain that to the commander. It would have put a different spin on their whole conversation and probably the outcome of their situation.

***

Commander Jiménez and the remaining FARC unit also prepared to leave their base. They usually kept an eye out for any army patrols coming up the river to show the people they still had a grip on the area. Recent incursions and probes by the regular Colombian army and the AUC had put immense pressure on the guerrilla group. The leaders had suffered a series of fatalities, losing many of their top commanders to assassinations and capture.

Commander Jiménez got the men and two women in his unit to fill up the two boats for them to move upriver to the next village. They would meet Comrade Isaza there after he had dropped off the travellers. Jiménez wondered if they were just foolish adventurers, clueless gringos. He had seen enough of their type, even kidnapped a few of them for ransoms from their wealthy families in America or Europe.

But these men looked like they could handle themselves, especially the one who called himself Frank. Something in his eyes told the commander he'd been in many tough situations and survived.

He shook off the thought as he stepped outside from one of the shacks and caught a repetitive hacking sound coming from behind the hill, which faded and then grew louder. He called to his soldiers.

"*Helicóptero!*" He gestured for them to get away from the boats.

A Colombian army attack hadn't happened in this area for years. How had they got so far north?

From the track further up, still thick with mud from the rainfall, came a shout:

"AUC! AUC!"

A jagged cracking sound bounced off the trees and the man fell, hacked down by bullets that ripped into his back. The commander turned and signalled to his soldiers, who were fanning out with AK-47s at the ready, making for the single row of houses. At that moment a black helicopter appeared, hovering just fifteen metres above the river line, the main door flung open.

Its heavy machine gun fire hacked into the ground, the arc of bullets churning up the mud on the riverbank, then mowing down the FARC soldiers like ninepins. The commander dived to the floor of the house as the wooden flats were pulverised by the chaingun hammering his position. He held his hands around his head and prepared to die. After a few minutes it fell quiet except for the low hum of the chopper that faded as if it were moving away.

He rolled onto his side and held his palm up. It was red from blood. He checked his chest, legs and arms and felt the wet patch around his thigh. He had been hit in the leg. Then the pain hit, and he found that he was unable to get up. A creak from the door and he turned to see an AUC officer sweeping his weapon barrel around the room before settling his aim.

***

The commander found himself surrounded by the soldiers of the AUC. Two of them hauled him to his feet, and he grunted with pain from his leg wound. A fist connected a massive blow to his face forcing him to reel backwards, still supported by unseen hands. Another punched his face again, causing a stinging rush of pain throughout his jaw and neck followed by a metallic tang of blood in his mouth. The punches continued to rain in, pounding his face, then stomach.

Mercifully, he lost consciousness. Then came round to shouts. He felt himself being dragged outside, his feet trawling across the ground until he felt his body thrown onto the mudbank.

It was the smell he noticed. The smell of death. He struggled to open his eyes; they were so swollen it was as if they were welded shut. Through slits, he saw bodies. So many bodies. His soldiers. Villagers. Children. A toddler crumpled, limbs at an unnatural angle, against the tree trunk he had been flung at.

He had failed, failed to protect his territory from these scumbag death squads, whose strings were pulled by the narcos and the ultra-rich in Medellín and Bogota. A drill of machine gun fire burst from another one of the stilted houses behind him.

Another murder.

He curled up in the foetal position waiting for another rain of blows.

"Commander Jiménez."

The FARC commander slowly opened the slit of his eyes, surprised to hear his name. He felt a stick prod his face, forcing him to look upwards. A short man with a vicious smile looked down through mirrored sunglasses. Beside him was a woman with tied-back blonde hair, dressed in black fatigues.

A moment later an AUC soldier stepped forward and proceeded to pour liquid over his face and body. The commander coughed and jerked his head to try and avoid the stream of what he realised was gasoline, stinging his skin.

"Tell me where the gringos are."

Ah, the gringos.

The man with the mirrored glasses crouched down to better hear his answer.

"What do you say, commander? Do you intend to burn right here on the riverbed for their benefit?"

The commander forced himself to focus and could see his reflection; the battered face, purple and puffy, caked with sticky blood. He already knew his decision. They were going to burn him, whatever he told them.

So he would tell them nothing.

Chapter 28

Apparently the situation was delicate enough for the Americans to cross the Atlantic and that gave Carl a feeling of confidence. What it was they actually wanted had not been disclosed yet but he could hazard a guess. Word had obviously got around that his man – Bowen – was in the field.

The call from Stark demanding a meeting in their most secure location in London irked Carl, but he went with it and made arrangements for them to come to the Limehouse studio.

They walked in and were quickly ushered to the meeting room where Carl had spoken with Frank just weeks before.

When Carl walked in, Wexhall wore an unsettled, impatient expression and cut through the pleasantries.

"Paterson! About damned time! You think we can get some coffee around here?"

Carl was about to bark back, tell him this was his turf and to stick his demand up his backside, but merely nodded, face tight as he picked up the phone.

"Sure, colonel. But I'll warn you, it's shit coffee, and that's without me taking a crap in it," he muttered, without humour, trying to break the dynamic Wexhall was setting.

"Sure, I'll take it how it comes —" Wexhall, replied, seemingly not hearing him.

Carl grunted into the phone in low tones and slammed it down before crossing his arms.

Wexhall leaned towards Carl. "This asset of yours, he's in play right now?"

Carl raised his eyebrow at the directness of the statement, but it didn't surprise him. This man was a blunt instrument, judging by their first meeting on US soil. He resisted inhaling through his teeth like a tradesperson overestimating the price of a job and lightly brushed the table with his palm instead.

"Why do you want to know about our asset? Is this an information-sharing request?" Carl asked in as casual a tone as he could muster.

Wexhall fixed a steely glare at Carl that he briefly imagined boring a laser right through his head onto the wall behind. "Information sharing is always welcome, Carl. But it may come to something more...involved."

Carl remained impassive. "Involved?" he repeated. "Sounds expensive," he added.

Wexhall stood up suddenly, pushing away the chair as if it annoyed him and towered over Carl for a second before turning to pace the room.

"Alright. I'll level with you. The situation is this. We had a leak at G13COMM; an operative took some sensitive data, and along with everything they know about our little enterprise, they are a clear and present danger. It's a situation that needs tidying up, quickly. We have our own players in the field of course," he glanced briefly at Stark who met his eyes with a steel-like determination, "but I'm hedging my bets right now. It's a tricky situation and I need you to start pulling some levers from over here, if you get me?"

This was interesting, to say the least, thought Carl. Still, he had leverage.

"What about me? In the scheme of things?"

Wexhall gave him a knowing smile. "I didn't come here expecting something for nothing, Carl. No, the world doesn't work like that; not our world. Give me what I want, and I'll make sure you get a seat at the table."

Carl nodded, resisting a wry smile at that. It seemed all his Christmases had come at once.

Chapter 29

Frank and Nero departed from the canoe at Puente America, another riverside village that was just a strip of shacks perched on a muddy bank. Comrade Miguel Isaza helped arrange another boatman for them, before getting himself ready to head upriver. They received a hot meal of crocodile stew from one of the locals as they waited for the boatman to come back from whatever errand he was on. Frank managed to get a look at another map that one of the locals had pinned up on their wall. As far as he understood, they were still deep in FARC territory. There was also the Urabenos, a murderous drug gang that operated in the area. Frank sighed and wiped his hand through thick, greasy hair. They were still cut off from any communications. No one in this cauldron of menace and isolation seemed to have a phone or way of communicating with the outside world at all.

It was frustrating as hell. He still had to get Nero to Medellín. That had been his last communication order from Rhodes in Panama City. But now it had turned into a hellish nightmare that didn't want to end. That helicopter and the AUC group had really wanted to take them down. Although they had lost them for the moment, Frank knew they could never keep a low profile in a place like this.

***

When Comrade Miguel Isaza reached his village, he knew something was wrong from over twenty-five metres away. A waft of smoke drifted across the river and there was an eerie silence. As he drew closer, he could see the riverbank strewn with bodies. An overwhelming sense of evil stalking the nightshades enveloped him. A terrible act that would live on in memory for anyone affected by it.

Miguel cut the engine and drifted closer to the bank a few metres away, reaching for his rifle as he slowly stepped off the boat. He made his way in a half crouch, sweeping his barrel from left to right, seeing only the staring eyes of the dead, the blood in pools mixing with the muddy ground. As he rounded the corner of the first shack, there were three of the children, face down in the mud. He knew all their names. What monsters had done this? But, of course, he knew, deep down. Who else could it be?

He saw the camouflage uniforms of his comrades laying scattered around the canoes on the bank as if mown down in a line; half of them were women. These were the comrades he had lived, worked and struggled with all of his adult life. He slumped down, hardly believing his eyes.

Dead. All dead.

Then he looked up and saw the bodies of the villagers and the children.

The smoke that he thought was the remnants of fire came from a charred corpse curled into a foetal position. When he stepped closer, Miguel recognised some of the blackened uniforms. Part of the face was still visible. The ear and jawline was the only part recognisable of his commander.

"Would you like to join him?"

Miguel swung around at the voice. It came from the darkened shadow of one of the shack doorways and in the gaps between stood a line of AUC, all aiming their weapons at him. A stout man with mirrored sunglasses stepped out, one hand behind his back, holding a stick. He jutted his head. "You'd better put down your weapon, *hijo*."

Miguel did so, dropping it onto the ground, his eyes darting to the soldiers lined up against him.

A sudden fear gripped his entire body. Never before had he faced the enemy this close. Without his comrades, he felt naked. He muttered prayers, his lips barely moving.

The AUC man walked up to him, his soldiers just a few steps behind. He booted Miguel's rifle away, which was immediately picked up by one of the men.

"What is your name, soldier?"

"M–Miguel," he stammered.

The AUC man smiled warmly as if the boy was his son and placed his hand on his shoulder.

"Tell me, Miguel. You took two gringos somewhere, si?"

Miguel nodded vigorously, realising this was about them. They wanted those men. Clinging to the last strands of hope, Miguel convinced himself they might let him live.

"Gringos? Two men. Yes, jungle trekkers."

AUC man sneered, turned his head and spat onto the charred corpse of Miguel's commander.

"Where did you take them, Miguel?" he asked, patiently.

Miguel was gently sobbing now. He told him what he wanted to know, then dropped his head. The AUC man with the shades clicked his fingers, a soldier stepped up with a jerry can, and all eyes turned to Miguel as he began screaming.

Chapter 30

The boatman called Zafro had finally arrived and appeared happy to take them further south in return for dollars. They agreed on a price and hauled their new supplies aboard. Zafro ran into one of the buildings, a flatboard abandoned schoolhouse then returned and clambered in.

Frank immediately noticed he had a pistol tucked casually into his shorts belt.

"For protection?" Frank asked in Spanish.

"*Si*. Many bad men."

Frank couldn't have agreed more. It seemed like they were in very shark-infested waters. He felt edgy without a weapon but was happy to see Zafro was packing.

Zafro fired up the engine and they headed down the broad river, the main artery into the heart of the jungle. They navigated along the river for a few hours until the darkness threatened.

"We stop and eat soon," Zafro said, pointing to the banks. "I know a place."

He pulled over at a row of three abandoned shacks that was often used as a stop-off for river travellers. They brought in their bags and a jerry can of gasoline and went into one of the huts. Inside, hammocks hung on the walls, a couple of old stools and a kerosene lamp in the corner. Graffiti was sketched out on the walls, an old discarded T-shirt and plastic bags littered the floor.

It was a simple but welcome shelter for the weary.

They ate sardines from a tin, sipped bottled water then lit the gas lamp and covered the gaps in the door to keep the insects away as best they could.

"You live in Puente America, Zafro?"

"Sometimes. I travel around, always on the boat."

"Makes you a good boatman," said Frank.

He nodded and smiled, smoking a cigarette. "We go at first light."

"Sounds good," Frank said. He moved the jerry can close to his sleeping spot, and they settled down for the night.

As the others drifted off, Frank went through their supplies. From what he recalled from memory of the map, the river led down through the left side of Colombia. A place called Domingodo ran parallel with a highway route that ran into the mountainous region of central Colombia and to Medellín, more or less. The problem was the sixty or so kilometres of jungle and lack of transport options in between.

Frank yawned and rested his head on the wall boards, listening to the light breathing of the others along with the usual night noises from the forest.

***

It was just before dawn. Moreno, his two best men and the female agent sent from his employers, were heavily armed in two canoes each fitted with 5hp outboard motors. As suspected, the FARCO kid told them where the gringos had been dropped off before he had personally ended the son of a whore's life. At Cacaricas one of his many eyes and ears, a boatman called Zafro, had approached him relaying that he had just left them at a rest stop. There weren't too many other options for many hundreds of kilometres.

He was close. Very close.

It was a shame their chopper couldn't be used to continue the hunt; the fuel for it was low and they hadn't time to replenish it. He needed to continue by any means necessary, primarily as the cash bounty for the gringos was such a large sum. It would ensure he could retain his position within the AUC forces, perhaps even help him make a bid for a higher command and do much more business with the narcos that had created the paramilitary force.

As they approached the next known rest stop, Moreno ordered the engines to be cut as the canoes slid silently along the final stretch. In the distance, they could all see a single lamp hung outside the first shack. With a clenching gesture of his hand, Moreno stopped the boats on the riverbank, less than a kilometre away. They disembarked and tied up the boats.

"Gomaz, you." He pointed at Evira. "Make your way to the front of the huts, check each one in turn." He turned to the second soldier. "Restrepo, head to a position behind the huts and keep your eyes out for them."

"I'd rather take the back route," said Elvira, icily. "And why would they leave a light outside? There is something—"

"Take off and do what I tell you. You're under my command here," he hissed in reply. He had not agreed with her being part of their hunting team, but that was what his employers wanted. As far as he was concerned, a woman should be at home with kids, scrubbing the floors, although he had to admit she wasn't a bad fighter from what he had seen.

"They're just stupid gringos. Probably afraid of the dark," he added. She stared at him long and hard but said nothing.

"Alright," he said, turning to the others, "I'll be just behind you. Vamos!"

Elvira and the two men moved along the river edge for a few metres, then Restrepo split off heading into the trees to get behind while the other two pressed on and stopped just shy of the huts. Gomaz turned to Elvira, who jerked her chin for him to continue.

Half-crouched in stealth mode they silently edged along the front of the huts. Gomaz took a position outside the first hut door and nodded to Elvira who proceeded to slowly open the door with the butt of her rifle. Then Gomaz ran in, his AK-47 in firing position.

All clear.

Gomaz quickly came out as she jerked her head to the side toward the next one. The soldier then tried the handle and opened it with ease.

Crouched low, Elvira moved inside her rifle at the ready.

All clear.

She backed out as a smell of something caught her nostrils…

At the last hut door an orange glow radiated from inside. Crackling wood.

"Wait—" she began, but Gomaz hurled his shoulder against the door which gave way to his impact easily. There was a crash, and Elvira just caught a series of snapshot images as if time stopped. A glimpse of the naked flame from a kerosene lamp. A jerry can clattering to the floor, spilling its contents –the gasoline she had smelled. Then a loud "whoomph" as a rapid escalation of fire engulfed the interior as well as Gomaz.

Elvira stumbled back, covering her face from the sudden on-slaught of heat, tripped and fell to the ground. She sensed a dull thud as her head hit something hard.

Her senses dulled, apart from the sound of the fire. She came around as agonising shouts gnawed at her senses. Elvira crawled away from the raging heat, coughing as her lungs burned with the acrid smoke. Her fingers gripped at the ground beneath her, head spinning. She needed to get up fast. As she lifted her head, she saw Gomaz had somehow made it to the river and had crawled halfway back out, his blackened uniform still smouldering.

Then Moreno stomped up the bank, pistol raised at the huts, his face contorted with anger. He shouted something she couldn't hear.

Over the roar of the fire, now rapidly spreading, Elvira heard a buzzing and realised it was a boat engine – no, two. Their boats! Moreno stopped and turned, looking into the darkness. A perfect target, silhouetted against the blaze of the huts behind him.

"Get down, you idiot!" Elvira shouted.

Too late.

A strafe of bullets erupted from the faint shadows of the boats. Moreno managed one useless shot at moving shapes before dropping to his knees as bullets ripped into his chest and neck. He clutched at his throat with one hand before slumping down into the mud as a stream of burning gasoline from the fires behind him snaked towards his prone body.

Elvira crawled to a clump of grass, her only available cover, the flames almost licking her feet from behind. Her AK was too far off, dropped on the ground somewhere. She pulled a handgun from her holster and aimed into the darkness. The sawing of the engines seemed further away, but she couldn't tell where they were, then she spotted the shapes on the far side of the vast river and fired off a couple of rounds. At this distance, it would only be a lucky shot to hit anything with a Glock 13. There was a flash from a muzzle and a return burst of fire sending bullets in her direction causing her to flinch and duck down to the ground. Then it stopped and the boat engines faded into nothing, swallowed up by the night.

***

A few hours earlier, Frank opened his eyes with a jolt, as if something was badly amiss. Had he just heard a boat engine in the far distance? He concentrated on the sounds but heard only the light buzzing of the jungle.

Then he noticed Zafro had disappeared and cursed himself for drifting off to sleep. Frank had suspected Zafro might be a "tip-off" guy on seeing his gun but had stupidly dismissed it. How else could someone like him afford such a weapon unless he was working for the gangs? Frank got up and shook Nero awake.

"We've got company, and our guide's gone. I don't think he went to get us breakfast."

"Great. Who's he gonna tell?"

Frank thought for a moment, his eyes dropping down to the jerry can that Zafro had forgotten to take. It had been too close to Frank, and he surmised the guy hadn't wanted to risk waking him. Outside was quiet, just the distant whining of the mosquitoes. Frank stared out into the slow-moving water through a gap in the door and heard a distant sound like splashing.

He held his hand up, motioning to Nero to keep quiet.

"I think someone's coming," he whispered. He held a finger to his ear. The sound was unmistakable; approaching boats. Although Frank knew slow-moving water always carried sound further, so he knew they had a little time. Five minutes max, in his estimation.

The chairs in the end hut; wood. And the jerry can.

Frank grabbed the jerry can and a kerosene lamp then they moved silently to the last shack of the three at the end of the row.

Once inside, Nero shut the door and Frank looked around. There were a couple of old stools and little else.

"Break one of them up for a fire distraction," said Frank, in short, clipped tones. Nero nodded and gave an OK sign. The stool broke apart easily, half-rotted from the jungle humidity. Frank grabbed the wood and built a pile in the middle of the room then poured a small amount of gasoline onto the broken wood and across the floor. He unscrewed the glass from the kerosene lamp, placed the other stool in front of the door and the jerry can on top facing inwards. It was possible just the fumes from the hydrocarbons would be enough to ignite a fire if it splashed across the floor, but the naked lamp would ensure it happened. The side window had a shutter that Nero eased open before climbing out.

Frank watched the river through the gap in the door, the silhouettes of two boats gliding closer on the muddy water. Then they disappeared behind a clump of trees, pulling into the bank a hundred or so metres away, leaving just the sound of Frank's heartbeat in his ear and the jungle crickets. His instinct was right. They were coming. He did a rough estimation. They were about two minutes away.

Frank climbed out and signalled to Nero, who had hidden amongst the thick foliage and trees. Half-crouched, they made their way into the jungle. They started to move in a semi-circle around the rear of the huts, heading in the direction of the river bank.

Frank, having taken the lead, held up his fist on hearing a noise nearby and they both crouched. Someone was approaching. The two men hid at the approaching footfall as that someone was not doing a great job of disguising their position.

There was a distant "whoomph" followed by the sound of crackling and a change of light; an orange hue lit up the trunks and vines from the direction of the river, quickly followed by a shout.

The party had started.

A soldier appeared, AK in hand, clear to see in the new light. He looked in the direction of the commotion and picked up his pace. Frank pounced from behind, grabbing his throat with one arm and jaw in the other. With a vicious twist and a crack, the soldier's body slackened and fell onto the ground. Nero helped him drag the body into the undergrowth before they stripped him of anything useful. There was the AK-47, an old Soviet Tokarev TT-33 pistol and a box of rounds along with other essential supplies in his bag.

Within a minute they were moving again, Frank checking the AK was loaded before they came across two boats tied up.

Ahead, Frank could see the glow glistening on the river surface as he untied the rope.

"We've got to go past the huts, so head to the far side, then along the bank."

They both frantically began pulling at the engine cords. Nero's fired up first, and he headed off across to the far side. Frank pulled, but it didn't fire. He tried again, and it caught. He steered his boat diagonally across towards the far side, crouching low. By now, the fire was illuminating the river, but there was nothing they could do about that. Frank let the boat tiller go and aimed his AK barrel at the river bank and the blazing huts. A figure was moving along the bank. Frank pressed the trigger, forcing the weapon down as it veered upwards on the sudden burst of loud gunfire. A single shot rang out, and Frank fired another salvo, getting a better handle on the weapon now and saw the figure slump, then fall from sight before being consumed by flames.

He put one hand to adjust direction, not taking his eyes off the huts. There was no one else in sight. Then, gunshots from a sidearm, the muzzle flashes coming low off the bank. Frank returned a burst of fire, just as the huts disappeared from view, leaving only traces of flickering light dancing across the river.

***

Elvira retrieved what ammo and supplies she could from the bodies and checked her collection: a Glock pistol, her AK, one box of ammo for each and her knife. She took one last look around and headed off along the bank after the fading boat engines. There was no chance of catching them now.

From her rucksack she fished out a satellite phone and dialled a number seared into her memory. She spoke a series of authentication identifiers until she was through to a company answering machine.

"Local Indians all sick – proceeding solo. Tangos at large. My co-ords unknown but estimate a few kilometres from Domingodo on the Atrato River." As she spoke, she spotted a shape in the reefs of the bank ahead through the clinging morning mist, then movement.

She cut the call quickly and crouched low, straining to get a better look in the low dawn light.

It wasn't likely they had stopped so soon, unless engine failure. She drew her weapon and stalked the distant shape, quietly stepping closer. It came clear it wasn't her adversaries; a local fisherman was cutting up fish for his crab traps.

She smiled to herself. Her transport beckoned.

Elvira stepped out of the undergrowth and clucked her tongue for his attention; he turned with a look of surprise and froze, only managing a toothless smile before a "thunk" from her weapon dropped him unconscious onto the ground, the sound of the fall sending birds scattering from the canopies above.

Chapter 31

Frank and Nero continued their long journey and, after another eight hours heading downriver, the boats reached Domingodo, the halfway point for anyone heading deeper into the jungle where Frank and Nero had just spent their harrowing days.

At the riverside town, a row of rusty brown corrugated iron shacks lined the muddy river.

Pigs rooted around in the alleyways, while children played on the steps to the flatboard houses that advertised Colombian beer with hand-painted signs. The population, almost all Afro-Colombian, regarded the two strangers, staring at their every move as they docked their piragua canoes. Children, some naked, jumped into the river from a jetty, laughing and shouting.

After a short rest, they traded one of the boats for supplies, procured a map and moved on, following the Atrato River in its snaking path of brown mud through the dull, dense green of the relentless jungle.

Frank studied the map carefully. There was a much smaller river that split off and cut across to Antioquia Choco, towards Mutatá and the prospect of civilisation with the Highway 62 that would get them to Medellín.

Both men thought the worst must surely be behind them now. The sparse, ramshackle hamlets now made way for river towns with more signs of modern civilisation in contrast to the savagery of the jungle.

After another full day of travelling, the relatively flat town of Mutatá with shacks and concrete block buildings came into view and they both inwardly breathed a sense of relief.

They found a sparse cafe and wolfed down their first full meal in what seemed like an age. Then Frank found a clothes stall, and they kitted out on basic attire: jeans, T-shirts and new trainers. Then they headed to the main street and boarded a packed bus destined for Medellín.

***

After taking the fisherman's boat and leaving his body in the reeds, Elvira headed down the river as fast as the basic fishing boat would go. She estimated that she could only be a few kilometres behind them. Spotting the fisherman had given her an unexpected and welcome piece of luck, like a portion of juicy steak straight off a BBQ.

Elvira could sense they were close and didn't let up until she reached Domingodo. As she cruised in, along the riverside shacks, cutting the engine, she watched the other moored boats closely. An old man in a dirty yellow vest was sitting on a makeshift pier that was nothing more than a slab of wood on metal poles.

"*Senor! ¿Has visto a mis amigos? Dos hombres,*"

He gave her what she assumed was his best ladies' smile as he pointed upriver. She treated him to her own alluring glance and then sped off in that direction. On the map, she could see the route they must take. A small offshoot in the river that led to Mutatá and the highway. There was always a chance they would try to put her off their trail by continuing, but that route looked like a long way, going deeper into the jungle and, besides, they would assume she had been left long behind without transport and couldn't possibly suspect she was so close on their tail.

At the split, Elvira headed towards Mutatá without hesitation, and after thirty minutes the dark shape of a boat appeared in her sights for a moment before disappearing around the bend.

At last. They were in sight.

She felt a rush of exhilaration and then realised the sound of her boat's engine might alert them and cut it dead. She drifted along the bank for a while before restarting it and cutting on through the murky water. As the hazy clinging heat seemed to radiate from the surrounding trees, Elvira tracked her prey, staying far enough back on the journey to Mutatá. When she arrived, she dumped the boat and moved through the tepee-style houses and single-storey homes that made up the town, with the looming familiar green hills behind.

The logical place the tangos would go had to be any transport hub. In this town, it had to be a bus terminal. She asked a local woman for directions and headed onto the main street, a wide concrete road with fruit stalls straddling the middle and the occasional store, where locals lounged around on plastic seats, watching their tiny world go by. Outside a cafe that served as a central gathering point, a small crowd of people waited in a queue to get on board. Then Elvira caught sight of them in the line. A moment later they had boarded, and the coach engine fired up. She quickly looked around, assessing the situation. It would be simple enough to find out the bus destination but, beyond that, there would be no way of knowing where they would end up. She spotted a white Jeep parked down a deserted side street and beelined towards it.

***

The monotonous six-hour journey brought them through the rolling mountainous countryside of Route 62 until the bus weaved around the snaking road that descended into the vast valley of Medellín. Skyscrapers and red-brick apartment blocks clustered the lower echelons of the city and higher up across the surrounding hillside, a cluster of distant squares – the shanty towns of the city's more impoverished barrios. Visions of the city flashed by through the grimy windows of the bus. A couple of olive-skinned, shirtless men covered in tattoos hung around outside a garage where a motorbike stood, half disassembled. A woman gesticulated while talking animatedly on a mobile phone.

At Terminales Medellín, the northern bus station, both men looked at each other and sensed each other's palatable relief, as if they were perhaps at the end of a nightmare.

"Maybe I'll buy you a beer," said Nero, with a mocking nonchalance.

Frank decided to call Rhodes first, then Carl. The initial plan was to head to an address that would be given by Rhodes on arrival.

But whom to trust?

His game of playing both sides was fraying the edges of his mind.

He bought a cheap mobile phone with a disposable SIM card from a store in the terminal and dialled the number.

A female answerphone voice asked him to leave a message. "We've arrived in MDE. Had major problems with the deliveries. I need that friend's address you promised, ASAP." Frank left his number then hung up before dialling the drop number for Carl Paterson at Ghost 13 where he heard a similar message service. As he was leaving the message, there was a click and Carl came on the line.

"Where the hell are— What is your location code?"

Frank reeled off a series of numbers and letters, the cypher code for Medellín; one he had memorised.

There was a pause as Carl confirmed it at his end.

"Alright. Now, listen carefully. Take Nero to a safe house in the city; I'll give you the location. We'll take it from there."

"What's going to happen to him?"

"None of your concern, Mr Milligan, but rest assured we'll take good care of him."

Frank felt a twist in his stomach. The thought of handing Nero over to his certain death seemed particularly nauseating after everything they had gone through. The struggle they had overcome; for this?

"You're not going to let me down, are you?" Carl asked, his voice full of suspicion.

There was a pause before Frank answered.

"Would I ever?"

Carl snorted. "Because there is an alternative: you solve the problem yourself. You have the means at your disposal, I'm sure," Carl said, his tone level and deadly.

"What about Liberatus? Won't this screw up that whole plan?"

"This is more important now. Things have changed."

Frank swore under his breath and looked across the bus terminal at Nero sitting on a bench, smoking. He met Frank's stare, smiled and nodded.

He would be stabbing the kid in the back.

He turned away, strolling in a circle.

"Send me the location," he said, dryly.

Frank cut the call and stared down at his mobile screen for a moment.

Next, he tried to phone Maria but there was no answer, so he left a quick message so she'd know that he was alright. For a moment Frank wondered if she even cared, but brushed it aside. Jungle fever was catching up with him, perhaps. Frank cut the call and returned to where Nero was waiting in the terminal.

Almost as soon as Frank had killed the call with Carl, the phone buzzed. It was Rhodes himself.

"Glad to hear you and our friend arrived safely, Mr Milligan. I'll give you an address. It's good for twenty-four hours. Then we'll meet for lunch or something. I know a great cafe our friend would love."

"That would be great."

After the call, they grabbed a taxi for Laureles, in the north-east of the city; a perfect place to keep their heads down while waiting for Rhodes, it seemed. Palms lined the quiet streets, a subdued calm at odds with the busy scenes they witnessed coming in. A fruit-seller pushed a cart shouting for buyers for his *plátanos, papayas y frutas de la pasión* with rhythmic *persuasión*.

At the address, a two-storey block, an elderly Colombian man greeted them outside the front door that had a barred gate and showed them inside an apartment. He left them the keys, explained the alarm system in Spanish and then left them to it. It was basic but clean and discreet with a small terrace looking out onto the quiet street below.

On a table was a package with about five hundred US dollars and a mobile phone.

Nero slumped down on the couch with a sigh of absolute relief.

"Hope this place is safe cos I need a shitload of sleep."

Frank smiled, concurring with a nod. "I'm gonna shower, then find out what the plan is. Then we'll get some food – and collect on those beers you promised."

After he had dried off and dressed in fresh clothes left on the bed, Frank found Nero crashed out fast asleep, breathing heavily.

Frank decided to leave him to it and ventured down the street to where he found a store. He loaded up on short-term supplies, snacks and added a pack of Club Colombia beer, then headed back to the apartment. He found Nero in the same position as he had left him and slumped onto a chair on the balcony, with one well-deserved *cerveza* and stared idly onto the street.

Grey clouds swirled overhead, and a sudden flash lit up the darkening hillside for a fraction of a second. Moments later, a heavy crack of thunder rent the air. A car alarm, set off by the concussion, began beeping loudly, birds squawked wildly in the trees and in the distance a dog barked furiously. Another series of rumbles rolled across the city overhead as if anger had manifested itself through nature. Then the slow pitter-patter of heavy raindrops before a rainstorm cascaded down in sheets.

"Hey, Frank." It was Nero, dark hair dishevelled. He took the spare chair, sat down and stared out at the rain with Frank.

"Takes you back to the jungle days, huh?" he added, watching as a man rushed across the street with an umbrella that flew outwards, turning into a useless flapping device.

"Happy never to return to that place, mate," Frank muttered, handing Nero a beer.

Nero shuffled in his seat and turned to look at Frank.

"So, any word on contact with Eaglecraft? I'd like to know what my position is and be safe, although I'm not sure here is the place."

"I'm sure Rhodes has considered every angle when it comes to security."

"Evidently not when it came to travelling here."

Frank took a long pull from the brown bottle. "Yeah, well. It could've been smoother, that's for sure."

They both laughed at that.

"I hope Rhodes is paying you enough, huh?"

"Not for that hike. I hope you're worth it, Mark."

Nero nodded, as if to himself, his face turning serious. "Oh, I'm worth it, alright."

They both watched as a woman on a scooter sloshed through the cascading water on the road, followed by a white Jeep that turned off into a side street.

***

The rain had eased, but water continued pouring off the roof across the windowless holes where the guttering had not been fitted. Elvira shuffled in her position inside the semi-finished apartment block. It gave her shelter from the elements at least and from her hidden position a narrow view of the balcony of their apartment.

Her options, as she saw them, were limited.

Take them out on the street, attempt clean kills. There were two of them, and they were both well trained so that ploy could be messy.

Or wait it out. Follow them and see if any other players appeared in the game.

Elvira swigged on her bottle of water and ate a cold empanada as she considered her options, then checked through her bag. A few rounds for her Glock 13 pistol, the AK long ago dumped for having been deemed way too conspicuous to be carrying around.

Only a few rounds. She'd have to make them count and settled down for a long wait.

As the cold light of dawn struggled to break through the thick cloud cover, Elvira decided to wait and see what crawled out of the woodwork.

Chapter 32

Frank and Nero left their apartment as a blue sky opened up overhead as if the previous night's rain had never happened. They hailed one of the city yellow cabs from Carrera 70, directing the surly driver to Envigado at the opposite end of the city. It seemed much longer than the actual thirty or so minutes to Frank with the radio blaring incessantly, spewing a mind-numbing mix of inane chatter, crappy music and canned laughter. He tried to tune it out, keeping his eye on the rear mirror from his passenger seat for any tails.

They headed along the Autopista Regional that split the city in two and veered off into the enclave of Envigado, the enclave that Frank remembered from his research had been the birthplace of Pablo Escobar, the notorious drug narco, who had been killed by the Search Bloc seven years before. They exited the cab on a quiet side street a few blocks from their RV with Rhodes.

"How do you want to play this?" asked Nero, looking down the street each way as the cab screeched off.

"Carefully. We don't know whether that bitch was alone or has an army of local gun-toting maniacs with her." They started to walk up to the main road.

"We left her in the jungle, I wouldn't worry," Nero said dismissively before slapping Frank playfully on the arm, "let's eat before we meet Mr Eaglecraft himself."

Frank half shrugged, "You're probably right. Still, I want to take a recce around the park and I'll meet you in the cafe in about ten minutes. Order me breakfast?"

They split up, each taking a separate side of the road. At Parque Envigado Nero took a right turn while Frank headed straight. Two multi-lane highways ran parallel on either side of the park, lined with a mix of stores, a bank and offices. Two paved pedestrian walkways connected the two roads, and through the park trees where fruit sellers and coffee carts were peddling their wares, Frank could see a white Greco-Roman Catholic church on the far side.

***

Nero ordered two breakfasts at the counter, then glanced around the cafe. It was empty; business must be slow. Through the trees and passers-by, he caught sight of Frank heading back towards him to the cafe after his recce. The thought had crossed his mind as to whether Frank was right to be extra paranoid. Whatever, he was just following tradecraft procedure; in which case he'd better do the same and check the back entrance.

"Where's the bathroom?" Nero asked the young gringo behind the counter, who was absorbed in a newspaper.

He thumbed to the rear of the building.

"Right at the back, outside," he replied, barely looking up at his customer. Nero walked down the corridor, passing a closed kitchen door on his right, the radio blaring inside. As he came through the back doorway, he caught sight of a woman a few steps away, making to move into a position behind crates that were stacked up in the backyard.

They looked straight at each other, the recognition instant as time froze.

Nero moved at her, feigning a left punch but shifting his balance quickly and lunging with his right. She sidestepped him and jumped, spinning in mid-air and landing a high kick right in his gut.

Nero crashed into a wall and, in a flash, she was coming at him, knife drawn.

Raising his arm, Glock in hand, Frank pulled the trigger. A loud crack echoed around the enclosed yard. Elvira's body pivoted as if attempting a ballet twirl but still managed to stay on her feet.

He had shot her arm.

With one wide arced throw she threw the knife in Frank's direction with a swish. He leapt aside behind the stack of crates as the blade hit a window frame just behind him, burying itself deep in the wood with a dull thwack.

Frank crouched low and went to fire again but just caught a glimpse of her leaping over the low wall to the street. He scurried over to Nero who nodded with a pained expression, clutching his stomach.

"I'm fine," he grunted, waving him off.

Frank moved to the back entrance and checked the road, just in time to see her turning, pistol in hand, about to fire back. Frank aimed at her centre body mass and squeezed off a round sending the sound of loud cracks bouncing off the neighbouring buildings.

Her weapon fell from her hand as she slumped onto her knees, a hand clutching over her stomach. Then she keeled over and collapsed on the ground next to her gun.

Frank exhaled and stared for a moment at the motionless form. He half jogged over to her body and bent down. Her eyes, half closed, gazed skywards. With a check of her neck for her pulse, he confirmed she was dead.

Whoever she had worked for had lost a good asset, that was for sure.

Then a screech and a white Audi turned the corner, heading in Frank's direction. The sound of a siren drifted over from the main road.

Frank ran back to the cafe backyard and waved at Nero, who had just hauled himself to his feet.

"I got her, but someone else is coming. We've got to move!"

Nero looked back into the cafe. "They might have the front covered."

Both of them looked at the high concrete blocks forming high walls on either side. There was no easy way out from the courtyard to any neighbouring buildings.

"Bollocks," Frank muttered, then he trained his aim at the rear wall. "Alright, get to the front, keep an eye on my six, and I'll cover."

On the street a screech of tyres as the vehicle stopped out of sight, then the sound of opening doors.

"Frank!" It was a shout from behind the wall, followed by the word, "Fire!"

Frank's body relaxed. It was the agreed counter-sign with Rhodes.

"Fury!" he responded quickly.

Then Rhodes appeared, flanked by a Colombian man; the Audi driver he had spotted earlier.

"We've got to move right now!" Rhodes demanded, gesturing to them both with his hand.

With the approaching police siren only a block away, Frank was happy to oblige.

***

It was a two-hour drive back up into the hills surrounding Medellín on the same route they had done on the bus. They turned up a steep lane and kept going for around ten kilometres, glimpses of the sprawling metropolis behind them.

"She tracked us all the way from the jungle," said Frank. "Must have followed us in the bus and waited it out. Had a tag on us somehow." He was thinking it through, trying to figure it out, then he turned to Nero. "You handled that well. I was surprised—"

Nero brushed it off. "Just keeping myself out of harm's way. This place we're going – it's secure, right?" asked Nero, looking at Rhodes.

Rhodes turned to face him from the front seat. "We have a network of safe houses, and I have contacts in the government here and in Venezuela. We can go through your future role after the information debrief. See how the information you provide can help us with what we're trying to do. The people who are unknowingly repressed need a counter against the rise of the state. You're playing a pivotal role in that, Mr Nero, a hero of the world's people."

Nero visibly relaxed, although his face remained impassive.

"I'm not doing it for the people," he countered.

Rhodes sighed. "Well, maybe you should be."

"I have my reasons, and it's not just about the money."

"Alright," Rhodes said in a tone suggesting he'd made his point.

The vehicle continued until they came to a fork in the road, where the lower track curved around a hillside out of sight. The car followed it around for two kilometres until they came to a terracotta-roofed finca surrounded by palm trees and a high wooden fence.

At the gates Rhodes slipped out a small grey remote. The gates swung silently open as they drove through and into a large enclosed courtyard. A grass lawn formed a semi-circle in front of the house that sported semi archways along the side, for an exterior balcony.

"Not a bad place, John," said Frank. He thought it looked like a high-class house for the aspiring rich.

"I'm not staying," said Frank.

"Please stay, Frank. It's too late to return to Medellín now."

Frank sighed. Rhodes was right, but he was eager to get home, to get back to normality and see his kids. One more day wouldn't hurt.

"OK, I'll check flights for tomorrow."

"And tonight we celebrate our coup," said Rhodes, smiling.

Chapter 33

The cut in Nero's hand, on the loose skin between the thumb and index finger, drew a pool of blood that he dabbed away with a tissue. Frank parted behind the skin with the sterilised tweezers and attempted to grip onto the microchip with the tiny pincers without success.

"Jesus, go easy, you got it yet?" Nero was taking in sharp breaths as Frank rooted around under the skin. Frank shot him a glance without moving his head, "I didn't exactly volunteer for this—"

Rhodes, standing back from the table, chimed in. "Sorry, Frank, I would have tried, but the old peepers aren't the same as they used to be."

"I'll get this, don't worry," Frank grunted. With another bite, he managed to get the object in the grasp of the tweezers and began easing it out of the blood, millimetre by millimetre, until it was free.

"Don't drop that now," said Rhodes, edging behind Frank to get a closer look. Frank was holding it up to the light, peering at the chip that looked like a miniature translucent pill no larger than a grain of rice. He then placed it down into a metal box.

"So all the data is stored on this? Impressive," said Frank. Impressive indeed, but not unsurprising.

Nero wiped the cut on his hand with an antiseptic-soaked wipe and nodded, glancing down at the chip. "Yeah, smart, right? It was a G13COMM project, the know-how gathered from some British scientist who implanted one a few years ago. They want to use them for all kinds of shit: location tracking and ID access but the technology isn't quite there yet. In their simplest form, they can hold a lot of information, and for this mission it was perfect."

"And getting the information off it?"

Nero bandaged up his hand and flexed his thumb, his face remaining hard.

"This doesn't carry the data itself. There's too much of a chance it would corrupt. There's a tiny antenna that transmits an ID key from the chip to unlock the data which is on a secure server." He allowed himself a wry smile, then looked at Rhodes, "You should have the right stuff...right?"

The old man nodded. "As you asked."

All three men moved silently out of the room into a hallway where Rhodes ushered them into an adjoining study. A bank of three screens faced them, placed on a long desk along with a plastic box filled with tech equipment sat on one of the chairs.

Rhodes moved it onto the long table and proceeded to log into a laptop, then handed it over to Nero.

"I'll do a preliminary check on the server, make sure everything is secure, connect to it, then we can unlock the key with the RFID," said Nero, casting his eyes over the screen.

"Am I needed for this?" Frank asked.

Rhodes shook his head. "This is going to take a while. Then I have to sift through all the data. I'd like you to hang around for a bit though."

Frank sighed. "Hmm, dunno. I'm itching to get home. I'll check the flights, then give Maria a call. See how it pans out."

Nero glanced at them both before returning his attention to the laptop.

***

As expected, it took several days for Rhodes to organise all the data Nero had unlocked and have it transferred to his server. To dig deep to see what he actually had would take a lot longer. He needed Nero around for explaining aspects of what they had, to answer questions. To wade through the information: the planned operations, codes, details of the covert military teams that were in the making.

And, of course, the danger. Rhodes peered out of the window onto the hills, the shades of green lush and vibrant. Would soldiers appear from those trees? Was it a matter of when not if?

Not that he was a stranger to it all. Rhodes smiled.

Stranger danger.

No, he could handle it although there was no doubt this was several leagues above his pay grade. There was real power having these files: he now had intimate working knowledge of the agency.

As for Nero, he would need to keep a low profile. He would be a wanted man for a long time, but Rhodes would have no problem finding him a new role. Rhodes needed all the help he could get to achieve his long-term goal: building an opposition to the octopus-like global state serving its own interests with the good of humanity at the bottom of its priorities.

Dangerous work, indeed.

Chapter 34

Nero watched the main house through the window of his guest house and the cascading rain outside. There was a glimpse of a shadow from Rhodes or possibly one of the García brothers from behind the blinds. Couldn't be sure but it didn't matter.

Bowen was about to leave, and pretty soon it would be showtime. Nero had given Rhodes enough detail about the G13COMM operation. Sketches rather than the final painting, but it would be enough to discredit them and pull the plug on the whole tub of shit without putting too many American lives at risk. A fine tightrope, for sure, and one that had to be navigated carefully.

As for Bowen, Nero had felt a kinship with the man who had done an excellent job despite all the shit that had been thrown at them. They had survived out there in the jungle, and he would miss the guy.

What a close run, though. When they had been captured and caged by the AUC paramilitaries, he had recognised Commander Moreno from the previous operation eighteen months before, waiting in the AUC camp as the two leaders arrived by 4x4. Had Moreno come closer to their "cage" and recognised him, the game would have been up right then.

Thankfully, they had managed to escape that night.

Moreno.

Just for a moment, the pattering rain against the window took him right back to that day. The Ecuador mission that followed, the FARC camp raid and subsequent capture of those young fighters left to fend for themselves.

Then, the burnings.

Poor bastards.

Draining the sea to kill the fish.

Every one of those captured had been burned alive by Moreno's sadistic hand while Nero watched, more intrigued than horrified. None of them told him where their commander might have gone. Or they just blurted out random names to try to save themselves. Whether they spoke the truth or not, the covert mission had to be wrapped up fast. There was no way they could have continued the hunt for the FARC commander, Jiménez on Ecuadorian soil that day.

How ironic he and Frank had run into Jiménez in that village. The very man, he had tried to capture on that mission.

Nero had been part of a CIA special forward group to assist with ground operations ahead of the plan while the influx of weapons and military training continued unabated in the background.

While "Plan Colombia" openly assisted the de facto Colombian state with nine billion dollars in military funding, all approved by Congress, an altogether more secret plan was about to be implemented using the combined expertise of the NSA and the CIA; surveillance and elimination. In its purest form locating and hunting down FARC leaders for assassination using the latest technology from the US.

Nero moved away from the window. That was all in the rear-view mirror now, as if obscured by the rainfall itself.

Only his current mission mattered.

Nero had been summoned by the CIA Deputy Executive Director, Kate Foster, at Langley five months before. He was already trained in the deep infiltration of networks and intelligence gathering. He was a young "rough diamond" in the world of CIA field ops. Foster had called him into one of the deep windowless rooms that had surveillance and cameras spotted all around the walls.

"Do you know why you're here?" she had asked with a stony face.

Nero had slumped back on his chair with a cool gaze towards the black mirror that took up the entire wall at the back.

"Tell me, please," he said, turning his head slightly, his dark eyes fixed on her.

"We have enemies abroad in the Middle East and domestic enemies right here at home." She slapped down a paper file and opened it with a little finger. "You'll have to read it in here and remember it."

Nero leaned forward to look at it with all the enthusiasm of a mouse accidentally walking in on a cat soiree and opened up the file.

"The next page," Foster ordered, then leaned over the table and flipped the page for him. Nero looked down at a US Army colonel. A grunt. Well, that was unfair. A grunt with power and a lot of it. The colonel was staring hard at the camera, with a craggy face and shaved white hair.

"Colonel Dean Wexhall is the most dangerous man to this agency today. Do you know why?"

Nero looked at it with renewed interest, his eyes scanning the text; taking in the various occupations, history and all the rest.

"I'm shaking with anticipation," he said, dryly.

"Wexhall has established Ghost 13 or G13COMM: a new, combined intelligence and military agency that is to amalgamate the G13UK operation. A big project and ambitious enough to rival our own." Nero whistled. "I had heard of it. This must have come from the top?"

"Pretty much. But it's all coming from a blacker than black budget.

Obviously you know whose feathers this is going to ruffle?"

Nero thought for a moment, looking down at the photo of Wexhall with a deadly serious expression, then looked up at Foster. "The Boy Scouts?" he quipped.

Foster shot him an icy look and tapped the files with her index finger. "Us! The entire fucking CIA. So familiarise yourself with this because you're going into G13COMM as our ears and you will be playing a game. Understood?"

Nero nodded, the smirk long gone.

"Your history will show a clean sheet at one of our partner security companies. When you're in, see what you can find out. We'll keep comms open during that period."

"Who am I gonna be?"

"Don't worry. We will make sure your legend is solid as stone. When you've cleared a few security levels get that data and make sure it's something we can sell."

"Sell? Are we working for the Chinese or the Russians now?"

"Not quite. The target is Rhodes of Liberatus."

"Who?"

Foster leaned over again, catching his eye with the look of a patient mother comforting a confused child. She flipped the page again, revealing a white-haired man in his late fifties or so. It was a photo taken covertly at a traffic junction, as he was about to step into a car.

"He's built an influential alternative media network that is revealing too many close truths across the board. His younger days were spent with MI6, and now he's fishing around his old contacts and trying to set up some intelligence network."

"Paid for by who?"

"We don't know, but that would be one of your tasks when you go in. Find out, but that's not your primary mission. You need to leave a nice trail that will discredit G13COMM. It needs to be blown open using Liberatus as the conduit. Nothing comes back to us. Understood?"

Nero nodded, exhaling slowly, taking it all a lot more seriously.

"When Rhodes contacts you, he'll be wary. You'll have to be convincing, show him some lead gems, a little sample of what you're offering. We'll get you some genuine covert photos to show him. If I was him, I'd have someone else run you around for a while, have you hung out to see if there are any other interested fishes."

"Great, so there's potential for a real-life shooting gallery," muttered Nero.

"When, and only when, you've delivered the payload to Rhodes comes the final act." She paused. "Then you need to take him out."

Chapter 35

Since Frank had left on Saturday morning, Nero had been waiting for the opportunity to hack into Rhodes' computer network to access any files relating to his organisation.

Now, at last, the chance had come. Rhodes had gone on one of his frequent hikes, along with the García brothers. The old man liked to stretch his legs regularly, and Nero had accompanied him once or twice at his invitation.

Nero let himself into the computer ops room with the key he'd seen Rhodes hide inside a book in the kitchen and softly closed the door. He was hoping to find more names of people involved, other locations the group occupied and, specifically, who funded them. That was a secret that had remained behind closed doors for some time.

Nero scanned the room, his attention focusing on one of the computer towers, lights flashing in the gloom.

Need to be quick.

He sat down into one of the chairs, tapping rapid commands onto the keyboard while he listened out for their return.

A noise outside spiked his attention and he jumped up to check through the blinds. He looked to the gate. Nothing. Then noticed an empty beer bottle had rolled off the outside terrace onto the ground.

He quickly returned to his work.

Just killing Rhodes without any access to this information would make it hard work for themselves when following up on any future mission to take down Liberatus. As expected, the files were mostly encrypted. It would be a headache for the geeks back at Langley to nail but that was not his problem right now.

Rhodes had the external network locked down, so Nero had to transfer any interesting files to an external USB flash drive. It was a risk, but he couldn't transmit the data without alerting Rhodes' network. He deleted the log files to hide his trail, then slipped the drive into his pocket and left the room.

Killing Rhodes was simple, Nero surmised as he returned to his guest house. They frequently conversed as the days had passed; he was gaining the old man's trust more and more. But Nero needed to time it perfectly. The García brothers were always around, and neither were at the top of their game as far as he could tell. The other consideration was that it had to appear as an accident. Still, there were numerous possibilities that Nero could think of.

Firstly, the natural option was an automobile accident. Getting access to the cars shouldn't be too difficult.

A second possibility was to get him during the morning walks and hikes. But Rhodes was a cautious man, and his guards were always with him. He knew what he was doing would attract an array of enemies.

Later that morning, Nero strolled onto the terrace, sipping ice tea. From what he could gather, Rhodes had employed the brothers through trusted contacts or he knew their family in some way. It had crossed his mind more than once as to how loyal they might be. Would they fight to the death for their gringo employer? It was an interesting question: one Nero couldn't answer just yet.

Nero took a seat at the small table and watched a pair of grazing horses in a field across the valley.

Poison? Or that zombie drug that Elvira had tried on him back in Las Palmas? Unfortunately Frank had gotten rid of it but if he could get hold of some more? Then he could slip Rhodes some and persuade him to jilt his guards. The old man would be putty in his hands.

Nero sighed. He would mull it over; let it percolate like the excellent Colombian coffee he had been enjoying. No need to rush into a decision, unless it was needed, of course. His training gave him the full confidence that he would succeed. It had been a rough ride getting here. The jungle run came to mind. Yet many bridges of trust had been established with Rhodes and his man, Bowen. Despite the G13COMM-backed muscle that had born down on them, they had survived. All the more reason to take down their little enterprise. Now he felt he was part of some internal clean-up operation. Cutting down internal enemies of the 'State', or people deemed enemies. Working deep against allied agencies. Still not his concern. He would do the job and move on.

He thought about Frank Bowen. The man was a capable opponent. Rough but resourceful and wouldn't be a pushover. He would have had to take care of him too, had he stayed around.

Fortunately, he hadn't, and Nero was glad.

Must be getting soft-hearted, he mused.

Just then Nero caught sight of Rhodes fetching something from his car and thoughts returned once again to the manner of achieving the man's death.

Chapter 36

Frank glanced at Rhodes and Nero through the side-view mirror, standing side by side watching him leave, and a huge rush of relief washed over him. Rhodes had his man and the data and would no doubt use it to throw a few spanners in the machine of the establishment.

Now he just needed to figure out how to deal with Carl. What were the consequences for disobeying him and the British operation of Ghost 13? Should he make up a story, spin a yarn about Nero being snatched from him by Rhodes? If only Carl were that naive to buy it.

Frank focused on the distant hills as the taxi weaved around the narrow streets that headed back into Medellín. There had been no flights available for several days so Frank had decided to stay in the city and look around. But he was also looking forward to getting home. To finally try to deal with all his personal shit and actually be there for his kids when they needed him.

Frank returned to the Laureles area they had previously stayed in and checked into a small hotel. Despite the heightened alertness at the time, he remembered it for its friendly local vibe. The streets were lined with trees and no one bothered him; it seemed to be a place where nothing much happened. Precisely what Frank felt he needed. The early afternoon sunshine, a steady twenty-five degrees in the city of "eternal spring", as it was known, changed into a predictable pattern of thunder and rain in the evening.

After a long delay, the line rang. A tone that sounded distant.

"Hello?"

Frank recognised the voice of his oldest son, Joe.

"Joe? It's your dad."

There was a pause and Frank wasn't sure if it was the line or Joe.

"Dad? Where are you?"

"I'll tell you all about it when I'm back...soon. So have a think about what you'd like to do. Anything you like...football matches, Alton Towers, Disneyland...whatever."

"OK, cool," Joe replied, excitement creeping into his voice.

"I'll see you really soon, Joe. Is your mum there?"

"Yeah, I'll get her."

Another pause, then Maria came on.

"Frank? Thank god. Are you OK?"

"Hi. Yeah, everything's fine. I'll be back soon. Just wanted to let you know."

Frank thought he heard a long sigh of relief.

"So you're coming home?" she asked.

"Yes. We'll work everything out. Don't worry about the money—"

A series of beeps and the line cut.

"Shit!" Frank cursed out loud.

Still, at least he'd spoken to her and Joe.

That night, around ten, Frank took to his bed and slept deeply; a series of images of him missing his flight and unable to get home seared into his dreams.

Chapter 37

Later in the afternoon on Saturday, Nero had driven towards Medellín, a few kilometres, stopping to make a phone call on the way . He then pulled into a supply store to pick up everything he needed. He pushed a trolley around the supermarket-sized store and threw in a spanner kit, pliers and a tubing cutter, then waited in his car.

After an hour of waiting, growing bored, Nero closely watched a Mazda pull up alongside and park. A man with a dark complexion, bearded with cropped hair, wound down his passenger window.

"You got a light, buddy?" he asked.

Nero nodded and got out of his driver seat, slipping into the passenger seat of the Mazda, handing over a lighter.

"Thanks. Zeus comes bearing gifts," he said, sparking his cigarette into life from Nero's lighter.

"Gifts are always gratefully received."

The beard jerked his head slightly and Nero turned to see a black gym bag on the back seat. Nero opened the rear door and took the bag, then returned to his vehicle without another word and drove back to the finca.

***

Frank awoke early and decided to call Carl from a public phone just outside a row of cafes and bars. It was time to face the music.

He grabbed a take-out coffee, then dialled the number for Carl's messaging service and waited, reciting his code number when it answered. There was a series of beeps, the cross Atlantic transfer routine, and Frank looked out onto the street.

A young couple climbed onto a scooter and took off down the road. A blare of Latin pop blasted from a passing taxi. An old torn poster for a Colombian film called *Los asesino* – The Assassin – covered an old brick building that was a half-built unfinished shell.

Carl came directly on the secure line.

"We've been trying to locate you for some time. What is your status?"

"Heading home."

"But we never received the asset."

"The asset is with your love rival, I'm afraid."

There was a pause. Whether it was simmering anger or frustration, Frank couldn't tell.

"You were intercepted?"

"No, I dropped him off."

"For fuck's sake. Milligan!" At least in his outburst Carl retained his legend cover. Another pause, and then a sigh.

"We'll deal with the consequences later. When did you last see Rhodes alive?"

Frank sipped his bitter coffee, frowning with confusion.

"Rhodes, alive? What are you talking about?"

"The asset is a sleeper agent. He's been allowing you to take him to Rhodes for a reason. To drop a certain amount of dangerous information but also to take him out, permanently."

The space around Frank seemed to close in, and he felt his heartbeat quicken.

"What?"

Was this a ruse by Carl? Frank quickly went through the options of what he could gain from this? He wanted Nero, of course, but why label him an assassin?

El asesino.

"I've had word. It's reliable, that's all I can say. He's in immediate danger," Carl said, gravely.

"If you're so sure, why are you telling me?"

"I may not be an angel, but this isn't going to help anyone."

"This isn't one of your games?" Frank asked, his tone increasing with worry.

"I promise you it isn't."

Frank was struggling to believe it. Nero an assassin targeting John, after the hell they'd endured together and the feeling of close camaraderie to have survived it.

Hard to believe, but not impossible.

The understated impression Frank had of Nero was of someone well capable of taking care of himself, not just a geek. A trained individual. He remembered the way he'd seemed calm on the *Anita* when he was grabbed from his room. The way he had handled Elvira out the back of the cafe.

Not the kid he thought he was.

"I'm going back, then," Frank said. The decision made. "This sounds like the real deal."

Carl sighed.

"Yes, and do what you were supposed to do in the first place. You get up there. Bring in the asset to us or get rid of him. It's on you."

***

Nero waited until early the next morning before making his move.

Based on his knowledge of the routines at the finca, he knew the guards would disappear around two or three in the morning. He silently let himself inside the main building and found Rhode's key fob hanging up in the kitchen, then headed over to the stand-alone garage and went inside.

Carefully closing the door behind himself, Nero glanced around inside. The Audi took up most of the space and, against the back wall, a tarpaulin half covered a motorbike, the bottom of the wheel just visible. Several wooden shelves held pots of old paint and jars filled with rusting bolts and screws.

Nero placed his tools and other items down by the front wheels of the Audi and popped his head underneath, facing upwards. He located the brake pipe, took out his spanner and started to loosen the hose. As the connector came loose, brake fluid began spilling out. Quickly Nero pinched the ends together, taking a small cloth to wipe up the liquid. Then he reattached the pipe with electrical tape. This would keep the brakes working initially, without immediately alerting the driver with a loose brake pedal before the inevitable failure.

Next, he got up and opened the driver door, slid inside and put the vehicle into gear. Back underneath he located the primary handbrake cable. He straightened and pulled out the split pin with pliers, then pushed out the clevis pin with a screwdriver. With a firm yank, the cable came free of the handbrake lever.

Now the handbrake would fail also.

Quickly and silently, Nero cleaned up the scene, packing away his tools into a sports bag and erasing any signs of his deed before slipping back out and returning to his guest house.

Inside, Nero closed the door behind him and paused, glancing around the small studio apartment where Rhodes had housed him. He cleared it of all his belongings and took the small training bag of gear he'd used for the car "adjustments" and the gym bag given to him outside the store. In it was a Walther P99 pistol with 9×19mm Parabellum rounds, new travel documents, ID cards as well as bundles of cash in different currencies.

He changed his clothing and cleaned up the guesthouse, removing any sign that someone had stayed there; folding up the bedsheets and pillowcases and bagging them to take away. He had been there too long for a thorough clean up, but fewer questions would be asked if it looked unoccupied. It was highly unlikely the Colombian police would carry out a forensic sweep of the property following a car crash involving a gringo. Most likely they'd file a report and follow the standard procedures related to automobile accidents; if they even bothered at all.

Nero wiped down the taps, door handles and surfaces anyway, then left with the bags and placed them in the boot of his hire car. He drove out along the curving track and pulled off the road in behind a patch of trees on a piece of scrubland. He had already carried out reconnaissance of the area earlier and pinpointed it as a hidden spot to watch the track entrance to Rhode's place.

Nero checked his watch. 5.30 A.M.

Even on a Sunday, routine in the Rhodes household usually kicked off around seven, so he estimated he'd have enough time to get into position to monitor and follow to check it all went smoothly. Then he waited, as the dawn broke.

Rhodes and his guards would expect Nero's vehicle to have gone that early as he'd already mentioned wanting to go for a morning hike knowing full well that Rhodes had other commitments and wouldn't join him.

Just after 7.30 the white Audi appeared and headed up the hill on his usual routine drive to visit his wife and boy. Troy, his five-year-old son, went to a playgroup with other local kids.

Nero pulled out and followed at a distance.

The route had been studied by Nero closely, explicitly looking for brake points or areas where the vehicle would be at maximum danger. The snaking roads led to a long, steep decline and a high probability of a fatal crash once the speed built after they reached the hill. From his observations Nero had noted that one of Rhodes' Colombian guards who drove, didn't exactly hold back on the gas.

Rhode's vehicle sped up the hill, around the bends that hugged the lush green hills. There was no way of estimating how soon the brake pipe would fail but the car continued up to the crest of the mountain and the descent beyond. Nero increased his speed to keep them in sight.

He needed visual confirmation of the accident, the kill.

The Audi turned out of sight. As it was the weekend, there was no heavy traffic. Their car was descending now, picking up speed. Nero reached the crest, checking his speedometer. They were reaching 120kph. The hazard lights came on, followed by a blaring horn.

The Audi overtook a slower van, narrowly missing an oncoming truck as it increased speed. It disappeared around another bend. When Nero had rounded the corner, the Audi weaved into the middle of the road and at the sight of an oncoming truck overcompensated by swerving too far.

There was a loud crunching bang as the Audi careened along a house wall, then smashed into a stationary car, spinning on impact. It flipped over onto its roof and slid to a standstill. The whole incident was over in less than ten seconds.

Nero reached the accident scene and pulled to a halt. He knew he had to act quickly. They were in an area with a few houses alongside the road. He saw the truck in the rear view slow, then stop, having seen the accident.

Nero grabbed his bag and ran to the upturned Audi. He bent down and peered through a cracked window.

Where the hell was Rhodes?

Just the two of his guards. Both were unconscious but alive.

Nero pulled out a small pack and a hammer. He broke in the window on one side and glanced up the hill. The driver, in a straw cowboy style hat, had jumped down from his cab and looked down at the scene. Nero pulled out a small zip-up bag and took out a syringe filled with potassium chloride and saline water solution; fatal for the heart. He jabbed it into the driver's neck and injected. Then he moved around the other side and carried out the same process. The driver was walking down at a fast pace but not running. Once the injections kicked in, both men would be dead. Any post-mortem would show heart failure for both of them. Not perfect, but it would have to do.

Nero would need to move fast.

He stood up and waved at the driver who was a few metres away.

"I think they're both dead. I'll go and get help," Nero shouted in Spanish. The truck driver looked shocked. He nodded and stared at the smoking vehicle. He knew the driver would likely disappear when Nero had left. Hanging around at a car accident for the policia to come and interrogate you was not a wise move in Colombia.

Nero jumped back into his car, turned it around and headed back towards the *finca* to go hunt down Rhodes.

***

Frank was running along across the main road, beelining for a gas station with a garage set just behind it as he held the phone to his ear, willing Rhodes to pick up.

Shit!

Rhodes still wasn't picking up. The call went to answer message again.

"John! Call me when you get this. Be wary of Nero. I've got good intel he may be out to harm you."

Frank hung up and arrived at the garage, walking up to one of the young mechanics.

"You have a car I can rent?" he asked quickly, in Spanish. The mechanic pointed to an older man standing by a VW Beetle with its rear boot open.

"My boss can help you."

Frank asked the boss the same question who glanced and gestured at a light blue Ford Aspire.

Frank looked at him with an expression of pain.

"Nothing faster?"

Twenty minutes Frank was heading as fast as the Aspire would go, back up through Envigado into the steep hills that towered overhead.

Chapter 38

Earlier that morning, John Rhodes showered, poured himself a coffee and noticed he was low on milk, not to mention bread and other basics. He made a mental note to call the García brothers before sitting down in front of his laptop on the kitchen table. The large windows overlooked the valley of Medellín, and he watched a small bi-plane come in from the east, appearing momentarily through the darkening clouds before it descended over the city towards Olaya Herrera Airport. His plan to take his young son, Troy, to the playgroup had to be aborted after a sleepless night of feverish hell. Whether it was a virus or from too much exertion, he wasn't sure, but it was bad enough for him to have to call off his plans. Instead, he had sent the García brothers to collect his wife, Evelyn, and Troy.

He picked up his mobile phone to call Santiago, one of the brothers. Those men had been reliable and dependable after Rhodes had disappeared into the mists of South America after the Pandora Red episode. A new start for his family and, thanks to help from his increasingly wealthy brother, Michael, a good set-up on the outskirts of Medellín.

The family home was separate for a reason. Close but far enough apart to keep his family out of harm's way, at least in theory. All his intelligence business took place at the finka. The comings and goings of his contacts or in the case of his recent coup, Nero, a place for them to work in safety, out of range from the ears and eyes of potential enemies. Through his network he had befriended an old Colombian family who had children at Troy's school. They had, like many other Colombians in Medellín, been brought up under the reign of Pablo Escobar. They were tough but smart and just wanted to make the best of their lives. Rhodes had offered two of the brothers, Santiago and Diego, the work of guarding him and keeping him safe. Rhodes knew enemies could always be potentially within reach.

The call connected.

"Santiago?"

"Señor Rhodes? We're just on our way."

"*Hola!* It's OK. I just called to check if you can buy some milk and bread on the way back?"

"Sure, no problem—"

There was a pause and a shout in the background.

"What's happening?"

"The car has no brakes! They don't work at all. I don't know if we can—"

There was a blaring horn in the background. More indistinguishable shouts.

"*¡Cuidado! el camión!*"

Rhodes could only listen in horror as they narrowly missed a truck.

"Santiago?" he shouted. No response.

There was a loud clunk as if the phone dropped onto the floor of the car. More muffled sounds and shouts.

"*El freno de mano está muerto!*"

Then a sound of screeching tyres, a loud bang and the line cut off.

Rhodes re-dialled the number with shaking fingers. A sickening feeling rolled in his stomach. They had crashed, no doubt.

No connection.

Rhodes hauled himself out of his chair to go and get dressed. He'd need to call a taxi. Go find them. The feeling of fever was pushed well out of his mind by concern for the brothers. As he went to his phone to call their family to go and see, it rang in his hand.

Unrecognised number.

Tempted to cut it off, Rhodes then decided otherwise and answered.

"*Hola.*"

"John. It's Mr Milligan."

Rhodes was relieved. It was Frank!

"Hey, I thought you were on a flight? Listen, something terrible has happened to Santiago and Diego. They were in a car accident. I just heard it while speaking to them."

"Why? What happened exactly?"

"I don't know; something about the brakes not working. Then I heard a loud crash."

"Alright, listen to me very carefully. I'm almost certain Nero is a Trojan horse. I spoke to Paterson. He found something; Nero is on a deeper mission to take you out!"

"What?"

Rhodes felt a rush of fear. Not only had he been tricked, but he'd also almost trusted Nero enough to let him in the whole way to their network.

"Are you sure?"

"I'm pretty sure. And now this accident."

"Then the car brakes?"

"Were meant for you. Probably. Were you supposed to be in that car?"

"I. Shit, yes, yes, I was," Rhodes replied.

"Right. Is he there at the finca?"

Rhodes shook his head. "No, no. He left. I saw him leave."

"Thank God! Right, as soon as he realises you're not in the car, he'll come back. You need to hide, get out of there. I'm on my way, but it's another forty minutes from here."

"Right, right," Rhodes started to look around, his mind racing. If he phoned the García family, they might be put at risk. He didn't want Nero rolling in and killing any more of his people.

"Goddammit!" he shouted, his fear forgotten, anger and frustration rising. The deeper he went, the more scumbags came out of the woodwork. Still, it only served to focus his resolve.

Always had.

He went to the window and looked up the driveway. It was quiet but too risky to head up that way. He needed to make for the hills.

"Alright, Frank. I'm going to take off into the hills to the north."

"I need to meet you somewhere. I need location!" Frank barked, the line breaking up.

Rhodes thought for a moment.

"OK, at *La Catedral* prison. It's on the map. There's a road that goes up to it, but I can reach it through a track in the hills."

"Alright. Do you have a weapon?"

"Yes, yes. I can get one, but—"

"OK, get it and move fast and I'll meet you there. Be careful, John!"

Chapter 39

Nero parked in his previous spot, behind the trees and scrubland opposite the track that led to Rhode's farmhouse. He took his bag and weapon, then walked toward the gates.

Had Rhodes been alerted or not?

It was possible he'd somehow heard of the crash and become suspicious. Nero cursed himself for his mistake. He should have put himself in a place where he could see who was actually inside the vehicle before following and wasting all that time.

It didn't matter anyhow. He would find the old man and finish the job. At least those brothers guarding him were out of the way.

Nero came to the gates and wall that sectioned off the property. He scaled the wall with relative ease, then looked around inside. The main house was seemingly devoid of life and the guest house that Nero had stayed in was also quiet.

He jumped down on the far side and remained in a half crouch, looking around before heading to the main building and checking the door. It was locked. He edged around the house, peering through any gaps in the blinds and curtains.

No sign.

Nero took out his pistol, went back to the door and smashed the butt of his gun through the glass, breaking it with a sharp crack. He reached in to unlock the door from the inside, then slowly pushed it open, across the shards of glass on the floor. Nero moved into the corridor, weapon now poised.

He edged into the kitchen, a smell of coffee still lingering and spotted the source; a mug and coffee pot on the kitchen table. He doubled back and checked the living room and the back room that served as the computer centre.

Creeping up the stairs, he kept his weapon aimed directly in front of him and edged around the corners, confirming each of the bedrooms and bathroom were empty.

Rhodes was gone.

Had he been alerted? Taken off somewhere? His guards had taken his only car. Unless he had been picked up by someone? The timeline from the guards leaving, the crash and Nero returning was just over an hour. If he had been picked up, that would mean he'd have arranged it pretty quickly, even if he did know about the accident. No, it seemed more likely Rhodes had left on foot. He was a keen hiker and knew the various tracks around the forests reasonably well, but if he needed somewhere to hide, where would he go?

Nero left the house and checked the guest house where he had been staying. All clean and empty as he had left it.

La Catedral? It was within walking distance. Not easy through those rocky paths but an option. Had he overheard Rhodes mention it to Frank at some point?

Nero was undecided.

Track him on foot or—

He moved across the manicured lawn and let himself into the garage. The motorbike was still under the sheet. After rummaging around for a few minutes, he located the keys hanging up and set about getting it started.

***

Rhodes walked hastily along the rocky path, coming to a fast-moving stream with dispersed rocks that he carefully navigated across. He had run into the nearby forest. Heading to the road risked coming face to face with Nero coming the other way. Much easier to hide in amongst the natural chaos. His plan, in this panicked last-minute dash away from danger, was to head to the beginnings of another road across the hills, around twelve kilometres away. He'd done it before, in about three hours, then he would call Frank from the mobile he'd taken.

After that, God only knows, thought Rhodes. He had been badly exposed. All his precautions had counted for nothing. A Trojan horse, an enemy of the most dangerous kind. Rhodes had spent the entire previous year setting up his hideaway and taking every precaution he knew to keep his whereabouts secret. The new identity, with all the corresponding fake information required to make it credible. But they had found him, through his own idiotic stupidity.

Lessons would have to be learned. If he ever survived this.

Then a horrifying thought came to him. His family at the other house. Maybe Nero wasn't even going to try to return to find him? Perhaps somehow he had found out the secret of his wife and son's location.

He had to move faster. But it would be hours before he got in any position to do anything. He tried his phone again, but the signal was weak and cut out intermittently.

Should he turn back and return to the finca? Try and flag down a car or phone Frank to change the plan or call the García family for help?

Rhodes stopped and took a swig from the water bottle he'd hurriedly snatched before wiping his brow, glancing down at the stream behind him. He decided against it. Getting back and then to the main road would take just as long.

Goddamnit!!

He moved off again at a half-jog as his journey became more urgent, panting loudly as the path became steeper, lined with hazardous tree roots and rocks jutting out of the dry soil. In his haste a loose rock dislodged his foot and a sharp pain shot through his ankle.

Shit!

He stumbled, then stopped, leaning over with his hands on his legs, panting. He wanted to shout out in pain, in frustration, but the risk of giving away his location stopped him dead.

"Well done, John. Well done, mate," he muttered under his breath before hobbling on up the path.

***

When he finally got onto the home run within five kilometres of the RV point, Frank tried calling Rhodes again but couldn't get through at all. He would have to trust that Rhodes could make it on his own. His wasn't exactly a young man, Frank thought. He followed narrow, steep roads for several kilometres, then came to a junction that had two houses and some shack-turned-bar that overlooked Medellín. Frank asked a local woman for directions and then continued up the winding *Caldra–Envigado* road until he found the gates of the old prison, *La Catedral*.

He parked outside, got out of his car and looked around. It was quiet.

He moved inside the gates that had been wrenched open, walked down a slope towards a half-sized concrete football pitch with small goalposts and nets where Pablo Escobar had invited the Colombian football team to play with him. There were remnants of furnishings scattered over the ground; a smashed china sink, taps, tiles that appeared to have been stripped and carried out. Overlooking the pitch on his left side were small buildings with steps leading up to a terrace wall, the windows smashed.

He crept along the wall and moved up the steps until he was on a terrace. He peeked through one of the building windows. There had been a large living quarters here, with remnants of the luxury that Escobar had once lived in, stripped since his death.

Frank checked around the back of the building and then returned to the terrace. From that spot he could see an old helicopter pad set lower down the hill, beyond it the golden hills spreading outwards towards another panoramic view of the Envigado enclave of Medellín, partly obscured by a mist that had begun to rise.

There was no sign of Rhodes. How long could Frank wait here?

Frank headed back down to the football pitch, along a walkway with other single-level buildings; all empty and trashed. He passed narrow steps leading down to the helipad and continued on round, past an old guard tower to a wide track that led into the jungle.

That would be the direction Rhodes would come.

Frank walked down the path, thick with trees on one side, the same expansive view of the golden hills as from the helipad on the other.

Frank half jogged down the track until it narrowed and split; the path heading down a slope would be the route Rhodes would come.

After around ten minutes Frank heard a rustling noise ahead and hid behind a nearby line of rocks and waited.

A distinct footfall, slow and lumbering, came nearer. It was Rhodes, holding a makeshift staff, limping.

Frank stepped out to show himself. Rhodes' face turned from surprise to relief.

"Thank God!"

Frank went over, checking his leg.

"Are you hurt?"

"Ah, just slipped and twisted the old ankle, it's slowed me down a bit, but he's back there somewhere, Frank. I know he is."

Frank took a look down the track, then back up to the way he had come.

"Alright, we'd better get moving as fast as we can." He went to help Rhodes, but the older man waved his stick ahead. "I'll be alright. Just keep eyes behind."

"Did you get a weapon?" Frank asked.

"Yeah, I got it." He held out a Glock 17 for Frank to take.

"Good. I think we're going to need it."

Chapter 40

As they approached *La Catedral*, the dark silhouette of the old guard tower loomed against a swirling grey sky. Heavy raindrops began to fall, splattering against the plants and ground before slowly turning to a steady cascade that soaked them both to the skin.

They moved onto the concrete path towards the first row of buildings. Frank had been keeping most of his focus behind but now had to be wary of what lay in the old prison grounds. Squinting from the raindrops running down into his eyes, Frank moved cautiously, aiming the Glock ahead at potential ambush points as they edged forward. He signalled Rhodes to stay close.

The first doorway led into a small space which looked like it had been a chapel, the remnants of wooden pews covered in dust and a stone statue of the Virgin Mary on a small altar. The roof had partially collapsed, and the rain now formed pools of water on the floor. Frank moved into the vestry, a small confined space at the back. He carefully opened another door and saw it led to the other side of the building.

They moved on, Frank methodically checking each potential hiding space.

The further they went in, past broken windows and dozens of blind spots, the more he realised it was looking like a turkey shoot. He didn't like it.

The pounding rain disguised their footfall at least, thought Frank. But it also would mask Nero's. The more rooms and buildings Frank cleared, the more his senses told him Nero was playing ghosts.

Rhodes' limp seemed to be getting worse. If they were in a situation where moving fast was required, it would be over. And, as Frank knew only too well, being stationary or slow heightened the chances of being killed.

Got to keep moving.

Rhodes limped ahead and Frank turned to check their rear; a gap on his right revealed the steps leading up to other buildings further up the hill. A light thud sound cut through the rain. Frank turned to see Rhodes had slipped down onto the pathway by a door.

Another thud.

Gunfire.

Frank dived to the ground.

Where was it coming from?

He belly-crawled over to Rhodes, who had frozen in place.

"It's him." Frank gestured with his hand. Rhodes began crawling back to Frank and the gap between the two buildings.

"Where is he?" Rhodes rasped. Frank glimpsed around the corner where Rhodes had slipped for any clue, then turned back.

"I think he's up in those buildings." Frank jerked his head in the direction of the single-storey buildings up the hill, out of sight from their position.

Rhodes propped himself up against the wall; pain etched on his face.

Frank wondered briefly why the hell he had to hurt his ankle at a time like this but kept his mouth shut. The only thing to do was for Rhodes to hole up somewhere while he hunted down Nero. He looked around and remembered the first building. The chapel.

"Alright, let's retrace our steps."

They headed back, knowing Nero was up in the higher buildings enabled them to move as fast as they could with Rhode's swollen ankle. Back inside, Frank had another look around. Alongside the pews was an old wooden table on its side and sheets of corrugated metal resting against the wall.

"Hide somewhere so you can see this doorway and window." He pointed at the space they had come through. There's another exit if you need it. I wish we had two weapons—"

Rhodes eased himself down on a pew. "He could've killed me at any time," Rhodes muttered.

"He needed it to be an accident, but I'm not sure he'll care, now." Frank was looking through an arched doorway to another space next to the altar. "Think Escobar prayed here, John?" Rhodes snorted as if he couldn't care less.

Frank gestured to him. "Alright, in here. Quick!"

Rhodes hobbled inside.

"You can see the door and window from here." Frank was standing at the doorway. "And there's an escape route." He pointed at another doorless space that led to the opposite side at the back then walked out into the main area. Rhodes followed him out as Frank pulled up the old table and quietly shifted it along to the doorway, leaning it upright to act as a block to that entrance. Then he grabbed the few concrete blocks on the ground and placed them against the underside of the table, while Rhodes took the corrugated iron, adding to the barricade.

"Won't last too long, but it'll buy you a few precious seconds."

"Keep an eye on both. He could come either way."

"So you're taking off on holiday?"

Frank checked his Glock. "Yeah, hear it's better food down south." He patted Rhodes on the shoulder and caught his eye, face deadly serious.

"I'm going to get him. If anything happens to me, you've got a clear run back into the woods. Just stay hidden and don't make a sound. We'll go with 'high' and 'five' to identify each other. Is that clear?

Rhodes nodded. "High—"

"Five," Frank finished.

"Thanks, Frank."

"Thank me when this shit storm is over."

Frank moved back outside via the more hidden rear exit, assuming a firing position as he headed along the exterior wall. At a gap between the buildings, he switched back to the main path, continuing in the same direction. The rain was coming down in torrential waves now. Frank duck-walked along the edge of the building back to their previous position within sight of the steps leading up the hill directly ahead. He carefully edged a quick look around the corner, but the visibility was almost zero. Nero must have the steps covered. It would be suicidal to take that route – had to find another way.

On the wooden door frame where Rhodes had slipped and narrowly avoided being shot, Frank saw the bullet holes. He was or had been on their left flank, up in the buildings that hung overhead, looking down on them from the hill and Medellín beyond.

Frank, half-crouched, moved around the building, back towards the path from the forest they had come through. He then cut back toward the prison grounds and headed back through the trees, up to a hill towards the buildings. He kept his eyes peeled ahead, glancing down at the ground to see if there were any tracks left by Nero.

What the hell had happened? How had he got ahead?

He shook the questions from his mind, treading through the undergrowth as he ascended the hill, pistol aimed ahead. The rain had begun to ease, the distant roar fading as Frank reached the peak to face the old red brick building that had once 'imprisoned' the most famous narco in the world. He edged his way to the rear, as far back as he could go before a mound of rock formed a sheer cliff reaching into the grey sky.

With his pistol continuously covering the edges of each wall against potential fire, Frank traversed and secured most of the east side but inside the buildings was another matter. Down to his right, he could see the single-storey blocks, with the church building at the end, where Rhodes was hopefully still hiding. Beyond the wall, steps and helipad lay the Colombian panorama, its vibrant green vista dulled by the dying rain.

Suddenly, a bullet whistled past him; the concentration of his effort shattered. He dropped fast and took a glance along the line. An exposed window, and a flicker of movement. Frank fired a burst, then leapt forward, closing the space to a pile of rubble and fell behind it. After a few seconds he rummaged around and grabbed a clump of loose concrete.

With a quick flick of the arm, he tossed it at the roof of the building. The concrete crashed into the tiles, causing a cascade of movement. Frank jumped to his feet, covering the final few metres to reach the wall of the second building next to the window, and slammed against it. He peered over the sill of the window and through the space of the glassless frame with the barrel of the Glock scanning the inside. A distant noise of shifting rubble caught his attention. Frank knew Nero had moved on and was no longer in the room. He opened the rusty window and proceeded to take a good look inside to check before hauling himself through.

Inside, Frank barely noticed the large, spacious area had been stripped of anything of value. He aimed his barrel and edged forward to a pair of double doors at the far end. Beyond, the floors caught the light from some unseen window. The rain had completely stopped now, leaving Frank feeling naked and exposed from the lack of covering noise.

He carefully moved forward to the side of the doors, lowered himself to his haunches and listened for any hint of Nero's position. However, all he could hear was the distant sound of birdsong from the surrounding trees. Frank edged his barrel around the doorframe into another space, a smashed-in window on the far wall revealing itself as the source of the exterior sounds and an upturned table.

Frank checked his arc of fire, left, right then moved inside in short sprints to the table, then swiftly moved again to the exterior window.

No sign. Frank began to worry.

He looked down to the church and decided to head back. There was a sudden bang, like wood hitting the ground punctured the air from the direction of the church.

Rhodes!

Frank descended quickly down the steps to the lower buildings in a trot. He moved along the bottom of the hill towards the rear of the church, then cut through a side alley to the main path.

Another crunch, a shifting of wood as if the barricade was being ripped apart.

The bastard had outmanoeuvred him.

Running at full pelt now, Frank caught sight of Nero as he climbed through the doorway of the church. Too late for a shot.

As he reached the exterior of the church wall, Frank slowed to a halt, crouched low just by the doorway. The barricade had been breached. The table top was shoved aside.

If Rhodes was still in there, he was dead.

With a sharp exhale, Frank swung his aim inside. He saw a glimpse of Nero's black shirt as he moved through the interior doorway of the vestry and fired a shot, bursting open a cloud of debris on the stone wall. He didn't hesitate and moved fast, straight to the wall he'd just shot. A light scrape sounded outside the rear door through the vestry.

With another swift move Frank stepped into the vestry room where Rhodes should have been hiding.

Except he wasn't.

Must have run out the back and now Nero is right on him.

Frank was about to go out after them but decided to go back to the front and pincer Nero. When he got to the door, he saw Nero crouched by the bottom of the guard tower aiming in his direction. He jumped back just as a bullet whizzed past the door.

He crouched low, pointed a blind aim and fired back in his general direction, then moved back inside and looked up to the collapsed ceiling leading to the roof.

Low enough.

He tucked his Glock into his belt, stepped onto the table that had been shoved aside, grabbed the exposed metal joists and hauled himself up with both arms. With a swing of the legs he was quickly on top of the chapel flat roof. He retrieved his pistol, got down on his front and crawled along to a decorated parapet with holes on the edge

Nero had moved to the right side of the tower, anticipating Frank to come at him from the rear of the chapel, then he glanced back down into the woods behind him, where Rhodes must have headed. Nero moved his focus back onto the chapel.

He apparently wanted to deal with Frank first.

Frank aimed for his body mass, taking his time, and squeezed the trigger. Yet Nero moved just as the hammer fell and the shot missed by a fraction but the bullet still caught the top of Nero's thigh, sending him reeling and stumbling to the ground.

There's another nice flesh wound for you, mate.

Alerted to Frank's new position, Nero returned a shot but it was way off, then he rolled across the ground in an attempt to hide. Frank fired again, hitting the metal skeleton of the guard tower.

Peeping through the parapet holes, Frank saw Nero hobbling away in the direction of the jungle path.

Run, you bastard, run.

Frank stood up, then leapt down the twelve feet or so to the ground, landing on his haunches. He scurried in a half crouch over to the tower, then sighted on Nero just as he crawled into a wall of the jungle behind a group of trees. Frank jogged to the edge of the trees on the same side, melting into the foliage, then set about stalking his wounded prey.

Step by step, he inched closer, gaining on his target fast. He caught glimpses of Nero moving away from him, just a few steps ahead now. Through a gap in the trees, Frank saw space in the vegetation and ran hard, then dived, tackling Nero around the waist with one arm and grabbing his pistol arm with the other. Both men hit the muddy ground with a jolt and a shout of pain.

Nero tried to roll Frank off, but his free arm was being jerked behind his back with lightning speed. Frank adjusted his stance and planted a knee onto his lower spine. Another grunt of pain.

"Release your weapon."

There was a pause, then Nero slowly loosened his grip on the pistol.

Just then, Frank heard a noise and looked up to see Rhodes appear through a cluster of jungle plants.

"Grab his gun!" Frank rasped.

Rhodes did so and pointed it down at their new prisoner. Frank rolled off, stood up and pulled out his pistol to train on Nero. Rhodes stepped forward and booted Nero in the waist.

"Aaargh!"

"You fucking killed my friends, you little shit!" Rhodes' voice was full of venom. He looked across at Frank. "Let's just kill him and leave him here with all the other ghosts."

He looked like he meant it.

Frank ignored him and jerked his pistol at Nero. "Get on your hands and knees." Then, to Rhodes, "keep an eye on him, I gotta search him." A patch of dark red was spreading through his combat trousers. "And check that wound."

Frank found no other weapons or knives and allowed Nero to bandage his wound with a piece of ripped shirt. Nero looked up and offered Frank a thin smile. "So, you decided to come back, huh, mate?"

"Just for you. We figured out your game, Nero or whoever the fuck you are. Is it CIA?"

"Does it matter? You think any intelligence agency would tolerate an organisation like G13COMM coming into existence?"

"Screwed up all your plans?"

Nero sneered. "Not mine. I don't personally give a flying fuck." His breathing quickened, spitting out the words, his face winching from pain, "The big sharks upstairs care though; a lot. I do the work required; used to be terrorists but I guess we're in a new era and some cleaning up phase; pinpointing internal enemies."

"You mean like my organisation? Publishing news you don't like?" said Rhodes, with contempt.

"Bullshit news and building whatever the hell the network is you're building with your survivalist buddies, Mr Rhodes?"

"I guess being candid with the truth would be beyond the pale for the likes of your type."

Nero flashed him a look of disdain.

"Let's go!" said Frank, levelling the weapon at Nero. He struggled to his feet and they walked slowly through to a small football field, Nero ahead with his hands raised, Frank behind while Rhodes stayed back. Frank turned his head. "John, you OK to drive? I don't want to give him any chances."

"Yes, I can drive. What are we doing with him?" Rhodes whispered.

It was a good point. Frank was now swimming in an unknown sea. Could he get Carl to help? He had a double agent on his hands, as well as effectively being one himself. His employers would want him back and what would happen to Frank or Rhodes?

Nero was now a few more steps ahead.

"Do you think your place is safe?" It was a rhetorical question. It was impossible to know. Certainly, Nero must have had plenty of chances while staying to update his employers on his location.

"No, but I know where we can take him until we get this sorted out," Rhodes replied.

They reached the car. "In the front," Frank ordered Nero. Frank quickly slipped into the rear seat just behind him, while Rhodes eased himself into the driver seat.

They headed back to the winding road, past sporadic houses that were perfectly positioned for views across the valley. Glimpses of Medellín appeared through the rain clouds that moved overhead. The narrow road widened until they came to the main route back to the city, joining the main flow of traffic. They drove in silence, the sound of pattering rain and the squeaking wipers frantically clearing an arched view through the windscreen that was steaming up.

Rhodes wound down his window halfway and rubbed a circle of condensation away from the screen. As they gathered speed, Nero suddenly pulled the handbrake, causing a screech of the tyres and the vehicle to slide at an angle on the wet Tarmac.

"What the—" Rhodes shouted, struggling to control the vehicle as it nearly collided with oncoming traffic.

Simultaneously, Nero slammed his seat back against Frank, pinning his legs, then half turned to grab Frank's wrist with the pistol pulling Frank forward while twisting his arm.

Rhodes slammed the brakes, too hard, sending the car careering across the road. It skidded side on against the flow of oncoming traffic. A speeding vehicle clipped the rear end of their Ford Aspire, sending it spinning until it hit a concrete post on the edge of the road with a loud crack.

The gun flew out of Frank's hand, bouncing off the edge of the passenger window, then out onto the road. He cracked his forehead on the seat in front and fell back dazed.

Through his confusion, he sensed the passenger door open. Rhodes lunged for Nero and missed. Frank saw the shadow of Nero move across the rain-washed window, then the weapon rose, pointing at Rhodes.

With all the strength he could summon, he slammed open the door hard against Nero who fell back onto the road but managed to keep on his feet. Frank began moving out of the car and saw Nero steady himself, raising the pistol toward his head.

A loud horn, screeching like the bellowing of frenzied cattle.

Nero turned to see the oncoming truck, but it was too late. His body fell under the huge engine grill and wheels with a dull thud as if mown down by a freight train.

The truck wheels screamed as the brakes locked, sending it turning across the road.

Another loud collision of metal as another car narrowly avoided crashing into it, only to careen into the vehicle in front.

The truck continued braking with a piercing screech until it came to a halt in a cloud of smoke.

Frank looked back at the road in front of him, the crumpled, bloody corpse of Nero lay twisted across the wet Tarmac.

"Jesus!"

Both ends of the road now had stationary cars that had come to an abrupt halt.

Frank leaned down, peering into the car.

"John! You ok, mate?"

Rhodes peered across at the carnage in the road, his face frozen in shock.

"We've gotta get out of here. Head to your friend's place on foot," Frank said, loud and clear.

Rhodes continued to stare at him, still seemingly paralysed.

"Come on, John. Move!"

The shout cut through, stirring him into action and he pushed open his door and clambered out of the car.

They moved across the road and Frank leaned down over Nero, his breathing shallow as he searched the wet red pockets.

"Wish it could've been so different, mate," he whispered.

He felt something and pulled out a USB flash drive.

"Thought so," he said, quietly.

"Come on!" It was John, by the side of the road, now fully alert to the risk of hanging around.

Frank jogged over and they both disappeared into the trees, away from the honking horns and growing sound of distant sirens.

Chapter 41

Frank, Rhodes and the García brothers' mother and father were sitting at a table, littered with coffee mugs, ashtrays and a bottle of Aguardiente, on the veranda of their house looking out across acres of farmland. Two chestnut horses grazed nearby. An idyllic scene in direct contrast with what Frank and Rhodes had been through hours before.

The mother broke out into sporadic tears as the father fought his grief with continuous coffee, booze and cigarettes, his face fixed with shell shock. They had only recently heard of their sons' deaths in a terrible car accident.

A young boy, no older than five, played with his trucks on the living room floor, oblivious to the grief that cast gloom over the household.

Rhodes leaned forward clasping his hands together, his own shock from earlier events erased by concern for them, and offered words of comfort. Their daughter, early twenties with jet black hair and light skin, looked equally forlorn as she bandaged Frank's forehead, then proceeded to check his other scrapes and bruises.

"*Gracias,*" he kept saying, unsure of how to console her.

The father's phone rang, and he spoke for a few moments in Spanish before ending the call.

"My sons are at the morgue. I need to go and make arrangements.

Please make yourselves at home." He looked over at his daughter. "Valentina will make up the guest room if you need it."

"Thank you, Mateo. We won't stay long," John said, gratefully.

"Stay as long as you like, but get your wife and kid here. It'll be safer," Mateo added. He patted John on the shoulder. "Please be our guests. You were very kind to our sons. And the man responsible is dead, yes?"

"Yes, he certainly is."

The father nodded, his expression becoming cold as stone. "*Muy Bien.*"

*****

Later in the evening Frank and Rhodes found themselves alone on the veranda as the evening closed in, sipping on their drinks. The rain had long dispersed as the sun set behind the far lush green hills.

"So what have we got?" Frank asked.

"Two good men dead. I hoped it wouldn't come to this."

Frank shuffled in his chair and nodded. "I still can't believe Nero—"

"His story was watertight. None of us could have seen that coming. I screwed up and nearly compromised the whole of Liberatus. What a mess." Rhodes shook his head and drained his glass.

Frank reached into his pocket and handed over the flash drive he had taken from Nero on the road.

"Before I forget. This is probably Liberatus data he was trying to steal."

Rhodes took it. "Thanks, Frank. That was fast thinking."

Frank leaned back, observing Rhodes with relief. "Well, you're still alive, thank God. You believe that he was CIA?"

"Certainly not officially sanctioned, that's for sure. But it makes sense. It has to be a small unit deep inside, operating without any remit to the official hierarchy," Rhodes mused.

"As bad as G13COMM, huh?" Frank said, laughing without humour.

"They fucking deserve each other. If they were out to protect the citizens, well, I wouldn't hate them so much. After all, I was MI6 once. But they're not. They serve their own interests, the military–industrial complex and that of their masters. They are run by psychopaths." Rhodes leaned over to the bottle of Aguardiente, offered Frank another who declined, and poured himself another one.

"I'm sure they have good people too."

"I'm sure." Rhodes snorted, "Well, the red dots will be circling our heads soon enough. We'll both need to lie low," Rhodes added, ominously.

Frank sighed. "So, I need to look over my shoulder."

"You'll be alright. Nero is dead. That female assassin is dead. You're a formidable force to be reckoned with. Your legends were solid from my end, but I can't vouch for Carl, of course."

Frank studied his empty glass. Another loose end he'd need to tie up. Still, he'd done what Paterson had wanted. Turned Nero into roadkill on the Tarmac. The vision of the carnage on the road flashed into his mind and he reached for the bottle.

"And the paramilitaries we came against, in the pay of G13COMM, no doubt."

"Can't be certain, but it makes sense. They wanted Nero dead for all the milk he was about to spill."

"You have all the data he gave you secured?"

Rhodes smiled. "Don't worry, Frank. I know what I'm doing on that front. Yes, it's secure. I made a call to get the farm thoroughly 'cleaned'." He glanced at his watch. "Should be nearly done."

"What are you going to do with it? The data, I mean?"

"Well, I'm going to be very careful right now, Frank. Very careful indeed." Rhodes sucked in air through his teeth. "Right now, it's leverage, that's all. But, if needed, it might serve a purpose."

"Hmm, very cryptic, John."

"What now?" Frank asked, sipping on the anise-flavoured liqueur.

Rhodes sighed and leaned back in his recliner, staring out at the misty haze.

"Well, it's over. I'll get your last payment organised, as arranged." He turned to look at Frank. "The car. We left it at the scene."

"Yeah, don't worry. I hired it under the alias you gave me. It'll lead nowhere, so I'll need a new one if you can arrange it?"

Rhodes nodded.

"I could use the one Carl gave me, but it might be a risk," added Frank.

Rhodes shook his head. "No, don't risk it. You don't know if it's compromised or what the bloody hell is going on between Ghost 13 in the UK and the CIA. Mateo has contacts here. We'll get you sorted out so you can get back home."

"What are you going to do?"

"I'll move on but stay in South America. It's easier to get lost here, stay under the radar."

"Just make sure you do. You're gonna have to be more careful than ever."

John sighed. "I know, I know."

Chapter 42

G13COMM. Colorado air base.

In the series of barren, dark cubicles, illuminated only by the fluorescent ceiling lights, the G13COMM teams working on Operation Darkwood hunched over their desks. Colonel Wexhall walked briskly along the corridor that joined them together, glancing through the glass of each one with a stony glare.

Nero and his handler, whoever the guy was, had slipped his grasp, gotten clean away and he needed to resume the trail. First, his own men had screwed up on the ship. Then the AUC couldn't even deal with them in their own damned jungle.

Wexhall entered his private office and paced around the room. He stared at the blank wall at the back. He should get a big painting up there, a battle scene and a damned glorious one. The phone rang. It was the encrypted internal line.

"Colonel Wexhall? It's Sergeant Major Stark" came the monotone voice. "Sir, I have an update on the field situation," he added.

"Go ahead."

"The one believed to be Nero was found dead outside Medellín. He stepped in front of a truck according to reports picked up on the police network. We're eighty per cent certain it was him."

Wexhall nodded. That was good. A stroke of luck however it happened.

"That's interesting. What about the other guy with him?"

"No sign of him, I'm afraid. Disappeared. But there's something else—"

"Yes, Sergeant Major."

"Nero was almost certainly a CIA agent."

There was a pause. Wexhall stared at the desk, momentarily frozen. That was messy. They had inadvertently been hunting down someone from the company.

Not good.

"We identified him from surveillance cameras on the chopper over the *Anita*. The photo recog only just came up with a ninety per cent match. We also got a match on the fingerprint from his house from our man inside. It's on the CIA database. He's definitely one of theirs—"

The line began beeping, indicating another call.

"I'll get back to you, Sergeant Major." Wexhall looked at the number, then tapped a button on the handset.

A low, husky whisper came over the line; faint but exuding power. A voice Wexhall recognised immediately.

"Wexhall. You know who this is?"

"Yes."

"Good. You need to close down Darkwood immediately, without hesitation."

"I don't understand?"

"There's nothing to question here. It'll have to wait for another day. There is a Senate enquiry about to happen and you'll need to appear and answer questions."

Wexhall sunk into his reclining office chair as if dealt a second body blow. "I don't understand. I thought we had everything covered—"

"We'll deal with that. In the meantime, you need to close down the operation; get rid of everything, and I mean absolutely everything."

The line went dead.

Wexhall slammed the handset down. He grabbed his china mug, filled with coffee, and threw it at the blank wall. The cup smashed, splattering the brown liquid across the paintwork like the blood from a gunshot wound.

CIA Headquarters, Langley

"This has to be Wexhall," said Fallon.

Brett Fallon, Deputy Director for Operations, and Kate Foster, the Deputy Executive Director, were in a small comms room. Fallon was sitting in front of the console while Foster paced, pausing occasionally. The large screen on the wall had the encrypted message lingering on the screen with the confirmation that their field agent had been confirmed dead. The snippets of information from the ground were sparse, the breakdown in intel over the previous few weeks had made the situation on the ground hazy at best. But CIA-backed Colombian sources on the ground had acquired pictures that clearly showed their agent dead in a traffic accident.

"We've lost a good man there. It's unfortunate. But not entirely outside the orbit of our profession," Foster said, in a matter-of-fact tone. "It's likely to have involved Rhodes. We just don't know."

Fallon held the expression of a man unconvinced and stared into the mid-distance.

"It's over, Fallon. Wrap this shit up. For now, our mission is nearly complete. Wexhall will fall, soon."

Chapter 43

"Jesus! You left him spread over the Tarmac?"

"I didn't personally chop him up or anything. It was an accident."

There was a pause as Carl considered. "Ironic, the way things work out considering he was trying to put Rhodes through the accident meat grinder himself."

"I liked him," Frank said, without thinking. "He just had his moral compass in the wrong place. I didn't want to see him die that way," he added, swapping the satellite phone to his other ear. He peered out through the farmhouse window across at the rolling Irish countryside. The briquettes needed bringing in, or the fire would die. It would be a right pain to get going again.

"Friends and enemies. There's an indistinguishable blur between them in our business,"

Tell me about it, thought Frank, his previous friendship with Carl coming into focus.

"So, we're wrapped up then," Frank said, wanting to finish the conversation.

Carl got what he wanted. G13COMM was sunk, and he retained his power base with Ghost 13 in London.

"Essentially. Although you did go off-piste and disobey orders."

"Naturally," Frank cut in.

"Handing over the asset to the wrong crowd. I'll never employ you again. You're talented, Frank, but you're ill-disciplined. I'll need a debrief in London ASAP."

Frank sighed. "Alright. I'll be seeing you, Carl." He cut the line, dropped the phone on a table, and headed outside to fill up a bucket with turf briquettes. He brought them inside and tossed them into the fire in the stove, watching the flames build.

There was some basic furniture still in the house, but he had driven over enough clothes, a sleeping bag, work tools and a small box of possessions to the house once the contracts were exchanged. He stood up and looked around at the walls. Some would need plastering, followed by a lick of paint. It was going to be great to focus on the straightforward work of refurbishing his new house. He was looking forward to it; the therapeutic act of painting, listening to music, switching off his mind to the previous escapades.

A news item on the radio caught his attention, and he went to turn up the volume. A Senate hearing had the spotlight on the intelligence community once again.

"Doug, the big question here is: did any US intelligence agency, CIA or otherwise, have connections with the paramilitary group the United Defence Forces of Colombia? Remember, this is a group that is rumoured to have been involved in numerous massacres, some extremely gruesome incidents involving beheadings as well as the brutal killing of women and children. Colonel Wexhall will be fielding questions from the committee about this."

The news moved on, and Frank switched it off with a wry smile. Perhaps John Rhodes had planted a leak somewhere, stirred the pot; the old man still dealing a strong hand even as he disappeared with his wife and son into the mists of South America.

Frank headed to one of the bags he had brought over and cut open the inside lining where he had stashed a brand-new legend passport, arranged when he had got back to London. He had decided to wrap it up in plastic and tape it behind one of the plasterboards when he redid the inside walls.

At that moment his mobile rang and he fished it out of his pocket, glancing at the display. He smiled seeing Maria's caller ID and answered.

Author's Note

False Flag

Way back in the misty depths of time when I was 21, I was backpacking around South East Asia and was struck with inspiration to write fiction. My locations in Thailand, Malaysia and Sumatra at that time provided the inspiration and so the very early notes on False Flag began. At that time it was an entirely different story: traveller gets inadvertently pulled into drugs smuggling operation, bad shit ensues.

When I was staying in Penang, Malaysia (designing T-shirts in the back of an apparel store) I had to renew my visa by doing a border run into Thailand. Unfortunately, everywhere to stay was booked up so I asked around and ended up in an interesting little place called the Bird House; a spot for tourists to bird watch across a jungle strewn vista. It was the same scene, as described in the story. I met the proprietor who gave me a key and left me to it The place was empty of tourists, no host, just an eerie quiet and the remnants of past guests in the guise of empty beer bottles.

Isolated and alone, yet inspired I wrote down a handful of pages of a chapter, set in that very place as well as an outline for the entire novel. I kept the notepad for another 20 years before revisiting the story with fresh eyes and a very different idea about what kind of story it should be.

I hope you enjoyed it.

Pandora Red

Pandora Red, the Frank Bowen follow up to False Flag, had been a long time coming. It started life in July 2013 and was a difficult book to write. Why? I'm not so sure but it was research intensive and along with a few personal life interruptions, Pandora just took a lot longer than I hoped it would.

Firstly there were major changes in the plot, characters dropped (goodbye Sergio) and others re-aligned. As the story developed and after really useful feedback from the editor, Cate Hogan we had to strengthen the difference between the official G13 mission and the mercenaries hired by Devlin who harboured more sinister plans for the whistleblower, Sarah Edwards (Codenamed: Pandora) rather than extradition.

After discussions between myself and lead editor, Jay Newton we looked at working in some changes. We made Frank and his associates work a lot harder to find the location of Pandora, whereas originally they were handed the info on a platter. That involved writing a whole new sequence of scenes and re-jigging a lot of other stuff which in turn pushed the release date back two months but resulted in a much stronger book. It's amazing what fresh eyes will do and that's precisely why we are looking to build up our beta reader core group.

So, as you've already read, the story takes place eight years after the False Flag story. Bowen joined 'the firm'; MI6 and has been through several years of training in surveillance and combat as well as having live mission experience. The intermittent Frank Bowen years between False Flag (1991) and Pandora Red (1999) will probably be covered by a short story or novella series in the near future.

Ghost Order

I didn't travel to Colombia in early 2017 to write Ghost Order. The story didn't yet exist in my mind but the way it came about dovetailed nicely with my journey at that time.

In December 2016 I had given away or sold most of my possessions, given notice on my day job and with a vague plan to be a travelling nomadic writer for as long as possible, headed to the embarkation point of the Nomad Cruise in Las Palmas, Gran Canaria.

This would be a two-week kick-off party to a plan that was vaguely centred around finding a sun-kissed utopia to write books and possibly freelance on the side. The cruise itself was for Digital Nomads, a creative mix of mostly younger, smart Europeans who made it their business to travel the world and work online. That cruise opened my eyes to the possibilities of the new nomadic lifestyle; one of moving from country to country, enjoying the fruits of each one while edging away from any winter nastiness.

The cruise arrived in the Dominican Republic just before Christmas, and I have to admit not having a great time there. An accident at a lagoon cut open my foot and I had my precious iPhone stolen days later. I was glad to leave.

My trip, followed in Frank's footsteps, was as yet unwritten. To the Caribbean by boat, with stops at Antigua, Barbados, St Martin and St Lucia.

I arrived in Cartagena, Colombia, with a determination to get back on track, with both my mindset and my work, and after a month went to Medellín, the city of eternal spring.

The subsequent trips I took while there, including a trek to the self-built prison of Pablo Escobar, La Catedal, would provide more inspiration. Those who have watched the Netflix series Narcos will be familiar with the background to that place. It became the setting of the showdown finale in Ghost Order, naturally.

At the time White Horse (the first book in the Dark Paradigm series) was with the editor, and I was deep in first draft stage with Red Horse (mostly set in Iran). So I was in a different world when it came to my fiction as opposed to my location. The dream is to be writing on location wherever my book is set. One day. But staying in Cartagena, on the Caribbean coast and then Medellín, certainly simmered the imagination, and the seed for Ghost Order was sown.

After my return (the digital nomad thing didn't work out!) in October/November 2017, I began piecing together the plot for Ghost Order and then saw that authorpreneur Derek Murphy had a spot going at his castle writing retreat in Rappottenstein, Austria. Yes, a sanctuary for writers during NaNoWriMo (National Novel Writing Month). Too good to miss and what a place to get stuck into Ghost Order.

So a group of writers spent almost two weeks in this fantastic location: writing, eating, drinking, walking in the surrounding forest, the occasional road trip to other castles and a border run to Czech, then more writing...lots of writing. By the end, I had a very rough first draft and the past year has been honing and reworking the story. It has been great to be working on a Frank Bowen story again after that four-year break.

There is, of course, a wider team behind the story. I also have to thank the beta readers, Diane and Dorene, who have been with me for several years now. James Newton who has spent a lot of his time copy-editing. Collaborative partner Jay Newton who mechanically dismantles the weaknesses and finds the missing parts. Thanks also to Nicky Lovick for the final edit.

So that is the story behind the story. And what next for Frank Bowen? There is undoubtedly a long gap between this latest episode in 2000 until the Dark Paradigm series, where Frank's offspring come into their own in the epic struggle to prevent an apocalypse. Let's see where the inspiration and ideas manifest next, and perhaps I will throw darts at a globe to find out where my and Frank's next destination lies.

Jay Tinsiano
   Bristol, United Kingdom

FREE Thriller

Exclusive offer. To grab your FREE Novella eBook (Blood Tide) head to:

http://jaytinsiano.com/secret-access/

PLUS you'll get access to the VIP Jay Tinsiano reading group for:

- Free Books and stories
- Previews and Sneak Peeks
- Exclusive material

Also Available

White Horse

(Dark Paradigm #1 by Jay Tinsiano and Jay Newton)

Half a world away in Spain and running from his past, a Los Angeles gangster unwittingly takes a train that's headed straight into a terrorist attack. He survives only to face an even deadlier threat.

On that same train: a virologist with clues to a deadly epidemic. Did his secrets die with him in the strike?

Raging in the aftermath, a foul-tempered police chief with a daughter caught in the attack thirsts for revenge. But against whom?

An orphan child without a name disappears down a dark, illegal CIA mind-control programme. Now trained in the ways of death, he prepares to do his master's twisted bidding.

From its first pages, the relentless techno-thriller White Horse drops you with a thunderclap in the middle of these colliding worlds. This tale of global conspiracy that threatens humanity itself will keep you guessing whether anyone can survive.

Available at all major eBook retailers
Paperback ISBN: 978-1-9997232-1-7

Red Horse

(Dark Paradigm #2 by Jay Tinsiano and Jay Newton)

Haleema Sheraz, a cyber hacker for the Iranian government, discovers her father has gone missing. Frustrated at the lack of urgency from the police, she investigates and soon reveals a kidnapping network that spans back to Operation Paperclip in World War II.

Meanwhile, her brothers join an ISIS-inspired uprising that is wreaking havoc inside Iran, and finding her father quickly becomes a mission to save her family.

Joe Bowen and Hugo Reese continue to prepare Liberatus for a wider global struggle and find themselves called to help one of their own secret assets–Sirus aka Haleema Sheraz.

Soon they will all be thrust into the battle zone and their lives will change irreversibly in this epic story of bitter struggle against the backdrop of total war.

Available at all major eBook retailers
Paperback ISBN: 978-1-9997232-4-8

Flight 313

(Dark Ops #1 by Jay Tinsiano and Jay Newton)

A group of men board flight 313 with the equipment and means to hijack the aircraft.

An air marshal who hasn't seen action for years finds himself dealing with a group of terrorists.

It's his chance to be a hero.

Except, nothing is as it seems.

A short military conspiracy thriller that will keep you guessing.

Available at all major eBook retailers

War Dogs

(Dark Ops 2 by Jay Tinsiano and Jay Newton)

As Ghost 13 begin to operate inside Iran, ex-SEALS Lieutenant Commander, Kurt Coleman comes up against an adversary that jolts him back to his first G13 op on the Syrian border. That experience left a bitter taste but the high-risk close combat missions are only just beginning.

Available at all major eBook retailers

War Lords

(Dark Ops 3 by Jay Tinsiano and Jay Newton)

With Colonel Stark out of the loop, Captain Coleman and the rest of the Ghost 13 squad are briefed on a Daesh plan to hijack and steal an Iranian government convoy carrying enriched uranium.

The stakes are higher than ever as Iranian intelligence begin to track the covert op inside their country.

Available at all major eBook retailers

www.ingramcontent.com/pod-product-compliance
Lightning Source LLC
Chambersburg PA
CBHW060935190726
48286CB00005B/1281